I0822187

AND THE

BOOK 3
HEALING FATE SERIES

ASHA NYR

ISBN: 979-8-9885350-6-5 (ebook)
ISBN: 979-8-9885350-5-8 (paperback)
ISBN: 979-8-9885350-4-1 (hardback case laminate)
ISBN: 979-8-9885350-7-2 (hardback dust jacket)

Copyediting by Misha Carlstedt, Verity Ink Editorial

This novel is dedicated to tem, who knows what they did. Thank you, tem.

Content Warning

Dear new readers, this novel contains adult content with scenes describing explicit language, explicit sex, violence, physical abuse, and psychological abuse. Reader discretion is strongly advised.

The Packless and the Fae Prince was originally exposure therapy for the sexual assault and abuse I survived. Due to popular demand, I've decided to publish it. More information is provided in the Author's Notes about why this was written. Please note that includes spoilers.

More information can also be found in the Author's Notes of *The Mistake and the Lycan King* and *The Dragon Knight and the Coveted*, the first two books of Healing Fate.

Acknowledgments

I have far too many people to thank for getting me through this last year. As usual, my therapist continues to work with me, guiding me through my major depression, anxiety, PTSD, and more—toward a life worth living. It is so much work, and I can only imagine what a challenge I must be to treat. And yet, no one has given up on me. My gratitude is overflowing.

I want to thank my social worker for her support, for helping me gather resources to better navigate my life. I struggled greatly to finish editing this book, and the changes she helped implement in my daily life is why I'm even wrapping this book up by the end of July.

Also, I need to acknowledge my street team, the Fourlight Pack, specifically Samara, who earned the title Coven Mother through her outstanding proactivity, experience, and dedication. When I thought it an impossible task, she swooped in and helped me build a street team. She's becoming my other right hand person—I guess I have two right hand people now between her and Beta Julie—and completely irreplaceable. More than that though, she's become a dear friend. I also have to give major props to my coronels, Allison, Amanda, and Sheena, three incredible women who instilled within the Fourlight Pack a pulse, a beating heart.

As usual, my love and gratitude to Beta Julie, the truest beta to have ever lived. She's now one of the few people who know who

I actually am, having earned that trust for huge responsibilities. She's the reason why acknowledgments pages exist.

Moonlight preserve you all, my readers, my shifter family, fellow survivors, the people who give me purpose. I can't thank you enough for giving me reason to hope. I love you all.

Love,
Author, artist, musician, and unyielding survivor,
Asha Nyr

Chapter 1

Hekla

Fog rolled through the trees surrounding the pack Ragna, Rakel, Soley, and I used to call home. The mist caressed all beneath it, and though I wouldn't be around, I knew the plants would glow with life once the Sun God showed Himself. He'd feed them, night would fall, and the cycle would start anew… depending on the time of year. Depending on the season…

About a month had passed since Ragna's coronation. Who knew a queen would have sprouted from these humble roots? I stared at the quiet houses dotting the woods, my mind a hazy reflection of the weather. Above the dripping treetops, smoke from chimneys drifted to the Sky Gods like lazy howls. We were lucky to have grown up here. Erik had been a good alpha to us, and the location helped us thrive. Winters weren't too cold, summers weren't too hot, and droughts were never a problem. Food was plentiful since there was always water around for the wildlife to prosper and for whatever plants we wished to grow. Looking at it all now, it almost seemed like the Earth Gods favored us.

We had it good here. Life was predictable, and it was safe.

Until Eysteinn happened.

"Hekla? Breakfast is ready!" My mother interrupted my thoughts, calling from inside my childhood home. Reluctantly, I returned indoors, knowing I couldn't escape the pull of time. This would be the last meal I'd share with my family for the foreseeable future, and that thought was almost enough to give a she-wolf a panic attack.

There weren't a great many things in the hall that told of my youth here, but I did pause to look at one such item. A straw weaving hung by the mirror, one I'd made with Ragna when we were pups. Two mismatching twigs had been added ages ago by Rakel and Soley, who'd wanted to contribute in their own silly way. They stuck out of either side like whiskers on a bedraggled wolf. Though humorous, the additions completed the piece the way the two she-wolves completed our sub-pack—our group of friends.

I pulled off my scarf and sat at the table with my parents, grandparents, and younger brother. We'd gathered with extended family yesterday, so it was just us this morning. Mother was in even more of a state than she'd been last evening, and Father comforted her the best he could, sitting close and doting.

Plates clattered onto the table, serving a hearty breakfast to nourish my wolf, but my human body didn't want to eat. Nausea gripped me after a rough, anxious night. I hadn't slept a wink, which meant hunger had struck well before dawn.

"Thank you for breakfast, everyone," I said to the table, not sure who had done the cooking this time. "It's delicious."

My father smiled as he held Mother's hand. "Just make sure you eat plenty so Eventide has energy to work with."

"Yes, you must make sure to eat when you reach the court. Can we get news of your safe arrival?" my mother asked, biting her lower lip and fighting off tears. She loved her pups. Gods, I felt so guilty.

"I'll make sure they get a message to you," I assured, hoping that I wouldn't forget to do that. I was so nervous that I'd be lucky if I left with my head still attached. "And thank you for letting me store my things from my old place. I don't know what to do with them, but I'm not ready to just throw it all away."

"We have the room," my mother replied sadly.

My grandmother slapped the table to—I suspect—lift the mood. "Well, I think she's going to be just fine! This Generic Blueberry person said he'd give you everything you needed!"

"You mean General Belenus?" I asked, correcting her while suppressing a smile.

"Yes, the gold one with the big ears," my grandmother clarified, pointing her fingers along her head to imitate fae ears. To my parents' dismay, she now enjoyed pretending to be senile. Even worse, my grandfather was starting to join her antics.

"I thought his name was Dennis," Grandfather grumbled as he took a bite of ham. I snorted into my juice, nearly choking on the tangy drink while my sibling laughed uncontrollably. A fae general named Dennis…

I smiled, greatly appreciating their attempts to lighten the mood, and said, "Yes, I'm sure his salary is more than enough to provide. I'll just have to figure out what to do with myself. I have no idea what career options I'll have."

My father nodded. "Don't rush it. You have an entire new culture to adjust to. There may be exciting trades we've never even heard of."

Mother furrowed her brows, looked from me to Father, and asked, "Do find a way to contact us if you get with pups or… er… what do they call fae pups?"

Huh. "I… don't actually know," I said, jutting my lower lip out in thought.

"Faebies," Grandmother answered.

"Little, tiny, bouncing faebes." Grandfather nodded, agreeing with her.

Somehow, I didn't think that was true. I smiled wryly at them and took another forkful of eggs. It was just a tiny bit, but their good humor eased my nerves. The jesting made it seem like this wasn't the last meal with my family, though I didn't know if that would make it harder to leave.

"I didn't think to ask him when he was here," my mother said, worrying at her hands until my father claimed one of them in his strong grip.

"He wasn't here that long," I consoled. "It was just the meal at the pack house to meet you all and Alpha Erik."

"I hope it won't be too hard for you to contact us from…" Mother choked on her words and held her hand over her mouth. Father reacted immediately, rubbing her back and whispering soothingly. They were a beautiful example of what a mated pair should be like, and I could only hope for the same with Belenus and me.

I waited until she steadied herself before answering. "I promise I will do everything I can to sort that out. Remember our Ragna's a queen now, and there's no way she's letting me go any length of time without news!" I grinned and reached over to pat her hand.

"What you pups have been through is remarkable," my father said, shaking his head in disbelief. "Ragna's banishment, the search for Rakel, and our little Soley—a vessel for the barkin' Sun God. That tiny, submissive little thing!" My father thumped the table with a finger. "I gotta say, I'm so proud of you little she-wolves!" He wiped a tear away with a growl and shoveled some ham into his mouth. "The lot of you are warriors!" It had been exclaimed with a mouth full of food, but he was far too emotional to care.

"I just can't believe they've all had to leave the pack," Mother said. "You all found your fated mates, but they couldn't be brought here…"

"Definitely not," I replied.

"It's better this way," my brother added calmly. "Go out, see the world, learn new things. I think it's exciting."

Mother rounded on him. "Nuh-uh! I don't care if your fated mate is a blessed mermaid! You're not leaving me too!"

Pretty much the entire table erupted into laughter. My poor mother.

Alpha Erik arrived at the hour he said he would, and he escorted me to the edge of pack territory, my parents in tow. My mother held my hand in a death grip, and though it threatened to go numb, I let her do it. She was clearly as stressed as I.

Actually, I'm going to need that paw to work, Eventide informed, and I chuckled quietly.

Just walk it off. You'll be fine, I replied to my wolf. *You said all your byes too?*

I did... and I'd be a crying mess if it were possible. But. We. Will. Be. Ok!

Alpha Erik slowed, and I sensed the border as we approached it—the edge of our pack's territory. It smelled different out there, felt different, but I knew some of what to expect. I'd left this place several times in my life—briefly. The first had been when the Sky Gods possessed me to aid Ragna. The time after that? That was when Rakel had been abducted. Soley and I had left together to find her, unwilling to lose yet another member of our sub-pack. Then we'd visited the Earth Gods' sanctuary. And then there had been the coronation...

Ragna had become our queen, Soley was now a rogue she-wolf living in the Lunar Coven, and Rakel had the grand beta to help her heal at the castle. I was the last to leave for a new home. Being the last, I suspected I felt the most guilt.

My alpha's stern face softened as he looked down at me. "It's a shame to lose yet another exceptional wolf, Hekla," he said, crossing his arms, thinking the exact same thing that plagued me.

"I'm sorry, Alpha," I apologized with all the sincerity I could muster and bowed my head in submission. "I felt like I had to make an impossible decision."

"I can't even imagine." He shook his head. "I don't hold it against you. It's one thing to find a fated mate, but it's another thing to leave behind everything you know."

"I am… scared," I confessed, and my mother released my hand to give me some space.

"The fae should be the ones scared," Alpha Erik asserted. "They will have a wolf in their woods." Even though he delivered them seriously, the words were meant to comfort. "As much as you'll want to blend in, never, ever forget about what sets you apart, Hekla. Use the tools they do not have, and do not let them know your weaknesses. You'll have to sort out who the predators and the prey are yourself. Do so carefully, because a buck you aim to hunt can still kill you."

Even though I was about to leave his pack, he continued to look out for me. That hit pretty damn hard. I wiped a tear from my eye and nodded, letting him know I'd heard every word. After that, the separation was performed without ceremony. I barely heard him speak as he severed my connection to the pack, and I stumbled into my father's grip, reeling.

Emotional and physical turmoil assailed me before the isolation could settle. The way Ragna had described it was accurate; a place that I never knew existed was suddenly empty. I felt hollow, scraped out. I hated it. Was this to be the rest of my life? How would I ever get used to this? Oh gods, how?

I called upon every ounce of control I had to not cry because I knew my family was doing the same. We were all trying to be strong for everyone else, but I knew we'd individually shattered. No, I felt more than shattered. My shards of glass had been ground back into sand and left to scatter in the wind. A part of my identity had just disappeared—all to be with my fated mate, one I barely knew.

Everyone embraced me for the last time, their warmth fighting my urge to hurry. Mother shook and shivered, and I knew that the sooner I left, the sooner she could let out her grief. After a last round of goodbyes, I departed from the only place I'd ever called home. I hoped that my family could find comfort with my friends' families because I honestly had no idea when I'd ever see them again. I had another realm to call home now.

It'd been a fair journey from my old pack to the castle of the lycan king and the wolf queen, but since becoming the vessel of the Sky Gods, I'd become a good deal stronger. Being the vessel wasn't what made me stronger; it was the days of traveling I'd undertaken with Soley that'd tightened up muscles. Survival was a brutal trainer.

Finally! We're here! Oh, I can't wait to see our sub-pack! I just want to goof off and lie around in the sun! Eventide cried.

I shifted a short distance from the castle and smiled while I dressed, looking forward to the planned reunion. It had been a while since we'd last gathered. I couldn't really count the cult battleground and Ragna's sanctuary since we had all still been in the thick of it, and the coronation had been a short affair. A relaxing day with our she-wolves before a life-changing realm hop was just what we needed!

I approached the castle guards and hailed, "Good afternoon! I am here to see Queen Ragna. She's expecting me. My name's Hekla Himinn, vessel of the Sky Gods."

The guards brightened at the mention of the gods and allowed me to pass. An escort met me once I entered the castle, and she walked me to where the wolf queen awaited.

"Thank you, by the way, for your part in freeing the Moon Goddess," the guard said quietly. "Because all the fated mate bonds got sorted back to normal, I met my mate two weeks ago, and we couldn't be happier." She patted her belly over her armor. "Think we've already gotten with pups too."

I gasped quietly and discreetly said, "Congratulations! That's wonderful news! Yes, I'm so happy that catastrophe is over. Embrace your new life and move forward with confidence." I nodded, smiling widely. Every new fated mating brought me the most intense sensation of joy, and I hung on to it ferociously. It helped ease the sting of the rocky start I was having with my own fated mate.

When we arrived at a garden, three over-sugared she-wolves ambushed me.

"HEKLA!" the small redhead screamed.

"You've got a twig in your hair…" the blonde said wryly, trying to hold me still while performing surgery.

"You're finally here!" the brunette breathed excitedly.

I'd almost fallen over from their attack and laughed heartily as they fawned over me. Had we all been in our wolf forms, we'd have been a pile of slobbering, whining, barking rapscallions. I made several attempts to calm everyone, but she-wolves would be she-wolves, and I was apparently sorely missed.

Finally, Ragna pulled everyone back and gestured to a picnic blanket surrounded by the autumn bloom and lightly littered by fallen leaves. We settled down and gawked at the spread of food. It had everything a she-wolf could want! I hovered over mouth-watering prime cuts of bison, fresh fish, nourishing greens, and fruit. Also, there was dessert… lots and lots of dessert.

Ragna gestured to a low table in the middle of the blanket and poured four cups of tea. We each grabbed one and waited patiently for her toast. She pressed her lips together in thought and looked away to find the right words.

Finally and decisively, she nodded. "Today is a day of great import! We celebrate our friendship and recognize that we will always be pack in our hearts, no matter the distance. Tomorrow, our dear friend Hekla leaves for her greatest adventure yet." Ragna wiped a tear from her eye and regained her royal poise.

"Don't cry, Ragna. You're going to make me cry!" Soley whined, squirming in her dress.

"Which will make me cry," Rakel warned, "because nothing is sadder than a crying Soley."

"T-tomorrow," Ragna continued, taking a deep breath, "Hekla will be escorted to the Realm of the Fae to live with her fated mate, General Belenus of the fae's Summer Court! We wish her safe travels, a cozy home, and a wild night of mating and marking!" The last part brought some giggles to the group, and my cheeks heated from the sheer thought of being naked with Belenus.

"I am dying to know what he's hiding under his armor." I grinned impishly, daydreaming.

Everyone took a sip of the tea, and Soley had to have her say. "May Belenus finally get the courage to look upon a sexy, naked she-wolf!" she toasted, and I laughed along with the others, albeit a little weakly.

We all took another sip, and Rakel cleared her throat. "So that they can finally do more than kiss, great gods," she toasted dryly, but I winced at that one. Rakel frowned and lowered her cup when she noticed the change in mood. "Gods! I'm sorry, Hekla! I shouldn't have assumed… I mean, I haven't kissed Rude either. You were just so aggressive about it, I thought for sure you'd have gotten him to cave by now…"

"He still insists on courting me… slowly," I mumbled, staring into my steaming drink.

"How long are fae courtships?" Ragna asked with a puzzled look on her face.

I shrugged. "I don't know. I've only seen him a couple of times, and that was to get things sorted for my move. At first, I was really confident about it, but as time passes… what if he rejects me? What if he's just buying time to gather the courage?" I asked my she-wolves, baring my fears before them.

"Not possible!" Soley exclaimed with a fervent shake of her head that sent her curls flying.

"He was desperately wanting to find his fated mate when the bonds were all messed up, Hekla," Ragna reminded, propping her head up with a fist.

"Yeah, when he thought you were his mate," I replied, gesturing to her. "What if he preferred you? What if he's disappointed that I'm his mate instead?"

Rakel gawked at me like I was a complete stranger. "Hekla, I can't believe what I'm hearing! I've never seen you so out of sorts before. Where's our confident Hekla gone?"

"It's just… more and more time has passed since we met. I'm starting to doubt his enthusiasm," I replied, doing everything I could to hold back tears. My eyes stung horribly from the fight. The novel insecurities that had grown over time—that I'd tried to ignore—encroached.

"The mate bond really does make you vulnerable, and you've both been apart for too long without marking," Ragna said thoughtfully and reached over to hold my hand. Hers were warm but nowhere near as warm as her heart. "Remember yourself, Hekla. This isn't like you. You're the most levelheaded of us. I need you to keep asking yourself what you would do, ok? We can visit each other, but you're going to have to rely on your strengths."

I sighed and wiped my sweaty palms on my thighs. "Right, sorry. I'm just so nervous. First, I leave my pack, and now I have to leave my realm! With someone I barely know! I've been more than obvious with my desires… I'm tiring without results…" I thought I was beautiful enough to seduce him, but it seemed he had more restraint than a male wolf.

"Trust in Belenus," Ragna said as she rubbed my back, trying her hardest to soothe me. "There's a reason why the Moon Goddess paired you two. Look at all the work she had in store for Zorian and me before we even knew we were fated mates. My goodness, I still wonder how we survived all that!"

"I'm hoping it won't be quite that intense," I said with a chuckle, wiping a rogue tear from my eyelash.

"We will come visit," Rakel promised, patting my knee. "We've seen him look sweetly upon you once. We'll witness with our own eyes how much he cares about you." She then went wide-eyed with Ragna, and they both doubled over into a fit of snorty laughter.

"What?" I asked with a nervous chuckle. "Trail being inappropriate again?"

Ragna scratched her ear and cleared her throat. "She just wanted to say he totally likes you. We've seen th-the way his p-pants look at y-you!" She barely managed to get the sentence out of her mouth before bursting into laughter. The rest of us were in stitches for a good five minutes.

"It's true," Soley said, giggling nonstop and wiping tears from her eyes. "He's always adjusting his pants around you, especially when you're being a horny tease."

I smiled a little to myself. "Perhaps I'm just thinking too much." Goddess, it was true there had been a lot of time to ruminate. Too much, admittedly.

"What are the fae like, anyway? We only saw Belenus," Soley asked, tilting her head at Ragna while she dug into a piece of bison. The rest of us began to fill our plates.

"Oh goddess," Ragna said and looked away to think. "Just as diverse as us, really. The women at the court are kind of… competitive, though. They kept trying to get Zorian's attention and attempted to embarrass me by asking how many lovers I had. Just shut those females down, Hekla. They're not even worth your time."

"Well, it's nice advice, but I doubt I'll ever be at court," I replied with a laugh. "Belenus is a general, so his house is probably in the surrounding city, if it's set up like our castles."

"Ah… yes. That's right." Ragna fiddled with a strand of her hair. "A general. No, I haven't been to the city. Your guess is as good as mine, I suppose."

Rakel sighed. "I wish we could have a run together. We still haven't done that, have you realized?"

"That's true," Ragna replied apologetically and grimaced. "Once again, I'm keeping us from doing that, aren't I? Sorry, my she-wolves."

"Let's just plan on doing it after you deliver your litter!" Soley stated cheerily. "It'll be safe then."

"We'll make an event of it." I grinned, glad for the distraction. "We'll have a party at the following full moon and let our wolves go nuts!" I nudged her playfully. "Get you started on losing that pup weight!"

"Hey!" she snapped, barely able to contain her smile, and threw a piece of fish at me. I snatched it victoriously out of the air and popped it in my mouth, grinning like a scamp.

I woke the following morning after a late night with my she-wolves, barely prepared for my visitor. Ragna came running into the guest room with a pile of clothes and jumped on my bed. For a moment, I had no idea where I was, surrounded by mostly foreign scents, but her excited howl snapped me to attention.

"Wake up! Today is the day, Belenus's mate!" she crowed. "Get up so we can put you in something sexy! The servants are bringing up breakfast!"

"Oh my gods!" I sat up a little too fast, and my vision greyed for a heartbeat. "Am I running late?"

"Nope! We have just enough time!" She pulled on my arm to get me out of bed. "Go bathe!"

I did just that, hurrying to get ready. Each minute poured more nervousness into me until I felt like screaming. When I was clean, but no less frazzled, I joined the wolf queen to regard my seducing options.

"I wonder what Belenus likes. Think he likes breasts or bottoms? Legs maybe?" Ragna pondered, eyeing me thoughtfully. "You have it all, though. My mate likes breasts, but I've noticed he enjoys me in leggings. Fae women do wear dresses, though. Should we put you in a dress? I don't know… What do you think?"

I glowed under Ragna's zealous efforts and thought about her question. I preferred leggings and tunics, but if I was entering a new realm, perhaps I'd make a better first impression if I tried to blend in with their culture. I could put my discomfort aside for a while. I was sure that as long as I was with Belenus, I'd be happy anyway.

"Maybe a dress then, just to be safe." I nodded decisively.

"With a low décolletage!" Ragna said with a feral grin. "I learned that word recently. It's like how you display your breasts… I think. Something like that." She dismissed the uncertain explanation with a wave of her hand, a gesture I didn't recall her using before meeting Zorian. She then dug into the pile of clothes and laid out several dresses. One was a pretty teal, and the other a sunny yellow. She pulled out a third in a vibrant coral. The lycan fashion differed from what the wolves wore, and they definitely had access to superior fabric. Caressing the elaborate embroidery, I knew that I'd always keep whatever I picked here, even if it no longer fit. Everything from here on out would be mostly tailored by fae.

"What do you think?" the wolf queen mused with a finger on her lips.

I held them all up to the mirror and agonized over the decision. "They all look nice…" I said, frowning. "Which one has the lowest décolletage?" I riffled through them and landed on the sunny yellow one.

"That one!" Ragna agreed and giggled as she helped me into it. The laces were confusing, but she showed me how to tighten them.

"Don't overtighten. I made that mistake once and almost fainted at a banquet," she cautioned and ran to the door to let the servant bring in several trays of food.

"My favorite…" I remarked, feeling sentimental at the sight of waffles and strawberries. Ragna was as thoughtful as always.

"And these will be here for you every single time you visit!" she exclaimed, shoving a syrupy forkful into her mouth. Overwhelmed and a touch speechless, I gave her an affectionate side hug. These were all lovely distractions, and she was the most wonderful friend for her efforts.

"I'm going to miss you," I eventually confessed. "We only just reunited."

"It will be ok, Hekla. It's ok to be scared, and it's ok to miss people. Remember," she said emphatically, "we will always be pack here!" She thumped a fist against her chest. "Always and forever."

Chapter 2

Hekla

My she-wolves and their mates walked me to where I was supposed to meet Belenus. A 'door' to the Realm of the Fae awaited me several miles west of the castle, and I welcomed the chance to hike off some jitters. My wolf did the best she could to distract me, and it was kind of working because she was easily distracted herself when not faced with responsibilities. Of all my she-wolves, I was pretty certain that my wolf was the… wolfiest.

Ah! What a good day it is to meet a mate! Eventide said with a very audible grin. *The leaves have started to fall, and the air has a crispness to it. Can you smell it? I just want to roll in a big pile of dry, dirty leaves!*

Pretty sure Belenus wouldn't like a mate smelling like dirty leaves, I replied, suppressing a smile. *Also, it's going to be summer... for the rest of our lives.* The realization had me crest-fallen, and I fought off another wave of anxiety. I was about to enter such a strange realm. Would I be able to handle it? How long would it take me to adjust?

Not true! Eventide growled. *I'm sure Belenus will be fine with us taking vacations in our original realm!*

That perked me up a bit. Perhaps she was right. I didn't necessarily need Belenus to come along either… but it would be nice if he could. *Maybe he could make time to come with us? I imagine a general would be pretty busy, but we'll see.*

We'll be ok in our new home! We just need fresh meat and a forest to run in! Then our fated mate to mount us every night!

Don't make me blush before we get there, Eventide! I chastised. *I refuse to have my friends' last memory of me be of my arousal!*

She just chuckled at that and went silent, sensing she was testing my sanity. I looked down at my dress, noting that the layers of skirts might actually help contain any scents that would give away my readiness. Perhaps there was something to wearing gowns after all. Did fae have strong senses? They couldn't possibly have a nose as sharp as a wolf's.

"Ragna." I moved to nudge her. "Do fae have a good sense of smell?"

She twisted her lips and looked thoughtful. "That's a good question. I don't actually know!"

"Drat," I said. "I hope I won't advertise as much as we do among wolf and lycan males."

She winced. "Yes, that is always problematic." She patted my back in sympathy. "I guess you'll find out the hard way."

I barked out a laugh at her playful—but brutal—honesty. Though it took me off guard, it let some of my anxiety trickle away, and Ragna looked quite pleased with herself. I linked our arms and briefly laid my head upon her shoulder as we walked, being of similar height.

"Just remember what I said, Hekla. Don't forget who you are," she murmured softly. "In our little sub-pack, you are spirited and wise. You're our guiding light. You're practically our alpha in a way!"

I snorted at her flattery. "Hmm, an alpha? Oh, totally."

Soley leaned over and added in a conspiratorial whisper, "Try commanding Belenus to do naughty and unspeakable things!"

Rakel overheard her and choked on a laugh. I glanced over at her mate, Rudesind, who pretended he hadn't heard it and was desperately trying to keep a straight face.

"Alright, alright, we're here," I said in a rush, spying a circle of tree stumps ahead on a hill. "Thank you, my she-wolves, for all your very helpful advice," I added sarcastically. We marched toward the unassuming realm door and waited for Belenus to make his appearance.

"We'll check in with you from time to time," King Zorian said. "Perhaps we can figure out a way of sending messengers. I'll have to discuss it with Belenus, but I don't want any ties to you severed. You were born a wolf in this kingdom, you're a vessel of the Sky Gods, and a close friend of my mate, my queen. I want to make sure you're safe over there." He let the tiniest, rare smile out for me. It wasn't something he did for just anyone. Unfortunately, that was when a rogue autumn leaf decided to fall on his white locks—the color of his lycan—and ruin his friendly façade. He growled and ripped it off, causing Rudesind, Rakel, and Ragna to break into chuckles. Koray just smiled and pulled his smitten mate, Soley, to his side.

I stopped hearing their well-wishes in my anxiousness and glanced around while wiping my sweaty palms on my hips. Whatever relief I'd obtained from that walk was getting overshadowed by the wait. I stared at the vibrant, ruddy autumn leaves under the deep blue sky, knowing that this was but a small moment in my lifetime. Right now, though, it felt like an eternity was passing with no end in sight. I wanted to scream, but I restrained all my howls, leaving them to pile suffocatingly in my chest. Departing my realm seemed unthinkable, and yet here I was, desperate to get it over with. I started when I felt Ragna wrap her arms around me and rest her head on my shoulder. Even Eventide paced restlessly.

As jumpy as a rabbit now, I accidentally knocked my shoulder into Ragna's jaw when the air distorted in the ring of trees. I apologized profusely to my friend while she nursed her face, and I swung around to see if it was Belenus who'd arrived. Indeed, it was.

I was hit by his scent first, which had my mouth flooding with saliva. I swallowed multiple times, gulping hard to make sure I wouldn't drool before my aloof fated mate. He smelled like a lemon tree and a summer storm. Lemonade and petrichor, the scent of rain evaporating off the hot earth.

I tried to keep my legs stable as he marched toward me, and Eventide did her best to strengthen them, making sure I didn't wobble and embarrass myself. Belenus was a fae… and he was the most beautiful man I'd ever seen in my life. I'd thought so the first time I saw him, and I thought so now.

He was tall, very much around Zorian's height but more lithe in his form, whereas Zorian carried the typically massive lycan bulk. Belenus was still very muscular, though, and I had a hard time not daydreaming about him working those muscles over my splayed body.

A masculine fairness chiseled his face, and his amber eyes flickered with a keenness, both enchanting and exotic in their almond shape. I wondered if all fae had such delicate features. His summery yellow hair was brushed neatly to the side and trimmed shorter around his pointed ears. Finally, wherever I could see his skin, there was a very subtle golden sheen, as though he powdered himself with sunshine after every bath.

I swallowed again as he stood before me and reached for my hand to kiss it. His soft lips pressed gingerly against my skin and sent sparks up my arm, nearly making me jump again. It'd been so long since he last touched me. Frustratingly, this was as intimate as we got.

He looked up at me through his thick blond lashes and straightened. "Miss Hekla, I hope you are well," he greeted formally and reached to take my bag for me. I handed it over reluctantly. I could have carried it…

"I am. Thank you, Belenus," I replied nervously, not feeling like myself at all. The she-wolf in me was going crazy, wanting to drag him into the forest and make him ride the nerves right out of me. She wanted to finally complete the mating and marking. We were not meant to wait this long. It just wasn't in our blood.

Belenus nodded at the group behind me, acknowledging my royal escort. Zorian cleared his throat, moved to shake my fated mate's hand, and said, "Greetings, Belenus. I wish you both a successful mating. As Hekla is a dear friend of Ragna's, I'd like to find a way for them to communicate. Could we perhaps discuss a messenger system in several days when you come to collect Koray?"

Soley whimpered slightly and clung to her unmarked fated mate, unhappy to let him go for any period of time. Belenus wanted to teach Koray sword fighting in the fae realm so he could better protect himself and his mate. The general felt like he owed it to him after Koray had been trapped in the Realm of the Gods, and the young man had accepted the offer. Koray would be away for a long time, and that was going to suck for Soley. She was probably going to get as agitated as me.

Belenus nodded thoughtfully. "I think that is a good idea. I'd like to expand communication in general. Let's have a lengthier discussion later."

I turned and sent a desperately sad look to my she-wolves, who acted immediately. They rushed to envelope me in hugs, tears, and nuzzles. The love draped over me was so desperately needed that I tried not to cry, but that was an impossible goal. The tears were simply forged from too many distresses. I was going to miss everything that I had in this very moment—my realm and my sub-pack.

I slowly stepped back from them, rubbed my tears away, and turned to face Belenus with a smile. He looked slightly sad as he held out his arm for me, and I had to wonder if he was sympathizing or regretting his decision to keep me.

Stop that! Eventide snarled, her viciousness snapping me out of it. *No assumptions!*

You're right, I'm sorry, I responded hastily and girded my loins. I took Belenus's arm, lifted my chin, and took a deep breath. *This is a new adventure!*

And maybe we'll finally lose our virginity tonight!

Oh my goddess, what did I tell you about flustering me? I reprimanded and tried hard to not think about that very thing.

Belenus waved with his free hand to my sub-pack and their mates. "Farewell, all. I will see you soon."

Ragna pointed her finger at him and said, "Remember what I said about the Sun God! You better worship our Hekla or I'll get Soley here to smite your bum!"

I looked up to catch an amused expression on Belenus's face as he nodded in understanding. I held back a sudden bout of jealousy at their inside joke. The emotion both startled and concerned me, having never felt something so ugly before. I needed to exercise better control over myself!

Belenus placed his hand over the one I had on his arm, making more tingles shoot through my skin, and we teleported out of my realm, away from everything I knew and held dear. Once my body arrived in the Realm of the Fae, I swayed slightly, dizzy from the intense transport. To have moved without moving was a nauseating experience, and I wondered if I'd ever get used to it.

I snapped my eyes shut, blinded by the brightness, so I let my nose and ears take in the surroundings first. Slowly, I opened my eyes to let my vision adjust. Not only had the location changed, but the weather had shifted dramatically. My skin was used to the crisp fall air, but it had been forced to thaw within seconds under the burning summer sun, and my bones ached from the change in pressure.

Belenus tightened his grip on my arm to stabilize me, and I could just barely make out his worried face. "Are you ok, Miss

Hekla? Queen Ragna had a similar reaction to the realm doors. I'll take you to shade and refreshments. Does that sound good?"

"That does, thank you," I admitted and looked around as my eyes finally adjusted to the fanfare of hot, golden light. We walked off the stone platform we'd arrived on and proceeded through the courtyard. Everything was so neat and tidy, not at all like the wilderness I'd called home, but I could get used to it. The emerald shrubs were trimmed to perfection, and there was hardly a speck of dirt on the perfectly laid tan flagstone. Fae guards equipped with spears were stationed throughout the area, and I only caught one or two glancing curiously over at us. The rest were as statues in their white gold armor.

We turned a corner, and I faltered at the sight of a stunning, gleaming castle looming before me. I swallowed heavily and asked, "A-are we going to the castle?" I knitted my brows in confusion and looked up at him. His jaw worked as he patted my hand.

"Yes," he said simply. "It is where I work, Miss Hekla."

That didn't really answer the question I had, but I realized I may not have asked the right question. *Is he taking us to work with him? That would be odd,* I said to Eventide, feeling uneasy. *I kind of just want to go to our new home and get settled.*

I guess we'll find out soon enough, she replied, too distracted by the sights and smells to be perturbed. She was already enjoying herself. I needed to do the same, but I was so tightly wound. I had so many thoughts and questions racing through my mind. Where were we going? Was I dressed appropriately? Would we meet his family? Oh gods, could I even read their literature? Did I have to learn a new language? What would tonight be like? Would we finally complete our mating?

Stop, Hekla! Stay in the moment! Eventide growled, and I released another long breath I hadn't realized I'd been holding. This was brutal.

I'm going to lose my blessed mind, I replied absently and tightened my hold on Belenus's arm. The fear grew hard to control, making my heart thump like a ravenous woodpecker.

I stared at the glimmering castle, its towers and enormous spires stretching toward the sunny, cerulean sky in a prayer. It seemed larger than our castles, but a lot of that may just be due to the decorative additions. Ragna had briefly described it as elegant, bright, and golden, and it was definitely all of those things. Lovely white stone made the majority, but pristine gold was generously worked into the trim and molding. The golden spires in particular seemed impossible to build. Well, apparently the fae were magical folk, and I supposed I'd learn soon all they were capable of doing.

That thought frightened me. I'd gone from being at the top of the food chain to somewhere unknown. With their magic, were the fae stronger than wolves? Was I now at the bottom of the food chain? I had no idea…

Belenus steered us onto a path that went to the right of the castle, and we soon entered a massive garden. I released a breath and relaxed a touch. This was familiar. Nature was familiar. Perhaps the garden was a touch too groomed, but it would do for now. Oh, it would certainly do. How I longed to take my slippers off and dig my toes into the soft grass.

The garden, also, was not what I expected—at all. My eyes grew rounder the farther we walked into it, exposed to the most beautiful and strange flora sprouting from the soil. I couldn't believe the variety of plants they had here! The different gardens felt like entirely different realms. Some paths brought us to cheerful, daydreamy patches of flowers while others toured through sections that looked positively ancient! How could all these species exist in one place?

Belenus's stride was more relaxed here too, and I found him smiling down at me. I blushed slightly under his kind gaze, enjoying the small break in my shattered nerves. However, upon us taking a new path, a different garden stole my attention—a small forest that looked just like home. Ferns popped out of the soft soil, acorns littered the ground, and moss clung to the trees. I tried to stifle a gasp, but it just escaped as an unfortunate-sounding squeak.

I couldn't resist. Perhaps it looked stupid, but I broke from Belenus's arm and ran to embrace a tree. Its scent settled on my tongue and in my lungs, prodding old and recent memories alike. I recognized even the sap that bled through the bark. If I squeezed my eyes tight, just for a moment, and pretended I was home, I could almost believe it.

"I had this section grown for you, Miss Hekla. It's… well... consider it my first gift to you," Belenus said from behind me. "I brought back some samples and had our gardeners work their magic."

I released the tree to gawk at him, unable to believe it. "Is that true? Thank you, Belenus!" It was an incredible gift—impossible, really. When I thought of gifts, I imagined little sentimental items. This, though… This was phenomenal. I knew Belenus was a general, but this was a part of the palace garden! What must the royal family think?

Appearing happy with my reaction, he gestured to a table I hadn't noticed and silently prompted me to join him. Still in awe of my surroundings, I asked another question. "Do we live far? I'd like to visit this place often, I think."

He politely pulled out my chair for me and said, "Er… no. We do not live far, Miss Hekla."

Not wanting to be rude, I hurried to sit so he could eat. The table had been set quite lavishly for two. A large number of what seemed to be fae delicacies were spread before me, still hot and somehow protected from the garden insects. I suspected magic had to be a part of that because I knew no fly could resist an open invitation. Perhaps the crested songbirds in the trees—nigh winged rainbows—did their part to cull the pests.

"Th-that's good," I replied and looked at the assortment of dishes. He pointed at everything as he named them, but it all mostly went in one ear and out the other. The names were as foreign as I expected, and I knew I'd forget them. I sighed and accepted it would just take time.

I nibbled on a small meat pie and groaned quietly at how perfectly the buttery, flaky crust mixed with the stuffing. Next, I tried something that I did remember the name of, only because I just thought of a lizard named Colin. It was a soup with smoked fish in it, and I smiled in satisfaction with every spoonful. I'd never thought to put fish in a soup. Eventide approved as well.

My fated mate tilted his head when he noticed. "Your eyes turned silver for just a second there. Was that your wolf?" Belenus asked curiously, leaning forward a little. My cheeks heated up from his attention, and I quickly took a sip of water.

"Ah… if silver, yes. Eventide was just showing her appreciation for this cullen skink. She loves fish."

"That's a pretty name. Eventide…" Belenus said quietly and looked down at his plate. He seemed lost in his thoughts. "Miss Hekla, I… have something to tell you. It's very important, and I'm starting to wonder if I should have told you sooner."

I froze at those words, and my heartbeat faltered. *Oh gods, what could it be?*

Just let him say it, Eventide replied.

What if he has a mistress he won't give up? Or what if he already has offspring? I guess that doesn't really matter. I could love them like m—

Hekla! Stop, you crazy female! Pay attention to our mate, or so help me!

I prompted Belenus to continue with a nod, feeling my lips press together in anticipation. He brushed his plate aside and interlocked his fingers on the table. Taking a deep breath, Belenus looked up at me and said, "We are at the castle because I work here, that is true, but I also live here."

Ok, not a wild start, Eventide noted calmly.

"I do work as a general, but someday my rank will rise… considerably."

I do wish it would, my wolf commented. *Tonight, preferably.*

I nearly choked on my water. *I thought you were going to help me stay calm!* I scolded. *I am barely keeping it together!*

"You see, Miss Hekla, my mother is the queen of the Summer Court," Belenus announced, and my water glass slipped right out of my hands. I fumbled to pick it up and shoved it back onto the table. Eventide had no interjection this time. She was just as shocked.

"S-so... you're a p-prince?" I asked, doing an incredible job of staying cool, collected, and calm. I reached for the other beverage that I'd left untouched and took a sip, but somehow my body couldn't process the flavor. It was too busy digesting Belenus's confession.

"Ah yes..." he looked up for a second like he was saying a prayer and then gave me a small smile. "The crown prince, actually."

I dropped the other glass, but this time I couldn't bring myself to collect it. It lay abandoned in the detritus, along with my wits. My hands slowly migrated to my face to cover my mouth. What was happening? Was this a dream? I patted my cheek, then pinched it. No, this was real.

Belenus, upset by my response, or lack thereof, came to kneel by my side. He grabbed one of my hands, and the mate touch took the edge off my shock. Quiet solace spread from him into me, and whether he was aware of what he'd done or not, I gratefully embraced the comfort.

"I am so sorry. Perhaps I should have told you sooner. I just wanted to get everything ready here and ease you into it as much as possible. I thought that telling you after the move would be better, but..." he sighed and bowed his head. "Well, you know now, and I'm sorry it distresses you so. Perhaps I was worried you'd run away if you knew."

He was worried about us running away? I said to my wolf, bewildered. *I wasn't expecting that.*

Belenus looked back up at me, his worried expression turning into one of newfound determination. His blond brows drew a firm line over his amber eyes, the eyes that reminded me of the pretty sap that crystallized on the trees of my realm. My realm… My old realm.

He grabbed both my hands and gazed at me in earnest. “Miss Hekla Himinn, I am addressing you now that you know who I am and what I will be someday. You have recognized me as your fated mate, and I have recognized you. I know our customs differ, but I must ask this question regardless.”

I held my breath and tried to get what comfort I could from his large warrior hands. “Will you marry me and accept your role as the next queen of the Summer Court when I ascend to the throne? It won’t be for some time. My mother, Queen Fedelm, still rules.” He added that last clarification a bit hastily, staring at me as if I was about to faint.

Perhaps we are, Eventide said woozily.

“Y-yes,” I answered simply, still in disbelief. It was an easy answer only because there was no declining. A decline would mean rejection, and I would not reject my fated mate! Belenus was mine! No one else could have him! The she-wolf in me was adamant about that!

Belenus released a colossal exhale and grinned up at me. That was the first time I’d seen him truly happy, and he was even more stunning. The handsome fae radiated joy as he kissed the back of my hand once more, looking so relieved. Had this secret been the cause of his aloofness?

“Thank you, Miss Hekla. I will prove myself worthy of you and do everything within my power to make my home feel like yours. This I swear,” he vowed adamantly, placing a hand over his heart.

“I admit I am overwhelmed,” I confessed, looking down at the gold-dusted hand that still held mine. He rubbed his thumb across my knuckles, so gentle and kind with his touch. “A new realm, a new people… one season.” I swept my hand around me nervously. “I will do my best to adapt, though. I promise.”

“We’ll do it together, Miss Hekla. I’ll be with you every step of the way.”

Chapter 3

Belenus

I laid my lips down on the back of her hand to kiss it once more and patted it tenderly, trying to bring her out of shock. I knew that as agreeable as Hekla was being right now, she was struggling to stay present. I could practically taste her fear; it was bitter, and I hated it. I could only hope she'd recover and allow me to make it up to her.

Had there been a right way to go about this? Probably. In all likelihood, I'd taken the coward's route. A part of me had thought it would have been easier to break the news in a prepared location, but now I felt like I'd tricked her.

Just another stereotypical, untrustworthy fae, I thought bitterly.

I released her hand, but before returning to my seat, I grabbed my glass of water and offered it to her. "Have some water, Miss Hekla. Maybe you can get a sip in before you drop this one?" I asked, relaxing enough to grin again.

Her eyes widened, and she carefully accepted the glass. "I'm so sorry about that! I'm not normally so… so…"

"Not normally whisked off into another realm and proposed to? Funny, happens to me all the time," I said as I sat, stroking my chin. She blushed and laughed before taking a long drink of cool water. After getting her fill, she handed it back to me with a small smile.

"Best you hold on to that then," she said, chuckling lightly. Ah, it was good to see her smile. Hekla was radiant... sublime. I took a moment to appreciate my fated mate now that my secret had been revealed and that my terrifying question had been asked.

"You are incredibly beautiful," I said as I studied her. "The most beautiful woman in history, I'd say."

"You... I... That's so... Um. Th-thank you," she stammered, unusually flustered. It was hard to believe this was the same woman who'd tried seducing me by eating sausages at Ragna's coronation. I had a lot of work to do. Her confidence needed to be rebuilt before she went under the brutal scrutiny of the court. Fortunately, we had all the time in the world for that. We just needed to complete our courtship and get married. I couldn't wait. I especially couldn't wait to bed her. I cracked my knuckles anxiously under the table at the thought.

Hekla was a perfect, ethereal beauty. The sight of her in the weeping autumn woods earlier had been enough to tie my tongue into absurd, impossible knots. There was something about her wild, lush nature that put fae women to shame—something so pure and honest. It seemed to run in wolves, but she wore it like a radiant gown.

Though it dismayed me to see her struggle with it today, I knew she had a great deal of confidence. Somewhere deep inside, I believed I could rely upon her as much as she could rely upon me, which was completely. I sensed that she was a natural-born leader and a true fit. I'd never known such deep, instinct-driven knowledge before, not even when Ragna had been everyone's fated mate, but I trusted it. I would follow it with dedication.

She was also a spirited little minx! Coupled with her beauty, she'd tempted me more than a dozen times, but I'd managed to stay in control. If she went back to her seductive ways, I wasn't sure I'd be able to restrain myself much longer. I just needed to get through this damnable courtship.

Great Sun God, her loveliness... Like other she-wolves, she needed not a drop of makeup to look like a goddess of the wild. She made me think of our royal flower garden in more ways than one. Her velvety smooth skin—that I desperately wished I could explore—was like our night embers daylilies, and her eyes—playful like a sprite's—reminded me of blackberry petunias. As umbral as they were, they still sparkled and caught the light like stars in the night sky. I also longed to run my fingers through her long, jet-black hair. The strands were vibrant, healthy, and reflected the sky's blues like an onyx odyssey hellebore.

Her flushed lips were my undoing, though—so soft and so full. I couldn't even think of a flower to describe them because all my mind could focus on was my desire to kiss them. I had to clench my teeth to prevent that much. I had to do things the right way. I had to treat her with the respect she deserved. She wasn't just another lover to be discarded. She was my fated mate, future wife, future queen, and the future mother of my children.

"H-how long is this courtship… anyway?" Hekla asked, the question releasing me from her thrall.

I raised my brows and said, "About a month." I nearly laughed when I heard the smallest lupine whine escape her throat, and she looked away in frustration.

"I assume the mating and marking is on hold until the wedding then?" she asked, trying to hide her disappointment.

I nodded, studying the range of expressions on her face. She wasn't happy, that was certain.

"This is not… how we do things, but we are in your land, and… I will do my best to abide by your customs." She sighed and brushed something off her skirts.

"Tell me how you do things," I said, resting my chin on a fist. She tilted her head, and I saw an ounce more of respect in her gaze. I made a mental note to research wolf customs. It seemed I had neglected to do that in my rush.

"We discover our mate. Unless we reject the other, we complete the mating. We mate and mark. There is usually no waiting, no marriage. The longer it is put off, the more difficult it gets," she said, almost growling the last part. "Sometimes it doesn't matter where. We could be in the woods," she added with a small shrug. "Many she-wolves enjoy a good chase."

Well, that made my pulse quicken. Shit. We definitely did things differently. Her way sounded a lot more fun. As unusual as it was, the thought of rolling around in the woods with Hekla was incredibly arousing. Something about it got my blood pumping—a deep sensation that reminded me of primal magic. Either way, I wasn't getting up from this table anytime soon. I sighed in aggravation.

"I regret that our cultures seem to be clashing, Miss Hekla," I said, taking a steadying sip of wine. "Perhaps if I were not the crown prince… but many eyes will be on us."

She looked confused by that. "It isn't anyone's business what we do to each other."

I immediately took another sip of wine, thinking briefly about what I'd like to do to her. "Court relationships are… tricky. Sometimes it seems as though no one has any privacy." I regretted saying that much when I saw Hekla's frightened face. Shit, I should have kept my cursed mouth shut! She didn't need to be more afraid than she already was. I was making this worse.

"To have others force restrictions on a mating… this is hard for me to accept," she murmured to herself. "What other restrictions should I expect? Am I not allowed to shift?" She looked up at me, speaking at a normal volume again. Her jaw was set, and her eyes glittered with either anger or tears. "If I am not allowed to let my wolf out, Eventide and I will do very poorly here, Belenus. It is akin to holding our breath after a long while. We will suffocate."

"I will personally make certain that Eventide will have the space to run," I said firmly, already making a mental note to expand the garden and get more trees growing. She looked comforted by my words, and I relaxed somewhat. This luncheon was having us sway between so many emotions and sensations, it was nearly enough to make a man seasick.

Remember her sacrifices.

She looked unwell now, listless and wan, and I knew this was the moment I needed to step up and care for her. "I know you haven't been here long, but would you like to rest, Miss Hekla? I can wake you in several hours, or by dinner if you need it."

She met my eyes and nodded. "Yes, please."

I hurried from my seat and held out a hand. She took it, and when she stood, I tucked her hand into my elbow. The walk back was quiet, and once we entered the castle, I stole a look at her, hoping to get a glimpse of her wonder. I wanted to take pride in showing her our grand architecture, but she seemed lost in thought, completely disinterested in my family's opulence. My heart sank. Hekla was not to be won by gold. I would have to try harder.

I led her to one of our most exquisite suites. It was reserved for princesses, especially ones in line for the throne, but I was no longer confident in showing it. Even though I tried to have it tailored to a wolf's tastes... perhaps I'd messed that up too. I opened the door and said, "Welcome to your room, Miss Hekla." I smiled, hoping she'd like the space, but when she wandered in, she didn't seem to see any of it.

She turned abruptly and asked, "We don't even share a room?" The tears in her eyes shocked me. "We can't share a bed? I promise I won't try anything, Belenus!"

"We don't room unmated together," I said with an apologetic look. I fidgeted with my hands, understanding now because of our luncheon why this must be upsetting. I was already forcing her to wait a month, and now she had to be alone every night. This must have been far from what she'd expected.

She swallowed heavily and took in the room for the first time. As large as it was, she looked upon it like it was a cell. “Thank you. It’s a lovely room. I appreciate your effort,” she said politely, gesturing weakly to the amenities I’d provided for her. “I like it.”

She took her bag from me and gave me a serious look. “One thing, though, in how you address me. Please, call me Hekla and not Miss Hekla. It makes me feel miles away from you,” she requested, and I nodded.

“Done. I will do so, my dear Hekla,” I said softly, bowing a little.

“And we wolves do not use the term ‘woman.’ That term is used to refer to pure humans... and fae, apparently. Shifters rarely use terms like ‘man’ and ‘woman’ for each other in our culture. Please show me respect by either calling me your female or your mate. I will also accept she-wolf if said in a positive manner.”

I shifted uncomfortably. “Those at court may find that a bit crude,” I said before I knew what I was saying.

Shit! Why did I say that? Just say ‘yes!’ Shit, shit, shit!

Hekla stared at me from beneath furrowed brows, her deep disappointment cutting. It hit me right in the gut and twisted hard, like an assassin’s dagger. “Then I suppose you should sort out who you care about insulting more,” she replied quietly. “Thank you for everything, Belenus. I recognize your efforts. I will take my rest now.” My fated mate then stepped forward and closed the door in my face.

In that moment, I wished I didn’t have the fae’s excellent hearing. I leaned my forehead against the door, mentally flaying myself. She was sobbing into her pillow. Shit.

I sniffled into my pillow after a bout of crying, pulled away, and wrinkled my nose, dismayed I’d made a soggy, snotty mess of it. Fortunately, Belenus had supplied me with countless luxurious cushions, so I threw it across the room with a growl.

Do you feel better now? I kind of do. That cry was what you needed, Eventide said. *Maybe you could let me out later?*

I looked around my sizeable suite, noting the various doors and hallways. I hadn't quite explored it yet. Perhaps she could do that for us.

Looks like there may be some space for you to do some laps... it could be worse, I remarked, trying to find some silver lining in our situation. I dragged my bag over and opened it to unpack the small things I'd brought from home. Belenus had given me an extensive list of items I wouldn't need, so I hadn't packed much.

The very first thing I noticed was two packages and a card that I hadn't put in there. There was no containing the broad smile that stretched across my face. I knew who the culprits were! I rubbed my nose and opened the card first.

"To our very favorite she-wolf, wisest of the wise and vessel to the poor Sky Gods who have to put up with your bossy bottom," I read aloud, finding comfort in my own voice. I laughed and hiccupped while rubbing away a fresh tear. I was not bossy! I was assertive... "It's our greatest, most wolfish hope that you are currently riding the general of the Summer Court, but if you are not, it is not your fault! We have all agreed that you are the prettiest of us, and he is just being a scared summer dandelion. Don't forget what we do to those!"

I furrowed my brows, not sure what was meant by that.

We pick them? Eventide suggested. *Blow th— Oh.*

"That had to have been either Trail or Soley!" I realized, letting out a very unflattering cackle. I rubbed away another tear, but this one was from mirth.

To be fair, Belenus does kind of look like a dandelion flower. No, dandylion. With a 'y.' Because he's fancy. Eventide snickered.

I grinned and continued reading. "To commemorate your brand-new adventure, we've put little sacrificial offerings to our beloved vessel of the skies! We hope to see you soon so you can tell us all about what snobs the fae are! Howl at midnight with us! All our love, Ragna, Rakel, and Soley! P.S. We wanted to sign with our paws, but there wasn't enough space, so we did our thumbprints. It looks kind of stupid, but there you go." I laughed again, seeing three inky thumbprints under their names.

There was an arrow, and I turned the card to read one last message. "Soley here! My gift to you is a potion! The witches said this will make Belenus… affectionate. It sounds disgusting, though. Good thing only he needs it! Pack always!" I smiled and looked at the list of items. It just seemed like a bunch of aphrodisiacs that were definitely not intended to be mixed together.

Oh, Soley… I'm not about to give my fated mate food poisoning.

I eagerly pulled out the two wrapped gifts, wondering which was from Ragna and which was from Rakel. I opened the bigger one first, which turned out to be a dagger sheathed in a beautiful but sensible leather scabbard. There was incredible, skillful tooling of four wolves on the leather, and I had no doubt who'd given this to me. I unwrapped the note from the hilt.

"Rude helped me get this made for you. I'm worried if you can't shift, you'll be vulnerable. Please be safe and keep this near. Give it an honorable name. I love you, sister she-wolf. Pack always. Rakel," I read. She was succinct as always, but her words made me shudder. I was getting the idea that maybe my new home wasn't as safe as I'd hoped.

Finally, I opened the small package, which must have been from Ragna. A shard of a stone fell into my hand, and I read the note that had been wrapped around it. "To my very first friend. I broke off a piece of the lunaite, and I'm gifting it to you. I don't know if you recall the night you came to me as the Sky Gods' vessel for the first time. They used Eventide to save me, then brought this rock down from the Moon Goddess. It was with me through my ordeals, and I hope that it will see you through yours. I truly cannot wait to see you again. As I write this, you haven't left yet, and I already miss you. Pack always. All my love. Ragna."

I held up the dark brown shard and stared at it. Sometimes the Sky Gods blocked memories, but most of the time They didn't. That night was painful to recall, and I didn't want to think about what would have happened had the Sky Gods not interfered.

I eyed the dagger and spoke to it. "What should your name be? Rakel said something honorable…"

What about a combination of everyone's names? Eventide suggested.

"What, like Heraraso?" I burst into laughter. "That sounds so stupid. No…"

Hmm… Fourpaw?

"That would be a faux pas, I think." I laughed again. Thank the gods I had a wolf with me. I couldn't imagine going through this ordeal as a human woman. I disrobed and shifted, allowing Eventide to do the exploring for us.

She hopped off the bed and sniffed around, particularly intrigued by the furs that decorated the floors. Some seemed to be bears, but we didn't recognize the others. She studied the unlit fireplace briefly, then placed her paws on the edge of a small dining table, smelling food. As soon as her silvery eyes fell upon an entire row of spiced, sliced beef, she snagged it.

Delicious, she murmured and continued to explore. We found a large bookshelf that had several rows of novels in our language, but the rest all seemed to be in a different one. It was probably fae. She nosed through a couple and tried to figure out if any were for language learning.

Not sure, Eventide, I mumbled. *I hope Belenus gives us a tutor. We'll probably have to learn to speak it too. Oh gods.*

Stay in the present, Eventide ordered and wandered into what we thought might be the bathroom.

That's a… big bath, she said, staring at the large pool and the shelves of soaps on the side. Rocks decorated the water's edge, and massive, lush ferns flirted with a small waterfall. The trickling created a delightful sound, and the candles about the space promised an exquisite, soothing atmosphere once lit. This wasn't quite like home, but I saw the obvious effort Belenus had put into it. I felt a moment of regret, wishing that maybe I hadn't closed the door in his face. He was trying…

I mean you can call this trying, but I'm pretty happy about it. I'd say he succeeded in this one thing! Eventide said, and I felt her urge to jump into it. She knew better, though. She'd get water everywhere with drenched fur.

You can jump in tomorrow before I bathe. Sound good? I asked.

Yes!

She turned and found what looked like a normal bathroom. This one had a large shower, a toilet, and a sink. It was certainly a relief that indoor plumbing was readily available, but it had me pausing a moment, thinking of my friend's trials.

Poor Ragna hadn't had anything like this through her ordeal. Maybe I needed to toughen up and snap out of my self-pity. Ragna said it was ok to be scared, though. I was torn. Was it ok to be sad? Was this maybe like grief? Can you grieve a realm like you would a loved one? How long would I feel this way?

You're rushing yourself. Remember what Father said. Stay in the present. Eventide sighed and trotted into another room. It was an office, a nice one. I supposed I could use it to write my letters to everyone when that process got sorted, hopefully in a couple days. I wasn't sure what else I'd do with it—maybe studying.

Eventide found glass doors behind some light green curtains and tried to open them, but since it was a doorknob, she couldn't get a proper grip. I shifted back into my body and opened the doors. Once I adjusted to the swathing summer heat against my skin, I was pleasantly surprised to find a large balcony. A stylish wooden table and two chairs sat by the balusters, a very nice setting for tea, I had to admit. There were some other objects I wanted to inspect, but I realized I was naked. I longed to feel the fresh air on my skin, but what if someone saw me? What if my nudity offended them, and they complained to Belenus? I doubted the fae accepted nakedness like shifters did. Humans were just as squeamish.

I withered in misery and retreated to the privacy of my room. Instead of returning to my dress, I looked for the closet that should have the clothes Belenus promised. Sniffing, I followed the scent of fresh laundry to another door, and upon opening it, I discovered a colossal walk-in closet that had more clothing than what all of my friends and family had—combined. I blankly took in the excessive collection, and after a moment of processing, I searched for some pajamas. Unfortunately, there were none... just nightgowns. I sighed and slipped one of those on, knowing I'd get tangled up in the middle of the night.

I don't think I'm up for dinner with Belenus. I... I'm tired. Maybe I'll just stay and sleep until tomorrow, I said to Eventide. It was more than that, though. I knew it was depression.

I'm tired too. I'm trying to be strong for us, but I'm feeling it. Thanks for letting me out, even if it was short.

I'll let you out whenever you want, whenever it's possible, I promised her.

My gaze settled miserably on the huge bed. I'd never seen such a large bed in my life, and I didn't want anything to do with it. It was too big to have to myself. Belenus should be in it with me...

I set my jaw, grabbed a bunch of pillows, a bedsheet, and all the furs, then went about making myself comfortable. He may have given me a bed, but I didn't have to use it. If this suite was mine, I'd make it mine.

Belenus

It'd been hours since I'd left Hekla to her rest, and I constantly checked the time to see if it was appropriate to fetch her for dinner. I desperately wanted to see her again and apologize. I felt stretched thin between trying to make her feel safe and keeping in mind the risks of court life. It would be harder to compromise on some of her desires, but perhaps that was a sacrifice I'd have to make. I wasn't a king yet, but I could try to influence where I could. I could handle a little trouble.

Deep inside, all this strife had me wishing that I'd moved to her realm instead. It sounded so simple, so honest. Her people said what they thought and meant what they said. Aside from the binding magic of a promise, the upper-class fae were a far cry from that.

I couldn't, though. I had to stay here. My people needed a reasonable king for when my mother's reign ended. She'd made too many selfish decisions after my father died, and the people had suffered for it. Hekla could help me piece the kingdom back together. She had it in her to be fair, compassionate, and firm.

I decided that it was late enough in the day for dinner and strode down to her suite. My heart thrummed excitedly to see her again, and I knocked on her door. I heard no footsteps, no call to wait, so I lingered a minute more before knocking again, a little louder. There was no response.

What would she want me to do? I thought, scrunching my brows. My hand went to the keys in my pocket as I considered my options. The appropriate thing would be to leave and have dinner sent up to her later, but I had a feeling she'd take that as a rejection. It certainly was not appropriate to enter and check on her, but I suspected she'd want me to do that. She made it clear that I had little to no boundaries with her.

I braced myself and tested the handle, which gave. She'd left it unlocked… that wasn't safe. That was something else I needed to warn her about without scaring her. Shit. If I posted guards by her door would that scare her too?

When I entered, she still wasn't in sight. I expected her to be passed out on the bed, but perhaps she was in the study? I wandered over to check, but no, she wasn't there either. Then I heard the trickling of the pool I had installed for her and noticed a note pinned to the expensive gold molding of the doorframe. I smiled at her casual destruction of the fine decoration and suddenly realized I quite liked that about her. She clearly didn't give a shit about finery. That in itself would make for a prudent queen.

When I read the message, however, my heart sank. It said she wasn't feeling up to dinner. Deep disappointment and guilt weighed upon me, but I understood. I had to be patient. I hazarded a quick look into the bathing room to see if that was where she'd hidden, hoping she wasn't naked in there. Oh, who was I kidding?

Instead, my heart broke just a bit more. I knew wolves were social creatures, but… was she that lonely? Already?

Behind the large ferns, she slept, buried in a nest of blankets. All around her were the rare pelts I'd ordered for her room, and she'd wrapped every single one around a pillow. She'd even cuddled up to one. Hekla, my fated mate, had made herself a little fake pack to keep her company, and I wanted to cry.

Chapter 4

Hekla

I woke to the sound of my name, followed by the scent of lemon trees and summer storms. When I blinked my eyes open, I found Belenus at the entrance to the bathing room. It was odd to see him there, like some invisible barrier kept him from coming to my side.

I sat up and gestured with a hand. "You can come closer to talk, Belenus. I won't bite," I said calmly. I left out my usual joke with him, which was to add an "until you're ready" to that sentence. It wasn't funny anymore.

"I… uh," he began, seeming to have a hard time looking me in the eye. I frowned and checked myself to find that one of my nightgown straps had slipped down an arm, giving him quite the view of my left breast. My nipple wasn't even exposed and yet my body was still able to break Belenus's brain.

Sensing this was the only power I had at the moment, I chose not to fix it. I simply stared at him and waited patiently for his wits to return. I had nothing else to do.

He cleared his throat and tried to be subtle about adjusting his pants beneath his belted tunic. "I, uh…" he said one more time. "I was going to dinner and thought I'd check on you," he said, pointing back toward the door. "You left your door unlocked, by the way."

"Why would I lock my mate out?" I asked, confused.

He hesitated, then finally replied, "We all lock our doors… it's just a safety precaution. Like how one locks their house, yes?"

I nodded, understanding but not liking that.

He then patted his pocket and added, "I have a key, though! Not that I plan on abusing it, I mean. It's… for safety."

"Abusing it?" I inquired, knotting my brow and rubbing my forehead with a palm. I knew what he meant, but honestly, why did he pretend that I cared about his sense of propriety? "Belenus, you can come in whenever you want. You're my fated mate. Stop talking like this," I growled softly. "In my culture we'd be 'married' by now, so your sense of what is proper only means something to you."

"Of course," he replied, just as softly. "I'll be more mindful of my words..." He glanced away and took a deep breath. "What I came here to say… I know you're not up for dinner, so I'll bring something back for you before I let you be. Any requests?"

That's sweet! Eventide chirped with excessive enthusiasm. *Ask for fish!*

I laughed into my hand, confusing poor Belenus. His lips twitched into a smile, but he obviously had no idea why I'd reacted the way I had. He had a lot to learn about wolves. I wondered if he'd be able to hear Eventide when we eventually marked each other.

"My wolf said she'd like fish. That's why I laughed, Belenus," I explained, unwinding after the last chuckle.

"Then the fair lady will get our finest fish!" he said with a playful, sweeping bow, also relaxing enough to send me a flirty grin. I nodded quickly to get him to go away, because his brilliant smile had sent heat straight to my core. When I heard the door shut, I groaned and curled into a ball. All I could do was squeeze my thighs together and press my hands against the ache, as though it could be pushed away and forgotten. Carnal needs were, unfortunately, impossible to ignore.

Oh great Moon Goddess, get me through this month!

By the time he returned, I'd gotten my body to calm. It took a lot of cold water, and there might've been a tantrum involved.

"A fancy, fishy feast for my dear lady, Hekla, and my favorite wolf… whom I have yet to properly meet, I just realized," Belenus announced, turning thoughtful while placing the tray of food on my small dining table.

"Thank you." I sat to eat, ravenous from my bout of sexual frustration.

"I will take my leave… I'll see y—"

"If you wish to meet Eventide, return at five to midnight, Belenus," I said while I cut my food.

"That is… rather late…" he uttered, looking away as though torn on his answer.

"It is a late hour," I agreed, stilling with a forkful of fish as I waited.

"I mean… late to call upon…" He stopped himself short and sighed. "I will be here at five to midnight."

My brows shot up in surprise, and I nodded in approval. "I will see you then, Belenus."

Belenus

I paced my room from about eleven fifteen to eleven fifty in the evening, then walked down the halls until I reached Hekla's room. My heart pounded, like it usually did when I was about to see her, and I groaned, rubbing my hands over my face. Why was I doing this to myself? Why was I at the door of my betrothed at this hour? A female who had enchanted my cock to salute her regularly like *she* was the general...

The door opened sooner than anticipated, and Hekla gestured me into her suite... still wearing that delicate nightgown.

"I-I was going to knock when it was time," I explained quietly after she'd closed the door behind me.

"No point hiding," she remarked with a small, wry smile. "I could smell you from miles away."

I tapped my nostril and grinned. "Your nose is that good, eh?"

She shook her head and chuckled as she opened the door to the balcony. "No, you just smell that good," she said, smiling over her shoulder at me, and moved to open the other door. I swallowed heavily. That was quite the compliment.

"And what do I smell like?" I inquired, forcing a confident grin onto my face. I licked my lips when the drawn curtains allowed the moonlight to shine through her nightgown. Great Sun God, I knew from her past teasing what she looked like naked, but her curves always stunned me like a blow to the head. I worked feverishly to keep my eyes on her face when she turned.

"You smell like my mate," she answered, leaning her head against one of the bedposts. The sight of my divine betrothed with the moonlight on her back had fire razing my insides. I must have been staring too long because she decided to expound. "Our noses help us determine things about our mates. They help us identify them and help males determine a female's readiness. I imagine the fae do not have this," she added quietly.

"We may be more known for our eyes and ears than our noses." I tilted my head. "It's not so hard to tell when a woman or a female is wanting."

"Is that so?" she asked curiously.

I stood and considered her. "Perhaps I can't smell what's happening between a female's legs, but I can see if her pupils are dilated," I answered softly, tilting my head in the other direction to stare into her sharp, entrancing eyes. I knew what I'd see there. What was I doing? I took a step forward. Why had I done that?

"I can also see if she's biting or licking her lips," I continued, gesturing to her sensual mouth. As though I'd commanded it, she licked her full lips nervously.

I took another step toward her. "Perhaps I'd notice a change in what's holding up her clothes." I gestured to how her hardened nipples made peaks in the nightgown. My desire to wet them with my mouth made something else harder.

One last step brought me close enough to feel her warm breath through my tunic. My eyes roved from her blooming cheeks to the curve of her hips. "I can see if a female's skin is flushed… as her flesh might be swollen elsewhere..." I brushed the back of my fingers down the loose fabric—careful not to press into her skin—and let my hand hover suggestively where her abdomen met her thighs.

I rested my arm against the bedpost, just above her head. "And it's easy enough to tell if her pulse and breathing accelerate." I placed my palm on her chest, just above her breasts, to feel her heart hammer into my calloused flesh. What was I doing? What was I thinking? I just touched her chest without warning.

I leaned over her like that for a moment, knowing her panties must be positively drenched. And me? My cock throbbed and strained for release, needing to get at my fated mate. Oh, it wanted her. She was so close. She was so ready. We both were. How was I going to survive a month? If it was bad for me, how bad was it for her? Did she suffer more? This was only the first day!

It had been a mistake to come here this late. It was too tempting. I wanted to bed her too badly. I'd already had to masturbate twice today, and it still hadn't been enough.

I needed to leave before this escalated. When I opened my mouth to excuse myself, she stepped back and checked the little magic clock I'd left on her nightstand.

"It's almost midnight…" she observed and backed farther from me. I immediately missed the tingling sensation of her skin under my palm. The mate touch was a phenomenal force of nature, both comforting and thrilling at the same time. I wanted more… I wanted so much more—on my cock, beneath my fingers, pressed against my mouth.

Hekla made sure the balcony doors were open wide, and in a move that had my jaw dropping, she shrugged off her gown straps, naked in less than a second as the silky fabric hit the floor. I was wrong earlier. She hadn't been wearing panties. My cock lurched, my fist tightened around the bedpost, and the small snapping of wood hit my ears.

"My sub-pack told me to join them at midnight tonight…" she informed in a low voice, studying my face. I'd lost the battle; my eyes were glued to her luscious breasts. "Meet Eventide," she introduced with a sad smile and shifted. It was a lot quicker than I expected, and I wished I'd been paying more attention.

In a blink, a massive black wolf appeared and walked up to greet me, wagging her tail excitedly. I squatted and patted her head, able to finally get a good look. The canine's eyes shimmered silver, and her fur was soft to the touch—a fine beast, indeed, and much larger than the wild variety.

"Hello, Eventide. You are a beauty, aren't you?" I complimented gently and scratched under her chin. I paused for a moment, wondering if this was appropriate. Eventide was also technically my mate, but I wasn't expected to be intimate with this form. Were head pats ok, or was she just like any other canine I'd met and lived for table scraps and belly rubs? Confusion hit me now more than ever.

I sighed and accepted some lupine kisses from Eventide before she went out onto the balcony, claws clicking on hard tiles. There went our first kiss…

I followed and watched the stars with her. Another clear night in the Summer Court graced our skygazing—one not too hot and not too cold. Simply a perfect evening for my intended to do what she willed. Something about joining her friends at midnight?

I had a feeling it was about to get noisy in a second. Eventide hastily retreated into the room and ran back out howling. She must have gone to check the time, and I grinned, finding that very cute for some reason. But great gods, Eventide had quite a pair of lungs on her! One could probably hear her all the way out to the Unseelie Court!

I chuckled quietly as I watched her howl at the twinkling stars and the passing moon. The wolf was excited, like she was truly connecting with her friends in the other realm. It was a nice gesture for them to plan this. It wouldn't keep Hekla from being lonely, though… I had to figure something out, but I still couldn't think of anything outside of what I already had planned. I had to introduce her to people slowly and to those I trusted the most. Strategizing in general was a long game and painful for those not used to patience.

Eventide eventually ceased her howling and trudged back into the room, visibly depressed. Then she jumped on the bed and shifted back into my Hekla. I held back a groan and forced my gaze from her starlit skin. She was too tempting, and I was going to lose control. Already my abdomen cramped and crackled with electricity. I pumped my fists in agitation, reminding myself I wasn't to touch her again tonight.

"It was good to meet her," I said, running a shaking hand through my hair. "She's as beautiful a wolf as you are a w—female." I grimaced, almost calling her a woman again on accident.

She nodded and rose from the bed. Was she going to try to seduce me again? I didn't know if I could take it. But all she did was pass me to enter the bathing room and crawl into her hidden nest.

"Good night, Belenus," she murmured, knowing I could easily hear her. "Lemon trees and summer storms."

"What?" I asked, leaning against the doorframe, not understanding.

"It's what you smell like… lemon trees and summer storms," she clarified, then yawned and curled into one of the pelts. I stared at her for a long while after that, watching her breathing slow until I was certain she'd fallen asleep. I wasn't sure what possessed me to do it, but I didn't want her to be alone until then.

The next time I woke, it was from a tapping noise. Sitting up slowly and feeling a touch disoriented, I rubbed my eyes to clear them. I'd dreamt of crisp air in my lungs and autumn leaves under Eventide's paws, which made me forget for a second that I was in the fae realm. The reality hit like cold water, but after a couple deep breaths, I shook it off, stretched, and went to find the source of the noise. It definitely wasn't a fist on a wooden door, and when I realized the sound was coming from the balcony door, I hesitated. Was someone out there? How? They didn't have dragon-shifters here, did they?

I rushed to slip on the nightgown I'd left abandoned on the floor and peeked through the curtains. Behind the glass hopped a colorful bird whose eyes simply begged to be let inside my suite. What a delight to wake to! I swung the double doors open and allowed the bird entrance, smiling as it flew about and landed on the bed.

"Look at you! Good morning, little bird. Are you here to wake me for the day?" I chuckled. It was a lovely little thing, like a wren with a long train of rainbow feathers. It hopped forward and tilted its head, seeming as curious of me as I was of it.

A swirl of what could only be described as a ribbon of light rippled about it, and a fully dressed woman appeared. The bird was gone, and it didn't take long to make the connection. I yelped in surprise and retreated a step, my skin prickling with every hair that stood on end.

That's no shifter! She's wearing clothes! Eventide gasped.

"Wh—" I began, startled; however, rage quickly quashed fear. My territory had been invaded—by a woman, no less!

"First rule," the beautiful strawberry blonde fae said, "is don't trust animals! Any one of them could be a fae in disguise!" She shook her head and tutted. "That's how assassins get to you!"

"Are you an assassin?" I growled and bared my teeth, letting her see my lengthened canines. I also raised a hand to make sure she knew that I had claws just as sharp. Eventide raged in my head, just as offended and ready to shift.

"Ooh! I like you!" She grinned, leaned forward, and rested her chin on her hands. Then, as if she'd just sipped on a fine tea, she scrunched her freckled nose in delight and hummed.

"You didn't answer my question," I said flatly. "Not that I have a reason to trust your answer. Get out, fae!" I pointed back to the balcony and took an assertive step toward her. I didn't care if she had magic; this was my territory! I would not stand for this!

"Maybe you'll survive court after all," she said thoughtfully, staring at me. She tilted her head and frowned. "Or that aggressiveness could get you killed."

I flared my nostrils and snorted. If she wasn't going to answer my questions, then there was no reason to ask more. My patience, already stretched thin, evaporated.

Bringing myself within a hair's breadth of her, I yelled, "I was forced to move away from my realm, I am utterly alone here with a disinterested mate, and suddenly, I have people invading my territory! The one place I have to myself! I won't tolerate further insult!" I grabbed her wrist to drag her out of my suite, digging my claws into her arm and not caring one bit if I cut her or not.

"Wow!" She gasped and whimpered in pain, allowing me to tug her along. The lock on the door jiggled before I could reach it, and Belenus stormed in, furious. He glared at the woman, cheeks flushed as he caught his breath. Had he run down here?

"Emer! I told you! I strictly told you not to do this!" he yelled, slamming the door behind him.

"Greetings, brother," she said with a pained grin, looking up at me to make sure I realized she was his sister.

Oh, we so do not care! Eventide barked.

"Adopted," he said through his teeth, making the muscles in his jaw knot.

I closed my eyes, took a deep breath, and tried to find myself again. Had I been too violent? I was on edge.

Maybe more than usual, Eventide noted. *Best let her go. Make sure Belenus deals with her.*

I opened my eyes to find them both staring at me, and I promptly released Emer, who examined the cuts on her arm. "Your bitch is incredible! Look at this! I'd say it's quite refreshing to see someone so honest."

I growled at her, which made Belenus start. He then rounded on Emer, scowled, and hissed, "Do not call her that! I've never raised a hand against you, but don't tempt me, Emer!"

"But it's what one calls a female dog… Oh, alright!" She smiled up at me. "I do enjoy bending rules, but I'll try to behave. It's a good thing I like you. Belenus is poor at picking bed partners."

That was a jab to my heart, and for a split second, I wanted to kill her. I knew many didn't wait for their destined mates, and that was fine, but I didn't like hearing about his previous women. I seethed, slowly and coldly, "Then it's a good thing we're not." In an agonizing amount of emotional pain, I dug my claws into my palms until they pricked skin—a bad habit among my kind. My chest had been squeezed by a vise, and my skin ignited. Eventide whined within me in solidarity.

"I figured," she said with a sigh and looked up at her brother, shaking her head.

This had gone on for far too long. "You are testing me on my territory. Get out. Immediately!" I yelled at her, then glared at Belenus. Lividity shook him, but he seemed frozen, like he didn't know what to do with himself. I wanted to order him out as well, but he didn't do anything wrong.

Finally, Emer brushed off her red skirts and left through the door without a word. I paced restlessly, squeezing my fists while trying to calm myself. Blood pounded and rushed in my ears, an annoyingly loud thunderstorm in my head.

Belenus explained quietly, and I strained to listen over my fading ire. "Once she found out you'd arrived, she wanted to see you straightaway. I told her no, but you can see she's great at talking… not so much at listening." He walked slowly toward me, hesitantly, as though I were about to attack him.

I had so many angry, immature, spiteful things I wanted to say, but none of it was like me, so I held my tongue. I just needed to calm down and think rationally. This place was poking at all my sore spots, but I couldn't forget who I was. What would Hekla do? That was what Ragna told me to think. I needed to hang on to that and remember how my friends saw me.

"Belenus, I will not attack you. I would rather chew off my arm than attack you. You seem wary," I said, watching him out of the corner of my eye. "Yes, I am furious. My territory was invaded. I'm packless now, and I feel vulnerable. I need to feel safe in my own living space if I'm without a pack or a mate." I looked down at my hands, seeing the bloody damage I'd caused in my own anger. Though I'd heal just fine, I took this as a warning. I needed to fight to stay in control, and I feared I was slowly losing that battle. Fire scalded my skin, and my muscles ached. My heart hurt.

While I stared at my hands, Belenus moved silently, standing in front of me before I realized it. He reached out, grabbed them, and rubbed his thumbs gently across my palms. The mate touch soothed me so potently, so immediately, that I let out a colossal exhale. Warmth spread into my hands, a different heat than the injury's inflammation, but it was the sight of skin knitting back together that surprised me. Not even Eventide could heal me that fast!

"Fae magic… now that I'm back in my realm," he explained softly. "It's stronger here."

"Thank you," I said, just as quietly. I stared blankly at where the cuts used to be. Now only red remained. Even so, I still felt like I was bleeding.

"I'm so sorry, Hekla. I'm sorry for everything," he apologized in a thick voice, and I could tell he spoke the truth. I nodded slowly, letting him know I heard him. He pulled my hands up and kissed them both. "You feel warm, Hekla. Are you feeling alright?" He placed a wrist over my forehead in concern.

"I think my body's still upset by some of the things she said. She-wolves are very territorial, Belenus," I said, looking away from him. Surprisingly, his hands slid down my arms and around my back to pull me into a hug. I went wide-eyed and froze as he pressed me close against his hard body. In my shock, I didn't know what to do, but I let my stained hands hang limply at my side, not wanting to get blood on his nice clothes.

He murmured into my ear, his hot breath stroking my skin, "Since the moment I met you, you became the only female I wanted to touch for the remainder of my life, Hekla. No shifter, woman, or fae woman interests or would ever interest me in the slightest. All I can see is you. Perhaps if tradition wasn't so strict, I'd have had you the night I met you."

His words and breath had me shivering, but the claim irritated me. "You offered yourself to Ragna when she was here," I accused without thinking and winced. I sounded like a jealous pup. Why had I said that? I should have let that go a long time ago.

Belenus sighed, and I thought he'd back away, but he just dug his fingers into my back. "I was desperate, Hekla. My time was running out. My mother was about to marry me off to a nightmare of a woman, and I saw Ragna as my only way out—if I could win her over, that is.

"I would have tried to claim her as my mate if we weren't fated. Being the Sky-Blessed might have been enough to change my mother's mind. Practically anyone was better than that fae, Hekla. Yes, Ragna was beautiful, and I pursued her so recklessly I came across as a bit of a bastard." He chuckled briefly and sobered. He laid his chin upon the top of my head and sighed, pressing his ribs into my breasts.

"But apparently she-wolves are beautiful in general," he said in a bored tone. "When I saw you, though," he continued, his voice warming with nostalgia, "you were so beyond beautiful that you rendered me speechless. I couldn't appreciate anyone after that. You made me want to risk my life on the raid that King Zorian was leading on Eysteinn's cult. That's how much I wanted to see you again. I wanted to stick around and see who you were. It was well worth getting stabbed, I'd say. I didn't even know you were my fated mate."

I jerked my head up to look at him. I had no idea! I hadn't known about any of that! He grinned down at me. "What?" he asked, feigning incredulity. "Never had anyone take a sword to get a chance with you? I find that hard to believe."

I simply gaped. "Certainly not. But you were scared to death of me!" I argued.

"And I still am," he said, his amber eyes penetrating me.

"Why, though?"

"Because you, of all the females and women in the world, not only make me feel like I'm going to lose control… you make me wish I could."

Chapter 5

Hekla

I let Belenus's words sink in for a moment as he held me. The revelation shocked me, to say the least, and I was a little embarrassed for assuming his lack of interest. He'd volunteered to join a battle just so he could stay around a little longer? Just so he could see me? He'd risked his life for just a little more time with me?

My cheeks flushed from a bevy of hot emotions. Flattering couldn't begin to describe it! I also needed clarification of that last statement. "What do you mean by losing control, Belenus?" I inquired nervously, biting my lip.

"What I mean, my dear Hekla," he began, grabbing my chin and forcing me to meet his hungry amber gaze, "is that I'm forced to live by rules, and you make me want to abandon all of them. That could land me in a lot of trouble, you know."

"Wh-which rules?" I asked, flustered. My skin heated as the flush traveled down my body, kindling an ache between my legs. Oh Moon Goddess, he was so close!

"You make me wish I could just run away from all this." He nodded toward the balcony. "Drop all responsibilities so I could give you all the time and attention you desire."

I shook my head, my instincts finding that unacceptable—even being packless. "No… your people require you," I reminded, intimidated by his intensity. "Alphas don't abandon their packs."

He continued as though I hadn't spoken. "And you make me wish I could ignore this accursed thirty-day courtship so I could bed you here and now." He jerked his chin heatedly toward the giant four-poster while his hands slid up my back to play with the nightgown straps. He twisted and wound the material, as if he was toying with the idea of slipping them off my shoulders. "You have no idea how hard it is to resist you. Especially when you're being such a shameless little minx." He wrapped the straps tighter around his index fingers as he spoke.

Oh gods! An embarrassing whine squeezed its way out of my throat, fed by my spike of arousal. Still, I couldn't tear my eyes from his broiling stare.

Is your face on fire? Eventide asked. *I feel like your face is on fire. Go find a mirror.*

I wouldn't be surprised if it was.

"S-so the rules really are that strict? You didn't put me here because you were disinterested?" I asked uncomfortably. "You wished we could share a room?"

He released a beautiful, clear laugh. "Oh, dear Hekla. I'm so interested that I'd put us in a room and throw away the key." A rakish grin swept up his lips, and his eyes glittered with eagerness. "I'm sure it'll be plenty clear to you on our wedding night just how interested I've been."

I heard Eventide swallow heavily. I followed suit.

OK, I'M GLAD WE GOT THAT SORTED, she yapped, like his stare had broken her brain. The unexpected loudness had me jumping in Belenus's grip.

He started and I blurted an explanation, blushing horribly. "Eventide startled me. Sorry! You've, uh… made your point clear to both of us." I sandwiched my lips between my teeth and tried to retrieve my wits. He smirked knowingly, briefly dropped his gaze to my mouth, and released me from his clutches.

"So, how do you feel about a tour today? Get familiar with the surroundings? We won't really be meeting anyone new... Just ease you into things," he asked, tilting his head and crossing his arms.

"I can do that. When do we leave?"

"Whenever you're dressed! I'll be waiting outside." He grinned and left, in a much better mood than when he'd arrived. I blinked and looked around, feeling very... something. Already this morning had been so eventful, dragging my emotions all over the place. I had been so furious earlier, but then Belenus completely disarmed me with his confession. I guess I was... feeling ok?

It's going to be a long month, Eventide sighed. *I don't know if we have the stamina for this ordeal.*

I groaned in agreement and went to peruse my wardrobe. I agonized over the choices; there were too many options. How was I to know what was appropriate? I grabbed an olive dress that seemed nice but wasn't too fancy.

I freshened up quickly and gave the dress a challenging glare. When I donned it and reached around to tighten the fit, I somehow tangled the strings. I stretched, twisted, and even tried pinching them with a couple claws, but the mess just worsened. At least it wasn't wool; a wolf losing to a sheep would have been mortifying. I marched to the door, opened it, and pouted at Belenus in defeat. When I coaxed him back in to help, he burst into laughter at the state of the dress.

"What, is this not how you do things?" he teased, retying the back. I growled quietly, which made him laugh harder. "There, all done. Shoes and let's go!" He smirked and leaned against the wall. Feeling his eyes on me, I quickly pulled on a pair of soft boots and grabbed his offered arm.

On our way out of the castle—and free from the initial shock—I was able to better appreciate the surroundings. The interior of the castle felt very much like a celebration of summertime. Windows, balconies, or skylights brightened the rooms, and pale colors allowed the sunlight to bounce around, illuminating the spaces naturally during the Sun God's waking hours.

Gold was… everywhere, as it had been outside the castle. It followed doorways, trailed along windows, or simply existed in little decorative patches on the walls and ceilings. The yellow invaded motifs of the sun and crept into the stone flooring, which was a light blue-grey and speckled with gold flakes. Polished to perfection, the floor felt like walking on a mirror. It also looked very slippery. I grimaced at the mental picture of Eventide trying to turn at a run only to slide into a wall. I hoped my imagination was exaggerating.

I paused whenever we passed the long stone planters that occasionally ran down the middle of the halls. They hosted a variety of flowering trees that attracted remarkable butterflies. Or perhaps they were moths? They were a little on the chubby side. Also, their colors shimmered so vibrantly that I felt like my eyes would burn if I stared at them for too long. I had to wonder how much of fae nature was as perfect as these tiny creatures.

I refocused my attention to where we were going, needing to remember every turn Belenus showed me. He gave me a brief tour of how to get to several important places like the dining areas and the library and where to find his personal chambers should I need him. I noticed there were more guards by his suite. Was the queen nearby as well?

After showing me where his chambers were, Belenus playfully whispered, "Don't get any ideas, my dear Hekla."

I raised my chin. "One has no control over their ideas. At least I have them."

"Oh, that was clever." He scratched his jaw with his free hand. "But at least now I know you think about me."

I raised a brow and showed off a canine to further challenge him. "If you've suddenly realized that, it was a waste to have paraded naked around you all those times. Perhaps I'll not bother again."

"Ok, you win that time." Belenus flashed a bright smile. "Please keep bothering."

I glowed, enjoying how this particular conversation felt playful, natural, and easy. Things seemed to flow better when matters of the court weren't involved, and now that some confessions had been made, Belenus had become relaxed and flirty. I wanted this to last. Aside from wild matings, this was how I pictured interacting with a fated mate. I'd imagined the simple, sheer joy of just being with them.

Belenus led me out of the castle where a carriage waited and my heart leapt. Would we get to see more nature today? Or maybe we were going somewhere else?

He helped me into the compartment, and I quirked a brow once he seated himself. A slight urge to rebel against yet another custom had me remarking, "It was not so hard to climb the steps. Do fae women have trouble with balance?"

He laughed and peeked out through the mostly closed curtains that seemed to block the heat. "That's a great question. Now I'm wondering if they've been needing help all that time. Devilish creatures, fae women."

The carriage lurched, and we left the castle steps with the clopping of large tan horses. Belenus waved a hand. "It's just polite. Men extend greater courtesy to women here. It's antiquated, from when men thought women much weaker. Or perhaps just in hopes of earning favor for a good time. How do you do things?"

I wasn't sure about the lycans, but I could answer for the wolves. "She-wolves accept that we generally do not have the same muscle mass as males, but it does not stop us from being the best we can be. Males encourage us to be strong. Some she-wolves can take many males down. Our Rakel was our finest," I said nostalgically, proudly. "But males treat us well, and we are respected." I frowned down at my dress. "Perhaps fae women would fare better with pants and boots?"

"No doubt," Belenus agreed. "A female's bottom looks fine in a pair of pants."

I glanced up at him with narrowed eyes, suffering a tinge of jealousy. He held up a finger. "Ah, ah, ah. Notice I said 'female.' You are the only female here."

He is playing a dangerous game, Eventide growled.

Feeling an intense rush of possessiveness, I left my seat and promptly sat in his lap, resisting the urge to bare my canines. I just sandwiched my lips between my teeth to keep the impulse at bay.

"Don't play word games with my wolf, Belenus," I warned, holding up a finger to mirror his. I subtly wiggled in his lap to tempt his cock as punishment. "She doesn't like competition. She doesn't like you thinking of other females. Or women."

Belenus leaned forward into my face. "Hekla... you don't want to start this game with me," he said in a rough voice. Barely hidden beneath his smirk was a severe countenance. His eyes glinted with warning.

"What game? The game where you try to make me jealous?"

I'm wondering if maybe we're overreacting a li— Eventide began.

Belenus moved his lips to my ear and said, "No... the game where we try to see who breaks first... she-wolf."

I laughed bitterly. "I've already played that game. You're unbreakable." I crossed my arms.

"So... you don't mind the fact that when we go out that door, all the fae women will see the size of my excited... royal scepter?" he murmured seductively, tracing my ear with a finger.

That's a very good point. This was a bad idea, Eventide declared.

I fell off his lap and scrambled to my seat, not wanting any woman to stare at what belonged to me. His scepter had better calm down right this minute! Belenus chuckled and brushed some imaginary dust off his pants, then adjusted it to ease the bulge that'd grown there.

I decided that the topic very much needed to be changed. "Where are we going anyway? Aside from insane?" I asked, placing my chin on the heel of my palm.

He took my hand, squeezed it, and pulled back the curtain. "To show you our people, my future queen," he said with a gentle smile as we entered a city full of the strangest creatures, sights, and scents I'd ever encountered in my life.

We're going to be queen of total chaos! Eventide bemoaned. *What is all this?*

I was speechless. Yes, it was a city, and yes, there were houses and shops. However, the sizes of said buildings ranged from birdhouses to barns, from rustic to sophisticated! The sizes and shapes of the citizens took on that range as well! My ears strained to sort through the distant noises, and my nose felt like it'd snagged on the aromata of a hundred species.

"Who... what... ?" I gasped, unable to formulate a single productive question.

"These are fae, my dear," Belenus informed, rubbing a thumb soothingly over my hand. The tingles and sparks of the mate touch soothed me but barely enough for me to pay attention to him.

"But they don't..."

"Look like me? No, they certainly don't," he replied, a hint of a smile in his voice.

It was as though they were all shifters but had gotten stuck mid-shift, though in a way that made more sense. I saw people with goat legs or antlers or wings, but then there were creatures I'd expect to see in the wild that were wearing clothes! A gopher in a satin vest carried a basket overladen with purple vegetables. Finally, I spied beings that weren't quite describable, creatures that were a mix of so many other species that they were their own unique... living thing!

They were all so different, and yet they interacted in a completely normal way. They chatted, laughed, or ignored each other, just like wolves and lycans did. No one gave anyone odd stares; if anything, I was the one being rude.

"Why do they look so different from the ones at the castle?" I asked, turning back to Belenus with wide eyes.

He regarded his people with an inscrutable expression and spoke in a low voice. "The fae of the court, like me, are mostly fair fae, though I'm not necessarily a fan of that term. It's self-declared beauty, isn't it? Royalty and those who tend to serve the court look more… like your humans; I suppose we could put it that way." He gestured to the bustling scenery outside the carriage and continued his explanation. "These people we call folk fae are often seen as inferior, being mixed with nature's… other traits."

"But they are so beautiful," I protested and pointed to a girl with blue-and-white butterfly wings and little fuzzy antennae. "Isn't she gorgeous? How could she be inferior?"

"Because she has wings, which makes her an ideal worker. Fair fae have no need for wings since they—er—we, have servants who do everything for us," Belenus answered. Thoughtfully, he murmured, "Cleaning the rafters…"

I muttered without thinking, "If anything, it just makes fair fae sound weak. Pick up a broom." Instantly, I winced and slapped a hand over my mouth.

Instead of getting offended, Belenus broke into laughter. He pinched his nose with a thumb and forefinger, possibly pushing back tears of mirth.

"Sorry," I said with a cringe and looked back out the window, distracted by a folk fae made of more branches than expected. Under the eaves of a furniture shop fluttered two… reddish faeries, I supposed. I recalled that's what Ragna had called the tiny winged ones. I leaned against the glass, trying to follow their frenetic movements until they fell from sight.

When the carriage rolled to a stop in front of a larger shop, Belenus squeezed my hand one more time. "Before we leave—whatever you do—do not say 'thank you' to anyone, ok?" he warned.

"That seems rude. Why?" I asked with a frown as he brushed his hair aside and straightened his coat.

"Because old traditions state that you will owe them something in return. We've abolished some of our more… mischievous laws, but that one is still legal, unfortunately," he said seriously. "Fae will take advantage of you. Just tell them to have a good day and be off. Is that understood?"

"Y-yes!" I replied, frightened all over again. How could they enforce such an odd rule? That seemed far too sneaky and manipulative for modern society. What happened to the people who visited and didn't know about it?

Belenus left the carriage first and held out a hand for me. I took it, grateful to touch his skin more than anything. I desperately needed the comfort. The strange rule had me looking over my shoulder, turning me into a nervous wreck. Again, where was I on the food chain here?

"So," Belenus said, capturing my attention with his charming grin, "I was thinking about how you're all alone in your room…" He pointed to the wooden sign of the shop we approached, but the painted words were in a different language. "What do you think about"—he opened the door to the shop and gestured me in—"getting a pet?"

I wasn't certain if my eyes could get any wider. There was a menagerie of some very strange critters in here, and my nose was assaulted by their equally odd scents. I gasped and stepped back from a cage that chirped.

"Oh Moon Goddess, startled by a bird!" I scolded myself in shame. It was the same bird Emer had turned into, and I narrowed my eyes at it. "I'm watching you…" I whispered, pointing a finger at its cute little face. It chirped again, happy as can be.

A growly voice cried out in welcome, but it was in fae, and I sighed in disappointment. It would have been nice to talk to someone else—someone new—and make an acquaintance. Then, I fell well past disappointment when I noticed this fae was a man with a wolf's head. He was almost like me! Oh, how I wished I could talk to him! The wolf-headed folk fae noticed the crown prince and fell to his knees in deference, bowing his head like an obedient pack member.

"Rise, Oscar. I'd like you to meet someone today," Belenus greeted, and the fae stood, taking a humble stance. "This is a wulver named Oscar. He owns this pet shop. Oscar, please meet my fated mate, Hekla Himinn. She is my betrothed, soon to be my queen!" He grinned down at me, beaming with pride.

For some reason, him saying that to a citizen made it seem all the more real. I blushed furiously and tried to put a hand to my face to cool it, but my palm was just as hot. The wulver's head snapped to mine, and he said something in fae, sounding surprised. I wasn't sure how he managed to speak with a wolf's mouth; there had to be magic at work. That was impossible!

"Oscar here says you smell like a wolf," Belenus translated, chuckling.

I mean... we better, Eventide mused.

"Hello, Oscar. It's nice to meet you," I said politely, then turned to Belenus. "Am I supposed to be a secret?"

He shook his head with a dry expression. "No, and I doubt you could keep your nature a secret if you tried," he replied before addressing Oscar. "She's a wolf-shifter from the Realm of the Humans. We're here to see if she'd like a pet. She's not used to being without a pack."

Oscar's shoulders fell, and he nodded in understanding. He whined quietly, then gestured to the cages, saying something that I had to assume meant, "Take a look around." I absorbed his reaction for a moment, feeling comforted by what I suspected was wolfish solidarity. Did the wulver have packs?

"What do you think, Hekla?" Belenus asked, turning with a hopeful expression. His eyes held an apology, like it was his fault we were even here. "Would you like a little companion to keep you company?"

"I... don't know. I mean, I have Eventide," I said, strolling past furry and scaly critters.

"But can you cuddle Eventide?" he inquired with a wry smile.

I snorted and shook my head. "No… not quite," I replied. "I've seen dogs being used at castles, and sometimes a pup will keep an injured rabbit they don't want to kill, but pets are not something we think about. We're already surrounded by nature in the wild. Maybe it is more common in our cities, but I'm from a more remote pack, as you recall."

"That makes sense," he mused and walked patiently by my side. "This was just a thought. Don't feel pressured if you don't wish to have one."

Pets, I imagined, were a lot of work. Aside from keeping me slightly less lonely, what would be its purpose? It was hard to consider yet another adjustment to my daily life.

Eventually, the wulver came back and asked Belenus a question, who then turned to me. "Apparently, he has more interesting specimens in the back that he saves for… important customers. Would you like to take a look?" he asked, tilting his head. "I admit, I'm curious."

"No harm in looking." I smiled at Oscar and gestured. "Lead the way."

Oscar took us around the back counter and through a curtained doorway. Larger cages sat back here, and the enclosed creatures carried a sharpness in their gazes that belied their innocent status as pets. I looked up at Belenus, who was studying the animals with interest.

"No doubt you have some very useful companions back here, Oscar. You do not disappoint. Cuilean-sìth, piseag-sìth, pygmy beithir…" he said thoughtfully, rubbing his chin. Oscar seemed pleased, and his ears perked up at the praise. At least I could read his body language. His expressions spoke the same as a wordless wolf.

Belenus traced the edge of a cage before he spoke. "My dear Hekla, what say you to something a little more useful than a simple bird or beast?"

"What do you mean?" I asked. One cage held black kittens with white spots on their chests, while the one next to it kept shaggy green puppies. They tumbled over each other to reach the front, eager for attention.

No cats, Eventide said firmly. *For so many reasons.*

Fair enough, I replied. *No puppies either. They look too similar to wolves; they'd hardly feel like pets.*

"Well, some of these could act as very good guard animals," Belenus answered, snapping me out of my conversation with Eventide. I hummed and continued to look around at the other options. I was intrigued, I had to admit. Fae animals were remarkable.

Oscar said something, and Belenus pointed to some small snakes with little legs. "These will detect poison for you. Good for court li—" Belenus started to translate, then froze. He closed his eyes tight and cursed under his breath.

"Poison?" I asked, my strained nerves finally manifesting into shaking. "Belenus, will someone try to poison me?" I covered my mouth, horrified by the disclosure. He placed both hands aggressively on my shoulders, but most of his fury seemed directed at himself.

"Not on my watch, Hekla!" he said, almost in a snarl. His yellow eyes darkened to gold, then narrowed, like he was trying to transfer his confidence to me. "Not on my watch."

I leaned into him while I fought for calm, and he hugged me tightly in turn. Without a pack, without a mate, I felt far too vulnerable to cope with a new threat. After a minute of clinging to him, I managed to get my shaking under control but left my arms wrapped around myself for comfort. None of this was what I'd imagined. Blindsided. I was blindsided.

We can probably sniff out anything weird, anything like poison, Eventide reminded weakly. *We'll be ok...*

I hoped so... I sincerely hoped so.

In an attempt to further distract myself, I wandered over to the next cage that had another strange bunch of creatures. These little beasts clung to long sticks in the fake habitat and somewhat resembled opossums. Each had the same pale face and black fur, but from the back sprouted velvety moth wings with eye patterns. Their whiskers had gleaming tips, as if dewdrops clung to each strand. Curious, I asked Oscar, "What are these?"

Belenus answered for him in a soft tone. "These are a breed of mac-talla." He slid his hand into mine. "When they bond with their owners, they can act as additional eyes and ears because they'll be able to speak to you. Now that I think about it, they might be a good choice because they could translate fae for you, Hekla. You'll learn it eventually, but it'll take a while."

"I think it's wise… I can imagine running into difficulties when I'm on my own," I replied, staring at the young things. "What's the story behind that one?" I asked, pointing to a larger, disheveled mac-talla with underdeveloped wings.

Oscar hesitated and began explaining to Belenus, who nodded along in understanding. "This one is… apparently unpopular. It's been returned a number of times. That's why it's older than the others. He doesn't recommend it."

Studying the raggedy thing, I asked, "Is it because its wings are stunted? That's hardly its fault." The others were curious about me, but the bulkier mac-talla just stared blankly at the back wall. Its moth wings were only several inches long, not nearly enough to allow it flight. It looked more like a bow tie than a pair of wings.

Oscar spoke, and Belenus relayed his warning. "Apparently, its personality is a little rough around the edges…"

"Wouldn't yours be if you were returned to your orphanage a dozen times?" I asked a little more curtly than intended. I wiped my brow, feeling a touch feverish again. I needed to get control of myself. Deciding with confidence, I pointed at the mac-talla that looked as lonely as I felt and declared, "I'm taking that one, and it's never coming back!"

"Are you sure?" Belenus inquired, not looking particularly perturbed by my decision, which surprised me. "Sounds like you'll have your work cut out for you."

Oscar said something, and Belenus translated again. "He's asking if you're sure too. It'd break his heart to see this mac-talla returned again. He's also willing to part with him for free—which will not be happening." The prince turned to Oscar and pulled out a coin purse.

It sounded like the wulver reluctantly stated a price and took the coin. The folk fae handed me a little booklet, which I assumed was a care guide. Unfortunately, it wasn't written in my language. Belenus would have to read it to me.

"Thank y—" I began out of habit, but my fated mate slapped his palm over my lips, while Oscar snarled to interrupt me, then submitted in apology.

Slowly, Belenus removed his hand from my mouth and said, "Remember what I said… just wish them a good day."

"That serious, huh?" I laughed nervously and wiped a trickle of sweat from my overheated brow. "Right… I remember." That had been rather embarrassing.

Oscar finally opened the cage and removed the strange winged opossum. The wulver gestured for me to hold my elbow up to allow it access to my shoulder. I smiled and hummed encouragingly to the beast who looked anything but interested. The mac-talla eventually released a defeated sigh and crossed onto my arm. Then, he settled on my shoulder and wrapped an arm around my head for balance.

"I have a good feeling about this." I nodded to Belenus, who appeared both relieved and happy that I'd picked a companion. Indeed, this had cheered me up immensely.

"Shall we get some breakfast then?" Belenus inquired, offering his arm to me once more.

"Let's!" I agreed, and we both said farewell to Oscar, who still looked worried. Oh, it would be fine!

Chapter 6

Belenus

I escorted my exquisite fated mate to my favorite café and nodded to my hidden guards, who posted themselves nearby in case of trouble. Every fae we passed bowed in deference, and Hekla's grip on my arm tightened by the minute. I patted her hand, trying to soothe her.

I couldn't imagine being in her position, and I was grateful I was able to get her a little companion who could potentially offer comfort. I'd racked my brain for hours trying to find a way to make her less lonely. If the mac-talla turned out to be more of a handful than she expected, I'd give it to one of our animal handlers who'd care lovingly for it during the remainder of its lifespan. Per my Hekla's desire, I'd make sure it wouldn't go back to the pet shop.

With a satisfied smile on my face, I watched Hekla devour a large breakfast. She even made for a beautiful glutton! I couldn't blame her for being starved, though. Stress burned a lot of energy.

I idly thumbed through the care guide as we ate. "Seems the mac-talla is most active in the evening and morning. It'll probably sleep during midday and late at night." It was all in fae, so I made sure to relay the important information to Hekla. I skipped over the section regarding the wings as this one sadly wouldn't develop them further. She nodded along to everything I imparted, then froze.

"Oh goodness, I feel so rude. What does it eat? I should feed him," she asked, blinking her long black eyelashes.

"Hmm." I flipped back to the beginning. "Seems like they eat most anything, actually. They particularly like fruit. They also… haha, uh-oh." I snorted and raised my eyebrows. "They'll also get into natural fibers like silk and cotton. Best keep it out of your wardrobe, my dear."

She picked up a piece of dragon fruit and handed it to the mac-talla. "Maybe we should buy some bolts of cotton while we're out." She chuckled as the mac-talla smacked and chomped on the snack, but when it returned to its listlessness, she frowned. "How do we bond anyway?"

I flipped through more pages and scratched the back of my head. "Looks like they bite your ear to inject their magic. Sounds like marking, kind of," I said, turning the pages and reading more.

"Great," she muttered, and I glanced up to catch a cloud darkening her expression. "My pet will bite me before my mate does."

I leaned forward and grabbed her hand. "Yes," I whispered so quietly that only she could hear me, "but it will feel *so* much better when I do it, hmm?" I smirked at her rouging cheeks and the subtle way she squirmed in her seat. Perhaps that was a bit mean, but I couldn't resist. My smile broadened as she quickly finished her food, obviously wanting to leave. I had to wonder how wet that'd gotten her panties.

I paid the bill and walked a flustered Hekla back to the carriage with my guards in tow. She hadn't seemed to notice the escort, which was what I'd wanted. When we settled in our seats to return home, the carriage began to bump along the cobbled streets of the city. The mac-talla crawled off Hekla and curled up to sleep on the bench cushion.

My fated mate dozed off too, obviously from stress and digesting a large meal. I wanted to carry her to her room when we got back, but that wasn't really appropriate. I sighed unhappily at the restrictions that seemed so pointless. We fae were not prudes; in fact, many of the unmarried had multiple lovers. It was an absurd standard to keep such a close watch on my courtship with my fated mate. We were meant to be; how could the courtship end in any way other than marriage? How could she not be the perfect queen for this court? The seelie should give more weight to the Moon Goddess's decision.

We arrived at the castle, and I wanted to kiss her awake, but—of course—that would be inappropriate too. I sighed again and called her name, urging her from sleep. She started and growled softly like she'd left a dream, and I hid a smile, finding that extremely adorable.

She departed the carriage carrying the sleeping mac-talla, and I walked her to one last location she should know how to find. Opening the door to my study, I gestured about the place. "If I'm not in my chambers, I'm likely working in here or I'm in a meeting. I'll make sure you have a copy of my schedule so you'll know where to find me."

I moved around my desk, sitting briefly to see if there was a duplicate somewhere. Hekla settled the drowsy mac-talla on one of the couches and started fidgeting. The movement caught my attention, and upon inspection, I noticed she appeared feverish.

"Are you coming down with something, Hekla? You're looking warm," I inquired in concern, leaning forward to better study her features. Her irises had nearly been swallowed by her pupils, and her skin was flushed. Her heart raced within her chest, and had I not known any better, I would have thought her aroused.

"I don't know, it just keeps getting worse," she said, pressing her hands to her face. She shook her head and came around to my side of the desk. When I palmed her hot forehead, she sighed in relief.

"What are you feeling?" I asked, worried about her heaving chest. Perhaps now would be a good time to summon a doctor… Though, I wasn't sure how well-versed ours were on wolf-shifters.

"It's just really warm and… I ache," she answered breathlessly.

"I'll send for the doctor." I attempted to leave my chair, but she pushed against my shoulders.

"Just hold me for a minute, please," she begged and lifted her skirts to straddle my hips. Then, she wrapped her arms around my chest and nuzzled into me.

I froze, not sure what to do. If anyone walked in, this would look… really bad. I sighed and patted her back, allowing this for a minute before fetching help. She groaned and squeezed me with her slender and strong arms. Great Sun God, her body heat radiated into my clothes. I palmed her back where the skin was exposed to cool her down, and she moaned her gratitude.

I clenched my jaw, becoming drastically affected by her noises and how she was pressed up against me. Maybe a minute was too generous. I grabbed her shoulders to stand her up, but she whined and grinded her hips against my lap.

"Ah, Hekla, best not do that, my dear," I warned through gritted teeth. I should really get her off me. Her clad core was dangerously close to my burgeoning erection, and I couldn't stop thinking of her delicious, firm thighs spread so eagerly.

"Just… ah… one minute," she said faintly, sliding her fingers up my back, kneading with little claws like a kitten. I took in a deep breath and held it, trying to stay in control. Blistering sun, why did her sharp claws turn me on so much?

She squirmed again in my lap, this time finding my expanding erection through my pants and pressing her sex against it. I felt her folds part, molding around me. I tilted my head back, suffered the crackling electricity of desire darting through my chest, and barely caught the guttural groan escaping me. Oh shit, she was so warm. So warm. What would it be like inside her right now?

When she pressed harder, her dampness seeped through my clothes. Had she been standing, she'd be weeping down her thighs.

The mental picture had my cock jutting well past the waistband of my pants, and it leaked liquid beads of excitement down my tense abdomen. Fortunately, my tunic covered my pulsing lust, though I doubted she'd notice in her current state.

"Hekla… we should get you to rest… and I'll g—Ahhh…" I was cut off by her rotating hips and soft moans.

It was her turn to tilt her head back, providing an up close, tantalizing view of swollen breasts. I tried not the stare at them, but they were too sumptuous, too luscious to ignore. Her arched back strained her neckline, and I swallowed hard, secretly hoping her panting would expose a glimpse of her nipples or the dusky circles that preceded them.

I tried to shake myself from my hopeful staring. What had gotten into her? I slid my sweaty palms down to her waist, telling myself I was going to lift her off my lap.

I was going to lift her off me… any time now.

Any time now.

My hands stayed glued to her body and wouldn't move, despite all the yelling in my brain. Hekla now grinded along my erection like a wanton, and I couldn't escape it. I couldn't escape it because I didn't want to escape it. This was exactly what I feared with her. She was making me lose control.

When she released the saddest little wolf whimper, I finally caved. "Sun's blaze!" I slapped my hands onto her hips to help her grind harder into my lap. Digging my fingers in, I yanked her down and along my cock with every one of her rhythmic rubs. I leaned back in the creaking chair and grunted as she searched for her pleasure, because she was definitely helping me find mine.

"What has… gotten… into you… you sexy… little minx? Uh! Ahhh…" I gasped as she rocked into me. Her pulse throbbed through her soft underwear, and it was only a matter of time before she would drench my lap with desire. All it would take was a slip of some cloth to slide into her. This was getting so dangerous. This could get out of control so easily.

It already had.

My hands twitched in their hard grip, desperately wanting to unbuckle my pants, lift her, and impale her heat with my starving length. I bet she'd ride it wilder than any fragile fae woman could. Would she howl? Could I make her howl? That would draw too much attention, but I was damn curious. I wanted to see just how much of Hekla was a sexual, lustful beast. Just how feral could this she-wolf get? My new obsession was exciting, fresh, and deeply invigorating. Perhaps I wouldn't mind consummating my marriage in the woods…

However, as much as I was enjoying this, I was too worried about someone overhearing our activity and didn't quite have the state of mind to create a sound barrier. It was time I satisfied my female, my she-wolf. Gods, referring to her as such was becoming quite a primal turn on. I'd never expected wanting to taste such wild words on my lips.

Mounting instead of bedding…

"Come on, my dear," I groaned. "Find your pleasure on me. Come on, Hekla, you filthy, filthy she-wolf." I looked back down at her as she rode me with rapturous intensity. Her full lips parted and panted, and her breasts jiggled with every fervid movement.

Sweat trickled all over her overheated flesh. The female, though wild and ravenous, still maintained that impossible ethereal beauty. Electricity sizzled up my groin, and I nearly cried out from a wave of arousal. She was too beautiful, and I honestly didn't think I was going to last much longer.

"What's it… going to… take… to make… you howl… female?" I snarled, bucking my hips into her to make her bounce on me. I fought for air as I strained to hold my load. My eyes squeezed shut as I started panting with her. This was going to get messy, but I absolutely did not care.

She began to shake and tense, but I couldn't hold back anymore. My sack drew tight, and I came blindingly hard under her. I bucked up and hissed through my teeth, trying to stay as quiet as possible through my euphoric orgasm. My cock unloaded under my shirt and onto my abdomen, releasing what should have been ejected into her. Each surge had me gasping for air, making me lightheaded by the time I spent the last of my seed.

Knowing Hekla wasn't done, I picked her up, laid her on my desk, and yanked up her skirts. I tried not to look where I palmed her, fearing I'd lose all control. Then, with the heel of my hand, I pressed through her undergarment and into the nub above her entrance, making her writhe with pleasure. I was not leaving my intended untended.

She fell into whining, panting, and moaning. I wanted to hear more; I wanted to make her howl louder than her wolf had at the stars. I loved it, oh how I loved her sounds, but I knew someone might hear it. I looked around for something to stuff her pretty mouth with, but there was nothing within reach, so I leaned forward and offered her my arm, willing to get the fiercest of bites for her release.

"Bite, you noisy she-wolf!" I growled quietly. "Bite and find your pleasure under my hand!"

She chomped down on my arm and was able to cry louder while being muffled. Her panting almost became concerning by the time she finally froze, arched, and yelled into my arm. I grinned in sweaty victory as I feverishly rubbed her orgasm out of her, making her toss and turn on the table, absolutely delicious in her throes of pleasure. I kept kneading her throbbing flesh until she was spent, melted on my desk like a snow treat on a hot day.

I finally removed my hand and lowered her skirts, still trying to catch my breath. Oh, great Sun God, I'd do anything to take her to my chambers right now for a sweet, naked nap.

"What… what have I done?" Hekla groaned, covering her face with her shaking clawed hands. "I don't feel like myself… Why am I so hot?"

"I'll say…" I wiped sweat off my brow. "Let's get you to your room, and… I'll find a doctor."

Shit, I hoped this wouldn't get us in trouble. It wasn't sex, though. It'd be fine… right? Technically, no rules were broken… I think? Shit.

I sent the nearest servant I could find, a young teenager named Bidelia, to fetch the three fae women I'd picked out to become Hekla's personal maids. I was going to introduce them to her later today anyway. After my salacious chair dance with Hekla, I was a damnable sticky mess and did the best I could to clean myself up before help arrived.

I rushed to the door upon a knock, let in the three maids, and returned to my fated mate's side. "Hekla?" I said softly, squatting by her feverish form on the couch. She looked up at me through her thick eyelashes and blinked slowly. "These are your three personal maids. They'll take care of you when we get to your room, ok? This is Talam, Ushka, and Spayr."

She nodded slowly and allowed Ushka and Spayr to help her to her feet. Bidelia snuck back in, curious as always, and pointed to the mac-talla. "Should I bring the beastie as well, Yer Highness?" she asked, looking hopeful. I would have smiled at her childlike enthusiasm had I not been so concerned about my intended. I gestured for her to take Hekla's pet, and Talam hovered by my side while we walked back to Hekla's chambers.

"What happened, Yer Royal Highness?" she asked, worrying at her hands. The brunette fae adjusted her bonnet around her small, red deer antlers as we quickly made our way through the halls.

"She's been getting progressively warmer like she has a fever. Can you go fetch a doctor and bring them to her chambers?" I ordered, and she sped off like the deerlike fae she was. I didn't want to mention the other… more personal symptoms until we were in private.

The other maids helped Hekla to her bed and turned to look expectantly at me. Ushka cleared her throat and spoke in a melodic voice, "If you can please give us privacy to work, Your Royal Highness. We will sponge her to keep her cool until the doctor arrives." She raised her brows, making the tiny scales at her hairline glitter.

I looked at the time and groaned as well. Kneeling by my intended, I said, "Augh, Hekla, my dear. I must leave for a meeting. Do not be afraid to talk to the doctor, ok? Everything is confidential. I will come and check on you later."

She nodded, swallowed, and shifted uncomfortably. I bit back an anxious sigh and left her chambers, knowing she was in good hands. I'd been extremely careful picking those maids out for her. None of them would ever admit it, but they were safe because they were some of the ones who disliked the queen the most. I scowled, hating that it had to be a factor.

After I freshened up and changed all my clothes, I strode through the halls and pushed the doors open to see my next appointment. She'd been very difficult to find over the last month, and finally, I could catch her up on my engagement.

"Greetings, my son," my mother said and gestured to the empty seat across from her. "Join me for tea." She sat regally in her indoor garden, dressed like a queen even though she had no appearances to make today. It's possible she wouldn't even leave her chambers. She'd become quite the recluse over the years.

I sat across from her, and a maid came forward to fill my teacup. I ignored the woman, knowing that my mother didn't like to acknowledge the folk fae. The things I put up with to keep the peace with her could fill a library.

"I have been trying to find you for a month, dear mother," I said casually. "Have you been busy?"

"As much as ever," she said—as distant as ever too. "What do you have to share, my son?" She took a sip, but her gold eyes never left mine.

"I informed you a while back that I've found my fated mate, so I thought I should let you know that she's finally been moved into the castle. You will be able to meet her now," I announced, glad to have the weight of the arranged marriage forever off my back.

"I'm not sure why I should care about that," she said calmly, but there was a vein of ice in her words. I frowned and took a sip of my tea, trying to formulate the right reply.

"What do you mean? She's my intended. Of course it would be appropriate to speak with her," I responded, straightening my shirt and jacket.

"No," she said in a tone that made it sound like she was chastising a confused child. "Eislyn is your bride-to-be."

The blood drained from my face at her impossible words. "Mother," I said, trying to keep my voice steady, "I had an entire month left to find my mate, per our agreement. I found her within that limit."

"You did not bring her here. You also have no proof you found her in the time allotted," she said, taking another sip. She was still so composed, so aloof with me. "You're late, so your marriage to Eislyn will go according to plan."

"You cannot be serious," I uttered, feeling the ice-cold drip of dread ripple down my spine. "My fated mate is here. I can marry no other!"

"You can't? I think it's rather simple. Say your vows at the ceremony. If you wish, you could keep your fated as a mistress, but I'll allow no children between you. They'll be destroyed if she conceives."

"My fated mate will be no one's mistress," I retorted heatedly. My teeth clenched in growing fury, and my stomach roiled with nausea. What was happening?

"Then return her to her people," my mother said, shrugging lightly and picking up a biscuit to nibble delicately. "There'll be no point in her staying here."

"You never intended to let me marry anyone else, did you?" I asked in realization. "This whole agreement was a blisterin' game! Even if I'd brought her here earlier, I wouldn't have been able to find you, and you'd certainly not believe any witnesses."

She ignored my accusation and adjusted her skirts in a prim manner. "Anyway, the contract has already been signed. There's no getting out of it. Eislyn will be here soon, perhaps in a couple days."

"No…" I gaped, horrified. "There has to be a way out! Mother, you cannot do this!" I threw my teacup, shattering it on a stepping stone. "She is my fated mate! I must marry my fated mate! We were meant to be, and she was meant to rule alongside me!"

My mother sourly regarded the shards on the ground. "I didn't have that luxury when I married your father, Belenus," she replied coldly, her gaze cutting to mine. "I didn't have the luxury of having a husband who didn't dally in others' beds. You should be grateful I'm allowing her to stay as your mistress."

"I. Am. Not. My. Father!" I snapped back, incensed. "How many times do I have to say that? You can't keep taking his actions out on me!"

She pursed her lips. "What I am doing, beloved son, is showing you the things you should be grateful for."

"Grateful for what? For pairing me with a vile creature for the rest of my days?" I shouted, slamming my fist down on the table and making the teapot rattle. "What's even the point? She's from the Spring Court! We're already on good terms with them. We certainly don't need more power or money. This doesn't make sense! Why are you doing this?"

"I'm doing this because it's the best decision for my court," she answered. "I can't imagine that after all the resources I've spent on your education you've forgotten about royal discretion."

"And this is what? A two-week courtship?" I asked, fury dripping from my clenched teeth. How much time did I have to fix this?

"Precisely, because she is not an outsider to seelie territory."

"You mark my words, Your Majesty," I warned slowly and icily. "I will marry my fated mate. I will get out of this plan you've made behind my back."

"I'm sorry to say you won't, my son." Calm again, she patted a pin that held back her long, brilliant hair.

I abruptly stood and left her table, reeling. With a hand on the door, I seethed over my shoulder, "You've made small efforts to abolish some of our worst practices, but you've done nothing about what you are."

I slammed the door and rushed down the hall, blind in my rage, panic, and despair. I was not a blistering pawn, and I couldn't lose Hekla. My racing mind steered me poorly after that encounter. I didn't know what to do or where to go, but regardless, I eventually found myself at Hekla's chambers and leaned against the door.

How could I tell her this? She was already so afraid, not to mention ill. I couldn't hide it from her, though. She had to be prepared for when that vile creature arrived. I needed allies. I needed to get a team together to research the laws and see if there was any loophole to exploit. I knew the contract was magically binding, so I needed people on that too. There had to be something...

I closed my eyes and took several deep breaths.

I'd tell her when she was feeling better, but now I was going to check on her and see what the doctor discovered. I knocked on the door, and Talam ushered me in silently. Doctor Elisedd sat on a chair at Hekla's bedside, writing on a notepad. The mac-talla was nowhere in sight, but that was the least of my concerns.

"Your Royal Highness," the doctor said, standing quickly so he could bow.

"How is she?" I asked, noticing that Hekla had fallen asleep. Her cheeks were still rouged, but at least she was calm.

"I'd like to request having an expert come to our realm to discuss the matter," the fae said. "I need someone to verify a theory and help me develop a remedy to get her through this."

"That can be arranged," I replied. "I'll ask the lycan king if I can borrow one of his doctors. What theory do you have?"

The fae sandwiched his lips between his teeth for a moment and sighed. "I suspect she's been poisoned."

What?

"What?" I asked, rushing forward to place a hand on one of the posts. I turned my gaze to her in shock. How had this happened?

The doctor sighed. "Well, like I said, I'm no expert, and we have very limited documentation on shifters. If she's anything like a wolf, she appears to be in heat. However, I suspect this is a false heat, but I need an expert. I've tested for various hormones and some have come out at levels that are… unnatural. I'm hoping it will work its way out of her system soon, but I can't be sure of the timeline. I would highly recommend having her guarded until she recovers, and we should test whatever she comes into contact with regularly."

"She just… got here," I uttered in disbelief and ran my hands through my hair, not caring if I looked like a royal mess.

"It's either through contact with a tainted object or someone dosed her somehow, perhaps while she slept," the doctor surmised, scratching at the white whiskers of his brows. I scrubbed my hands over my face, willing them to not shake. I couldn't appear weak.

"Alright, I'll have guards posted at her door and balcony." I turned to Hekla's personal maids and said, "Two of you are to be here at all times. Is that understood? If someone needs a break, call Bidelia. She's not yet corrupted by the queen." I knew it was inappropriate to speak of the queen in that manner, but I couldn't care less. She'd long since lost my respect. Today, she'd lost any love I had left for her.

Chapter 7

Belenus

I looked around the suite for a moment and asked, "Where's Bidelia? Did she go back to her duties?"

"I'm back here, Yer Highness!" a young voice squeaked from the office, and when I walked in, she hastily explained. "He went after the linens, so I'm tryin' to set him up here!"

She was placing sheets of cotton on the ground for the mac-talla, who scraped at the fabric to shape it to a nest of his liking. A bowl of water and some fruit were also shoved up against the wall. Seemingly appeased, the mac-talla idly gnashed on the edge of a sheet, staring up at me.

I gestured back at the main entry door and said, "I see, Bidelia. Right now, I need you to run to the stables and tell them to get my horse readied and brought to the front. Fast, Bidelia!"

I watched her scamper out at top speed, then I squatted in front of the mac-talla to stare into his unnervingly intelligent eyes. He slowed his chewing as he returned my gaze. The black eyes contrasted sharply against his facial fur, which was a shock of white, paler than his previous cage mates. He finally stopped chewing altogether, as if waiting for me to speak.

"Things are about to get really dangerous, mac-talla, and I'm relying on you to help keep my future queen safe. That woman—I mean—that female in that bed," I said quietly, pointing to Hekla's unconscious body, "is Hekla, my fated mate. I don't believe you're as undesirable as what we've been told, and I need you to pull your weight. You're never going back to the pet shop, so I'm—"

I was interrupted by the mac-talla heaving a lethargic sigh, standing, and crawling up my body to swing onto my shoulder. He dug his teeth into my ear, and I hissed at the unexpected pain. My ear turned hot for a moment, then seemed to go back to normal. The mac-talla then jumped off and lay back down on his nest of fabric.

Ah'll believe it when it ne'er happens, the mac-talla said darkly.

"You bonded with me." I grunted and felt around my ear for punctures. There was a little blood, but I'd take care of that later.

Sae ah can talk, ye big numpty.

"Right..." I murmured, rubbing my ear and processing the sass I'd just received. "One cannot prove a negative, mac-talla, so you do your job, and I'll fulfill my end of the bargain. I suggest you stop wasting your energy on waiting for us to abandon you."

I stood and walked away from the creature, who seemed to have nothing left to say. Giving Hekla one last worried look, I left for the castle's entrance where my golden stallion, Haul, waited. I mounted and hurried him along to our door to the Realm of the Humans. The guards, ever at attention, watched me guide Haul up the stairs, and we traveled across realms to the hill where I'd collected Hekla.

A surge of emotional pain struck my chest the same time the autumn air met my lips. I almost wished I'd never brought her back to my realm. Perhaps it would have been better had we stayed here. I could have renounced my claim to the throne and led a simple life... but I knew Hekla wouldn't have liked that.

Alphas didn't abandon their packs; that was what she had said. I sighed, haunted by everything I couldn't control, and encouraged Haul to run the several miles to the castle of the lycan king and the wolf queen.

Lycan guards ran to meet me, and I slowed Haul down to address them. "I'm Prince Belenus from the Realm of the Fae. Can someone please announce my presence to King Zorian or Queen Ragna? This is in regards to an urgent medical matter of their friend, Hekla Himinn, vessel of the Sky Gods," I stated, trying—yet again—to appear relatively calm. On top of everything distressing me, I also did not enjoy going places where iron metal was commonly utilized, and it seemed to be everywhere here.

One of the guards gestured for another to deliver the message while I was escorted to the castle entrance. I waited nervously and stared at the massive doors, white-knuckling the reins. When I saw Ragna wave me in from the doorway, I released a held breath and hopped off my horse.

"What happened?" Ragna asked, gesturing me along as she brought me to a sitting room. "Is Hekla sick?"

"I have a doctor with her now," I informed in a rush, "and she's stable, but the doctor thinks she may have been poisoned into something called a…" I snapped my fingers together, trying to remember the term through my distress. "False heat. Have you heard of this? He told me he needed a medical expert on wolf-shifters to verify and help make medicine."

Her green eyes widened, and she looked away for a moment while holding up a finger. After a second, I realized she wasn't pondering but talking to someone. Ah, the enviable mental link wolves and lycans had within a pack. If only fae could communicate that efficiently outside marking.

"I've summoned our doctors, and hopefully I can urge someone to go with you! I-I'll order if necessary… but I don't like doing that. I'm still not used to feeling like… such an alpha," she said, whispering that last part like a confession. I laughed, but it came mostly from my shattered nerves. Ragna then inquired,

"How do they know it's a false heat? I mean, heat is heat. I've learned it starts about a month after recognition, though it depends on the she-wolf's cycle and how much they've been together or apart. I didn't get mine because I already was pregnant. Anyway, the female… well, she gets excitable, and the male goes a little crazy because of her pheromo—"

"What do you mean by the male goes crazy?" I interrupted, trying to wrap my head around all this breeding information. "I have not felt an ounce different. It's probably a wolf nose thing, yes?" It seemed a lot more intense than fae women, but perhaps that part of my education was left wanting.

"What's a wolf nose thing?" an older female doctor asked, walking in with two male doctors.

"I think he wants to know if—because he's a fae—if he should be able to sense Hekla's pheromones if she was in real heat," Ragna answered for me. "You know Hekla, our vessel for the Sky Gods."

"I doubt he'd smell them the way we do, but there's no doubt he'd be stimulated by inhaling them. He'd notice something was different for certain," a redheaded doctor said, sitting between the taller male and the female.

"So, what happened?" the tall one inquired, opening a notepad.

I explained everything the doctor had told me, and they discussed between themselves while I turned to Ragna. "So, can you really loan me a doctor, just until she recovers? I need to have someone train our doctors on wolf health too. I really should have thought about this in advance!" I lamented, scrubbing my hands over my face.

"No one saw anything like this happening so fast!" Ragna consoled. "I can't blame you too much. You both have huge adjustments to make for each other."

"I'm trying, I really am. She's so lonely, and the cultural differences ar—" I began and looked up to see King Zorian enter the sitting room with his beta in tow. I rose to greet him, and he joined us at the table, looking cold and slightly murderous.

"Ragna caught me up. Poisoning? Assassination attempt already?" he interrogated.

"No, not if someone is trying to trigger her heat." I sighed, needing to explain something. "A thirty-day courtship is mandatory if the intended is from outside the Seelie Court's territory, which includes spring and summer. It's a paranoid trust issue. Since Hekla is not from our realm, it's what we must do. In addition, we cannot mate or mark until the marriage ceremony. If sex occurs, Hekla will be sent back home, and she'll lose her right to marry me."

"What is the point of that? That's absurd!" Ragna protested, aghast. "Oh, poor Hekla!"

"The point is to avoid manipulation from anyone outside seelie territory. Sex is legally considered a form of manipulation in official engagements," I explained bitterly. "I wanted to introduce her to all this over time. She's already so overwhelmed."

"So, if someone gets a drugged Hekla to tempt you into a disallowed act, they'll be able to get rid of her. That means someone else has designs on you," Zorian said, toying with an abused pen.

"My mother has already interfered," I hissed and further explained what she'd done. "So, you see, it could either be her or someone else."

"It's someone else," Zorian said with finality. "The queen already has her solid gambit. She doesn't need to find another way to remove Hekla from your kingdom. She won't muddy the waters. I don't think it's your forced intended either. If she's signed a magical contract, she's probably feeling confident. I suggest you look into others who may be interested in you. Past lovers can be a thorn in one's side." He growled out that last sentence, and Ragna leaned into him, offering her comfort.

"I can't believe your own mother would have you reject your fated mate," Ragna mumbled, staring off and tapping her lower lip. "That's atrocious."

Zorian leaned forward and folded his fingers on the table. "I recommend a regular delivery of letters between our realms.

Send someone to the stump circle every day at noon to swap any letters that are ready. Have them present the password, 'Because King-Fucking-Zorian says so.' The messenger will provide a different password every day. Does that sound good? Also, we'll send a doctor back with you. Have them train yours."

Ragna melted in relief at her mate's words and turned to see if the doctors were done discussing. "Thoughts? Volunteers?" she asked hopefully.

"I'll go," the female doctor volunteered, gathered the notes the other doctors had written, and introduced herself. "My name is Doctor Egres. Allow me to pack, and I will return momentarily." All three doctors took their leave, and that was when two more individuals walked hesitantly into the sitting room.

"General Belenus?" Koray asked as Soley peeked out from behind him. I waved an invitation, and they joined us at the table. "We got word that someone poisoned Hekla, and I was wondering if—since you're here—should I go back with you today? I can help keep watch after training. Soley and I already discussed it..."

Soley leaned over to land her head against her mate's arm with a thunk, looking despondent.

"Oh, Soley…" Ragna said sympathetically to the wolf-shifter with the ember curls.

Casually, I said, "That's up to you, Koray. I have guards assigned to her." I avoided mentioning how lonely Hekla was. I didn't want to guilt him into coming up early.

Koray looked down at his fated mate and sent her a questioning look.

"Go…" she whimpered miserably, like she was sending him to his death. "She's my dear friend. Go make sure she's ok…"

He took a deep breath, exhaled, and turned to face me with his determined, royal blue eyes. "Alright, let me grab my things, and I'll meet you at the entrance." He quickly stood and helped up his depressed female.

Zorian shook his head. "Had Hekla been human or fae, I would have told you to bring her back, but as you can see," he noted, gesturing to the departing couple, "wolves loathe to be separated from their mates. Soley will be a weepy she-wolf for a while."

"Was Hekla really struggling waiting for me?" I asked, furrowing my brows and looking over to Ragna.

"Oh, you got her doubting everything," she said with knowing, wide eyes. "She was certain you were going to reject her."

I sighed and scrubbed my hands over my face again. "So much I don't know about wolves," I muttered.

"If she's a fraction as forgiving as Ragna, you'll be fine," Zorian said, looking down at his queen thoughtfully, who returned his gaze with a bright smile.

Hekla

I woke to a warm, soft kiss creating little sparks on my hand and forced open my dry eyes. Several people waited by my bedside; Belenus was the closest, and I scented the next person before I looked at her.

"A lycan!" I croaked and sat up enthusiastically but became light-headed as a result.

"Slow, slow," Belenus cautioned.

"Don't get up, sweet one," the older female ordered kindly and moved to my side. Belenus provided a chair and hovered next to her. "I'm Doctor Egres. King Zorian and Queen Ragna asked to have one of their doctors attend you. I've spoken with… Doctor Elisedd," she said, gestured to the fae doctor—who sat at the foot of the bed—and cleared her throat uncomfortably. "And I just want to ask a couple questions. First, how are you feeling?"

I turned my attention inward. "I feel a little more alert after resting. I'm still hot, though," I said, pulling at my nightgown to unstick it from my body.

So sweaty… we need a bath, Eventide complained.

Oh, there you are. You've been quiet, I remarked, perking up to hear her voice.

Don't feel right... pay attention to the doctor, she replied, then went quiet.

The fae who'd hummed to me before I'd fallen asleep brought a bowl of cold water and began to wipe down my forehead, arms, and neck. I sighed from the cool relief while the doctor went through her notes.

"And do you give consent for your mate to be here or should we send him away?" the lycan doctor asked, making the three maids gasp. I tried to hide a smile. It was good to have a lycan here who wasn't intimidated by royalty. I supposed being Zorian's doctor would toughen up any healer.

"I give my consent," I answered.

"Ok, good. And are you still feeling sexually aroused or has that dissipated?" she asked next. Belenus shifted uncomfortably and averted his eyes to stare out the balcony windows. His face had gone completely red, and his mouth moved silently in what I suspected was an ardent prayer.

"A little," I admitted, chuckling quietly at Belenus's prudish reaction.

He didn't stay that virtuous and proper when you rubbed him out in that office chair. Eventide smirked. She wasn't wrong...

"And have you experienced a higher fluctuation in emotions?" the doctor inquired.

"Yes... actually," I answered, kind of relieved there'd been a reason for that... aside from moving to a new realm and discovering that my mate was the crown prince.

The doctor asked a series of other questions that made Belenus more embarrassed by the second. Finally, she turned to him and asked, "And you have noticed no change in your libido around your mate? No additional sexual response?"

Belenus, mortified, shook his head aggressively. "Nope. Nope," he said quickly. "Nooope."

Oh, if he wasn't so upset, I'd be dying of laughter, I said to Eventide.

Trail will eat this story up. She snorted.

"So, I'll have to agree with"—she cleared her throat and jerked her thumb back toward the fae doctor—"Doctor Elisedd. I checked some bloodwork while you were asleep, and it does seem like you've been dosed with hormones to trigger a false heat."

My jaw swung open at the news. "I… didn't think it was heat because Belenus wasn't affected!"

"Normal heat produces pheromones; this false heat only affected your hormones, so he wouldn't have noticed a thing."

"Oh…" I replied, a sickening dread coming over me. "So… someone poisoned me?"

"It's the only explanation for the levels we found in your blood," she said simply. "I will work with… Doctor Elisedd to sort out a medication to help ease your symptoms until your body returns to normal. Speaking of which, have you had your first heat yet since recognizing your mate?"

I shook my head.

"Ok, well, you're due for that too…" she said, writing something down.

"What do I do for that, though?" I asked, suddenly realizing the implication. "I can't have sex for a month!" It came out sounding more desperate than I would have liked, but the doctor seemed to have expected my intensity.

"You may have to find alternate means of release to get you by." She looked back at Belenus. "As her fated mate, you will have to assist her."

"What if I can't?" he asked, visibly wary.

Doctor Egres answered in a clinical manner. "She will experience similar symptoms to this. It is obviously your choice, and should you choose to not assist, I suggest you maintain your distance so you're not exposed to her pheromones. It will affect your ability to reason."

This courtship is getting worse by the minute, Eventide groaned.

"One last thing before I leave," Doctor Egres said, closing her notebook. "I know this place is new with a lot of different scents. Even I am overwhelmed, but try to get familiar with the scents of those you trust. I recommend attempting to find traces of a scent of anyone you don't know in this room. They probably administered this in your sleep. If you find someone who matches that scent, I recommend you report it to authorities."

I frowned and shuddered. The thought of anyone being in my room while I slept was horrifying to me and had me feeling more vulnerable than ever. I got out of bed slowly and walked toward Doctor Elisedd. I'd already memorized Egres's and Belenus's scent. I trusted those two completely.

At first, I couldn't quite figure out what kind of fae Doctor Elisedd was. The slightly older man had several white whiskers poking from his brows and streaks of black in his brown hair, which was tied at the nape of his neck. He didn't have any claws…

I leaned forward and took a deep breath to memorize his scent, getting a whiff of cat. I realized his ears did look a little fuzzier than Belenus's. He was definitely a folk fae.

I moved to smell the maids, getting a faint deer scent from Talam, a subtle fishy scent from Ushka, and something avian from Spayr. I nodded in satisfaction, having memorized everyone. Perhaps I'd subtly sniff my guards later…

"Bidelia?" Belenus called out, and a small smile tugged the corner of his lips. "Are you here?"

An aggrieved sigh came from my study, and the young fae teenager trudged in guiltily, hugging a cranky, but freshly bathed, mac-talla.

"Are you shirking your duties?" Belenus asked, raising a blond brow.

She opened her mouth to protest, but then looked at her toes and nodded. "I thought maybe I could be the royal pet assistant…"

she mumbled, turning pink at the cheeks. I bit my lips, finding this to be the cutest scene I'd ever witnessed.

"We'll talk about that later," he replied dryly and shook a reprimanding finger at her. "In the meantime, let Hekla smell you so her wolf can recognize you."

"Wolf! Like the Sky-Blessed!" Bidelia exclaimed and skipped toward me. "If ye want, ye can call me 'pup' too."

Oh my gods, let's adopt her, Eventide gushed, instantly won over by the small thing.

"Ye don't smell like a pup!" I said, making fun of her accent and sniffing the top of her head as she laughed. "Ye smell like a bug!" I tickled her sides, making her squeal and run away with the mac-talla. I tapped my nose and warned, "But now I know what you smell like, Pup, so you can't hide from me!" I grinned a feral grin, and she moved to hide behind the fae doctor, giggling.

"Alright, well, that seems to be everything," Doctor Egres stated, standing and grabbing her large medical bag. "I'll check on you later, Hekla. Get rest and hydrate." She turned to leave, and Doctor Elisedd rushed to open the door for her.

Belenus gestured to the maids and Bidelia, saying, "If you can please give us a moment. I have something important I need to discuss with my… mate. You be on your way, Bidelia." The maids left, dragging the pouting 'pup' out with them.

"I'm relieved it's only a false heat," I said as he sat down next to me. "I could have been poisoned with something much… worse." I rubbed my dry eyes and took a sip of water. "I may have nightmares for a month."

"Hekla…" Belenus began, sounding strained, "we must talk about something that occurred recently."

I winced, horribly embarrassed about my earlier behavior. "I'm so sorry about what happened in your study. I hones—" I said, but he cut me off with a wave of his hand.

"It's not that. I met with my mother and…" He slapped his hands down on his knees and looked out the window, as though he still debated whether he should tell me or not. Maybe he was just trying to find the right way to say it.

"What happened?" I asked, scooting over so I could lay my hand on his.

He hung his head and pinched the bridge of his nose with his other hand. He stayed like that for a while, and dread nestled in my belly.

"Belenus? You're scaring me. What happened?" I repeated slowly, squeezing his hand. My heart started to pound, adding to my discomfort. Was he going to reject me?

He took a deep breath and released a whirlwind of bad news. "My mother doesn't want me marrying you and has arranged a marriage behind my back with a princess from the Spring Court, who will be here in a matter of days. The contract was signed without my knowledge, and my wedding to this fae is to be in two weeks, but I will fight this with every resource I have! I swear, Hekla! I will get out of this somehow!"

I felt like I'd been slapped in the face. "What…"

What! Eventide screamed.

"But… we're fated…" I said blankly, stating the obvious.

"She doesn't care," he replied in a broken whisper. He still couldn't look at me.

"But… the Moon Goddess… She put us… together…" I was simply too stunned to sort out what I was feeling. "A goddess… Belenus…"

"She… she doesn't care." He leaned forward and covered his face.

"I don't… I don't…" I kept repeating, frigid shock coursing through my body. "Am I having a nightmare? This can't possibly be real." I hugged myself. I was so cold now...

"I promise," he croaked, "I swear to every god in the sky and on the earth that I will get out of this somehow. I don't want anyone else but you, Hekla! Do you believe me? I need you to believe me!"

I nodded, emptiness eating at my insides. "I believe you," I whispered to the man who now felt so very far from me. Everything felt far, even the tears on my face. They traced the contours of my cheeks to fall from my chin, and Belenus wiped them away with his calloused thumb. Despite his efforts, they kept appearing.

"Wh-what happens if you break the contract?" I asked, staring at Belenus's guilt-ridden face.

"It's a serious offense in fae society to break contracts; they are magically binding. As the offended party, the Spring Court could ask for anything of equal value. Something this large… they could also demand torture or execution as a worst-case scenario. You're basically in their debt until their injury is balanced out with something else."

My face went cold at the implication. Could Belenus be facing execution if he didn't marry this fae? That brought out a rage in me. Something meaner than a furious Eventide threatened to claw its way out and murder everything within a mile of us. My possessive she-wolf instincts wouldn't allow this. I'd go mad if Belenus mated with someone else.

"But you're mine!" I growled, my canines lengthening. "This is blasphemy! They can't do this to us!" I dug my claws into the sheets, fighting the intolerable, itchy urge to mark Belenus this very moment. "I won't let them hurt you! I won't let them take my mate!"

"Then fight it with me," he begged in a thick voice, placing his hand on the bed to reach for mine. "Be strong and fight for us, ok?" His eyes brimmed with tears as well.

I white-knuckled the sheets and snarled, barely able to keep my mind intact. My gaze locked onto his with a predator's intensity, and my voice came out cold, layered upon a heavy growl. "I confessed my fears to my previous alpha, and he told me that the fae should be afraid of me instead. I will make it very clear that there's a wolf in their woods now, and she. Will. Not. Be. Denied!"

Chapter 8

Hekla

Belenus tended to me, listened to my raging, then held my hand when I finally broke down into spiraling sobs. The false heat drained me, wore me down into a chaotic mess of emotions. I knew I had to recover my strength to defend my place as Belenus's rightful, true mate, and he soon left me to plan his strategy. It was a colossal relief that he was taking it as seriously as a mate should.

My maids helped bathe and feed me, then two of them set up cots so they could keep watch overnight. I stared at the shadows of the guards on the balcony as I tried to sleep. Every single time I recalled what the queen had said, I became sick to my stomach from stress. What would these guards think about the situation? Would they sympathize or were they so loyal to the queen they wouldn't dare stray from her stance?

The folk fae whose smell reminded me of the sea and its aquatic dwellers stirred and came to my bedside. I hadn't memorized my maids' names yet… I'd have to do so soon. I was just too overwhelmed to add more information to my mind. Eventide could remind me, but she'd been quiet through the false heat and especially after receiving the bad news of Belenus's new engagement.

The fae asked for permission to sing me to sleep, and I allowed it, knowing that her magic could force me into a slumber. I desperately needed it. I doubted resting was possible without her help.

I woke to pain on one of my earlobes and snapped my eyes open to find the mac-talla waddling off my bed. Did he just bond with me? Why'd he run off? I groggily felt my ear, noticed the wet punctures, and scented the metallic tang of blood. As my sleepy mind cleared, I realized the creature just needed more time to develop trust. I couldn't blame him; I'd be wary after consecutive abandonment.

Abandonment… I remembered the events of yesterday and curled up, wishing for sleep to steal me away again. I just wanted to hide a little bit longer… get a little stronger… and a little braver…

Or perhaps I was just a coward, afraid to discover how strong the fae were. So, I ran from it for hours, trying to stay unconscious until my maids woke me for a bath and a change of bedsheets. I wasn't one to require lavish attention, but their doting made me feel like we were in a small pack, and it was comforting. I was the she-alpha, my maids were my pack, and sweet Bidelia was an adopted pup—who was constantly stealing time from her duties to tend to my aloof companion, the mac-talla.

The doctors came by to administer the first dose of medication to help reduce the hormones plaguing me. I still experienced bouts of heat and arousal, but it wasn't as bad as before, and my maids worked diligently to keep me cool. Gratitude wanted to escape my mouth, and it was a battle biting my tongue to avoid saying 'thank you.' I'd have to find some other way to show them… something positive. It couldn't be gratitude.

Belenus arrived in the early evening to check on me, and I beamed, so happy to see his handsome face. And though he smiled in return, it was strained.

"What's wrong?" I asked, fearful of more bad news.

"There's a banquet, and the queen has invited us both…" he said, brushing his sunflower-yellow hair back into place. I knew it sounded like good news, but it definitely wasn't.

"You think she's planning something?" I twisted my lips and tried to sort through my own theories.

Belenus nodded but shrugged. "We don't have to go. It's not like she can make us," he said. "I've stopped giving a shit about her wants."

I shook my head. "That's not how we do things," I replied firmly, girding my loins and showing a canine. "Wolves face opposition. I will go if you go, my mate." It was the first time I'd called him anything but his name, and he flushed, looking pleased. Though we hadn't mated, we were fated.

Belenus gestured to the maids and nodded. "I suppose you three better get her ready. Dinner starts in an hour." He turned to face me. "I will come by to escort you in fifty-five minutes… my female," he said softly and rubbed my hand with his thumb. My heart may have swelled a bit, and I fought back emotional tears. Then he gave me a tender look and left me at the mercy of my maids.

I had never been so poked and prodded in my life, my maids working as ruthlessly as I'd feared. Knowing I was the vessel of the Sky Gods, they insisted that I make my debut looking as such. I was forced into a midnight-blue gown that had tiny little rocks sewn into it. I'd heard of diamonds before because of how Zorian doted on Ragna, and I guessed it was what they were. I could see why the maids had picked this dress; I certainly twinkled like the night sky.

The wispy sleeves concerned me, having the potential to slide into food while eating. I also hoped I wouldn't trip on the long trailing cape made from the softest, silkiest, gauziest material

I'd ever seen in my life. I almost thought I'd donned a length of morning fog.

They left my hair down but tamed it a bit and decorated it with diamonds, charms, and little silver links. The maids placed diamond jewelry around my neck and wrists but were dismayed to find I had no holes in my ears for earrings. I informed them that she-wolves didn't think about those things because they already had to spend time shedding clothes to shift. Adding jewelry would just slow the process, and it'd probably get lost.

Finally, they somehow procured a diamond collar for the mac-talla, but I told them to wait while I turned to the creature. "Do you want to wear this?" I asked.

A'll nae be caught playin' deid in they, he replied in a mind-link. I sat there for a moment, processing my impending evening with this creature translating for me. I could barely understand it through its thick accent. I asked for this...

"Ok," I said finally and turned to shake my head at the disappointed maids. When I offered my arm to the mac-talla, all three cried out, and I jumped back, startled. One ran off, then returned with a leather shoulder pad that buckled under my armpits and around my neck. It rather ruined the graceful appearance, but I supposed they'd rather not have the mac-talla shred my dress to ribbons. However, a maid tapped the leather straps, and the entire harness disappeared.

"Glamour magic," the maid with the antlers explained, smiling and sighing in relief. I gasped at the magic that was cast so casually, reminded of Ragna's blessing to turn invisible at night when untouched by moonlight. The fae had the same power a goddess had. That terrified me.

The maid then placed the creature on my shoulder, and I left the room, deciding to wait in the hall for Belenus. When he strode around the corner in his dinner jacket, his mouth parted, and his wide eyes took in my appearance from head to toe. He fidgeted nervously with his cuffs and blew out a long, unsteady breath.

"You… um," he stammered, turning a little red, "you look… stunning." Even his pointed ears pinkened; that was rather cute.

"Is this what fae battle armor looks like?" I asked, deeply pleased by his response, and gestured to my dress.

"If it is, I should declare war more often," he breathed, briefly adjusting his belt before offering me his arm.

I laughed and accepted his arm. However, as we departed for dinner, it didn't take more than a minute for me to realize what I was about to encounter. I'd spoken aggressively before, but I was still scared. Even wolves feared the unknown; it was nature's warning to tread with caution. I clutched Belenus tighter, and he placed his other hand over mine to offer comfort.

When we reached the banquet hall, a porter opened the door for us, and my heart stumbled at the number of fae dining. I hadn't expected so many. Were these all the… I didn't know the word… court officials? The chatter at the table slowed, and the majority turned to look curiously at us. There were only two empty seats, and they seemed to be placed as far apart as possible. I looked for the guilty party at the front of the table and found a fae woman who absolutely had to be Queen Fedelm.

I could see Belenus in some of her features, and she was fair, like the rest of the fae, but she glowed with something… extra. Her golden hair shone brightly, the glare of a fresh sunrise, and there seemed to be power radiating from under her skin, reminding me—in a way—of summer thermals. Despite the warmth of her energy and her overall appearance, her countenance was the coldest I'd ever seen. Eventide's nervousness intensified at this powerful living contradiction; this was no alpha, but she still had half a mind to submit. I wouldn't, though. This woman deserved none of my respect.

"Greetings, my son," the queen said, lifting her glass in recognition. As expected, she ignored me.

"Your Majesty," Belenus returned coldly. "I'd like to introduce my fated mate, Hekla Himinn."

At the introduction, I nodded in slight deference. That was all these fae would get from me. They would have to earn this wolf's favor.

One fair fae spoke out in another language, probably fae, and gestured to us. The mac-talla promptly translated. *The eejit asked aboot ah fae named Eislyn. Said they thought this wus ah engagement dinner. Eejit.*

It took me about ten seconds to figure out what the mac-talla said and had to suppress a laugh. Then what he'd said sunk in, and instead of a chuckle, I held back a scowl. It was only several minutes into dinner, and I was already struggling with mixed feelings.

Queen Fedelm replied calmly, "This is an engagement dinner. Belenus will be married to Eislyn in two weeks' time. The contract has been finalized."

Another fae asked a question, one a bit younger who couldn't control his staring. I avoided shifting uncomfortably, needing to appear strong, but I did not like the eager look in his eyes.

The horny erse asked if ye were available then, the mac-talla said.

Belenus tensed next to me, and I could almost taste his anger. The queen merely nodded once, as though giving him permission to 'court' me. Eventide woke a little and bristled. The insults were stacking.

"I believe the queen is mistaken about all of that," Belenus announced and walked me to the table. The spot near the queen was probably labeled in fae with Belenus's name, and I was pretty sure that the empty seat at the end of the table—basically at the end of the room—had my name on it. Instead of taking his assigned seat, my mate walked with me to mine, tapped the person seated next to my chair, and ordered the fae to switch places with him.

Before Belenus could sit next to me, the queen snapped, "General Belenus, return to your assigned seat at once, or do you defy an order from your queen?" The fae at the table gasped and fell silent. The reaction made it painfully clear that the queen never had to raise her voice.

Belenus stared straight at her as he plopped into the chair next to me, defiance flashing in his eyes. The queen then gestured to a servant, who hurried over and whispered something into Belenus's ear that sobered him. His eyes flickered to me, and he swallowed heavily. When I glanced at his hands, they were fisted tight under the table.

They said the hoor queen wull order ah floggin' fur ye if he willny move, my companion said and adjusted his position on my shoulder. Flog?

Is she threatening to whip me? For sitting next to my mate? I snarled to Eventide, spiking her desire to come out and remove the queen's throat. My claws and fangs elongated, and a small growl formed in my chest.

Belenus immediately grabbed my hand and shook his head. His wan face glanced furtively around the table. In the quietest whisper, he warned, "No violence, Hekla. That is not how we do things."

Enraged, I fumed through my teeth, "She threatened violence first!"

"She's the queen. She'll get away with it. You won't," he argued, slowly moving to stand.

"Then I'll take the whip!" I hissed. "I'm not afraid to m—"

He shook his head and left to sit next to the queen, sending me the most sorrowful look. I took a deep breath and sat straight in my seat. Yes, I would project confidence on the outside, but my insides writhed in turmoil. I did not like the way they did things here.

At home, she'd be considered an abusive alpha, and someone would try to defeat her to become the new alpha, Eventide said, reeling from shock. *We may be out of our depth here.*

The queen's aff her heid, the mac-talla said helpfully. *A right hoor.*

I restrained a whimper as the servants brought out the first course.

Belenus

I knew it would be dangerous to stand up to the queen, but I hadn't expected a flogging threat for changing my blistering seat at the table. I glanced over at Hekla, choked from all the emotions trying to escape me at the same time. They were bottlenecked in my throat, and not one of them could decide which feeling to release first.

My female sat tall and proud, but I knew her eyes by now, and I saw her vulnerability. I truly did believe she'd take the whip to stay at my side, but I couldn't let that happen. I had no idea how far my mo—the queen would go. I glanced over at the tyrant and took in her calm demeanor. No, she was my mother no longer; I didn't know this wicked person.

Emer nudged me, and I sent her a dark look, not wanting any of her nonsense at the moment. She whispered, "Did you find out who dosed her?"

I scowled at her, and through clenched teeth, I asked, "How did you know about that? Were you the one who did it?"

"Pft! I may be a touch naughty, but I'm not cruel like Mother," Emer declared, loud enough for the queen to hear.

"You best be careful, Emer. She's not who we once knew," I warned in a hush. "You may be the next one at the whipping post." I curled my lip in disgust.

"Who's to say I haven't been there already?" Emer asked, casually checking her nails before taking another bite of her salad. I looked sharply at her, but she ignored me. She exaggerated but did not usually lie—not to me. "Anyway, think it was a past lover?" she asked quietly, returning to the prior subject.

"That's what one of my… friends thought," I said, glancing bitterly around to see if any of them were at the table. "Unfortunately, there's a great number of those."

"See who approaches you in the next couple of days. That should be a hint."

"Glencora, Ronat, Lynet… Cutha…" My eyes raked over the diners as I tried to remember all my court dalliances over the last fifteen years. I doubted it'd be anyone else past that time. They would have long since moved on to other lovers.

"Augh… Lynet? What were you thinking?" she snarled. "Vile, shameless hussy."

I held my hands up in defeat. I had no good excuses for that one. As though she could hear us—which was impossible—Lynet looked at me, tucked a strand of her wheat-blonde hair over her shoulder, and bit her lip in a suggestive way. It was a good thing that Hekla was seated too far back to see the woman. She probably would have ripped Lynet's lips off her face. The other past lovers gave me a mix of glances; Glencora looked sad, Ronat looked jealous, and Cutha looked like she thought she could seduce me for one last romp. No, these women had not moved on for quite some time.

I sighed. I just wanted my Hekla.

Hekla

Even though I had the mac-talla, I did not want to be approached by anyone, so I kept my eyes glued to my plate. I didn't want anyone to look at me, talk to me, or touch me, and I tried to project that through my body language.

I don't know if we've ever been at a more uncomfortable dinner, Eventide mumbled. *Every second of this misery feels like an hour.*

Tattie, if ye wud, the mac-talla requested, poking my neck. I stared at my plate, trying to puzzle out his words, and finally forked a potato.

"This?" I asked quietly, and he snatched my offering, mashing away with his furry snout.

Mm, guid tattie.

The fae to my right, fair like the rest, said something in his language, and I warily waited for the mac-talla to translate. *This naff fae is Finnbarr, an' he wants tae ken if ye'll dally wi' him tonight.*

I gasped and recoiled slightly, horribly tempted to bare my canines and claws in displeasure.

Dae ye want tae reply wi' ah nae? the mac-talla asked.

Yes! Eventide and I hissed at the same time. My companion spoke the fae words slowly, and I repeated them word-for-word to Finnbarr, who grew progressively more shocked. He stood with a face flushed red with fury, threw his napkin down, and stormed out of the banquet hall. Anyone within hearing distance gaped at me like I was a barbarian.

Well, that seemed like an overreaction... Eventide observed slowly, befuddled.

The mac-talla rocked slightly on my shoulder, as if he was laughing.

What... what did I actually say? I asked, realizing I'd been duped, but my companion remained silent. I cleared my throat and returned to studying my food, my cheeks flushing with embarrassment.

I brought this on myself, I repeated calmly. *This was my fault.*

From the corner of my eye, I spied someone taking the empty seat next to me, and I withered, hoping it wasn't another man looking to 'dally.' The only one I wanted to 'dally' with was Belenus. Gods, I wanted him so desperately. I sighed and tried not to squirm as thoughts of my fated mate's embrace triggered false heat symptoms.

Damnation. Please help me, Moon Goddess. I fanned my face and took another bite of food.

"Your mac-talla appears to be playing tricks on you, I see," the fae next to me said, speaking fluently in my language. I glanced over to find it was the one who'd asked earlier if I was available to court. He grinned and swirled a glass of… something. It smelled a bit like wine.

Just. Want. Belenus! Eventide snapped.

"Maybe I meant what I said," I replied shortly, not wanting anything to do with him.

"So, you definitely meant to tell him that if his cock was as limp as his manners, you'd rather not jump into his lap?"

That had me inhaling a small vegetable, and I coughed until tears rolled down my cheeks. The fae slapped my back, the vegetable came out, and I spat it angrily into my napkin. Quite fed up at the moment, I growled very quietly, and the mac-talla stiffened. The creature was outside my glaring range, but he knew he was in trouble.

"Y-yes," I answered weakly, clearing my throat before pouring an entire glass of water down it. "Well, his sniffing about wasn't appreciated."

"This sounds like a wolf thing. Exotic. And what is the appropriate way to sniff a woman?" he asked with a flirty grin. I frowned when I caught his eyes devouring my flushed chest.

I don't think I can do this, I said to Eventide. *There is no point in staying here, especially with my heat symptoms. There are too many horny mal—er, men here.*

I agree. Let's ditch this garbage.

I stood, carefully gathered my sleeves and cape so I wouldn't trip on them, and left the banquet hall without a word. I fisted my hands, trying to hide the claws that ignored my mental commands, and since my canines had elongated, I kept my mouth firmly shut. Had there been any victory tonight? I made an appearance to take a stance, but it didn't seem to matter. It had only added to my distress.

From behind came the sound of boots slapping on stone, and I scented Belenus. My posture drooped in relief, glad that he at least had thought to check on me.

In the torchlit hall, he grabbed my hand instead of offering his arm and asked, "Did anything happen? I saw several men talk to you, but I couldn't hear what they were saying."

I squeezed his broad hand, liking the more affectionate touch. It meant so much to me that he'd initiated it. "Just… annoying fae sniffing about," I explained, scrunching my nose in distaste. "The mac-talla drove one off, but I left after the second one took his place. Not to mention my heat is returning a little." I blew out a breath and fanned my face to fight what couldn't be fought.

"Shit. Well, I know who they are. I'll warn them off," Belenus growled. It wasn't a wolf growl, but it was masculine all the same, and it aggravated the throbbing between my legs.

"I just want to return to my chamber. I've had enough socializing for one night," I said and continued toward my room. Belenus followed faithfully, escorting me while offering comfort. His grip on my hand stayed strong and reinforced how seriously he took our rebellion. The gesture, though small, meant everything.

As we approached my suite, I noticed something new on the door. A nameplate had been added with a small note tied under it. My blood turned frigid as I waited for a translation.

"They gave this suite to Eislyn," Belenus snarled, ripped the note off the door, and read it with a furious face. His chest heaved the more he read until he finally shredded the paper. "They moved your things into another room, and it's all the way in the servant's wing." Flushed from rage, he forcefully kicked the door, leaving a dirty scuff on it from his boot.

So that's why she invited us to dinner! So she could oust us! Eventide fumed.

I relayed what she'd said to Belenus and covered my face with my hands. This couldn't be happening!

Breathe, breathe, Hekla! Eventide urged.

"She's edging us out, little by little!" I panted, then placed a hand on my belly, suddenly unable to breathe in the dress. Panic fought to sicken me, and it was winning.

"Hekla! Hekla!" Belenus grabbed my arms to steady me. "No! She's done shit! She can't change how I feel about you, ok? Don't let her kill your morale! This is how she works!"

"It's not how we do things!" I cried in frustration and scrabbled at my dress to untie it. I needed to breathe!

"Hey, hey, hey! Let's get you to your room, and I'll help you with that dress, ok? Just stay with me! Let's go!" He grabbed my hand and hurried us through the halls.

"Please just let me stay with you!" I begged, tears welling in my eyes.

He shook his head fervently. "You know I can't do that. You need to stay strong for us."

I was at a loss for words. There were so many things I could have said, but my mind simply wasn't working. Too much distress. Too little air.

Belenus led me farther from where I stayed, and the castle gradually became less lavish. I didn't need fancy paintings or exotic flowers, but the stark difference was a brutal reminder of how little the queen cared for folk fae and other servants.

My fated mate opened a room, and we walked into a small bedroom that contained only necessities, which were a bed, toilet, sink, bath, and an empty closet. My belongings from my original realm were here, but all the clothes Belenus had collected for me were gone. I walked to the bed to check my bag and let the mac-talla jump off. Nothing seemed to have been stolen. The gifts from my friends and my other personal effects were safely stored within it.

"I don't need fancy things, Belenus…" I murmured emotionally. "But my territory and my… p-pack were taken from me… all over again." My gaze fell upon the wooden floor, its boards darkening from teardrops.

Belenus didn't say anything. He just moved closer from behind and started loosening my dress so I could breathe. I moved my blank stare to the windowless wall, feeling like I'd been locked in a cage. Wolves didn't do well in cages.

Chapter 9

Hekla

Belenus placed his consoling hands on my shoulders, and the sound of his deep inhale filled my ears. "I'll make sure the doctors know where you are. I'm also going to check and see if I still have privileges to assign your maids and your guards back to you. I'm not sure what orders the queen has placed regarding that."

My sorrowful heart could only think of one question. "If she ordered me to hold my breath until I died, would you let her, Belenus?"

"I'd *never* let anyone hurt you like that," he protested, his voice thick with pain.

My breath caught when he slid his arms under mine, hugging me just beneath my breasts, and rested his chin on my head. We just stood like that for a while, listening to each other's heartbeat, his novel embrace filling me with want. This was new, but I wanted more—so much more.

"Belenus… you tell me to be strong, but all that does is allow her to abuse me. This place… declaws me. I don't understand it. I don't know what to do. I know how to submit to an alpha, but to her… she's… not the same at all. It's like everything is a game. It's cruel."

"It's because everything here is a game, Hekla," he murmured. "Court life is not simple, it's not clean, and it's not honest."

"What scares me the most, other than losing you, is losing who I am," I replied. "I was confident and secure in my decisions before coming here. Now… maybe the false heat is making it worse, but I feel like such a scared little pup. I don't think I've ever cried so much in my life. I don't feel like a wolf. I don't recognize myself."

While removing the mac-talla's leather perch from my shoulder, he said, "This is what it feels like to go to war, Hekla. I've seen the bravest of souls petrify under the pressure of battle. The court… it's none of the gore but all of the mental scarring. This war is going to hurt, and we're both going to receive injuries, but we can't give up." He further loosened my dress and slid his large, rough palms down my neck to slowly sweep the straps off my shoulders. His stronger intake of breath brushed down my neck when my dress fell to the floor, but he simply collected the clothing to hang in the closet.

Belenus averted his gaze, as I wore only a bra and a pair of panties, and I couldn't ignore it. "Still can't look at me?" I asked, as much longing as hurt in my heart.

"You know why, dear Hekla." His voice softened as he removed his jacket. "I'll lose control and bed you. It worsens by the day. That's how much power you have over me."

I knew that already… I supposed I just needed to hear his want too. Then he took off his shirt, exposing a part of him I hadn't seen before now—a view of rippling muscles.

Now I truly knew what he meant by control; I held back a whimper as my underwear dampened, my own restraint flickering like a faint star. I forced the extra saliva down my throat but couldn't pry my eyes off his hard chest and the enticing, beautiful carvings down his golden abdomen. I wanted to touch them, mold my hands around them, but I could not.

He handed me his white dinner shirt while I stared. "Something for you to sleep in for now. I'll bring you clothes tomorrow."

"Thank you…" I said quietly and slipped it over my head. It hung just beneath my bottom, and that worked just fine for me.

Belenus pulled back the sheets and gestured for me to sit on the bed where he proceeded to remove all my jewelry. He was especially careful with the ornaments in my hair, trying not to snag any strands that had become entangled. His fingers ran through my locks to loosen them, and I closed my eyes in bliss, pretending for a moment that we were already mated.

"Lie down, my female," he urged quietly, lifting the sheets so I could slide under them. He tucked me in and stroked my hair, staring at me in silence. Though I closed my eyes, he remained by my side, comforting me until I fell asleep.

I sorely wanted to sleep through the next day, but a key jiggling into the lock told me that I had a visitor. From the scent leaking around the loose door, I could tell it was Bidelia instead of Belenus. She padded in but stopped tiptoeing once she saw my open eyes. Still moving quietly, she placed food and water down for the mac-talla and climbed on the bed to snuggle against me.

I swung an arm over her and closed my eyes, grateful for the extra warmth. Whenever my false heat had subsided last night, I realized that the room was quite cold. Even though wolves ran a little hotter than some other species, it was uncomfortable without a fireplace, and I'd shifted into Eventide to stay warm. Even the mac-talla had given up his aloofness to curl against my wolf.

Speaking of the mac-talla, I realized I'd forgotten something important and felt quite guilty about it. "What's your name?" I asked the creature, who was gorging himself on fruit and… grubs. I made a face.

Ah dinna huv a name, but ah huv mony names, he answered grumpily.

"He doesn't have a name," I shared with Bidelia.

"What do ye want to be called?" she asked curiously. The mac-talla froze for a moment, and his wings twitched. I doubted he had been asked that by previous owners.

Erse, he answered darkly.

"Erse? Ok…" I said, looking over at a giggling Bidelia. "Looks like he wants to be called Erse."

"His accent is thicker than mine! Why does he wanna be called Arse? That means 'butt.'" She continued giggling, and I looked over at the mac-talla with a raised eyebrow. I wondered if he could feel my stare on his back because he shifted uncomfortably. He also didn't answer Bidelia's question.

"I think he's waiting for me to get fed up with him and return him to the pet shop," I said with a yawn. "It's not going to work, Arse." Bidelia broke into another bout of giggles.

"That sounds so stupid. I like it!" She laughed manically, rolling about a bit in her mirth. Then, she howled in pain and sat up, quickly reaching back to adjust something under her servant's uniform.

"What happened, Bidelia?" I asked, crawling around to see what was wrong with her back. She shook her head and shifted away from me.

"Bideliaaa," I growled a warning and exerted whatever dominance I had into my voice. I was no alpha, but I could sound strong.

"My binding shifted," she whimpered in defeat and pulled her dress over her head. "Can ye fix it? The other maids usually help."

I couldn't help the angry growl that rose in my chest when I saw her back. She scented like a bug because she had beautiful gold, emerald, and sky-blue butterfly wings. I growled because they were crinkled from being bound by a gauzy tape. The skin around the base of her wings was slightly inflamed, and tears immediately flooded my eyes.

"Why?" I gasped, tensing in outrage.

"The queen doesn't like to look at folk fae parts if it can be helped. They demand winged to be bound while on floor duty," she said simply, like it was a completely acceptable reality.

"Can... you still fly?" I rubbed angry tears from my chin before they could drip.

"I'm not sure. I haven't tried."

My hands shook with sadness and fury as I touched the strap that'd become cockeyed. "Bidelia, I don't want to fix this! I want to take it off!" I confessed, trying to make it sound like I wasn't crying.

"Ye have to! I'll get in trouble!" Her fearful answer cracked my heart, and I carefully moved the band back to where it used to be, trying not to further damage her wings. "Thank ye. I'm sorry ye won't be queen anymore. I feel like ye would have been a good one."

Not even Bidelia thought I had a chance? The crack in my heart splintered from growing doubt, and being unable to cope with that, I forced a change in topic. "Best get to your duties, Bidelia."

She crawled off the bed but froze upon standing. "Oh! There was a human guarding yer door last night! Black hair, blue eyes? Do ye know him? Never saw a human before. At least I don't think I have."

Was that Koray? Oh, thank the Moon Goddess! Someone sane to talk to! "Do you know where the training yard is for the warriors?"

She nodded, staring blankly at my tear-stained face.

"Can you take me there?" I asked while taking off the shirt to throw on the fancy gown. It was all I had. She nodded once more, tightened my dress for me, and watched me race to freshen up.

I followed her out of my room and out of the castle where we took a right turn leading to an expansive training yard. It contained a massive number of sections for different specialties, even including an area for fae to fight on horseback. I'd never seen anything like this in my life, not even at Zorian and Ragna's castle; though to be fair, horses didn't like shifters riding them.

Bidelia ran off to fulfill her duties, and I searched the crowd of fae for Koray's familiar face. I scrambled through the yard past yelling trainers and found Koray getting… well… getting his butt handed to him by an older fae man. I waited anxiously until Koray was allowed a break and ran up to him. Thank the gods he saw me coming because I would have tackled him whether he noticed me or not.

Oh, thank the gods! Thank the Sun God, and the Sky Gods, and the Earth Gods, and the Moon Goddess that someone from our realm is here! Eventide sobbed. *I can't believe I missed the smell of a human!*

"Hekla!" Koray shouted as I embraced him, stunned. He hugged me in return and stepped back to study me. "You're out of bed! Thought you'd be resting after everything Belenus told me last night."

"No… no… a little fae girl gave me a wake-up call," I replied breathlessly, waving away his idea. "It's so good to see someone from my realm." I choked up and fanned my face. "Sorry, I'm just emotional right now. Oh gods!"

Koray gestured to a bench, and we sat while I gathered myself. With a sympathetic look, he said, "I'm truly sorry to hear about the engagement. I was planning on writing a letter to the Lunar Coven to ask if they had any ideas."

Touched by such thoughtfulness, I nearly burst into tears. What was wrong with me today? This was so much worse than the false heat.

This would be a really bad time for our real heat, Eventide bemoaned.

"That is… so… I'm so grateful for that!" I hesitated for a moment when I thought of something. "I just realized… do you think it'd be worth taking a trip to see the Moon Goddess?" I asked, then added hastily, "I don't want you to think I'm taking advantage of you! In fact, I could maybe ask Zorian if he could escort me."

He frowned and brought a fist to his mouth in thought. "I don't know if She'd be of any help. She just assigns the mates, but I can't imagine a trip doing any harm. I'm not keen on going back for any old reason, but I think this is important enough to try," he said, nodding slowly as he worked out his thoughts. "I couldn't imagine losing Soley like this. I think I'd go mad too."

"Um, just think on it. You don't have to decide right away, and I know you're busy… getting your butt kicked." I gave him a feral grin and pointed to his trainer, making him laugh. He glanced back to where he'd been practicing and wiped some sweat from his forehead.

"Yeah… it's a start. I'll get better I'm sure." He then moved his gaze to the castle and added longingly, "Though I'd love to talk to some of the magic trainers here. I know I'm just a human, but I can't help but be curious. I wonder how different it is from witchwork."

"Oooh, you should ask Belenus to introduce you to them!" I said excitedly.

He looked shyly at his hands. "I don't know… he's already given me a lot…" he replied in a quieter voice and nervously licked his lips.

"Um, excuuuse me, Koray, but you were trapped in another realm for years. I'm preeetty sure you could ask him for a lot more!" I lectured, poking his insecure shoulder. He nodded but remained visibly uncertain. "Well, if you won't, I will!" I stood and grinned. Before he could protest, I turned on a heel and strode off.

It felt so good to have a couple things on my agenda! Aside from my symptoms, I was starting to feel a little like myself again. I fanned my face and prayed that my real heat wasn't coming. I had things to do!

Belenus

The morning was a nightmare. Not only did I receive last-minute notification that Princess Eislyn had arrived, I also hadn't quite found where they'd moved Hekla's clothes yet. Certainly, all that finery wouldn't have been thrown into the trash. It had to be in a storage closet somewhere. I grunted in anger as I returned to my room, changed into my formal attire, then left to meet the princess.

She was waiting by the main entrance with the queen, who forced a broad, loving smile onto her face when she spotted me. "Ah! There is my handsome son. Belenus, come meet your bride-to-be! Doesn't Eislyn look simply ravishing this morning?" the queen said with a glint of warning in her eyes.

I regarded the princess. Dressed in a wispy pink dress, she curtseyed demurely and shyly fluttered her eyelashes. She was a fair fae from the Spring Court, pearlescent in skin and hair. Most would likely call her the fairest of the seelie territory, but I felt nothing. I would have felt nothing had I never met Hekla. This woman had never been rude to me, but I saw how she acted when she thought no one was looking, and she was a horror. The thought of a lifetime with her almost sent me retching to the nearest bucket.

And yet, I was forced to be civil. "Looking radiant as ever, Princess Eislyn," I greeted, then clenched my teeth when she held her hand up to be kissed. She blushed and waited for me to cave. *Damn you.*

I took her hand and lightly kissed the back of it, thankful for the silk glove that kept my lips from her skin. I stood up straight, placed my hands behind my back, and waited for the queen to speak. I wasn't volunteering any friendly discourse.

The queen beamed and clapped excitedly. "Don't you both make the fairest couple in all the courts! I simply cannot wait for the wedding. Oh, I do wish it could be sooner than two weeks, don't you?" She smiled at Eislyn who nodded enthusiastically. "Maybe we can discuss it with the court and seelie!"

"Mother," I said, choking out the word, "we should abide by the courtship rules. You made it very clear the other day how important they were."

She ignored my steeliness and dismissed me with a wave of her hand. "He's just nervous! He's been raving about what a beauty you are!"

After a lifetime of tolerating her cold disposition, it was surreal to see her acting like this—jovial in her lies and manipulation. I stood between two very skilled actors, and I couldn't say a blisterin' thing. And of all the acts she could have chosen, the princess had picked the most annoying personality to play. Eislyn tittered idiotically over the lie and stared up at me through her lashes.

The queen placed a guiding hand on her shoulder and said to me, "Do show her around, my son! Let her see her future kingdom. Make sure she knows where the servants' quarters are too."

I shot her a nasty look, but her gaze conveniently averted. That was way too far. I'd not allow her to target Hekla any further. I'd have to speak to her later about that.

Eislyn gave me an expectant look, and I lifted my elbow to escort her, forcing a smile on my face. Movement outside the castle caught my attention, and it turned out to be Hekla watching from a distance. My smile faltered and cold horror filled my stomach. I hoped she hadn't seen the entire encounter, including my own acting, but her shocked expression told me otherwise, and she backed out of sight.

Shit.

My heart hung angry and dark in my chest as I strolled down the halls with Eislyn. I didn't say much as she chatted, and I hid my scowls whenever she'd make camouflaged, disparaging remarks about the folk fae servants who crossed paths with us.

"I'm surprised to see some horns and antlers not thoroughly covered," she rambled innocently. "We make them wear the same hoods or bonnets, but we're quite strict. It's important to display a consistent uniform."

I gritted my teeth and hummed a noncommittal response. She continued to babble about other 'important' things and the changes she'd make here and there.

Genuinely wanting to know if she could even answer the question, I asked, "What do you think about some of our laws that are a bit outdated and problematic to visitors? We could increase tourism if we removed the 'thank you' bait and other entrapments. Perhaps we could work to build trust with our neighbors in the other realm that way?"

"Oh, I think that's a horrid idea, if you'd forgive me for saying as much, Your Highnes—I mean, my husband-to-be," she replied with a simper. "If we remove all traditions, we'd lose our identity as a people, don't you think?"

"If our identity relies upon trapping others for selfish reasons, then we're doomed as a species, Eislyn," I replied sternly, refusing to call her anything but her given name.

"Hmm." She pouted and put her other finger to her lips. "I don't think so, but that's why you'll have me! I'll make sure we make the right decisions, my beloved."

Just kill me, I thought miserably. *Someone just come along and put a sword through me.*

Hekla

Seeing Belenus kiss that fae woman's hand felt like someone had put a sword through me. When my mate's gaze fell on mine, I staggered backwards and retreated to release my emotions elsewhere. As I searched for a private corner, I placed a hand to my heart and labored for breath, suffering a surge of panic. The stress ravaged me inside and out, clawing like a shift gone horribly wrong. Though embarrassment burned and shock froze, neither worked to soothe the other.

He's just acting. That's how they do things here. It's all a game, I reminded myself as my vision blurred from tears. I rubbed the water away with a scowl, my emotions running as hot and cold as my body.

It still hurt, Eventide said. Her aggrieved voice twisted the sword that had not yet been pulled from me. *I want to rip her apart!*

Eventide's jealousy brought out mine, and I grew angrier. I hated feeling like this! This wasn't me! I knew better! My face and body flushed, and I sank to the dirt to lean against the cool stone wall and fan my chest. I was becoming more miserable by the second. My sex throbbed, needing to know that Belenus still wanted me. My brain knew better, but my body didn't seem to be on the same page, and I felt lost again.

I need to find the doctors... I said, the fever crawling deeper. *Maybe they can help.*

A fae soldier passed by and froze. He turned his head around like he was looking for something, then his eyes fell on me. "A-are you ok, miss?" he asked nervously.

"Do you know where the doctor is?" I asked, just cutting to the chase. I could have said I was fine, but I honestly wasn't.

"I know where the castle medical ward is, miss. Would you like an escort?" he asked, taking his helmet off and straightening his hair. I glanced at his dilated eyes and noticed the state of his pants. He seemed... affected.

Is this our real heat? Oh, please no! Now is NOT THE TIME! Eventide howled.

There was no helping it, though, and I answered his question. "Please." I gave my bleary eyes a rub and stood carefully, not wanting to display any more vulnerability than I already had. He politely offered an arm, but I declined, disappointing him a great deal. I followed him into the castle and down several halls, where he finally opened a door for me.

"Than—" I began, then froze. I'd almost thanked him. Oh, that could have been bad! "I hope you have a good day," I stated to his extra-disappointed face.

"My name's Ferchar, if you're ever… lonely," he replied, shifting anxiously. Realizing I wasn't going to encourage him, he hastily bowed, licked his lips, and rushed back down the hall.

No thanks again, Eventide moaned.

I approached the ward's front desk to greet an aquatic-looking fae organizing some documents. She noticed me through her pile of work and smiled hesitantly. "Can I help ye?" she inquired, moving the documents to the side. I had to wonder if she knew who I was. Did anyone?

Nearly begging, I inquired, "Is Doctor Egres or Elisedd in? I'm not feeling well, and they'd want me to see them…"

"Let me see if they're with a patient," she replied kindly and shuffled out of the room. I didn't have to wait long before she came back, blushing and flustered. "They're, um, on a break. I'd say to give them fifteen minutes… maybe?" she squeaked out and went back to her desk. "Just, um, take a seat. I'll check to see if they're don— I mean ready! In a minute!"

I had no idea why she was on edge, but I had very little energy to care. I sighed and curled up into a chair, wishing I had a cold cloth for my face. All I could do was sit, wait, and try not to replay the image of Belenus kissing that fae's hand. My eyes searched desperately for something else to fixate on but found nothing. I should have brought the mac-talla.

Finally, the doctors were available, and I was brought back to an examination room where I was greeted by two very… flushed and visibly pleased doctors. Doctor Egres briskly opened a drawer to collect some tools while I relayed my symptoms to both of them. She took my temperature and nodded.

"Yes, sounds like your real heat is here," she informed, and Doctor Elisedd continued a normal exam by checking my ears, pulse, and throat.

"Can I take that medicine you made to help with the symptoms?" I asked hopefully. Doctor Elisedd shook his head, and Doctor Egres crossed her arms, her brows furrowed in sympathy.

"I'm afraid not," Doctor Elisedd answered for them both. "We don't want to manipulate your natural hormonal cycle, especially now that you're recovering from being dosed."

I sighed miserably and buried my face in my hands. "What are my options?" I groaned. "I can't just writhe around in a room all day!"

"Cold water and masturbation helps," Doctor Egres said while washing and returning tools to their cabinets and drawers. "If your mate can't help, you can get some relief that way. It won't cure it, and it only lasts so long, but it's better than nothing."

"He definitely can't help," I grumbled nastily. "He's busy kissing some other fae's hand."

The fae doctor sighed regretfully. "Yes. We've heard about the engagement," Doctor Elisedd muttered, peeling off his gloves before washing his hands. "I'm terribly sorry to hear about it."

My surroundings clouded from a worsening mood, and I barely noticed the lycan clearing her throat. "Back in our realm, at the castle," Doctor Egres said, "we have counseling should you choose to reject him and look for another mate."

That was too much to hear. That made failure sound far too close, too real, and I broke down into tears. The doctors patted my back sympathetically and left the room to give me privacy, telling me to come out whenever I was ready.

Eventide tried to pull herself together for both our sakes. *I know we're emotional and this sucks, but we're getting ahead of things. Focus on the present.* Her tone wavered more than usual, and I knew I had to be there for her too.

I rubbed away my tears, straightened my shoulders, and left the medical ward with a body burning up from heat. I wanted to take a walk through the garden, but I didn't want to run into any men, so I just decided to return to my windowless prison and crawl back into bed. Maybe I could figure out how to sleep forever, because I was getting crankier than… well, there might not be anything crankier than a wolf in heat. I bared my teeth at the empty hall and turned right into the servant's wing.

My steps faltered when I nearly ran into two fae. Horribly self-conscious, I ducked past them, keeping my gaze to the floor. Before I could get far, one of the two, an angry woman, snapped at me. "Excuse me, servant! Apologize for rushing into us!" Despite what I wore, she sneered the word 'servant,' and cold fury flooded my veins. Oh, she had chosen the wrong time of the month to mess with me!

I looked up, and the cold fury momentarily fell to shock. Belenus was telling her something in a stern voice, but I couldn't hear him. I couldn't hear anything. All I could see was her arm wrapped around his arm as she raised her chin to glare at me. She seemed to ignore Belenus's words and snapped, "I'm. Waiting."

I stared at Belenus, who was sending me an apologetic look and tried to tug away the fae woman. Had he been a wolf-shifter, he would have thrown her against the wall and threatened her with death for speaking to his fated mate like that.

But that wasn't how they did things here…

"She's not a servant," Belenus warned her gruffly. "Please refrain from talking to her like that."

The woman batted her eyelashes at him. "If you let non-fair fae act like this, they'll walk all over you," she replied sweetly. "I'll help you sort this issue out after we're wed, my husband-to-be."

She looked back at me expectantly. I glanced at Belenus one more time, but he only looked angry. He didn't drag her away, and he wasn't going to protect me. Was this what he meant when he asked me to be strong? Did he mean for me to accept abuse?

I think not.

I let my canines and claws extend, then showed her exactly what I thought of her expectations by baring my teeth. I marched up to tell her to back off, but Belenus stepped in front of me and grabbed my wrist. I gaped in disbelief. He then shook his head warningly, and my fight utterly evaporated, leaving nothing in my heart but betrayal and heartache. How could he take her side?

He frowned, leaned down the tiniest bit, and his nostrils flared with a sniff.

"Are you in...?" he mouthed at me.

Our heat? Yes. Thank you for only caring about that, Eventide snarled, outraged by this entire scene.

I ripped my hand out of his grip and walked away, not understanding what the... the... fuck just happened.

Chapter 10

Belenus

I knew the moment I'd stepped in front of Hekla I'd done significant damage. Dread sank uncomfortably into my stomach as she stormed off, entered her room, and slammed the door behind her. She still wore the evening gown, reminding me of a task I'd failed. Shit! I needed to find her clothes. At this rate I might as well request new ones.

And, of course, Eislyn wailed dramatically. "Oh! Did you see the way she attacked me?" I heard her fanning her face, likely pretending to feel faint.

I just stood there and stared at Hekla's door, ignoring the dramatic creature behind me. How was I going to explain all this to my fated mate? How many times would it work to say that it wasn't how we did things here? Touching the princess would have gotten her whipped!

"She didn't even breathe on you, Eislyn," I said to admonish her theatrics. "Stop making up stories."

"That's because you saved me!" she exclaimed and ran to embrace me, pressing into my back and wrapping her arms around my abdomen.

I pulled her off me and retreated several steps, disgusted. "Maintain your distance, Eislyn! This is still a proper courtship."

"Oh! Of course, Your Highness," she apologized and dipped into a curtsey.

I gritted my teeth and turned to look back at Hekla's door one last time. I desperately wanted to go to her, to make sure she understood what was happening, but I still had to tour this wretch about the palace grounds. I was also worried about her heat; she had to be in it now because I felt shockingly... stimulated.

"Let us go," I directed sharply and moved us toward the training grounds. Perhaps I could find a nice and muddy path to take.

When we stepped outside, Eislyn batted her eyelashes and asked, "So, who is she?"

"Someone I'd rather you not bother, Eislyn," I answered sternly and tried to distract her by pointing out the different sections of the training grounds. There was a lot to see out here, plenty of topics that weren't Hekla.

"I heard you had a dog for a fated mate," she said sympathetically. "She certainly acted like one. Was that her? It must be her. Oh, what a terrible thing to be paired with one such as her!" She squeezed my arm with her hand, as though showing her emotional support.

I took a deep breath and ground my teeth. Eislyn knew the right buttons to push; she was very good at this. "I think we should focus on topics around the castle and our engagement, should we not?" I asked, bringing my other arm behind my back so I could white-knuckle it out of sight.

Don't shake, don't shake, don't shake... Calm down, calm down, calm down...

"So, have you rejected her yet? When will you do so? Perhaps I should be there to watch and support you?" she inquired, ignoring what I'd just said.

What a sadistic piece of shit.

"I would advise you to leave my personal matters to me, Eislyn," I warned, leading her right over a soggy puddle where she stumbled and splattered mud all over the bottom of her dress. It wasn't a big win, but I'd take it.

"So, she is the one!" Eislyn cheered, like she'd tricked the answer out of me. Then she frowned and tried shaking the mud off her skirts.

Oh, you figured it out fifteen minutes ago. Don't try to scare me with that tactic.

I spied Koray, and he hailed me from a distance, looking like he had something to say. I waited while he weaved through soldiers to approach us, grateful for any excuse to ignore Eislyn. His brow was beaded with moisture, and his training shirt stuck to his torso, both evidence of his hard work. That pleased me. I was fond of him and knew he'd make a fine warrior once we got him properly trained.

"Hey, Belenus!" he said breathlessly and brushed some sweat from his jaw. "Have you seen Hekla? I don't know if she asked you yet or not."

"Ahem!" Eislyn uttered from next to me, and Koray didn't skip a beat.

"Bless you," he said, then looked back up at me.

I didn't think I could have been any prouder of him than I was at that very moment. "I saw her, but we didn't talk," I answered, nervous about what this question might be.

Eislyn interrupted again. "Excuse me, but you really should bow before royalty." She returned her gaze to me, grimacing in sympathy. "I suppose it's too much to ask to train humans. Such trouble."

"Koray bows to no one, Eislyn," I corrected, then nodded to the young man with the long blackbird hair. "What's the question?"

"I was wondering if maybe I could get an introduction to one of the magic instructors? I just… I was curious, and… well… Hekla thought maybe I should ask you…"

The nightmare of a woman next to me tittered again. "A human has no use for magic, you poor confused thing. I doubt you'll get the permission you're wanti—"

"Permission granted," I said quickly to Koray, irritated that she was trying to demean yet another person who was important to me. "I'll make arrangements tomorrow if I can, but I will see to it. Thank you for asking." Though I'd warned him about gratitude here, I wasn't worried about the entrapment with Koray—the young man had one of the purest hearts I'd ever encountered.

I also thanked him to annoy Eislyn.

Koray beamed brighter than the sun and hopped a bit on his feet. "That's incredible! Thanks!" He turned away but not before giving Eislyn a disapproving shake of his head. I smiled internally, liking that kid more by the minute.

I also made a mental note to pull Koray into my investigation team. He would see the situation with fresh eyes. Perhaps he'd find something I was missing. I needed to get a copy of that marriage contract… As of today, I had two weeks to get this wedding cancelled.

Hekla

I lay in bed for hours. Sometimes I dozed; other times I stared at the wall. Most of the time, I writhed from the burning and forced myself to take cold showers, which were agonizing. Icy water flowing down feverish skin felt like being flayed. Bidelia ended up being a lifesaver, intermittently bringing the mac-talla and me meals from the kitchen. I wasn't sure how I would have handled the day without her help.

Adding to my misery, my pheromones must have escaped the room because fae men knocked frequently on my door, asking if I needed anything. They all seemed a little confused—probably wondering why they were drawn and inexplicably aroused. Some even tried to find a reason to enter, but I swiftly halted those encounters. I eventually stopped answering, shoved a towel in the crack under the door, and prayed to the Moon Goddess that they'd all leave me alone. My mind might be hurt, but my body still wanted Belenus.

The hour grew late, and I changed into the shirt he'd given me. It smelled like him, and I tried to calm myself with it, but all I could think about was where he was right now. Was he entertaining the princess? I rubbed away tears and dragged the protesting mac-talla into my arms for a comforting hug.

Canny, Hekla! Dinna footer aboot!

"I don't know what you're saying, so I can't help you, Arse, but I need a cuddle," I grumbled. The mac-talla sighed and gave up, knowing I'd won this time.

A rapping at the door had me freeing Arse, and I went to check the visitor's scent, hoping Belenus had finally come to visit. Had he gotten away from that terrible woman? I nudged the towel aside and caught a breath of the hall air. Nope, no scent of my mate. I opened the door warily to see some fair fae guard, but he wasn't wearing the usual armor. His skin also had a pearlescent sheen instead of the summer gold.

"Miss… Hekla… Himinn?" he inquired, flaring his nostrils and clearly distracted. "The Princess Eislyn requests your…" His voice cracked when he saw my bare legs. I supposed I should have worn a towel to the door. I couldn't put that dress on every time someone knocked. "Requests your…" He tried again. "Presence." He palmed the door and leaned forward to get a better look at me.

"Tell her she can kiss my butt," I snapped. I was not a wolf to be bullied!

He grinned slowly and pushed on the door. "Do you mind if I did that for her?"

"Um, yes!" I growled. "I mind a whole lot!"

"Oh, come on, who else is going to do it? Our princess has your mate by th—"

"By what?" I heard Belenus say from the hall. I sighed in relief and shoved at the stupid overgrown fae blocking my doorway.

"N-nothing, Your Highness!" he stammered, straightening to attention.

The air crackled with Belenus's lividity. "Get out of here! You shouldn't be in the servants' wing at this hour. Don't let me catch you doing this again!" he yelled, sending the guard running.

I turned and flopped on the bed, glad to be rid of the pushy messenger. Oh thank the gods Belenus was here!

The summer prince walked in with an armful of clothes and shut the door behind him with a boot. Then, he shook his head and groaned like he was in pain. "Shit…" he uttered, and as soon as he hung the clothes in the closet, he hurried to the door.

I gaped, bewildered. "What? Are you leaving?" I knew I was in heat, but we had to talk about what happened today!

"I can't!" With an arm over his nose, he left and slammed the door, stunning me.

"Thanks… for… the clothes… I guess…" I said blankly, in shock all over again.

In the words of King Zorian, 'What the fuck!' Eventide yelled.

I rubbed at my chest, feeling an incredible jab of pain. The burn burrowed deeper, like silver pouring into me. Belenus had spent all day with the princess, but he couldn't even give me five minutes?

He still cares about us… right? I asked Eventide. She didn't reply; she was much too angry.

"What do I do?" I snapped at the door. The door knocked in reply, and I swore I jumped a foot into the air, startled out of my wits. Deciding not to open it this time, I yelled, "Who is it?" My nerves couldn't seem to find a single moment to heal.

"Koray!"

Finally, a sane person! I popped my head out the door, a little worried that my heat would bother him too. "Hello, did you ask Belenus about the magic trainer? He just left..." I inquired, pointing down the hall in case he wanted to catch up.

"Oh! Yeah, he said yes. I'm really excited! Thanks for the encouragement," he replied enthusiastically.

I grinned, happy that someone was having a good time. "That's great! See? I knew it'd be fine! So, what's going on?"

He took a deep breath. "So, I think I'm good to take you to the Realm of the Gods. We could do the trip tomorrow after training or the day after if Belenus does my introduction tomorrow. He wasn't sure which day."

"Oh, Koray, that's so kind. Are you sure?" I asked, brightening up.

He nodded. "It's not a big deal compared to what you're going through. I saw him escort the princess around the training grounds, and wow... she is... extremely unlikeable."

"She seems to have Belenus wrapped around her finger." I averted my sudden scowl to the floor, feeling simultaneously convinced of it and ashamed of myself. My emotions fought so hard to corrupt my logic.

"Did something happen?" he asked, shoving his hands into his pockets and drawing his brows in concern.

"Oh, just... it's hard to watch him kiss her hand and smile at her. She tried to mistreat me today, and Belenus didn't stop her. Then he came by, dumped my clothes off, and left with hardly a word," I vented, my vision blurring with tears.

"Well, to be fair, your room reeks of pheromones. If Soley was that bad, I wouldn't be able to resist." He shrugged. "But the rest of that sounds awful. I'm sorry, Hekla. I'm sure it's all a show. Belenus wouldn't cheat on you."

"You're right..." I said, letting out a long, withered sigh. "It's so miserable to sit and wait for him, which was why I wanted to try to do something. But now it looks like he won't be visiting anymore..."

He patted me on the back in an attempt to comfort and encourage. "I'll check in with him for you, ok?"

I smiled in bone-deep gratitude, his reliability lifting some weight from my shoulders. He needed to know how much that meant to me. "I'm so sorry you have to be away from Soley right now, but I have to admit, I'm so damned glad you're here!"

We both laughed, and he said good night before wandering off to wherever he was going. I curled up into bed, but another knock came from the door, nearly making me scream in frustration. I wanted all these men to leave me alone! However, I relaxed when I heard a key jiggle in the lock. It was just Bidelia. She tiptoed in wearing her nightgown and locked the door behind her.

"Help," she mumbled sleepily, lifting the back of her dress so I could untie her bands, and I hastily assisted her. The poor thing didn't deserve this. If that rotten fae became queen, I had a feeling Bidelia's situation would eventually worsen. I needed to keep my sanity intact for her.

She sighed in relief and eased her wings through the slits in the nightgown. Then, she crawled into bed with me and snuggled into my shoulder. "I'm gonna sleep here, ok? It's cold."

I smiled and wrapped an arm around her. The mac-talla crawled onto the bed and curled up next to Bidelia. "Of course you will, Pup. You're in my wolf pack. You and little Arse over here." I poked the mac-talla's rear end, making him start in surprise.

I grinned at her giggling and fell asleep, praying to all the gods for strength and courage.

Belenus

The very first thing I did in the morning was to try to hunt down the queen, but she was unavailable; what a big surprise. I gave a message to her two chamber guards that I was demanding a copy of my marriage contract and needed an audience with her.

I eyed them both, making sure they saw how very important it was to their future careers that they relay this message as soon as possible. After getting my 'yes' from both of them, I left only until one saw fit to shift uncomfortably.

My mind buzzed with tasks that needed doing, but many of them relied on other people's availability. I'd send a summons to my chosen team once I got that marriage contract to peruse. I needed to ask Koray for his help too; I had to find him now before Eislyn found me.

That reminded me of last night. What in the blazing sun's rays was her guard doing at Hekla's door? I wished I had thought to ask, but her pheromones had hit me like a battering ram to the face. I hadn't been able to think for the life of me. I just had to deliver her clothes and run.

Shit, I knew that'd done a lot of damage too.

With a jaw clenched in aggravation, I turned to look for Koray. I probably had time to introduce him to the magic instructors. Something good needed to come of today, and that was by far the easiest task to achieve.

I spied Koray from a distance, put my fingers to my lips, and released a shrill whistle, startling damn near everyone. Koray looked around until he saw me, and I waved him over. After placing his claybeg in the weapon's rack, he jogged over, grinning like a kid expecting candy.

"Mornin', Belenus!" he greeted once he reached me and placed his hands on his hips, slightly out of breath.

"Let's go see if any of the magic instructors are around," I replied, turned, then smirked as he nearly tripped over his own feet in his excitement. "I have just enough time to go with you."

"Busy day?" he asked, catching up and shoving his hands in his pockets.

"Busy day avoiding a certain princess," I mumbled under my breath so only he could hear me.

He replied just as discreetly. "Speaking of that, I told Hekla I'd check in with you. She said you disappeared last night."

"She's in heat. I can't risk being around her," I reminded but still felt a pang of guilt.

"That's what I told her. Still though, she mentioned some other stuff, and well, she's not doing so well," he disclosed, true to his compassionate self. "Hate seeing her suffer so much."

"The court is a nightmare to navigate." My mood darkened as I guided Koray up a flight of stairs. "One wrong move could get her flogged, and everyone thinks they can handle a flogging until it actually happens."

He tilted his head before responding, his face contorted in skepticism. "One wrong word from a mate could make a wolf feel way worse than being whipped, Belenus. I think Hekla would still rather take the whip than some of the things she's going through alone," he argued. "If you keep taking everyone's side but hers, you're going to lose her. Wolves can't survive conditions like that."

"You seem to have become quite the expert on wolves, Koray," I said, raising my brows at him while opening a door to the study halls. Was what he said true? Could I really lose Hekla with the long-term strategy?

"Well, I've been around Soley almost nonstop since the day we all met our mates. She also talks a lot about her friends, including Hekla. You've hardly been around Hekla." He shrugged. "You just have some catching up to do."

"I'm sure I do," I replied with a groan. Then, before going any farther down the hall, I pulled him aside to change the subject. "I also wanted to mention," I said as quietly as possible for human ears, which were not as sharp as fae. "I've asked for a copy of my marriage contract to be sent to me, and I'm gathering a team to see if there are any loopholes or weaknesses we could exploit. Since there's a magical aspect to these contracts, I'd appreciate it if you could be an extra pair of eyes."

"Sure," he answered. "I've actually already drafted a letter to the Lunar Coven, asking if they have any advice. Just let me know when you're meeting." He then glanced around nervously, but I knew there wasn't anyone within hearing range.

"I'm impressed, Koray," I remarked, taking a step back to study him. "Very proactive. I appreciate that."

He shrugged, unaware of his rare combination of morals and motivation. Well, it was rare in fae court life. It could take decades to build trust with a courtier—an issue cultivated by long lifespans, endless intrigue, and of course, boredom.

I turned to lead Koray to a study that belonged to the head of our magic department studies. The master instructor was in, and the older, thin man scrambled from his desk to bow before me. Only several lizard scales at his temples told of his folk fae heritage.

"Good morning, Dumnorix!" I greeted and gestured to the eager young man beside me. "I'd like you to meet my good friend, Koray, the Lunar Key to the Realm of the Gods. He has some knowledge of witchwork, and I'd like you to design a curriculum for him so he can learn about magic theory. He is a human, so keep that in mind, but I want him to be as educated on the topic as any apprentice.

"He does train with the soldiers during the day, so see if you can sort out how you'd like the time to be split. Sounds good everyone?" I asked, clasping my hands and looking from Dumnorix to Koray, who both nodded vigorously. "Excellent. Treat him like you would my brother, Dumnorix! Have a good day!"

I waltzed out to let them get acquainted, happy to have something positive checked off my list. However, I slowed down when I reached the main floor and stared in the direction of the servants' quarters. Maybe Hekla's heat had calmed. Koray's words had speared past my defenses, and now I was truly worried about how she saw Eislyn and me.

I turned to head down the servants' wing and pumped my fists nervously. At the very least, I needed to know if she was ok. When I turned the last corner, a disgusting scene ripped my face into a scowl.

"What in the shit is happening here?" I snapped furiously, and about eleven men fell into deep bows. "Why are you all hovering at this door?" I pointed at the fae closest to my mate's door to get an explanation. Ashen faced, he seemed completely unprepared to answer the question, so I barked again, "Why are you at this door? Answer me!"

"Y-Your Highness, we just… er… well, it sounds bad to say it out loud," the fae stuttered.

I took another step toward the group, seething. "And yet I'm still asking you to say it out loud. Why are you making your prince repeat an order?"

A different fae finally snapped under the pressure. "There's a woman in there who smells really good, and we're trying to see if she wants to have a good time, ok?" He planted his profusely sweating face in his hands and groaned, knowing that what he'd just said had sounded incredibly disturbing. The others regarded him miserably like he'd just signed their executions. They were lucky this wasn't the Winter Court.

I stormed to the door, stationed myself before it as a barricade, and faced them. "If I see any of you bothering this person again, you will be fired on the spot. Am I understood?" My tone added to the warning—low, cold, and clear.

"Yes, Your Highness…" they all answered with strained voices.

"Get out of here," I spat and gestured them all away from me. The dismissal had them fleeing like they'd heard a cù-sìth. Somewhat mollified—but not in regards to worry—I turned and knocked on the door. The only response from inside was a mumble and a groan, so I put my spare key to the lock and let myself enter.

Hekla's pheromones penetrated me like a rabid wolf's bite, and I knew that closing the door had trapped me with them. I scrubbed a hand over my face, fought an intense and sudden need for her body, and tried to decide whether or not I had the self-control to remain. I had to though. I had to check on her.

The room was uncomfortably warm, a fire kept stoked by her body. Though Hekla immediately noticed me entering, she couldn't seem to stay still. She writhed on the bed, her gaze heated, almost angry, and her body covered in sweat and misery. The tunic had long since been soaked through, glued to her shapely breasts, and it looked like the only other item she wore was a pair of panties. Though my mind fractured with conflicting emotions, saliva threatened to drip from the corner of my mouth. My pants tightened. My heart pounded. The sight was a burst of adrenaline straight to my libido.

Do not bed her, do not bed her, do not bed her!

"Hekla," I growled, blinking fiercely and trying to stay focused. "Were you aware there were men outside your door?" I fisted my hands, trying to not let jealousy rise in my chest. Gods, my heart slammed against my ribs like a battering ram. I couldn't think in here.

"They've been there since my heat started! At least they're not kissing my hand," she snapped breathlessly and rolled away from me, squeezing her thighs together and moaning quietly.

My rebellious eyes focused on the shape of her bottom and refused to look elsewhere. "I hate Eislyn, Hekla! I hate that vile creature!" I retorted, moved to her bed, and rested a knee on it. I leaned over to try to get her to look at me.

"You sure seem to protect her well for hating her so much!" Hekla seethed, glaring over her shoulder at me and showing a canine. Sweat dripped down her temples, framing her furious eyes.

I placed my other knee on the bed to straddle her and returned her scowl. "Do you understand what would have happened had you touched her, she-wolf? She could have gotten my mother to have you whipped! Whipped!"

"But why did I have to go that far, Belenus? I had to go that far because you wouldn't make her stop!" she snarled up at me, her words angry but her body wanting. Her heat seemed to be tearing her in two.

"You could have left at any point! You should have! I wasn't going to let her do anything to you!"

Her eyes widened. "Do you know how hard it is to leave when a nasty woman is clinging to your mate's arm like she owns him? When she's calling him her intended? It's torture! It's fucking torture!"

I took her hands and pinned her wrists to the bed so she wouldn't scratch me in a blind rage. "You know what else is torture? Having to go through all this shit with an axe over our necks when all I want is to marry and bed the shit out of you!" I countered viciously.

Hekla cried out, from what I didn't know. It was a nightmarish mixture of frustration, despair, loneliness, and arousal. She bucked under me, trying to get out of my grip, but I held her down, feeling like I was also losing my mind. It was so damn hot in here. I glanced down between her legs, unable to tell what was sweat and what was from her core. I bet if I licked her clean, I could tell.

"Did you see the doctors for this?" I asked through clenched teeth, trying not to rip her underwear off and shove my tortured cock into her. I shuddered and my hips jerked slightly, like my body was telling me to get inside her already and start thrusting. My groin ached, and my abdominals and hip muscles screamed to begin their sexual workout. Sweat trickled down my brow from the effort of fighting for control. It dripped onto her collarbone with a satisfying plip and mixed with her own salt water.

"Yes! And because my mate can't help, they said it's either cold showers or masturbation!" She gave a cold, bitter laugh. "And it's very short, very temporary relief. Thanks for asking!" She growled a soft, wolfy growl that made me harder than I'd ever been in my life.

My blood simmered, coming to a boil, but I couldn't tell if it was from anger or lust. "Hekla, I would love to help. You know that!"

"If you won't be useful, then go away! You're just making it worse." The female groaned and squeezed her eyes shut. She truly looked like she was in pain.

"Useful? Oh, I can be quite useful, my dear she-wolf!" I fumed, angry despite the hurt I felt for my suffering fated mate. I moved both her wrists into my left hand so I could slide the right one down her stomach and straight into her panties.

Chapter 11

Hekla

"Ahhh!" I cried out as quietly as I could. Belenus's hand was in my panties! His hand was in my panties! It aroused and startled me, but most of all, it thrilled me. Fear lingered in the back of my mind, muffled by emotional overstimulation.

His fingers danced around the dark curls between my legs, playing and searching while his palm slid lower. I bared my teeth to the ceiling as anticipation wrung me into a state of torture. His fondling finally reached my swollen sex, and he massaged along my folds in hard, broad strokes, somehow knowing that I needed a heavy hand.

The novel act shocked me, and despite my excitement, I succumbed to a burst of shyness. Someone was touching me! Someone was touching my most intimate spot! He'd palmed me through my undergarment before, but now he was beneath it. The tingles from his fated touch carried stimulation and intimacy to an entirely new height; I could close my eyes and know it was my mate because of those sparks of pleasure. A comforting hum wove through it all.

Still, I clamped my legs shut. There was something entirely different about grinding through clothes and… this!

"What are yo— Do you even want this relief?" Belenus hissed in bewilderment and adjusted my wrists in his grip.

"Y-yes!" I moaned. "I-I've just never been touched d-directly!"

His expression softened. "Yes… you waited for me." He released my wrists, removed his hand from my underwear, and rolled his shirt up and over his head. "Shit, so hot in here," he mumbled gruffly.

I swallowed when I saw that his cock was no longer completely covered by his pants. Having only been fully hidden by his long shirt, it'd grown and jutted up well past the beltline, tucked tight against his stomach. I blushed and squirmed at the sight. My instincts wanted that golden, impossible thing inside me right now. I whimpered and licked my lips, hating this heat and wishing it were a physical monster so I could murder it. It was torturing me at the worst possible time!

"C-can't you just g-grind? I could pretend… I-I want you over me…" I begged with a light but feral growl, wiping my sweaty palms on an already drenched shirt. Damnation, nothing was dry! I thrashed my head in sheer frustration and moaned from the agony of an endlessly throbbing core.

"What? You want a repeat of our time in the study? You filthy female," he reprimanded harshly and yanked my underwear off my legs. "I can do better than that!"

I watched in disbelief as he lowered the front of his pants to let the golden beast that was his cock spring out of confinement. It looked heavy, but somehow the man's body could hold it up. When he lifted my hips, my attention snapped back to his actions, and I fell into a panic.

"B-Belenus, we can't! Don't m-mount me! I'll get sent back!" I protested, suddenly frightened. I knew I complained about it, but I wasn't stupid.

"I know that!" he snarled furiously, glaring at our sexes and how close they were. Shockingly, he placed the length of his cock against my folds and slid along in one long grind, nearly making me shriek. "I kn-know… ahhh," he repeated, moaning and tilting his head to the ceiling. He pushed harder, making sounds of pleasure and disbelief with each extended rub between my folds. After I adjusted to this new act, I arched into his hard member, panting. His carved, rolling hips had me sobbing with desire, and I stretched and squirmed beneath him, dying for more. This whole situation was terribly unfair.

"Will we g-get in trouble for this?" I whined as tears trickled down my cheeks. This wasn't enough.

"It's not intercourse!" he answered roughly, his glide seeming longer each time. Every stroke was wetter than the last, and his movements finally smoothened. If this felt euphoric, what would it feel like with him inside me? I dug my claws into the sheets, arched my back in pleasure, and let him massage the swollen flesh between my thighs. His cock was so much harder than I thought erections became. It was stone beneath soft skin. Oh Moon Goddess, I loved it.

My heat was bringing out all of my emotions—rage, despair, happiness, and too many more. I swore my heart would burst if I couldn't purge my feelings. I craved turning feral, tackling Belenus, wrestling and snarling at him until he overpowered me… but I knew that would lead to sex. I had to hold on to some shred of my mind while he was here.

I arched again, but I lifted too high as he swung back, and his cock hooked to notch against my opening. We both froze instantly—simultaneously—shaking and struggling to maintain control. Belenus's scowl softened, and he stared at where we were almost joined. His hand gripped his length, and he rubbed the head of his cock around my opening, moving it in slow circles.

"You'll get taken away if I push in right now… and if I mark you, I could be executed for breaking the marriage contract…" He shook his head violently, backed off, pulled up his pants, and dragged my hips to the edge of the bed. His next words were almost too quiet to hear. "I'm sorry, Hekla, you don't deserve how you've been treated."

"What are yo—" I asked, craning my head to watch him and wondering why he was kneeling between my legs. When he tucked his hands under my butt and brought my sex up to meet his lips, I quickly understood.

"Ah!" I slapped a hand over my mouth to stifle my surprise. Nerves quivered as I encountered new sensations. His tongue pressed firmly against my overheated skin, cold in comparison but just as wet. I might have balked outside of my heat, but I couldn't bring myself to complain about his face being down there—not right now!

I tried not to squirm as he licked a ring around my opening, but the erotic attention had me on the edge of losing all restraint. Oh gods, his tongue was so soft, so slick, and so smooth. I had not expected that! I sobbed again, overwhelmed with emotions and sensations. The tingles from the mate bond sank into my sensitive flesh and lit me like the sun did dry summer grass. Belenus had started a wildfire and each lick fed it.

What made it worse, so much worse, were the noises coming from his throat. Between the sounds of wet flesh lapping and the occasional slurp, Belenus groaned lustfully. I gaped in disbelief and felt my face blush hotter. How he could possibly be enjoying my sex like that? There was no way it tasted good!

And yet, Belenus dug his face in deeper, wrapping his lips around my hyper-sensitive nub while pulling and sucking. He moaned as he squeezed my butt cheeks with his hands, like he was lost in something amazing. I panted as I watched him work, unable to take my eyes off the lewd scene. This large, gold-dusted warrior was hunkered over my core, acting like he was partaking of the most delicious feast he'd ever had. Even his pointy golden ears were blushing!

"Hnnng, ahhh!" I cried through my teeth, trying to be quiet. He tightened his grip in warning, then massaged lightly with his thumbs, being rough and tender at the same time. My abdomen tensed from the spreading fire. More muscles tautened one by one in anticipation. "Belenus! Ah..." I whispered hoarsely, and he groaned huskily into my flesh in reply.

I noticed that he was taking the same path along my sex now, repeating a pattern that focused the fire where it needed to go. My legs shook as I leaned into him, helping him find the right spot, and he moaned appreciatively in response, gripping my butt possessively. He buried his face in deeper, gorging with abandon. His grunts were muffled but were very much from his own arousal. Though Belenus was not a wolf, this was the level of obsession I'd expect from one!

I grabbed my pillow and started crying into it, thrashing as the summer fire came to eat me alive. My body broke out into a heavier sweat as Belenus lifted me closer to the sun. Finally, his determined growl threw me into the bright lights.

My orgasm careened into me, and I muffled my scream with the cotton pillow. Pleasure blinded me as rays of sunlight scattered. Wave after wave hit, and Belenus's greedy lapping kept me trapped between the wildfire and the thrashing sun. I knew euphoria then, and for just a moment, the perfection made all else seem unreal.

Once the last ray had spread through me, my spent body went limp. A tortured, guttural sound hit my ears, and I looked up to find an agonized Belenus fisting his shaft. He fumbled toward the bathroom, but I said, "No! Here!"

He turned to see me patting my stomach as I lifted my tunic. I wanted to catch him. If I couldn't have him the way I wanted to, then I wanted this. I craved his scent on me. I needed it.

"Shit!" he uttered through his teeth and straddled me again, pointing the head of his cock down toward my stomach. He groaned as he ran his hand over his sticky length, and his eyes flickered from the skin of my belly to my face. Having found some relief from my heat symptoms, I decided to reward him with some mischief.

I lifted my tunic higher to expose my breasts for his pleasure. His eyes snapped wide open, his nostrils flared, and he bit his free hand to keep from making a sound. His stare was as hungry as his mouth had been, and it didn't take more than a minute of gaping at my breasts for him to hiss through his teeth and come. The crowded muscles in his abdomen flexed, and he spasmed as he released ropes of pale seed onto my belly, grunting hoarsely from every burst.

I could appreciate the sounds he made now that we'd climaxed at different times, and I watched the entire scene with interest. I'd gladly see him pleasure himself again. Or perhaps he'd let me do it for him. Watching this powerful man melt before me offered a different kind of euphoria.

Belenus spent the last of his offering onto my belly and collapsed next to me. It was a tight fit on the small bed, but somehow, we both managed to stay on it.

"So… not appropriate," he whispered hoarsely as he tried to catch his breath. The words caught me off guard, and I placed my hand over my mouth as I burst into a fit of giggles. A small smile curled the corner of his lips.

When I sobered, I turned my head to look directly at him. "Belenus?"

"Hmm?" His lids were closed now, and he looked relaxed. That made me happy.

"Do you think about me? When you don't see me?" I asked.

He mumbled all too casually, "Ask the dozens of cum-filled rags in my trash that question." My face contorted into a stupefied expression, unable to decide whether to gasp or laugh. He opened his eyes, saw my expression, and chuckled quietly. "Crude as that may be, it's a fact. But, yes, I miss you terribly."

"I'm glad it's not just me then," I said softly, studying his pretty face. He was so unlike a wolf, and I had to wonder why I was paired with him. The current challenges made it hard to get to know him, but our interactions were perfect when we could forget about the court. I could only hope we could free him from his forced engagement soon. I wanted to get to know the man meant for me.

"Of course it's not," he replied, stroking my arm with a lazy finger. We lay there for a while, taking a moment to find comfort in each other. He eventually adjusted an arm under his head and looked directly at me. "I just remembered something I was going to ask. Why was that Spring Court guard at your door?"

I was loath to think about that man and his message. "He said his princess wanted to see me. I told him she could kiss my butt. Unfortunately, he took that literally, offered to do it himself, and that's when you came along." I lowered my gaze, feeling my heart sink once more. "Everyone's taunting me about losing you…"

"You're not losing me," he declared firmly. "And I don't want you alone with that princess."

"What if they force me? You won't let me defend myself," I argued.

"You defend yourself by not attacking. And if they force you, send the mac-talla to find me. I'll interfere," he answered and went back to stroking my arm affectionately. "Avoid her as best you can. She's friendly with the queen, who holds all the power here. I can only do so much. I can't override her rules. If the worst-case scenario happens"—he took a deep breath—"you'll have to flee while I hold things down here. I think, as of today, you should have your bag ready at all times, ok?"

"Alright…" I said, not wanting to know what the worst-case scenario was. "I'll send Arse if they drag me away…"

His lip twitched. "Who?"

"Arse named himself," I said, jerking my thumb over to the closet where the mac-talla was curled up, asleep. "He's still trying to get fired."

Belenus buried his face in the mattress and erupted into tired laughter. He then turned his head to face me and rubbed one of his sleepy eyes. "If anything, I should start giving him a salary." He gaze wandered across my features as he stroked my cheek, making me smile. "That's my female," he murmured, returning my smile. "One day at a time."

Once Belenus gathered the willpower to leave my side, he departed, barely able to contain his lopsided grin. Though the spring in his step was cute, I hoped no one saw him leave my room looking so sated. I didn't want to invite more trouble during my heat.

Closing the door behind him, I sighed in relief and slid down the door, enjoying the temporary abatement of my symptoms. I shrugged my soaked tunic over my head and wiped the sticky mess off my belly. I stared at the substance of Belenus's pleasure and felt a sense of wonder; it truly was remarkable how this innocent-looking liquid could create life inside me. I smiled, hoping someday his seed would take root within me to make a pup… or a fae, I supposed. What a bizarre concept. If someone had told me I'd potentially birth a fae baby someday—or a faeby, as my grandmother dubbed them—I would have called them nuts.

Well, that was nice, Eventide chirped happily. *Finally got a good look at his cock. Must have gotten a gold trophy serving his kingdom because bow a-wow!*

Ye were shamefully quiet, Arse chastised, and I chuckled, looking over at him. *Get me ah bonny mac-talla female an we'll show ye how it's done.*

"Do a better job translating, and I'll find you a mate," I said seriously, pointing a finger at his nose.

He rocked a bit, hissing like he was laughing. *They'll no huv me. Ah'm deformed.* He waddled to rest under the bed, and I slowly removed my foot from my mouth, so to speak.

The next day continued to have me in the shackles of my heat, but I did the best I could. Sweet Bidelia helped cool me off several times last night by laying cold, wet towels on my body.

I wasn't sure how I'd get through the next four days, so it was a blessing to have help. I owed the young fae so much already.

Koray told me to meet him at the front of the castle around noon, and I was beside myself with excitement. I'd heard Ragna describe the Realm of the Gods, but I couldn't wait to see it with my own eyes. I knew it'd be a life-changing experience.

Koray waved and smiled when he saw me, and he led me to the tower where the door was guarded. He pointed up at the daylit moon and said, "That's where we're going. Isn't that crazy?"

I shivered and laughed nervously. "That is… beyond comprehension, Koray! I'm not sure I can even think about it too much."

"Ragna was shaken too," he said, sounding nostalgic. "I can't imagine a person who wouldn't be."

The tower was an exhausting climb; the stairs spiraled up for what seemed like an eternity. "Why…" I panted, "is it so… high… up?" My heat was making the climb hotter and way more painful than it needed to be.

"Apparently," Koray answered, "the door was discovered off the ground, so they had to build up to it. Really, there was no other choice."

"Oh!" I said and nodded in understanding. "That… makes a lot of sense. Wonder why the gods put it up so high…"

"Or maybe the ground wasn't always this low." He chuckled, and we finally reached the top to see a stone platform sandwiched between two pedestals. A guard stood to the left of the platform and nodded at Koray.

"Lunar Key," he acknowledged, and Koray waved in a friendly manner. When the guard looked at me, recognition registered on his face. "Vessel of the Sky Gods, an honor!" He nodded in deference to me. "You may proceed," the fae said and gestured to the platform. I smiled, enjoying the moment of civility, then followed Koray and waited for him to do whatever Keys did.

The still summer air stirred into a breeze that dragged the shadows from beneath our feet. Everything darkened up to several paces from us, and the darkness spilled into a deep shade of blue. It was like a bubble of night, and only the moonlight could touch us. The glare of the summer sun beyond the sheer moonlight made my eyes throb, so I averted them, wincing as a headache formed in my brow.

Koray reached back to grab my wrist and lead us through a door that I wasn't quite sure if I could see or not. My eyes still ached, and I had to close them once we passed through the door so I wouldn't be blasted with light again.

Cool air enveloped me, and I slowly opened one eye at a time, holding my breath in anticipation.

"We're here! Welcome to the Realm of the Gods," he announced, grinning at me.

"Oh my goddess..." I breathed and immediately lay down on the cold, springy moss that caressed the sides of a creek. "It's so cool here. I love it!" I squealed, instantly energized and wishing I could stay here for the duration of my heat.

"Yeah, the Summer Court is... not fun when I have to wear armor, I'll tell you that. I don't know how these fae do it..." Koray confessed, looking around and giving me a moment to get my dress dirtier. I sighed reluctantly and stood, brushing off the moss and soil I'd collected in such a dignified manner.

"What a delicious place," I noted with a grin. "I smell game in the woods, and everything seems fresh, completely untouched." It was a stark difference to the stuffy confines of my current room, and I sniffed so hard, so enthusiastically, I fell into a coughing fit. If I could bottle this air up, I totally would.

Maybe the Moon Goddess has a jar, Eventide joked.

Koray led me through the peaceful woods to a thatched cottage that blended perfectly into its surroundings. We went to knock on the door, but it swung open first, and a white lycan loomed over us. The hairs on my neck stood on end, and I bared my canines out of instinct.

Then I froze and sniffed. "Rakel?" I asked, confused. Shouldn't she be at the castle with Rudesind? And she wasn't a lycan...

The lycan huffed and stepped back, holding the door open for us. *No, I'm just using her likeness to receive you. I have no physical form you could comprehend, my most commanding daughter.*

"Oh," I replied vapidly and walked in, a little stunned to be entering the Moon Goddess's home. "But Rakel doesn't have a lycan form."

I needed hands to brew tea, the Moon Goddess explained and closed the door behind Koray. *It is good to see you again, Koray, my Lunar Key. Have you marked my sweet Soley yet?*

Koray blushed and stammered, "A-ah… no… I'm a human, and I c-can't mark… so… not yet?"

The lycan who was the Moon Goddess laughed another growling huff. She didn't reply to Koray's nervous answer and gestured for us to go into the next room. I went where She directed and froze when I saw another Eventide lying down on the couch.

Imposter! my Eventide yapped, and I took an involuntary step back into the hall.

I am so lucky to have so many guests today, the Moon Goddess sang happily. *Please find a seat. Sky Gods, you are hogging the couch.*

Oh, Eventide said. *BUT THIS IS WEIRD. DON'T LOOK AT ME. I CAN'T.*

I smiled nervously and averted my gaze from the Sky Gods who were using our likeness. I knew this wouldn't be a normal visit, and here was a whole lot of 'not normal.' The goddess placed two cups of tea down for Koray and me, making this seem far more like a family visit than one with a deity.

Yours will help with your heat, Hekla, my poor daughter, She said in a motherly tone. *Koray, that'll ease some of your training aches. You've been working hard! I'm very proud of you. I wish you were one of mine. I'd love to take credit for such a fine, outstanding soul.*

Koray blushed again and grinned into his cup, looking like he'd just received the best compliment in the world. I supposed it was. The white lycan crouched into a padded wicker chair that was easily twice the size of the one I'd claimed.

So, you are here, She said and gestured for me to talk. She likely knew everything already, but I spared no detail in explaining my situation. When I stopped recounting, She nodded in sympathy, but Koray looked angry. The Sky Gods were impassive, simply listening with the calm of a quiet sunrise.

I lifted my hands helplessly and lamented, "I guess… what I'm asking is… how is fae magic allowed to supersede your will? It doesn't seem fair, and I'm terrified I'm going to lose Belenus to rules that don't make sense to me. This would never happen in wolf society!"

The goddess gently shook Her lycan head. *It's not possible to answer why something isn't fair, my daughter. Fairness is subjective and at the mercy of Fate and Chaos. Chaos is what Fate wades through as It works. It simply is.*

And I only pair souls, She continued. *I cannot force them to end up together. It's why you have the option to reject a mate to begin with. Some never find their fated mates because Fate put them too far apart. For Its own reasons, of course. That's extremely rare, though.*

"So Fate could have a plan where I'm not supposed to end up with Belenus?" I gasped raggedly as tears rolled down my cheeks. My breathing accelerated uncontrollably, and I put a hand to my panicking heart.

No, no, no! Not acceptable! I screamed to Eventide. Instead of telling me to stay in the present like she usually did, she simply moaned in despair and slunk away to hide in the back of my mind, unable to accept the goddess's words.

There's usually a little wiggle room with Fate, pup, the goddess comforted. *I don't know what Fate has in store all the time, and if I do, I don't divulge it unless something critical has occurred. My relationship with Fate is fragile at best; I've nurtured Its trust in me for eons. I must be cautious so I can care for my wolves and lycans. The gods can only get away with so much.*

I was outright sobbing at this point, and Koray left his seat to crouch by me and pat my arm. He asked, "Is there nothing she can do to help her situation? It's bad enough she's in heat, but it sounds like these fae play dirty."

Hekla, do you think you can even do anything to assist Belenus with the legal or magical aspects of the contract issue? the goddess asked.

I shook my head miserably. "I-I don't know a-anything about these l-laws, a-and I kn-know nothing a-about m-m-magic," I said, hiccupping and rubbing my swollen eyes. With my heat, simple concentration was a colossal undertaking.

Then perhaps you can't do anything. Perhaps you should focus on something else while Belenus takes care of it, She advised. *Just a thought. Waiting sounds atrocious, does it not, Sky Gods?*

Indeed, They said, offering nothing else.

Have you forgotten? the Moon Goddess asked Them, blinking slowly.

I have not. She will ask when it happens, the Sky Gods replied.

"When what happens?" I asked, dread curling into my belly.

You'll see, They answered without answering. Fear stopped my tears short. See about what?

Well, then I suppose I'll do my part while she's here, the Moon Goddess said, not giving me a chance to press more about the vague statements, and stood from the chair. She gestured me up, so I drained the last of my tea and rose to face Her.

Hekla Himinn, my daughter, my little guiding light, would you accept a blessing from the Moon Goddess? She asked.

The jitters sank into my skin, Her words striking like a painless slap. Oh gods, a blessing? Ragna said hers wasn't that bad, but Zorian's blessing had almost killed him! I bit my lip nervously and looked over at Koray, as though he had all the answers. He just shrugged and gestured for me to pay attention to the goddess.

"I..." I began in a hoarse voice and licked my lips, "I accept your blessing, Moon Goddess." I squeezed my eyes shut, knowing it probably looked stupid, but I was terrified I'd be clobbered an inch from death.

Relax, Hekla, She said, laughing in my mind. *I won't kill you, my daughter.*

She said She wouldn't kill me, but She didn't say She wouldn't hurt me. I tensed further but opened my eyes to face my fear. Yes, I was terribly hormonal, but Hekla wouldn't shy from this. I had to remember who I was.

I had to remember what Hekla would do.

As I waited, my heat continued to radiate from my body, but it stopped replenishing. Instead, I grew cold and shivered as a chill settled deep within me. Next, I ran out of air. I looked around in a panic, my chest muscles fighting to take in anything, but there was no air to pull into my lungs. I staggered to lean against the wall and stared at the Moon Goddess, asking Her silently if this was normal. She didn't reply but continued to watch me struggle. I prayed to the gods that weren't here, asking them to please catch me if I succumbed. My vision tunneled, and I glanced down to see my flesh swell. I only lasted several more seconds before my eyes gave up, and I fell unconscious.

Chapter 12

Belenus

"...and in several days the soldiers will head out of the city again and run scenarios in the field, which I usually supervise since I'm still the general," I said after sipping my tea, a brew currently flavored with irritation and impatience. Eislyn insisted on refreshments today to get to know me better. She also insisted on having it in the garden where she somehow knew to make snide comments about the small forest I'd grown for Hekla.

"Fascinating," Eislyn replied, obviously not paying attention. "So, have you rejected the dog yet?"

I took in a slow breath and held it to keep from striking her across the face. I couldn't let her rile me up; that was what she wanted. If she got me into a position where she could demand compensation, my fated mate would suffer her hand. Simply put, upsetting Eislyn meant hurting Hekla.

"As I said before, Eislyn, it would be best if you left my personal matters to me," I replied calmly. There, I did it. I said something without ripping her head off her shoulders. Oh gods, how much longer was this dreadful tea going to go?

"Oh! Belenus! There you are!" Koray's voice came from down the garden trail.

I looked over my shoulder at him and flashed a brief, world-weary smile. "Koray," I acknowledged with a tilt of my head, grateful for the interruption.

"Belenus, I n—" he began, but Eislyn cut him off as expected.

"These humans have no sense, interrupting royal tea," she said with an aggrieved sigh and looked kindly at me, as though I had the hardest job in the world managing just one.

"Hey!" Koray snapped. "Shut up!" He mimed locking his lips and turned to face me. Eislyn's eyes grew wide, exposing a murderous countenance. I was a bit shocked myself. I'd never seen him this upset.

"I need your help, Belenus. Hekla…" He looked askance at the fae woman and became more discreet with his wording. "Hekla is not well. I need you to come with me."

Eislyn snapped a warning. "Absolutely not! You can't just order the prince about! I will go to the queen about this." Though she spoke to Koray, her words were directed at me. I couldn't be seen caring about Hekla.

"Take whatever resources you need for this person," I instructed dismissively, keeping a wary eye on Eislyn. "I need to remain here."

What was wrong with Hekla? Was it her heat? Should I send my sister?

Koray's hands dropped to his sides, and I finally met his stare. Then he straightened and tilted his head like he was seeing me for the first time. I scrubbed a hand over my mouth nervously and raised my brows in question.

He remained stunned for several heartbeats before he curled a lip in disgust and said, "I'd tell you to not forget who your real mate is, Belenus, but it seems like you already have." The young man turned and jogged off to get help elsewhere. Mollified, Eislyn began chatting about something else in a chipper voice, but all I could think about was that I'd just made a huge mistake. Again.

The first thing I noticed was that I was wet and thirsty. How could I be both? Certainly, whatever had made me wet would quench my thirst.

Where are we? Eventide asked groggily, her voice nudging me from my delirium. I turned my head, licked my dry lips, and slowly opened my eyes. *Oh, back in our windowless cage,* she said with disappointment.

"When did we get back?" I croaked and tried to untangle my sweaty legs from the blankets so I could get up and shower.

I don't remember. There's a big ol' blotch of black in our memories.

"Are you here, Arse?" I called weakly while shuffling to the bathing room.

Ah am, he answered, and I heard him crawl out of the closet.

"Are you ok? Did someone care for you while I was gone? How long was I gone?" I asked, rubbing my throbbing temples.

Wee Bidelia fed me, aye. Ye cam back twa days ago. Day ye left, Arse said with a surprising lack of sass.

"Two days? I was unconscious all day yesterday? Oh gods. It's only nine days til the wedding now!" I fretted and jumped into the shower. I scrutinized my body and winced when I found little bruises peppering my skin.

What did the Moon Goddess do to us? Eventide gasped.

"I don't know..." I murmured, studying them while scrubbing gently. "We should find Koray..."

I put on a clean dress, buckled on the mac-talla's leather perch, and let him climb onto my shoulder. I strolled out of the castle and wandered toward the training grounds, hoping to find him there. The fresh air was welcome, but I was a little worried about attracting the men's attention. I'd have to be quick.

A familiar little bird landed on my free shoulder, and I growled quietly. "Do you need something?" I asked it, really not wanting to deal with Emer right now. A swirl of light told me she was now strolling by my side.

"What I want is to look after my dumb brother's mate while he's off making horrible decisions. He's dumb, I mean. Not you," she said wryly and lifted my arm to study the little bruises. "Rumor has it you went to the Realm of the Gods a couple days ago."

"This Rumor fella seems to be correct," I returned, searching the sea of soldiers for someone with long black hair.

"Glad your wit didn't get bruised along with your skin. Augh, tch! Stop moving, bi—I mean, she-wolf," she said and tapped lightly along my arm. I stared as the bruising cleared, and she repeated the process on my other arm and legs, although she only tapped along my ankles for 'modesty's sake.' I was less shocked about what she'd done than the fact it was her who'd done it. Emer's personality had more depth than I thought.

"We'll have to do the rest in private," she informed with a shrug and followed along, not bothering to ask about my errand. Occasionally a soldier would approach and try to get handsy, but before I could even say anything, Emer got rid of them with a well-placed foot to the butt.

"Men. This is why I won't get mated. They're all after one thing," she grouched.

"Male wolves are very honest about their wants. I think you'd find it refreshing," I said with a small grin. "None of these stupid fae games."

"I'll tell you what," she began with a scowl, "if Eislyn becomes queen, I'll just follow you back to your realm. The soul of the Summer Court will be gutted in weeks. Maybe I'll just let a male wolf-shifter ride the pain out of me. That sounds nice."

Tears brimmed in my eyes, and I angrily wiped them away with a palm. The princess couldn't win. She just couldn't!

"Looking for your human? I don't see him," Emer noted, scanning the crowds.

"He did say he was going to study magic. Maybe he's with an instructor right now," I said with a sigh and turned back to the castle.

"Awww! A human man learning magic? That's terribly cute. I like that!" Emer exclaimed with a wicked grin. It was almost feral enough to be a wolf's grin.

"Well, I'm sure he'll find a way to do something with i—"

"Best get a move on, General Hekla," Emer interrupted in a militant voice. "Horny enemies on our tail!"

I looked over my mac-talla-free shoulder to find a handful of curious and eager fae men approaching at a pace faster than our walk. I grimaced at Emer, hauled Arse, and we broke into a run, making a mad dash for my room. We fled into the castle halls, and upon reaching my room, I slammed the door behind us and fell laughing to the floor, high off adrenaline. Arse, properly ruffled, wobbled off to drink some water.

Once I caught my breath, I looked over at the snorting, giggling Emer, and asked, "Do you know who cared for me while I was out? Did Belenus ever visit?"

She sobered and grew uncomfortable, a side of her I hadn't seen thus far. "He said he… didn't have the time. He sent me to check on you and report back to him when he was alone. I believe he's also assigned Bidelia to be your full-time maid. She's not a basic servant anymore, which is nice. I always thought she was a good, hardworking folk fae. She said your human stopped by a couple times, just to see if he was needed."

With each word, my heart sank deeper, and when she was done speaking. I placed my face in my hands and held back a gasping sob.

Emer's hand patted my back—gently this time. "The court is a bitch. It chews fae up and spits them out… alive but wishing they were dead. But where is that wolf who's an even bigger bitch? I want to see that one, the one who shredded my arm. That was amazing."

All I could do was laugh at her absurdity as I wiped mucus from beneath my nose. I was so tired of crying.

"Speaking of shredding, get that dress off so I can treat the rest of those bruises, you mad adventurer."

She scanned me from head to toe, healed all the bruises she could find, and took off, promising to make her report to Belenus. That wasn't what I wanted, but I'd have to accept it. Why couldn't he visit me? I frowned and sat down on my bed, fanning myself miserably and wishing my room had a window at the very least.

A while later, a key scraped inside the lock, and Bidelia stepped in with a hesitant smile. "Oh, I'm so glad yer awake! I have to get ye ready for dinner…" she said, shuffling forward and moving to look through the options in the closet.

"Dinner?" I asked, worried. Was this another wretched banquet?

"Yes, there's a banquet tonight in honor of the new royal courting couple, ye know," she answered sadly and glanced back at me while chewing her lip.

Damnation. I can't do this.

"Why am I even invited? It makes no sense." I worried at my hands, which were already sweaty. "And I'm in heat! Surely, they know that. I'd be a distraction!"

"I can't speak for Her Majesty," Bidelia replied in a gloomy voice. She pulled out a dark green gown and looked questioningly at me. "This would look lovely. Hide yer sweat too."

"That's clever, yes. Thanks, Bidelia." The words left my mouth before I realized what I'd said. We both froze and stared at each other like we had no idea what to do. "I… it just came out," I whispered and clapped my hand over my mouth.

She suddenly rushed forward, terrified, and said, "Ye cannot say that to anyone else, m'lady! Ye have to be more careful! Just wish them well! Ye must!"

Taken aback by her aggressiveness, I nodded rapidly. She blew out a breath and said, "Ye scare me with how little ye know! Ye must be more careful!" She helped me into the gown, and I kept waiting for her to drop her demand, but she never did. It floated there in the room, unspoken but not forgotten.

Bidelia pinned my hair and put some larger curls into the locks she decided to leave untucked. She did a rather nice job, and I tousled her hair before leaving with Arse. "No one's... coming to escort me, are they?" I asked quietly and Bidelia shook her head, looking down to scuff her worn shoes on the stone floor. "Are you sure I have to go?" I pressed.

"I'll get in t-trouble, m-m'lady." Her eyes glittered, moments from weeping, and I crouched to pull her into a hug. I knew she hadn't wanted to say that.

"Ok! Ok! I'm going! Don't cry. I won't let anyone hurt you!" I kissed her on the forehead a couple times, making big smooching sounds to get her to laugh, then I stood with a determined face, and marched toward the banquet hall.

I took a deep breath.

What would Hekla do?

Belenus

Eislyn had been here for five days now, and I was about ready to murder both her and the queen. I'd finally received a copy of the marriage contract, and I'd been poring over it with my experts to find a way out, but so far, we'd made no progress. Some information was 'need-to-know only' and was heavily blotted out with ink. As the groom-to-be, I was certain as shit that I was someone who needed to know.

The worst part—the part that I'd feared—was the section that outlined the retaliation agreed upon by the two parties. What I'd read had shaken me, and I was constantly fending off panic attacks. I didn't know how I'd sleep for the rest of this blistering war. The section for retaliation was heavily redacted but specified that an execution would occur if I were to break the marriage contract. If I didn't find a way out of this and broke the contract by trying to run away with Hekla, someone would be executed. If my name was in that redacted section, they'd hunt me down, even in the other realms. Hekla's name could even be in there.

So, what were my options? Kill the princess? Start a war? Lead my people to die over a marriage? Should I try to kill my mother? She was stronger than me. She was more dangerous, and she had the resources as the queen to do what she willed. No… none of those seemed feasible. There had to be another way. Shit!

There was also the question of why this union was so damn important to 'the court.' We didn't need anything from any other court! Aside from the rare drought, we were fine, so why force me into a lifetime of misery? That seemed pretty need-to-know as well!

Koray had come to assist today with some of the other experts, but he was aloof and didn't talk to me more than necessary. On top of disappointing my friend, hurting my mate by trying to save her, and struggling to get out of a wedding, I still had an army to run and fulfill my duties as a prince. I was under pressure, and I felt like I was several strikes short of crumbling.

I swirled through my thoughts like I swirled the contents of my glass. I didn't feel like drinking tonight, not even to drown my sorrows. There was too much at stake, and nothing could cut the misery. Eislyn chatted excitedly with the queen, but her annoying voice was as muted as the rest of the voices at the banquet table. I wasn't present; I didn't want to be.

I set my glass down and pushed it away from me, not even wanting to smell the hard honeysuckle. The sweet wildness reminded me of Hekla, and I ached for her presence. I began to smell what I could only assume was her natural scent when she went into heat, and it was the perfect aroma of sweet honeysuckle mixed with something... warm and woodsy. The scent of flowers wrapped around a sunbaked garden lattice was much more sophisticated and mouthwatering than the drink before me. Perhaps if I was a wolf, she'd always smell like honeysuckle nectar. I wouldn't be able to keep my lips off her if that was the case.

Every day without her was miserable, and somehow there was always someone watching me when I wasn't in my chambers. Eislyn waited for me to slip. Maintaining my distance from Hekla was the only way to keep Eislyn's attention off her. It only solved part of the problem, and my fated mate continued to suffer.

I pinched the bridge of my nose, wishing to speed up this farce. "Are we waiting for anyone?" I asked Emer in a bored tone.

"Only the designated virgin sacrifice," she uttered under her breath, annoyed.

A chill dripped into my bloodstream. "What?" I hissed.

"You heard me." She took a huge gulp of hard nectar.

One of the banquet hall doors opened and Hekla—beauty personified—strode in wearing a velvety, forest-green gown and her potent heat. I cursed under my breath as her pheromones reached my seat, instantly stimulating me. I stared at the queen, who appeared unperturbed and only raised her glass the moment Hekla seated herself in the last chair. Every single unmarried man in the room stared lustfully at her, forcing her to drop her gaze in discomfort. I ground my teeth in anger and jealousy. She was not their female to look at!

The queen's voice was barely able to rip my attention from Hekla. "I would like to make a toast to my son and his lovely bride-to-be! It may have started a little rough, but it truly has been a pleasure watching them grow closer by the day. I admit I was a little shocked by what I saw in the garden yesterday, but that is young love for you!" She gave a believable, reserved titter, and my gaze shot to her in bewilderment. Several of the guests chuckled. The easy reception of such a personal lie disoriented me, stunned me.

"What in the shit is she talking about, Belenus?" Emer hissed, snapping me out of my thrown state.

"I don't know! She's lying!" I protested under my breath. I glanced over to try to deny it to Hekla with a gesture, but her gaze was fixed on her hands. Her face flushed, and her hands shook beneath her heat and humiliation. The mac-talla had his prehensile tail wrapped around her neck, as though providing an emotional shield for her. Shit! This was bad.

Emer snapped back at me. "Well, I know that, but you need to say something!"

"I can't! She'll lash out, and you know who she'll target! Why do you think she was brought here? You always forget to look five steps ahead, Emer!"

My younger sister deflated, knowing that what I said was true. She didn't like it. She didn't have to like it, but there was no denying that we both knew what the queen was capable of doing.

"And since Belenus is the only male heir, I've given them both my blessing to attempt to conceive before the wedding. It is a rare exception, but one I think is acceptable," the queen said, and I felt as though I'd been slapped in the face. This entire situation was well out of control. That made no blisterin' sense! Was Eislyn really unable to wait a little more than a week? No, this was something entirely different, an obvious attack on Hekla, but at least I couldn't be forced into it. I restrained a gag at the thought of Eislyn in my bed.

At least one lie was something I could address. "I don't recall agreeing to that… Your Majesty," I said, loudly and clearly.

The queen chuckled, encouraging more members at the table to laugh with her. "You have ever been the shy thing, my son! No one here judges you for asking, especially with someone as pretty as our sweet Eislyn, yes?"

"Pretty like a muckie's muddy ass," Emer mumbled.

"I did not a—" I protested between my teeth.

The queen wouldn't hear another word. "So, a toast to our happy couple and our blessings for a swift conception!" she declared, and the courtiers toasted, shouting their good wishes. Eislyn tapped my shoulder, smiling shyly and lifting her glass to clink with mine. I ignored her stupid act and turned to Emer.

"Can you please, for the love of all things good left in my miserable existence, check on Hekla for me when the food gets here? Subtly?" I whispered to my adopted sister, and she nodded, downing the last of her nectar and summoning a servant to pour a second—or a third. It looked like Emer was prepared to get drunk on my behalf as well.

I glanced over at where my fated mate had been seated. It was obvious the queen knew she was in heat and had placed her by unmated men to further distress her. My blood started simmering when Hekla had to tactfully fend off a fae who'd attempted a groping under the table. I half wished she would ignore all the warnings I'd given her and scratch him because the mate in me was trying to claw its way out to protect her. I was disgusted, jealous, and dying to rip the man's hands off for touching her. On top of it all, her pheromones almost made me not care about the repercussions.

But I had to care about them.

Another fae man stopped by her side of the table and offered her an appetizer off his plate. As he leaned over, his hand tried to creep toward the side of her breast, but the mac-talla executed a perfectly timed sneezing fit and sprayed mucus all over the handsy fae, who departed quicker than he'd come. Arse continued to be vulgar in the very best way, but something vulgar was still trying to claw its way out of me now.

I was near shaking with rage, and the longer I was around her pheromones, the harder it was to focus on anything. The primal creature that I never realized was inside of me wanted to correct everyone's idea of who was going to be mated to whom. I had obscene thoughts of bending Hekla over the dinner table for everyone to see and thrust my cock into her until I flooded and marked her. I wanted to have my way with her the way I wanted to and show all these other men that she was not theirs. The additional slap in the face to the queen and the wretched princess would be a beautiful bonus. Perhaps it'd be the perfect, utopian moment that would make the penalty of my death so worthwhile.

After the fae on her other side tried to whisper in her ear and kiss her neck, she got up and started to leave the banquet hall.

"I did not excuse you, mutt," the queen said shortly, and I snapped my head around to glare furiously at her.

"Do not call her that!" I hissed under my breath. The queen ignored me, and Eislyn's countenance turned into one of annoyance, not appreciating my outburst.

Hekla paused for a moment, but she didn't look back. After a heartbeat of hesitation, she continued out of the room, ignoring the queen's order completely. A handful of fae discreetly left the table—one by one—to follow her out as quietly as possible. I stood to intervene, and the queen said, "I did not dismiss you. It'd be wise for you to stay, my dear, sweet son." Her eyes gleamed with a promise, but I narrowed my eyes at her.

"I am a general, and I see about a half-dozen men about to assault a woman. It's my duty to interfere. I don't tell you how to do your job; don't pretend you know how to do mine!" I snapped and rushed out to help my mate.

Shit, shit, shit, shit!

I stormed down the hall, caught up, and roared at the stalking men to get their asses back to the banquet. They scattered like mice, and I hurried to a panicked Hekla. I couldn't get a word out to my wild-eyed mate before hearing the slapping of slippers behind me. Emer appeared, obviously concerned about her, so I grabbed Arse and handed him to my sister. I snapped, "You keep watch!" Then I opened the nearest door—which turned out to be a supply closet—and dragged an emotional Hekla inside with me.

I summoned a ball of light to keep us from the pitch black of the closet and grabbed her arms to steady her. "That was brutal," I said to my shaking, sweating mate. "The queen is a monster, and she lied about everything, Hekla. You know that!"

"So, why haven't you visited me, then? I've been unconscious for days!" she cried, looking up at me with her dark, hurt eyes.

"Eislyn's got eyes on me! I can't go anywhere without being watched! I told you we'd receive injuries in this war! I told you we'd have to be strong!" I reminded her, passion swelling in my chest. Her pheromones were quickly filling up this closet, and I was starting to have a serious problem with my desire. I backed her into the wall, caged her, and leaned in to take a deep breath. "Gods! Stop smelling so good!" I snapped. I couldn't think! I fisted my hands and thumped one against the wall.

"So, what do I do?" she protested. "Put myself in a box until you have this all figured out? I'm being tortured! I almost believed what she said because it feels like you've forgotten about me!"

"I haven't!" I yelled in frustration and smacked the wall again, making my palm sting. "Shit, Hekla! You have to hang in there! This is going to get ugly! This is how fae do war at court!"

Chapter 13

Belenus

Breathlessly, Hekla lamented, “I hate how things are done here. This is so much crueler than pack life...” She uttered a moan, and the tilting of her head freed several tears to trail down her cheeks.

I shifted uncomfortably and looked away, knowing that moan wasn’t only from despair. She slid down the wall a little, then back up, like she was rubbing her scent on it. Her skin flushed deeper—a hearth sat stoked within her.

I couldn’t… get distracted. “Hekla, we have to go back! I’ll seat my sister next to you, ok? She’ll get you through it!”

Hekla bristled and gritted through her teeth, “I can’t! You don’t know what it’s like! They can’t keep their disgusting hands off of me!” She squeezed her eyes shut, bared her canines, and gripped her head with her clawed hands. “I hate this heat! Why can’t I simply have my mate fuck me through it? Agh!”

Lust roiled through my stomach from her words, but my worry for her kept my wits intact. “Shit! Turn around, Hekla! Let’s take care of this problem so we can go!” I growled, spinning her to face the wall. She wept quietly and stuck her butt out like she wanted me to mount her. Oh, I desperately wished I could. I'd gladly 'fuck' her through her heat as she'd put it. I'd have to make sure that word meant what I thought it did.

I pressed up against her, reached around, and lifted her skirts until I could access her underwear. I jerked my hand into her panties, found her wet center, and started stroking her folds. My fingers were immediately coated in her slick, which was good; it'd help my fingers glide across her skin. I heavily massaged the larger mounds first, then moved inward to rub the ones closer to her entrance.

She bit her arm to muffle her moans, but the sounds she made pulled noises out of me as well. "Shit!" I swore, getting excessively turned on by her swaying bottom and the sounds of her pleasure. Her wetness only reminded me of when I'd feasted on her core, and a surge of saliva filled my mouth. I'd gladly get lost in between her succulent thighs over and over again. Gods, I wished I had time to savor her, but we needed to be quick.

I circled her opening with a finger and asked in a strained voice, "Have you ever had anyone inside you, Hekla?" I knew already but waited for her answer, hoping I could speed up the process by delving into her dripping heat.

"N-no!" she growled quietly and spread her legs a little. Her body was one step ahead of my question, and I found that incredibly erotic.

"Do you want me inside you, Hekla?" I hissed and dipped my finger slightly against her wet entrance.

"Yes!" she sobbed angrily.

I slid my finger into her and swirled it a little to gently stretch her virgin tissue. She hissed in discomfort, and I rubbed her back comfortingly, hoping the mate touch would make up for the pain. Then I slid my other hand into her panties to massage her mounds while I pushed my finger in farther. She hissed again but wiggled her bottom against my pants, aggravating my own personal situation. The strain on her threshold had not diminished her desire—that was obvious.

"Stop it, Hekla," I snarled quietly. "You're making me hard!"

"I wish it was that easy!" she retorted, but her raw, sensual growling only made me harder. My cock strained against its confines, desperate to experience what my finger was enjoying.

"Gods dammit!" I yanked my hand out and gave her rump a good smack.

She jerked her head around to look at me in shock. "Did you just spank me?" she shriek-whispered.

"Yes! Stop misbehaving and let me finish you, she-wolf!" I snapped and shoved my hand back into her panties to continue rubbing her swollen folds. "Shit, you're as hot as the sun down there!" My breath caught as I feverishly pumped my finger, her sighs and moans stuttering with every forceful jerk. I grimaced and restrained an aroused groan. Feeling her tightness, wetness, heat, and texture, I didn't have to imagine too hard now what a dip in her sauna would be like, and that almost had me breaking. "Are you ready for a second finger?" I interrogated through my teeth, pressing my other fingertip against her opening as a warning.

"Of course I am, Your Royal Hiney!"

I gasped and pulled my hand out to spank her again. "Don't call me Hiney!"

"Just do it!"

I slid my second finger in slowly, swirling it like I did with the first. I groaned and leaned my forehead into her. "Gods! I want to squeeze my cock in there! Bed you til I burst!"

Her juices gushed a little onto my fingers, and I moaned in synchrony with her. The sexual frustration between us was unendurable. She sobbed with the same carnal need I suffered and scratched the wall with her claws.

"Stop t-teasing m-m-me!" she cried into her arm.

Arousal continued to drip its agonizing fuel into my abdomen, and I held my breath through a wave of lust. Restraining my ardor was too hard, and as soon as I felt like she was used to two fingers, I started pumping both aggressively into her. She hissed for a second before she relaxed into it and pushed back against my hand. I used my hips to push her forward to the position I needed her in, but that just ended up making her grind against me.

I choked on a cry, surrendered, and spread my legs, lowering my hips so she could massage my erection better with her rear. I closed my eyes and pretended that my penetrating fingers were my cock as I allowed her to stimulate my swollen length.

I gasped into her back, "Shit, Hekla! Does this feel good? Do you like it? Do you like my fingers in you?" The need for her swirled around my head, muddying my thoughts.

"Y-yes! Ah! Ahh! I'm getting there! Ah!"

The primal, vulgar creature within me now had direct control of my mouth. "Pretend it's my cock, Hekla. Pretend I'm going to impregnate the shit out of you!"

She gasped, "Your cock must feel weird!"

"Don't make me spank you again!"

"Ahhh!" she cried, and I felt her body knot up with tension. Her legs shook violently, the sign she was just on the edge. "Ahh! More! More! Harder!"

I dug my wet finger around her swollen nub, and my fingers pounded her with wild abandon. The squelching sounds of her desire were a buildup to her climax, and she finally yelled into her arm. I shuddered in delight as her walls clenched around my fingers, pulsing hard. Oh, that would feel so blistering good on my cock.

I exhaled in relief and slowed my rhythm to help her ride out her pleasure. "That's it, you filthy she-wolf. Let your heat go. Your mate chased that bastard off for a bit," I uttered between pants, still suffering from my own overly hard erection.

When her core calmed, I removed my hands and gave her a moment to recover. I stumbled to the side and leaned against the wall, wiping my hands on my pants and prayed to the gods that no one would notice the slick. I groaned in dismay, willing my erection to go away because there was nothing in here to catch my release.

"Gods, gods, gods, I can't go back with a claymore in my pants!" I snarled beneath my breath. I gritted my teeth and held a whimper back, trying not to remember Hekla's channel and how much I wanted to slide into it. My brain buzzed with arousal, and I couldn't think at all.

"Get…" Hekla panted. "Get your golden ass over here." I felt her tug at my pants, and my eyes shot open to find her rushing to free my cock. "I'll be quick! I think? I don't know what I'm doing! Ragna told me this was a thing!"

"Wha—" I asked, trying to follow her words.

Hekla hissed in surprise when she yanked my pants down, startled by my heavy cock springing free. "Moon Goddess, how…?" She grabbed my cock, and I bit my lower lip to hold in a cry of pleasure. She looked at it in concern from different angles, then leaned forward to slide it between her lips and into her mouth.

Staggering. The mate touch was staggering. Between her tight lips, the sensation of our destined connection had my vision greying. The tingling sparks of her skin on mine challenged my restraint, a heartless tease of what waited between her legs.

"Ah gods! Ah gods! Great Sun God, Hekla! You don't have to d—Ahhh! Ah!" I scrunched my face up, trying to say everything in a whisper-yell. "We n-need to hurry or they'll get s-suspi—Ahhh… Ahhh…"

Her response was too muffled to make out, and she moved her lips up my shaft, massaging with two hands what she couldn't fit into her mouth. My panting became heated, and I fisted my hands, trying to keep from gripping her head and thrusting into her beautiful mouth. I stared down at her, watching her full lips stretch around my girth as she sucked and slid. Oh, it was a euphoric sight. Such a shame she was wearing clothes.

"Oh, shit… Ahhh… you are so good… so good. How are… Ah! How are you so good?" I grunted between my teeth, unable to hold back the quiet sounds of my pleasure. She sped up the pace, and I gaped at the ceiling, feeling my sack tighten and cock tingle. I squeezed my eyes shut and ran my hands through my hair, going mad from her ambitious and amorous attention. I hung onto my last thread of control, trying not to buck into her mouth.

"Hekla!" I said under my breath. "I'm going to come. Are you sure?" She moved faster with her mouth, and I grew weak in the knees. "Is th-that a yes?" I hissed, starting to shake. She gripped my cock and massaged consistently while sucking on the head. Once she added her tongue, I was conquered.

I bit on my arm to hide a yell of euphoria, then gripped her head with both hands to steady myself as my seed filled her mouth. I hissed through my teeth, swallowing my cries of ecstasy while Hekla swallowed its proof. My hips pumped slightly with each ejaculation like they had a mind of their own, but Hekla didn't seem to mind. She just received my load through her silenced lips, keeping our dalliance a secret between us. After my last release, I grabbed her arms and crumpled to the ground with her, trying to catch my breath.

"We..." I panted, "really should go back."

"You dragged us down here..."

"You're... right." I groaned and threw an arm over my face.

After a minute she said quietly, "Back to pretending I don't matter."

I reached over to hug her and bury my face in her neck. "Back to protecting you, Hekla. My dear she-wolf. My female. Once I'm king, I'm going to change this brutal summer. I'm going to make it safer for you. Safer for everyone."

"Please don't fall in love with her," she whispered tearfully. "Please don't give up on us. I'm terrified. I'm so scared, Belenus."

"Never going to happen," I said, brushing her hair from her eyes. "That is impossible."

I helped her stand, and we both tried to sort out our clothing and hair. Once we were ready, I held both her hands in mine, squeezing them once before dropping them and opening the door...

…to find the queen, the princess, and five guards as my sister lay face down on the ground, bleeding from the head.

I was stunned to find the queen and the nasty princess outside of the closet but beyond horrified to find Belenus's adopted sister lying in a small pool of her own blood. I choked on a terrified sob and ran to her while my mate roared, "What have you done?"

I fell to Emer's side and gaped at her head injury. Someone had knocked her unconscious but may have cracked her skull in the process. It wasn't a big gash, but it was bleeding quite a lot. After I tilted Emer's face away from the floor so she wouldn't drown in her own blood, I moved her hand to prop her chin up gently and keened over her.

"Oh, she fell," Eislyn said innocently, and I jerked my head to gawk at her. "It was a terrible sight! I was just about to call the guards when I heard a ruckus in the closet! What… what were you doing in there with the dog?" A low growl began in my chest. How could she just move on like that?

Belenus's fists blanched at the knuckles, and he shook in fury as he addressed his mother. "Why aren't you more upset? This is your daughter!"

The queen didn't seem moved. "Adopted. Your late father brought her home. I didn't," she said coldly.

"And Eislyn," he continued to shout, "you think I believe your story about her tripping? This was an attack. Don't try to pull the wool over my eyes! I've seen some shit in my days during wartime! Who assaulted her?"

"I'd advise you not to speak in such a vulgar manner around your intended, my son," the queen said in a crisp tone. "Now answer me this. Did you have intercourse with the mutt?"

"Don't call her that! And no, I didn't," he seethed, pumping his fists. "Where's the medical team for your adopted daughter?"

"I'll call them in a minute," she replied calmly.

"Call them now!" I snarled, growling louder. "She's seriously hurt!" I turned to look down at Emer and stroked her strawberry-blonde hair. I could hear her heartbeat, but I had no idea if she'd suffered any brain damage. I was terrified for her and had no idea if I should put pressure on the cut. I looked up at Belenus and began to ask, "Belenus, can you heal h—"

"Stand before me, mutt!" the queen snapped, and I snarled back at her, letting her see my canines.

"No! I'm doing your job! I'm looking after your daughter! Kiss my ass!" I hovered protectively over Emer, feeling my wolf instincts lock onto Belenus's sister like a wounded pack member.

Protect her, protect her, protect pack always! Eventide growled. In our loneliness, she'd been looking for anything we could call pack at this point and hung onto it with the ferocity of a mother wolf. *She healed us; we protect her!*

I will protect! I affirmed, unleashing my claws.

"Guards," the queen called and gestured to me.

"Stop!" Belenus yelled. The queen ignored him, and two of her guards flanked me to grab a wrist each, making sure I couldn't scratch them. I betrayed my instincts by halting halfway through a swipe, knowing it'd make things worse. At least that was what Belenus said would happen.

I was jerked before the queen, whose face was so still and cold that I'd have taken her for a statue. The spring princess hid behind her, never once dropping her traumatized mask. It was truly embarrassing to pretend to be a coward in order to obtain power. She was the opposite of any shifter I'd ever met. We didn't value weakness. We protected the weak, but we didn't use it as a weapon. That was utterly pathetic. What a disgrace she'd be if she were a wolf. She'd end up a rogue in a heartbeat, and no pack would have her.

Belenus's mother parted her lips, but I couldn't quite catch if she said anything or not. A long, thin wooden staff appeared in her left hand. The top of it looked like a little oak tree, and each branch seemed eager to grow in a blink should it be commanded.

I frowned as she curled a finger against the staff and coaxed a small strip of wood from it. She flicked her finger, and the wood snapped around my neck faster than I could blink. I recoiled in fear, surprise, and a deep sense of violation, like its connection seeped deeper than skin. I struggled, worried that something terrible was about to happen. I felt movement, and several buds seemed to sprout from the wood. I could barely see them at the bottom of my vision.

What in the name of the Sky Gods is this? Eventide yelped.

I don't know!

I looked around, trying to find Belenus for comfort, but I couldn't see him. He must be standing behind me. I bit my lip and tried to get my panicking under control.

"Hekla, answer me truthfully," the queen stated, staring at me with pursed lips and narrowed eyes. Her gaze was a razor, as sharp as any alpha I'd met. I pressed my legs together, willing myself to not lose control of my bladder from fear. "Have you masturbated with my son in the last five days?"

What? Eventide asked.

I don't understand her question, I replied, confused.

Does she mean us pleasuring each other or us pleasuring ourselves in front of each other? Eventide asked, more perplexed the more we thought about it.

I don't know! Technically, isn't masturbation solo? I don't know how to answer this! I replied and found my panicking over a question like this completely absurd. I almost let out a manic laugh.

"You mean pleasing our own selves or ea—" I began, trying to get more clarification.

"Answer the question!"

"I mean, technically…" I cringed and gave my best guess. "Technically, I'd have to say no?"

A bud beneath my chin blossomed orange, and the queen shook her head. "Lie. Next question. Have you had sexual intercourse with my son?"

"What? That wasn—"

"Answer the question!"

"No, I have not!" I spitted, snarling. The second bud blossomed blue. The queen frowned and continued her interrogation. "Have your sexual organs touched?"

Great goddess, this is getting personal and graphic. Eventide blanched.

All I could do was tell the truth and hope it wouldn't end my life. "That'd be a yes," I said, feeling like I was about to vomit. I grew lightheaded and suspected that the wooden lie detector was making me ill. It was like invisible roots had invaded my skin, and I tried to blink away the black dots dominating my vision. I barely registered that Eislyn had put her hand to her forehead and made a big scene about how she was feeling faint. The absurd show further provoked my wolf.

"Oh, queen, this cannot be so! You and I know that Belenus loves me, truthfully. This wicked dog lured him in with her heat! You saw how he followed her out with all those other possessed men!" Eislyn wailed.

"It seems like she's done you a wrong, Princess Eislyn. She's forced herself upon your intended. Do you wish to exercise your right to retaliate?" the queen asked, putting a comforting hand on her shoulder.

"No, I didn't!" I choked out, appalled by the lies. How could they get away with saying whatever they wanted to say? How could lies run so rampant here, breeding like rabbits? Did the people know that this was how their court operated?

Eislyn's chin trembled with perfect execution, and she nodded, squeezing out a couple tears for the full effect. I tilted my head and tried to find Belenus again. "Belenus… I'm confused… you said that as long as it wasn't intercourse… I asked you if I'd get in trouble! D-did you lie?"

I still couldn't see him, but I heard him speak in a tense voice. "I'm feeling more clear-headed now, Eislyn. There's no need to take it out on the poor thing. Wolf nature is base. Let's not kick an animal for its nature. Let her go, and let us return to our banquet. This has wasted enough of our time together."

Please tell me this is an act, Eventide whispered.

It's an act, it's an act, it's an act, it's an act, I chanted and squeezed my eyes shut at the agony of forcing a thought upon myself that I wasn't sure I believed. I was so confused. My people spoke plainly, and this was like trying to run through a maze that grew scarier by the heartbeat. I was starting to worry that there was no end to the maze and that I'd be trapped forever.

"So, I think the second and third answers contradict themselves, don't you, Eislyn?" the queen asked, raising her chin. She ignored what her son had said as though he wasn't there.

"I do!" Eislyn sniffed weakly.

"Since it's unclear whether you had sex or no—" the queen began saying to me.

"Oh, it's blisteringly clear!" Belenus snapped, interrupting her. "She answered that question truthfully!"

"Since it's unclear," she repeated in an icy tone, "you can choose between three punishments, mutt, instead of being banished from the Summer Court."

"That is so generous, Your Majesty!" Eislyn simpered.

"So, mutt, will you choose a lashing with this beautiful aconite whip I made… just for you?" She gestured to a guard who held a braided brown whip made from a plant.

Hekla, Eventide warned in a hush, recognizing it, *that could kill us. You remember that Ragna was only bound with it, and she was helpless.*

I clenched my teeth and stared the queen down, trying hard to pull myself together.

"Or," the queen continued, gesturing to another guard who held a slender silver collar, "you could choose to wear this beautiful silver collar I had the blacksmith create… just for you. I must say, it'd look beautiful at my son's wedding to Princess Eislyn."

The silver would rip at my flesh and silence my wolf…

No… Eventide croaked.

"I have to say, I'm a little late getting caught up on mutt-shifter biology, but I think these are appropriate punishments." The queen braided her fingers together and tilted her head to look down at me. "Or thirdly, will you choose to reject my son as your fated mate?"

No, no, no! Eventide howled in despair, and her sorrow forced several tears out of my eyes. I scowled in fury, hating the impossible options she set before me. I had to discuss this with my wolf.

What do we do? I asked her, trying not to feel defeated.

Take the collar, take the collar! Eventide wailed, knowing it'd muzzle and weaken her spirit. *I don't want to risk dying, and I don't want to lose Belenus! We can't risk him accepting our rejection!*

I… agree. I sniffed and furrowed my brows. I was torn in half. I wanted to go on a murderous rampage, but I also wanted to crawl into the darkest corner I could find and weep until everything went numb.

"Collar," I decided, bitterly raising my chin to offer my neck. Now I'd know how my sub-pack mates felt when they had been collared. Only little Soley had been spared that torture thus far, and I hoped to the gods it'd stay that way.

"Eislyn, this is completely unnecessary. This is like shooting a stray dog at the market. Let's just kick her out and be done with her," Belenus insisted.

The words wrenched at my heart.

It's an act, it's an act… it's an… act… I chanted, but my belief wavered. I knew what he'd told me, but the words stabbed. They cut deep and provoked a heavy bleed. I was raised to trust words, and these were so hard to dismiss. My heart felt like it'd received yet another crack.

The queen and Eislyn ignored Belenus, and a guard approached with the silver collar, a device of true wolf-shifter torture.

I screeched at her, bucking to pull back from the guard, "You're going against the will of the Moon Goddess! I'm the vessel of the Sky Gods! Your reign is an embarrassment and an insult to the gods! Sacrilege!"

"I'm not afraid of those gods. We're children of Faete," the queen dismissed, completely unmoved by my warning and insult. What was she talking about?

I hope she regrets those words, Eventide murmured bleakly.

"You won't break me," I warned, swallowing heavily and eyeing the hinges that the guard opened. "You may call me a mutt, but I'm a beautiful, strong mutt."

"The ugliest fae is more beautiful than you," the queen replied like an instructor correcting a pupil.

On those words, the guard snapped the collar around my neck.

Oh… The pain... The pain!

It was better described as a hot fireplace poker trying to choke me. I snapped my teeth shut, but a hiss escaped through my lips. The hiss became a tight, sustained, high-pitched groan, but I couldn't hold it back any longer.

I spasmed and screamed from the deepening burn. I shrieked and thrashed, trying to get out of the guards' hold. My eyes squeezed shut, but I couldn't escape the pain. I tried stretching and angling my neck differently to get some air between metal and flesh, but the scalding silver grabbed and seared. The white-hot pain!

After riding another wave of agony, I recalled something my sub-pack mate had told us. Rakel said it'd gotten easier after the outside flesh had burned black. That had created a dead shield of some sort, so I wept while I waited.

The torture barely let me process anything around me. The queen and Eislyn discussed, and I believed I heard Belenus speak, but the environment otherwise swirled in a fog. A swell of exhaustion fell upon me, and grey dots cluttered my vision. Also lightheaded from shrieking, I panted heavily to catch my breath.

Belenus... I can't do this anymore.

Chapter 14

Belenus

Nothing I said made any difference whatsoever. It was as though I was a ghost throughout the entire interrogation. Perhaps I deserved it. I shouldn't have taken the risk with Hekla. I should have never touched her. I thought it'd be fine on a technicality, but I was completely wrong. It was a stupid mistake, something a young, lusty fae would have made. It'd be embarrassing if the consequences hadn't been so devastating.

The truth was… she was never safe here.

I hadn't thought so many steps ahead to avoid this. This trap had been so carefully woven. The queen invited Hekla to dinner during her heat and provoked her with an extreme speech. She surrounded Hekla with single men to overwhelm her into retreat. She knew the men would go after her, and she knew that I wouldn't be able to resist following to protect her. She knew that in order for Hekla to return, she'd have to be free of her heat by being sated. She knew that I wouldn't be able to resist sating her instead of letting her masturbate, and she knew I'd have to do that somewhere nearby due to rushing after her.

All she had to do was send someone out to follow us and wait. Then she'd expose our activity in front of the princess who wouldn't have been able to resist punishing my fated mate for "sullying her courtship."

That was what…? Ten steps ahead? I'd been blindsided like a fool! The queen had been reading up on wolf-shifter biology much sooner than she'd said.

Also, what were those punishment items? Were aconite and silver lethal for wolves like iron was for us fae? I'd nearly murdered one of the guards in my attempt to get to her, but the other ones converged on me before I could kill him with my bare hands. He was lying facedown on the floor in his own blood, a mimic to my sister's prone form. I could have killed them all, but the queen would have pinned me down with her magic by then.

Gone are the days of the benevolent summer fae.

The queen sighed at the two bodies and waved her hand at a guard. "Go fetch the doctors, please."

"How long?" I croaked out, staring at Hekla who was on all fours now. She was whimpering and occasionally shrieking in agony.

Her screaming would haunt me for the rest of my damned life.

"I think that depends on how you behave," the queen answered, and I knew in that moment that my time was running out sooner than anticipated. I had to find a way out of this marriage right now. More importantly, though, I needed to get Hekla out of the city and somewhere safe.

The queen continued to speak, interrupting my frantic planning. "You know, I thought she'd be a good way to control you when you became… difficult, but now I see that it's much worse. Keep your best groom face on, my dear son, or I'll execute her."

I asked, so shocked that my tone was almost one of wonder, "Who are you? I don't know you. I always thought you'd get better after Father died, but you got worse. Now I don't even recognize you…"

"I'm your mother. I thought that was fairly obvious. Perhaps you should let the doctor look at your head." She moved to return to her dinner. "Do escort your beautiful bride-to-be to the banquet hall now. Care for her. I'm sure her nerves are in tatters."

I stared at her back, wondering how we'd gotten here. Then, I looked down at my bleeding sister and to my writhing fated mate. It had never been more obvious that something larger was going on behind the curtains. I needed to think on this and formulate a new strategy—fast. I needed to figure out where the heart was so I could destroy it.

I tried to go to Hekla to comfort her, but Eislyn intercepted me and hooked her arm around mine. Her eyes were threatening as she said, "I am ever so woozy, Your Highness. Let us go back to our banquet."

I pointed to the guard and hissed, "You make sure she gets medical care too." He didn't seem to hear me, and I scowled, fighting the urge to cleave his head from his shoulders. I looked around, wondering where the mac-talla had gone. Perhaps he'd find his way back to Hekla.

I returned to my seat and pushed the food around my plate while the two nightmares dined happily. There was no way I could eat, being too nauseated and wrung tight with stress. Hekla's screams repeated in my mind, over and over. Guttural, they'd sounded like they'd erupted from her very soul, and I swore I had almost felt her pain. I rubbed my eye like it itched, but it was only to conceal a tear that'd escaped. How was all this real?

About ten minutes later, Hekla was forced into the banquet hall by a guard. He pointed to her seat and prodded her forcefully. I turned to the queen, beside myself with horror, and whispered, "You can't be serious! Let her go. Don't force her to be here!"

"But even a mutt needs to eat, my son," she said calmly and poked at her salad. "No need to be cruel."

I wasn't certain if I was surprised or not, but the room definitely had a strong opinion. There was a large commotion among the unmated men who'd noticed her state, and they were not happy. Now that her heat had subsided for a while, the men were more attentive than aroused and were trying to figure out what had happened to her. Hekla wouldn't talk to any of them, but there was a swarm of fae hurrying to make her more comfortable.

"Your Majesty," a fae named Odran said, "what happened to the vessel of the Sky Gods, Miss Hekla? Who did such a thing?"

"Marred her beautiful skin," another fae griped in deep disapproval, but I couldn't see who it was.

The queen replied simply, "She is being punished, Odran. That is all you need to know."

"But for what?" Patraic whined.

"It is none of your concern," she said, lacing steel into her voice.

"I'd say it is. She's a pretty, single woman. What if one of us wants to court her? Did she murder someone?" Beathan inquired.

"She doesn't look too good. You should remove it..."

"Why is she even here if she's being punished?"

"I'm... very confused right now."

"I think we have a right to know if she'll cut our balls off in the middle of the night!"

"Just remove the damnable thing. I'm sure you've made your point, Your Majesty..."

The table fell into an uproar, and that was the moment Hekla raised her red, swollen eyes to meet mine. Was she waiting for me to make my protest? I glanced to my right to find both the queen and Eislyn staring at me, so I looked back down at my plate. How did I know what would make things worse, what would get her executed? I needed Hekla to survive the night so I could get her out of here tomorrow. So, I swallowed heavily and shoveled some food in my mouth. It tasted like ash.

When several fae stood to argue, the queen rose and yelled, "SILENCE!" She pointed at the guards and snapped, "Get her out of here at once!"

I tensed and nearly stood. Get her out of here... but to where? She hadn't specified, so that must mean her room. She should be safe there. Bidelia knew to care for her. I slumped in my seat with my heart in my throat. I'd told Hekla that violence wasn't how we did things here, but I'd allowed violence to happen to her. I'd steered us both so wrong.

Shit.

Never again. Something shattered inside my mind, clearing my vision, letting me see much farther, past what I'd been told to believe and live by. I'd been too naive. King Zorian was right. As he'd put it to me a while back, I had to "grow the fuck up."

Hekla

The guard escorted me down the hall, and a scrabbling preceded the form of the mac-talla running around the corner to reach me. I scooped him up without breaking stride, not wanting to be yanked by the guard for falling behind. I held my pet to my chest and cried softly as he sniffed and prodded the collar.

Whit in the blazes is this scunner? Ye neck is burnt a'ower! Arse asked in surprise.

Don't touch it! I begged, sobbing from the pain of him adjusting it. *It burns me! It's silver.*

He was quiet for a moment, then said, *Ah'm sorry ah cudnae help ye. We were ambushed. Ah'm fair puggled.*

No, I'm glad you escaped. Emer wasn't so lucky. She was bleeding from her head, but the doctors are looking at her now, I said, patting him gently on the head. He wouldn't admit it, but he was shaken. His little body quivered from either stress or fear. *You're safe now.*

The guard stopped me at my door but made me pause before I could grab the handle. His dark blond brows were set, and his jaw was tight. He uttered in a low voice, "This isn't who we used to be, vessel. We never needed laws to control... certain fae. Could be that it's time for change."

"I can't help you with that," I said carefully, speaking on a soft breath and trying not to move my throat too much. "Tell that to your prince, but he'll likely be as helpful to you as he is to his fated mate." My eyes watered as bitterness coiled in my chest. I resented Belenus's silence as much as I resented my words about him. This world confused me.

"General Belenus is a good man trying to get his beloved army through a wicked... battlefield," the guard returned surreptitiously.

When the fae realized I had no reply for him, he stood back from the door and gestured for me to retire. I closed the door, slid down it for the hundredth time, and let the mac-talla go eat. Bidelia, already here, was sitting on the bed with a couple trays of food and nervously poking her fingers together.

When she looked at me, her eyes watered, and when I told her everything, the tears fell. I stared blankly at her for a moment as she bawled, then pulled her in for a hug. She accidentally brushed against my collar, and I screamed through my teeth, startling the poor thing. I nearly fainted from the pain and gasped for air. Bidelia scooted back, terrified, and I looked apologetically at her while panting.

"I'm sorry, little pup. Do you think you can help get me to bed?" I asked quietly, feeling my voice start to go from all the screaming. My throat... raw inside and outside. Irrational fear had me worrying my head would fall off.

Bidelia's chin quivered as she nodded and went to grab one of my nightgowns. She helped undress me, slid my nightgown on, and sponged the sweat from my skin. She offered to try to squeeze a cold, damp towel between the collar and my skin, but the gap just wasn't big enough, and I accepted that my flesh would be charred by dawn. I hoped that what Rakel said was true. I felt closer to Ragna and Rakel in that moment, taking solace from the fact that they'd both been silvered and survived. I pictured them with me, cooing and petting their comfort in the way she-wolves did.

I told Bidelia to sleep in her own room because I knew I'd be screaming throughout the night, but she refused repeatedly and curled up next to me and the mac-talla. We were a strange little pack, a bizarre mix of wolf and fae creatures. I stroked Bidelia's soft hair and vowed I'd grant her any favor I could if I survived this ordeal. Maybe I could send her to live at Zorian's castle. She could study there, and she'd be a good nanny when Ragna gave birth to her litter. Yes, she'd flourish there. She'd do much better under Ragna's care.

"You're such a good pup, Bidelia…" I whispered.

I was useless the next day and close to wishing for death. My wolf couldn't help me heal any faster for she was locked away now. I only slept briefly when I passed out from the pain, so I was terribly sleep deprived. I stared at the door all afternoon, memorizing every pattern in the wood while I rode out my heat—and torture sentence. I ached from staying on my side, but I dared not move. Though the black, charred flesh had finally numbed, the surrounding skin was excruciatingly painful and itched like mad.

Some of the pain was an antidote to my heat, though not one I welcomed; it was hard to be aroused when waves of white fire intermittently tore through my neck. Other times, the pain would feel cold on the lighter burns. I didn't know that burns could feel so cold. Some of the waves reminded me of when Ragna challenged me to lick ice when we were pups… but infinitely worse.

The doctors never showed up to check on me either. The queen had probably ordered them to stay away. I doubted they could have done much anyway.

Please Sky Gods, give me strength. Is this the moment you mentioned? Will you help me now?

There was no voice in my head. The Sky Gods remained silent. Short of death, I wasn't sure how much worse it could get.

Belenus

I didn't sleep last night. I could have sworn I felt Hekla's agony, but it was probably just trauma working its way through me. I had planned on pretending to be sick today, but I was closer to being sick than I'd imagined. Perhaps my body couldn't handle telling one more lie.

I sent word to the queen that I would not be available for social calls as I was ill today. I didn't want to give anyone an opportunity to take something out on Hekla before I could get her to safety. We just had to survive until tonight.

The guard who'd escorted Hekla to her room last night, Drust, came to give me a very, very unofficial report. He'd risked his life because I could have easily charged him with treason had I not agreed with his sentiments.

Apparently, there was dissent among the soldiers, including some of the castle's senior guards. There were many disagreements on a number of topics, mostly including the queen's growing hostility. It'd snuck up on those who'd initially taken it as her grieving for her late husband, but too many years had passed for it to be tolerated, especially as her behavior worsened.

On a more specific, personal topic, news had spread of the queen's abuse of my fated mate. Though it was somewhat understandable to have my engagement cancelled to marry into another court, it was appalling to torture someone for reasons the guards and soldiers couldn't unravel. Fated mates were incredibly rare, and they had anticipated her being treated with some dignity, especially since she'd soon lose her soulmate to another woman.

Though Drust understood that Hekla had been forced into the role of a hostage, he felt the need to impart to me the men's moods. They were disappointed I hadn't taken action yet, more specifically, action outside the rules of the court. It'd been made clear to me last night that not even the court followed its own rules, and I knew it was time for me to break from them as well, even with it risking death.

I was still shocked that there was any number of men willing to commit treason at this point. If we could organize them without exposing our intent to those loyal to the queen, we might have a chance to take the throne. Even so, there was still the question of how to dissolve the contract.

If I executed the queen, would that…? I shut my eyes tight, not sure I could think about that at the moment. She was still my biological mother, but… she was also a monster. I had more time to ponder that. The original date still stood; it was just about a week now.

I ordered Drust to get a broad idea of how many were willing to revolt. At this point, I could tell fairly well if someone was lying, and Drust appeared genuine—enough for me to take a risk. I crawled into bed to begin my planning, pulling out maps of the castle layout. I also tried to sort out safe places to harbor Hekla, Emer, and Bidelia. I needed to protect the lycan doctor as well. King Zorian would have my head if Doctor Egres died under my watch. If Emer was stable by then, I'd have her moved out just prior to the potential rebellion. I didn't want to give the queen any reason to suspect that something was being planned.

A knock on the door around sunset had me freezing for a second, but then I quickly shoved my plans deep between my two mattresses. "Who is it?" I snapped irritably. The door opened, and Eislyn walked in carrying a bowl of soup. I glared at her and said, "I didn't say you could enter. Get out. I'm sick today."

"I know, my husband-to-be," she said with a sympathetic, demure smile. Gods, I hated when she called me that. She probably knew too. "The queen insisted I practice playing housewife and feed you some soup!"

"I don't want your soup." I snorted, narrowing my eyes at her. What was her game? Poison?

"Aww, my sweet man is grumpy from being sick. That's ok. I'll help you feel better."

I stared at her, completely baffled. "How do you keep up the act? You know that I know this is all a game. It's just you and me here. There's literally no one to perform for!"

"Goodness, you must have a fever too. You're saying the strangest things." She swirled the soup, spilling a little on the cloth she had under it to protect her hands from the heat. "Oh dear, where is your trash?" she asked, looking around.

"In the bathroom…" I said, eyeing her suspiciously.

"One minute. I need to dump this and wash up," she replied cheerfully and disappeared into my en suite.

What in the shit is she doing here? I thought, trying to sort through her actions. I looked out the window as the sky darkened. I just needed to tolerate her a little longer, then kick her out of here.

She was in there for a while, a lot longer than she needed to be, so I'd have to have someone sweep it for spells or something. Shit, she was such a nuisance. Finally, she came out, stirring the soup that was still magically piping hot.

"Come on, have some soup! It'll make you feel better," she said with a bat of her eyelashes. When she leaned forward to put it near my mouth, I recoiled, scowling.

"I don't want your soup, woman!" I protested angrily, holding a hand up to block her. She giggled and tried to go around it.

A knock on the door seemed to startle her, and she spilled the bowl of soup on my shirt. I shouted and yanked the now-scalding shirt off of me. "That was hot, you b—" I yelled but changed what I was going to say when she went to answer the door. "Eislyn! Don't just ope—" I began to hiss, but then she yanked at her bodice to expose half a breast and messed up her hair right before she opened the door. The blood drained from my face. I knew who'd be on the other side, and this entire scene looked bad. It looked really, really bad.

Hekla stood in the doorway, staring in shock at Eislyn's disheveled appearance. Her eyes widened even more when she saw me in bed without a shirt. Her mouth dropped open, and her jaw quivered in horror.

"Hekla! This was a trap! Remember what I said!" I cried, scrambling out of bed to go to her. Her eyes went back to Eislyn, and she took a sniff, then braced herself against the doorframe as though she was having a heart attack.

"You… bedded her?" she asked in a whisper, stumbling back a step. "Belenus… did… you... use me?"

"I know the message said it was from my betrothed, but I summoned you to offer you work, Hekla!" Eislyn said cheerfully. "I want to make things right. I was hoping you could be my lady-in-waitin—"

"Stop lying, Eislyn!" I roared at her, furious. How many steps ahead was this sham?

"Oh, there's no need to hide us anymore, my love," she said, patting my shocked, shaking shoulder while I gaped at her. I recoiled and brushed her hand off, but it was delayed. "At least you had your fun with her. Just don't slip ag—"

My mind tried to shut off from sheer shock. "Hekla, look at me! She's not telling the truth. She spilled s—" I started to explain, and I reached out for Hekla. Before I could finish my sentence, she took one last heartbroken look at me, choked on a bone-deep sob, and fled. "Hekla!" I screamed and made to run, but Eislyn tugged at my arm. I could have dragged her, but instead, I shoved her violently to the ground.

"Guards!" I yelled at the top of my lungs. Two ran in, and I pointed to Eislyn. "Arrest her for assaulting a citizen!" I said to one, then I turned to the other and said, "If the queen gets near the dungeon, tell her that Eislyn's been taken to the doctors and needs her!" The first part was a blatant false accusation, but it'd cause confusion.

"I have diplomatic immunity!" Eislyn screamed.

"I don't give a shit! Kiss my ass!" I yelled, mindlessly repeating Hekla's words as I shoved my boots on and ran after Hekla, not certain that the second guard would follow my orders. I had asked him to do something treasonous. Eislyn didn't have any power here except for her relationship with the queen. She may have diplomatic immunity, but she'd still have to go through the process of being arrested first if the queen didn't get to her fast enough. Hopefully the goose chase would delay that part long enough. I needed to buy time to snag Hekla, get her out of here, and explain. Shit!

I ran into Koray in the hall and felt some relief upon seeing a reliable ally. What I didn't expect was his violence when he shoved me against the wall. "What the fuck did you do? You slept with Eislyn? What the fuck! Why would you do that to her?"

"No, I didn't!" I yelled back into his face. "Eislyn spun yet another elaborate damn trap!"

"Then why the fuck did Hekla smell your cum on her?" Koray seethed, looking like he was ready to throw a punch. My body straightened in surprise.

"What?" I blurted, bewildered. I couldn't have heard that right.

"She smelled your fucking cum on Eislyn, you lying asshole!" Koray snapped, spitting in rage.

It took me a moment, and then I made the connection. "Serves me right for throwing my sessions in the trash," I said in amazement. I didn't want to think about how Eislyn went about it, but it was probably one of the most disgusting things I'd ever heard of a woman doing.

"What?" This time, Koray had asked it, shaking his head and narrowing his eyes.

"Eislyn took an awful long time in the restroom while I was trying to kick her out. I throw my damn emission rags in the trash there. I told the queen I was sick, so she sent Eislyn to my room with soup. She spilled the damn soup on me, so I ripped my shirt off, and here we are!" I spread my arms wide in disbelief. "Tonight had been too late to get her out… I waited too long!"

"How the fuck do I know you're telling the truth anyway? I don't have your damn fae senses," Koray snarled. "You've destroyed Hekla, and this is going to break my Soley's damn heart!"

"Well, if you care so much, then figure the truth out for your Soley, Koray! You're smart! I can't prove shit! The queen is obviously a million steps ahead of me at any given moment! Where's Hekla? I need to explain this shit, and she can probably tell if I'm lying or not!"

"She's gone," Koray said coldly as he stepped away from me. "You messed up one too many times, Belenus. I warned you. I *warned* you!"

"Gone?" I asked, just above a whisper, deeply apprehensive. "Gone where, Koray?"

"I don't fucking know. I could barely make out what she was saying…"

I shook myself to clear my head and pinched the bridge of my nose. Steps needed to be taken, starting now. "I'm going to give you three options Koray, and you can take them or ignore them," I said in a low voice. "You can help look for Hekla, and take her somewhere safe. You can stay here and work with Drust, who's gathering soldiers for an uprising, or you can go home. I don't recommend staying casually because you'll be caught in the middle of a war zone."

His mouth parted in surprise, even though he was still furious. "You're going to do a takeover?" he whispered before looking over his shoulder.

"I don't have a choice!" I spat. "I thought following the rules would keep my loved ones safe, but it's done everything but that!" I leaned in closer. "And you can be sure as shit that Eislyn is on my list of hostile invaders."

I pushed Koray away and ran to Hekla's room, needing to see it to believe it. I shoved open the door, and all that was there was Bidelia sobbing on Hekla's bed. She jerked her head up in surprise and scowled. "Go 'way!" she shouted. The ire nearly struck me as much as Hekla's absence; so much had the young fae's love been for my fated mate that she'd yelled at the crown prince.

I stared at the floor, still unable to process it. My love's bag was gone. Koray came up behind me and released a deep sigh; other than that, he remained silent.

I addressed him numbly, "I'm going to find her, and I'm going to fix everything. If she ever listens to me again, I'm going to tell her the exact moment I fell in love with her. I never got to share that."

"And if she doesn't?" Koray asked in a low voice.

"Then I'll say I deserved it and take care of her from a distance. She has a right to never forgive me for this. Goodbye, Koray. Choose well and be safe."

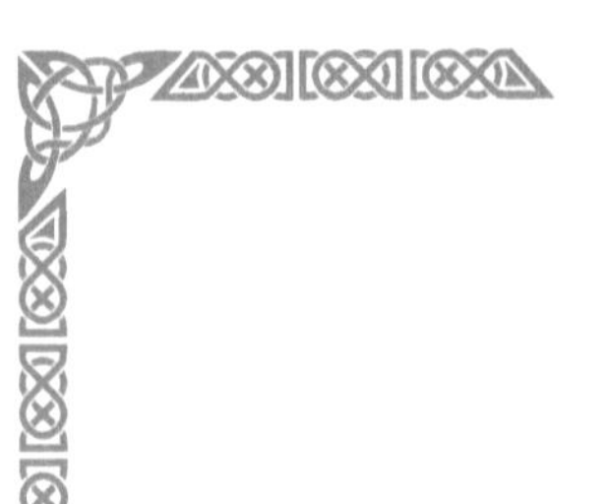

Chapter 15

Hekla

I ran away from my new 'home.' I ran away from my room, from the castle, and from my fated mate. I ran from Bidelia, Doctor Egres, and poor, injured Emer. I ran from the nightmare I'd been living, but the pain followed viciously. My neck blazed, and I sobbed from the fresh burns I continued to receive with every impact of my feet on stone. Though the fit was tight, the collar jostled and spread its agonizing fire.

Worse yet, my heart was in tatters, and I could only think with my emotions. The soul that should have joined with him had been shredded. It was now being dragged through the mud, broken and bleeding. Belenus… I couldn't believe it. Belenus had betrayed me. He had used me and abandoned me.

I was supposed to be the most precious creature in his life. He was supposed to worship me as much as I worshiped him. He was supposed to eventually love me as much as I'd eventually love him.

The courtship lengths made so much more sense now. How convenient mine was to last a month while Eislyn's was two weeks. I should have known... he didn't want to share a room because he was waiting for another female to warm his bed. I'd never been invited to his room... and yet there was Eislyn, making an heir with Belenus within days of arriving. Fucking each other... No wonder.

He must have not wanted a she-wolf after all. What was the word he'd used? Crude.

I knew what I'd seen, and I knew what I'd smelled, but I just couldn't believe it. Belenus's scent had been all over Eislyn, and she'd been disheveled like she'd been rolling around in bed. I couldn't smell between her legs because of her skirts, but her cleavage reeked of Belenus's seed.

I squeezed my eyes shut for the briefest of moments while I ran, trying to restrain the emotional torture, but it continued to erupt out of my broken heart and drain through my eyes. How much had they tangled? Was she covered in his pleasure? How many times had they fucked before I'd been summoned to Belenus's room? I hadn't seen him all day. Had they been fucking all day?

I screamed through my teeth and grabbed my head, hyperventilating. My claws dug in as I tried to reject the memories and assumptions that threatened to kill me with grief. The shrieking didn't help the cacophony in my head; the mac-talla had been swearing unintelligibly since I told Bidelia and him what'd happened.

"I begged him," I sobbed to myself as I fled down the main road from the castle. "I asked him not to fall in love with her! I asked him not to give up on us!"

That roaster's aff his heid! Bum's oot the windae! The bawbag's maw's a boggin, bowfin, lavvy heid! Arse ranted and raved from his spot in my bag. He was being rocked about from my running, but he didn't complain for a single second.

In my shock and despondence, I'd forgotten to try to head back through the door to my realm, so I ran to the only other location I knew. It wasn't until I saw the lights of the fae city that I realized I would have needed a fae to take me through the realm door anyway. I doubted I could have convinced a guard to do it. Also, the thought of facing all I knew in my original realm, sharing my humiliation… I wouldn't be able to bear it. Ragna was happily mated to a doting Zorian, Rudesind was obsessive in his nurturing of Rakel, and Soley and Koray? They were deliriously in love. Why me? Oh gods, why me?

My feet met cobblestone when I entered the city, and I was dismayed to find that many fae were still out, enjoying their evening. Everyone who saw me stared, and I could only imagine my frantic appearance. Here was a wolf-shifter in heat, running into their town and sobbing with a mac-talla peeking from a bag. With the collar, I had to look like an escaped prisoner. Several concerned fae tried to stop me, but I dodged and kept racing to my destination. My lungs screamed, chilled from the night air, and I started to feel faint. It was all too much.

I came to a stumbling stop when I reached the pet shop. It was closed, but I banged my fist on the door, crying and begging for Oscar's help. It looked like there was an apartment above the shop, and I hoped to all the gods that it was the wulver's and that he was home.

The shop light eventually turned on, and through the window, I spied Oscar's head peeking around a corner, wary at the sound of someone pounding on his door.

Ah'll spake tae him, Arse informed.

I slowed my pounding on the door and looked down at him. "You bonded to him? I guess you've been here long enough for that to eventually happen."

Aye, Arse said simply, and the door opened, revealing a surprised Oscar. He submitted, and I shook my head, gesturing for him to get to his feet. I rubbed my swollen eyes and whimpered while I waited for Arse to explain, unable to silence my overflowing grief. The wulver looked down at the mac-talla as he listened and then urged me to enter, locking the door behind us.

Oscar took us upstairs and sat us at a table. A she-wulver said something to Oscar, and they spoke in fae for a minute. Then, he hurried out of the apartment, and the she-wulver draped a blanket around my shoulders. She rushed into the kitchen and returned with some tea and a thick stew-like dish. When she nuzzled the side of my head in a wolfish way, I crumbled. It almost had me thinking I was home. I leaned into her and started howling in emotional pain. She patted my head and rocked me for several minutes while I sobbed, but then pushed the food toward me and growled in fae.

She insists ye ett yer stovies. This is Oscar's nighean. Erm, that means 'daughter,' Oisin, Arse said. I placed my hand on my chest and whimpered, "Hekla." I was nauseated from my stress, but I knew I had to fuel myself for… wherever I was going. I wanted to run away, far from here. My wolf would settle for no less than the wilds right now. Maybe the wulver would let me into a remote pack.

By the time I finished my food, Oscar returned and spoke in fae, gesturing for me to follow him. Oisin gave me a hug, and I whined wolfishly as I returned it, speaking the only way I could in the moment and left to follow Oscar.

We departed the shop and hurried through the city, turning this way and that to get to wherever Oscar wanted to take me. He kept looking down at the mac-talla and glanced up in occasion at me. He growled and whined randomly, and I quickly realized that Arse must be telling him the story. I didn't care anymore for my privacy. My heart had been shredded. Nothing mattered.

Oscar rapped on another shop door, and we were let in by a fae man with bull horns and cloven hooves for feet. It was a weapons shop, but we were rushed through and out the back where a forge rested under a sturdy stone roof.

Oscar saiz Fearghas wull tak ye collar aff, Arse translated. My tears started anew in gratitude, and I leaned my head to the side so the fae could get a good look at the lock. He snorted in disgust and bit his lip in consideration. Then, he spoke to Oscar—who pulled my hair back—before prompting me to lean my head to the left.

Fearghas worked over my collar for what felt like an eternity, and they eventually gagged me with a cloth because I'd started screaming. Finally, the silver ring came off, and I all but fainted. Noticing my shaking knees, Oscar caught me and Fearghas grabbed my legs to set me down on the floor, propping me against the wall. The bull fae retreated, then returned with a medical kit to tend to my neck. I cried hoarsely as he applied cream to my burns and shock brought me blissfully back into its numb embrace. I was offered water and pills, which I accepted without question or hesitation.

When I was more composed, Oscar escorted me to the east end of town. It was the farthest point from the castle, and I stared into the deep shadows past the city. I couldn't wait to sink into the black-blue of the night. Black and blue… the colors that were beaten into my wretched heart; I found that darkly appropriate.

The wulver watched me as I spoke to the mac-talla. "What do you want to do, Arse?" I asked with a voice that was barely working. "This is it. I'm leaving from here."

The mac-talla turned his black gaze to the night, then back to the castle. He was uneasy, and I understood his fear without him needing to explain. He was prey, he was domesticated, and the wild might be too harsh for him. As much as I might need his help communicating, I didn't want to consign him to my lonely fate.

Ah'm wirried aboot wee Bidelia, he said, sounding strained.

I smiled softly and petted his head, accepting this was where we parted. "Would you like Oscar to take you to her? You should keep an eye on her for me," I asked quietly. Another piece of my shredded heart disintegrated, but if I worded it this way, he wouldn't be made to feel like a coward.

Ye'll be alone, Arse pointed out uncomfortably.

"A she-wolf is never alone. I have Eventide. You know that," I reminded. "Bidelia will be under a brutal queen soon. She'll need you, my friend," I said, my voice breaking when I uttered the word 'queen.'

It was supposed to be me… I thought bleakly to myself.

Aye… tha'she wull, he agreed and began to clamber out of my bag. Oscar seemed to be talking to the mac-talla as I handed him over and undressed. I shoved my clothes into my bag, secured it to my back, and shifted into Eventide. Her entire body shook, her trauma displaying as extremely as mine. She still hasn't spoken.

Hekla, Oscar saiz he'll tak me tae Bidelia, Arse said.

The wulver crouched in front of me and stroked the side of Eventide's head, just under her ear.

How could he? I sobbed to him and let Arse communicate that. I knew that as a wolf fae, he'd understand the importance of honoring mates.

He saiz he dinnae think he did, Arse replied. *He saiz that's nae the Belenus he's kent fur oer a hunner years.*

But she smelled like his seed! I wailed, feeling sharp sorrow spike through my numbness.

He saiz she wants tae be queen. The fae can mak a' sorts o' things happen, Arse translated darkly.

Eventide whined and fidgeted. She was ready to run away, and so was I. We were ready to be forgotten.

Goodbye, Oscar. Arse.

Eventide darted out of the city and released a gut-wrenching howl. Not long after we disappeared into the shadowy fae wilds, Oscar responded with his own call.

Sky Gods! I begged the night sky. *Has it happened? Is it time yet? Please, is it time?*

It is time, They said, finally breaking Their silence.

Belenus

I wasted no time leaving the castle. I ran straight from Hekla's room to the armory and grabbed what I needed for the road. There was no time to gather meal provisions; I could hunt and forage for myself. When I raced out to the stables, I heard footsteps running after me and nearly cleaved Koray in half with my sword.

"Shit! What are you rushing at me for in the dark? I almost killed you!" I said, breathing heavily. I returned the blade to its sheath and leaned against a post. "Thought you were a blisterin' spring guard or some shit!"

"I think…" Koray whispered, holding a hand out while he caught his own breath. "I think we're being summoned to the Realm of the Gods."

"What?" I replied, giving him a speculative glance. "I know you're the Lunar Key, but what makes you think that? I thought only the vessels could talk to the gods."

Koray glared at me and looked toward the horses. It seemed like he was trying to sort out something for himself. He gestured to his head and growled, "I feel this prodding in my damn head, and no matter where I turn, it's always on the side facing that realm door. It's not fucking going away! Happened as soon as you ran off."

I groaned through my teeth and kicked a bale of hay to the other side of the stables, startling a couple dozing horses. "I don't have time for this!"

"Well, I'm going! Bye! I just came to let you know because I think you're supposed to come with me!" he snapped and stormed out of the stables, looking as tense as I felt. I glanced back at Haul, scowled in frustration, and followed Koray to the realm door at the top of the Sun Tower. We were both in abysmal moods, and I was going to get a lot angrier if this turned out to be a waste of my time. I needed to catch up to Hekla.

Koray rushed us through the realm door to where the goddess called home, and we jogged through the woods to Her abode. The door opened before I could knock, and a white lycan stood just inside to greet us.

"King Zorian?" I blurted but grimaced because that couldn't be right. He was the only white lycan I knew, but this didn't seem like his lycan. This one seemed far calmer and… well… I glanced down and verified. Yes, that was a female.

Definitely not, Prince Belenus. The lycan laughed. *Enter, please. It's good to see you again, Koray.*

"You too, Moon Goddess," the young man replied with a sigh and ran his fingers through his long black hair. He seemed calmer now.

"My apologies, Moon Goddess," I said, entering Her home. "I've never met you in your realm." I moved to the sitting room and stared at the couch where I had my meltdown over a month ago. That was when I'd found out that Ragna was pregnant and couldn't be my mate after all. That was when Zorian had told me to grow up, and yet that was the beginning of our tenuous friendship. How ironic that I'd found myself here… I hadn't grown up in time, I supposed.

"The Sky Gods left, I see," Koray said, seating himself, and the lycan gave a growling hum.

They are with Hekla at the moment. It is finally time, as They said, She replied, and Koray nodded, rubbing at his lower lip in thought.

"Hekla?" I asked, moving to the edge of my seat to address the goddess. "Is she in this realm? Where is she?"

Not in this realm, no. She's going where she needs to be, the Moon Goddess answered.

"So… I'm sorry, but I'm going out of my mind right now. Was there something you needed? I know you said she's where she needs to be, but I must find her. I really… messed up. I really hurt her," I said, utterly losing my composure before the deity who'd gifted me Hekla, and I buried my face in my hands. I couldn't meet Her eyes. Humiliation, horror, despair, guilt… I wasn't sure what I felt more.

Why do you say that? She asked. She didn't sound curious; She didn't sound confused… She sounded like She wanted to drag something out of me, but I didn't know what that was.

"I kept letting her get hurt!" I gestured out the window, picturing her alone in the dark somewhere right now. "I let people get between us! I thought if I played by the rules, moved cautiously, patiently, everything would be safe, but it wasn't!" I said, finally narrowing my eyes and speaking through my teeth to try to keep the brimming tears at bay. "And I fell to temptation…"

I should have never touched her.

The goddess moved to the kitchen and began to boil water on the stove. *Let's say a pup grows up in a home where they teach him that it's ok to bite. Is it the pup's fault when he bites someone else's pup?*

"Ah…" I hesitated. Where was she going with this? "No? I suppose I'd blame the parents?"

Imagine that, years later, he brings a mate home to his family. He thinks that if he plays by his family's rules, he can keep his mate safe. He knows that it's wrong to bite now, but he bites to keep his family from biting her. He's somewhat comfortable with it, because he grew up biting, but she doesn't understand it at all. It's scary for her. It's also scary for her to watch him bite others, the white lycan said, setting steaming cups of tea down for both Koray and me. I glowered at mine, thinking of the last time I drank tea. *So, is it really surprising that, at some point, no matter how hard he tries, his mate gets bitten?* She asked.

"I suppose not, but maybe he shouldn't have brought her there to begin with," I argued in a quieter voice, starting to see where She was going with this. "It was irresponsible."

You didn't have a choice, Belenus. You had to bring Hekla into chaos. A true alpha doesn't abandon his pack. You just didn't realize how bad it really was until your biting mother was provoked. You were outnumbered, and your opponents fought dirty. Though she got hurt, you did the best you could to keep her safe in the manner you were raised to. That's all you knew. Those were the only tools you had to work with. You knew no other way. Your family strayed from the rules you were raised to follow. One does not truly grow up until they live life outside their upbringing. That is where gathered wisdom grows.

Had you taken her anywhere else, She continued, *she would have been safe. The fae courts hurt her, Belenus. You did not. You were one man against an entire army of biters. She also hurt herself for not trusting you when you warned her it'd get that bad. In the end, blaming is a waste of time. We live life in grey, and it's time to move on. Focus your anger on your true enemies.* The deity spoke more like a mother than mine ever had.

I was stuck on what She'd said about facing an army. "A general should know when to retreat when outnumbered, though. I don't know if I believe you," I gritted out with tears streaming pathetically into my hands. There was a shift in weight on the couch, and Koray's sympathizing hand landed on my shoulder. I wondered if he believed me now.

You don't need to, She said simply. *Remember, your family used the threat of execution against you both. Drink your tea. What is your plan now?*

I frowned, cleared my throat and rubbed my eyes. "I'm going to start tracking her as soon as I leave. I've lost a lot of time, and I'm afraid she's long gone by now."

Are you going to use the gift you made for her?

"I… had considered but…" I looked away and shook my head. "I'm not sure if it would be… effective…"

She tilted Her head again, staring intensely at me; it was as though She was trying to measure my worth. *Would you accept a blessing from the Moon Goddess, Belenus?*

Eventide ran out her distress across the dark fae wilds while I spoke to the Sky Gods. *What do I do now?* I begged. *I'm going mad! Please give me something to do!*

I have children in this realm. Follow the Eventide star, the Sky Gods directed. Their presence in my mind nudged, aiming Eventide and me.

That's my name, my wolf said shakily. *Is this a bad omen?* I wasn't surprised that she'd see it that way. We were hurt in the worst way and saw the world through cracked, bleeding glass.

Eventide is the first, brightest star on the horizon at nightfall. It will take you east. Pass through winter and the wild fae—if you can—and look for the night, They instructed.

But what do I do when I get there? And what do you mean if I can? I asked in a rush. I knew nothing of this land or its people. I was afraid, but I embraced that. I'd rather be terrified for my life than think about…

If they still live, I expect you to herd them home. Is my will clear, Vessel?

No, it's not! How do I do that? What happened to them? I had too many questions.

I don't know, They said simply. *I haven't heard from them or seen them in an eon. Do what I cannot.*

I will. I will do that, Sky Gods. At least we had a specific direction to flee from our nightmares. I knew I had more questions, but my mind met its limit. Helpful thoughts evaded me. Reason drifted out of reach.

Watch out for what you might refer to as monsters, Hekla. The creatures here are older and more twisted than any you've met. Starlight preserve you, my vessel. We shall keep one of our many eyes on you the best we can.

MONSTERS? Eventide screeched, and she stumbled in her gait. My wolf slowed and crouched to the ground, getting as low as possible. Her entire body dissolved into violent shaking again. There was no point in asking the Sky Gods to clarify. Their presence was gone.

She sat in a patch of heather for what felt like a year, listening to the wind blowing through the solitary trees and over the moorland. Branches creaked and rustled as the air moved, making us feel like something large stirred out of sight.

Eventide eventually moved—a paw at a time—slinking through the spongy ground with her tail tucked between her hind legs. We started imagining things. Little shadows moved in the corner of our vision, and vague sounds promised to be any number of beings. Something sounded like either panting breaths right behind us or wood being sawn a mile away. Frightened, Eventide and I tensed by the second, on the threshold of terror. In the end, all it took was a single twig snapping to send her racing east. Her fear soared, and I knew I had to be the rock now.

Calm! Calm! I urged, trying to soothe her. *Slow. Just keep a steady pace, and we'll rest when we find a safe spot. Let's just follow your star.*

My star... she said weakly.

Yes! Look at you! I wish I was named after a star, I replied, sickened from forcing out positivity. *Not to mention, you're one of the brightest ones up there! You lucky pup.*

Lucky...? she asked. *I-I think not... I don't think either of us are v-very lucky right now,* she replied, breathing hard as she angled left to move around a soggy pond that seemed to come out of nowhere. *H-Hekla... I don't feel so... good...*

Oh no. It'd been too soon. I shouldn't have shifted right after getting that silver collar removed. I should have known Eventide would be weak. What was I thinking?

Eventide, find a place to hide before you pass out!

She lost her balance and stumbled toward a cluster of jutting rocks and shrubbery. Eventide discovered a dark corner to settle in and curled into a ball. Shudders vibrated her as we thought of monsters in the dark, but it wasn't enough to keep us awake. A deep, vulnerable sleep claimed us... in the rustling fae night.

Chapter 16

Hekla

Eventide stirred, blinking slowly and yawning as we came to our senses. The first thing we noticed was the blurry haze of sunrise, and something warm and tingly pressed against us. Eventide froze, and her heart hammered in fright.

Hekla... she warned, pausing her breath as she tried not to move. *Something is behind us. Something that wasn't there last night...*

Oh gods, I replied, trying to shake the sleep from my mind as well. *It can't be that dangerous, though. It could have eaten us in the middle of the night... right? Let's just move slowly away,* I suggested, trying to calm her with reason.

Wait... we both said at the same time as we recognized the scent.

Eventide scooted slowly on her belly, extremely confused, stressed, and scared. Before she could turn around and see what was behind us, something settled on top of her to halt our escape.

Ahhh! Heklaaa! Eventide wailed.

Stay calm, stay calm! I hushed. *It's not hurting us!*

YET! she cried in a panic.

A new voice somehow popped into our head. *Now where do you think you're going, you sexy thing? Mmm, you smell so damn good, Eventide.* It was smooth, devilish, and... arousing?

Who are you, and why do you smell like Belenus? Eventide whined, scrabbling to get away from whatever was pinning her to the ground.

I smell like myself, sexy thing, he purred, and we heard sniffing by her ear. *And I must say that your scent is wild.*

Oh gods, oh gods, oh gods, oh gods! Eventide moaned. I watched her big black paws rake at dirt and rocks as she tried to escape.

Yup, you'll be saying that to me again someday... and we'll be in the same position too, he chuckled.

AHHH! Eventide was about to lose her mind. The weight shifted, and she darted out from the creature's teasing clutches.

Now is that any way to treat someone who brought you breakfast? Guess I'll have to eat this enormous elk all by myself... the voice lamented playfully. Eventide slowed, and her stomach rumbled.

Should we look? I asked. *I'm scared... I don't know what we'll see.* She whined and shifted uncomfortably, trying to decide. *Should we run or should we investigate?*

Unable to fight our combined curiosity, she turned to see who the Belenus imposter was and shrunk to the ground, tucking her tail between her legs again. There was an enormous elk, like he'd said, and standing next to the offering was an enormous blond wolf. He stood tall and proud, the breeze sending gold ripples through his luxuriously soft-looking fur. We were not a tiny female, and Eventide wasn't particularly submissive, but we both balked at his size.

Like what you see? It's all yours. Now come over here, and eat my... meat, he said suggestively.

What did he say? Eventide choked, dumbfounded. *Wha...*

What is happening? I added unhelpfully.

Eventide crawled toward the kill and stayed as far away from the golden wolf as possible while she tore open the elk. I didn't caution her away. She was ravenous from our being silvered, and I doubted we could outrun that imposter.

This must be some kind of fae smell-alike... I murmured. *I don't like it. I don't want to think of... his scent. Eat fast and... let's leave?* Memories of Belenus and Eislyn tore at my heart. It made me want to cry all over again, but I couldn't as long as Eventide was in control. I supposed it was for the best; it'd only dehydrate me further. At least we were getting fluids through the elk's meat.

My heart aches too... and my lady parts are starting to as well. I'm afraid that... that wolf is triggering my heat, Eventide lamented, worried. *What if he tries to mount me? What if I want him to mount me?*

The words shocked me. What was coming over her? *Oh gods, Eventide, I'm in no place to emotionally handle that. Seriously, eat your fill and leave.*

The golden wolf padded toward Eventide and brushed her ear with his snout. *Do you like it?* he asked seductively. Neither Eventide nor I knew for sure if he was referring to the meal, but she shifted uncomfortably and slowly heated.

He instantly noticed. *Oh, now that's a smell I can... get behind,* he growled and leaned to sniff between her legs. She yelped and tucked her tail, keeping him away from her lady parts.

B-behave! she yapped at him, raising her hackles and kicking back with a paw. She then yelped loudly in pain when that action shifted some of the burned flesh on her neck. It'd started healing, but it needed more time and was still so very painful. The wolf growled in anger, and she froze in place with a heart that threatened to give out entirely.

When he nudged her thick fur aside to look at her injury, he snarled. *Silver,* he said in disgust. *Belenus should have killed her.*

What did you say? Eventide gasped and jerked away from him. *And why do you also smell like him? What's going on?*

We don't want anything to do with Belenus! I cried out to her. *Run, Eventide!*

Without waiting for his answers, she bolted. She veered toward the morning sun, hoping that it was roughly the right direction, but before we could get much farther, the gold wolf caught up to us. He simply ran next to Eventide, which surprised us but also made us wary. We'd expected him to tackle us again, but maybe he didn't because he knew she was injured?

I don't understand any of this, I said numbly. *I just want to forget about Belenus, but it's like he's haunting us now. How is he mind-linking us?*

He knows Belenus, but he can't be Belenus. Belenus isn't a shifter, Eventide sighed. She addressed the golden wolf, barking, *Go away! We want nothing to do with you or Belenus! He's dead to us!*

Pft! He's innocent, he said with a snort. *He'll probably never touch soup again for the remainder of his life, hahaha!*

You don't know anything! she shot back at him, snarling.

Oh, I know everything, Eventide and Hekla Himinn, vessel of the Sky Gods, he said with a smirk in his voice. *Hekla is quite the little... minx.*

Who are you? Eventide practically shrieked at him.

He knows too much... This exchange unsettled me more by the heartbeat. I couldn't have imagined anything this bizarre.

I'm a devilishly good-looking wolf named Escort, he answered. *You can decide for yourself which kind of escort you'd like me to be...*

Oh gods, oh gods, oh gods, oh gods, Eventide gasped. *Hekla, he is arousing me. Help!*

I can't help you with that! I yelled, almost feeling betrayed by her response. Eventide spied an outcrop up ahead and made it look like she was moving right of it but feinted and turned left at the very last second, putting the stone and shrubbery between them. I gave her a little energy to burst her speed, and she raced toward... more moorland.

There is no place to hide! I can't... I can't escape him! she cried.

Should we shift? I have Rakel's dagger and my own claws... I replied, but I was uncomfortable with the thought of attacking him. He hadn't hurt us... yet.

No... no... She groaned and plopped down on the ground in defeat. *Maybe we can keep traveling, and he'll just... be a weird shadow. I hate this. I hate smelling Belenus, but I love smelling Belenus. My heart hurts. Oh gods, it hurts!*

My heart hurts too, Eventide. I feel shattered, I said quietly. *Everything has changed.*

Escort trotted over to us. *What are you thinking about, lovely lady?*

That I hate your scent, she grouched. *That Hekla's and my dream has been destroyed. That I feel like I'll never experience joy again. Is that enough or would you like to hear more? I can go on for hours.*

What was your dream? he asked, standing before Eventide. *My dream is sitting right in front of me.*

Augh, make him stoop! she whined to me.

I can't help with that! I repeated.

Eventide just stood and walked in the direction we suspected was east. We held on to the small hope that if we ignored him, he'd eventually go away and bother some other fae creature. It was a very small hope... the size of a pea. He seemed too invested in us. How in the name of all the gods had he gotten all that information?

As she began her lope, Escort made his way into her peripheral vision. She snorted in aggravation and continued to ignore him, though it was hard with our heat returning. She groaned and scented something on the wind that—once again—reminded us of Belenus.

I smell a storm... Eventide informed unhappily and looked around the moor for any sort of cover.

I scent a wood fire over those hills, Escort noted. *Could be someone has a home with a barn. Let's look. I'd love a good roll in the hay with you.*

Starlight preserve my miiind, she lamented and followed him through the purple heather. When we reached the top of the hill, there were several very sad-looking towers. One had a small pillar of smoke rising from the top, but the other two appeared quite abandoned, dilapidated at best.

We entered the worst of the three, and Escort deemed it stable enough to last. A crazed, grated shriek startled Eventide from behind, but Escort sprang forward to address the threat. A tiny, lean, man-like creature was pinned to the ground before the wolf ripped its ugly head off its shoulders.

Ahhh! Eventide and I shrieked in unison. Escort threw the head out of the tower and tossed the body out with it. A pikestaff and a little red cap lay at Eventide's feet, and she gave an internal grimace. What was that creature? Was that a monster? Escort looked like he was about to reply when we were ambushed by six more little men with the same weapon.

Eventide! Everything has a throat! Everything has a belly! Rip into them. Just stay away from the pointy bits! You can do this! We've trained to handle rogues much bigger than them! I yelled to her, giving her all my energy to defend ourselves.

I must have helped flip a switch in her because she emitted a deep, powerful growl and bounded to the creature on the outside of the group, jumping over a pikestaff thrust and grabbing him just under the rib cage to push him into the other small men. About four of them toppled into an angry, sputtering pile of violence.

Eventide managed to gut two of them, finding their small necks too difficult to grip. Escort killed three, but the last one seemed to be missing. Where'd it go? There was one more!

I saw movement at the top of her peripheral vision and shouted, *The stone landing!*

Eventide's eyes flickered up and spotted the mean creature jumping with its weapon pointed down, aimed for Escort's neck.

She snarled, bunched her muscles, and sprang into the air to bite the incoming staff just behind the metal head. The tiny man went flying and hit a wall where Escort proceeded to rip him to shreds.

He paused, his ears moving as he listened for more. *Stay here,* he ordered and left the tower.

I don't want to stay here... Eventide gagged at the pile of wretched bodies and wrinkled the top of her muzzle. She turned to go outside, saw lightning hit a nearby tree, and turned right back around to enjoy the company of the gentle dead.

Girding her loins, she began tossing out the corpses, trying to throw them far enough where she couldn't smell them as strongly. They reeked of blood, and it wasn't necessarily their own. Each one somehow contained the scents of dozens of other creatures' blood. When she picked up one of the red caps they all seemed to wear, she almost threw up her stomach contents. That was where the smell originated.

Redcaps, Escort's voice said from the entrance. *Goblins. They have to kill travelers and keep drenching their hats in their victim's blood or they'll die.*

That's... a pitiful existence. If they hadn't tried to murder us, I'd almost feel bad for them, Eventide murmured as she dragged the pikestaves out of the tower. *This probably was their territory.* She sighed. *I should have scouted it better before entering. This was foolishly done.*

You are showing your wise, fair side again, Escort said, tilting his head. *Your fighting was excellent too. Can I mount you now? There are no more goblins.*

N-no! she gasped, appalled. *I think not!* She tucked her tail as he laid his chin across her back, chuckling.

Alright, but you'll come begging to me soon when your heat hits you, he said slyly. She groaned and tucked herself into a corner, starting slightly when thunder rumbled over the tower, and rain came down like a wall of water.

Summer storms... is it just impossible to escape our nightmare? I asked Eventide sadly. She whined and set her chin down on her paws. Escort settled his massive blond body next to hers and began removing the blood from her coat with licks and nibbles. She grudgingly accepted it, finding some small comfort in the grooming as the storm roiled above the old tower.

Eventide sulked as the rain poured. *How long is this going to last?* she sighed, not really looking for an answer. Escort continued to clean her, sometimes licking a little harder than we suspected was necessary. The tingling continued with each touch; that couldn't possibly be the mate touch, though... could it?

What are you thinking about, stardust? I like that one. I think I'll stick with stardust. Sexy stardust, Escort said while nibbling at the middle of her back and around our bag. Eventide gave a withering sigh and flattened with her snout on the ground, like she was a flower with too much sun and too little water.

How do you know Belenus? You keep avoiding answering that, she grumped and added, *and there's nothing about me that looks like stardust.*

Nope, you got little white and grey hairs in there. I'm snout deep in you. I should know, he said lasciviously.

You're killing me. She scooted away from him. *Now answer my question, because it's all Hekla and I can think about. We came here to run away from what broke our fucking heart!* she snapped, snarling out the last sentence. *Your presence torments us!*

Belenus didn't do anything, Escort argued, nipping her leg lightly. *You assumed and broke your own heart, stardust.*

Eventide stood up at that and growled, showing her teeth aggressively. *You weren't there! Don't speak of things you don't know, imposter!*

Escort just laughed and rolled onto his back, submitting playfully. *Oh, I very much recall watching Eislyn bully her way into Belenus's room while he was planning his takeover of the throne. He had designs that very night about sneaking you out!*

That little whore snuck into his bathroom, snagged one of those emission rags he told you about, and stuffed one down her dress to fool you. All she had to do was get him shirtless by spilling soup on him and make herself look like she'd just been ravished. I admit, it was perfectly executed. Belenus should have killed her too, he said more soberly. *I hate these fae women...*

You're a fantastic storyteller, but you have no proof, Eventide growled more quietly as we digested his words.

What will make you believe me? he asked curiously.

Nothing! You're a liar who got his hands on some... very specific information! Eventide snapped, but she sounded uncertain. *He knows too much, Hekla,* she said quietly to me, eyeing the large wolf who was still lying on his back, swishing his tail.

And yet I haven't told a single lie since I snuggled up to you last night and kept you safe from all those night crawlers, he replied, amused. Eventide shuddered at the thought of monsters sneaking up on us while we were sleeping. Had he kept them away from us?

So, tell me who you are, Eventide said, slumping a little from the exhaustion of dealing with this wolf.

What? It's not enough that I'm Escort? It's not enough that I'm a fine, strong male wolf who wants to please and provide for the she-wolf he wants? He rolled back onto his feet.

But you smell like Belenus, and you know things that Belenus would know, and your touch is... like a damned mate touch! Eventide protested.

So, I'm not allowed to just be Escort for a day? he asked flatly. *Fine, take him back then. As much as you say you don't want Belenus, you seem to be pretty obsessed with him.*

A swirl of light rippled across Escort's coat, and Belenus stumbled into sight where the wolf had disappeared. He was donned in armor, with a sword at his side and an unstrung bow on his back. "Shit! Blisterin' wolf..." he grumbled. Then his hopeful almond-shaped eyes fell on Eventide. "Oh, gods, I'm so happy you're safe, Eventide and He—" he began, but Eventide shot out of the tower and into the pouring rain.

How? How! she choked out as she raced across the thundering moorland. Her paws splattered unevenly into the boggy, sodden soil. I reeled. No, it'd been an illusion. We were still asleep. This was a nightmare.

Yet I couldn't ignore it. *How can he have a wolf? That's no shape-shifted fae form. That's a wolf! That's a shifter wolf soul! How?*

Emer shape-shifted... Eventide reminded, but we just didn't have enough information. *And maybe they can mind-link too...*

But then why didn't he tell us he could do that? I asked. *Unless this is still a monster in disguise.*

No... No, Hekla. That was Belenus. That was him, and he had a wolf! she insisted.

Then what's he doing here? Shouldn't he be off fucking tha—

Eventide's escape was cut off by a blur of blond fur, and she yelped in surprise. Neither of us were paying attention to our surroundings, and Escort herded us left, back toward the run-down tower. *Leave us alone!* I shrieked at the wolf, who was looking more golden brown under the pelting rain.

No! he roared back at us. *Not until you talk to Belenus! And there's a storm! What are you thinking? You can't be out on the moors right now! You want to be struck dead?*

It'd feel better than betrayal! Eventide cried, sobbing inside her heart and soul.

You were never betrayed, Eventide! How m— Escort froze, and his gaze darted to the direction we'd come. His fur bristled, and a low growl formed in his throat. Fear pricked at Eventide when she turned around to scan the hazy moors.

Wh-what is it? Eventide whispered, shuddering from the downpour and the thought of something stalking us.

Back to the tower. The main one. Now, Escort said quietly.

Eventide remained frozen, though, trying to find what he was sensing. The mist from the rain was so heavy that we couldn't see much at all over the thrashing purple heather. We were hoisted up into a colossally strong grip, and she started to yelp when a large, rough hand wrapped around Eventide's snout.

"Quiet!" Belenus hissed into her ear and ran toward the towers. Eventide's eyes rolled around in fright and finally spotted a figure, maybe two, in the distance. A third seemed to flutter down from the air, beginning a slow roaming in our general direction.

Belenus raced past the two more damaged towers and locked us into the third. "Close all the windows!" he commanded, and Eventide panicked, shifting back into me so I could follow his orders. Damnation, I didn't want to be near him! Swallowing a sob, I raced up the tower stairs and shut all the windows. Fortunately, Escort had been right. No more redcaps remained to attack us.

I stayed at the top of the tower, huddling and shivering in a corner just to be away from him. I cried quietly into my hands, feeling defeated. Why couldn't he just leave me alone? I kept remembering… I kept seeing them together in his room. I clutched at my heart and placed my mouth over my arm to muffle a scream of anguish.

Footsteps scraped up the stone steps and stopped several feet from me. A warm palm landed on my shoulder, and his scent filled my lungs. I squeezed my eyes shut, waiting for him to speak but willing him to go away and let me suffer in silence.

"Hekla…" he said quietly, "I got a fire going downstairs. Let's talk. You'll catch cold up here."

When I didn't say anything or look at him, I felt my nude body being lifted and secured to his chest before he made his way back to the bottom floor. I stared blankly at the roaring fireplace, distantly appreciating the heat that fought against the chill in my rain-soaked skin.

He placed me down on a small, clean blanket, took my backpack off, and started gently wringing the rainwater from my hair. I wrapped my arms around my legs, wishing to wake from this torment. I heard him take a deep breath, and I braced myself.

"We need to sort this out right now, my dear," he said softly, brushing his fingers through my strands to detangle them. "Wolves can tell when others lie, yes? You can do this?"

I couldn't bring myself to speak just yet, but I nodded an affirmative.

"If I let you ask me any question—as many as you like—you can tell if I'm lying or not?" he asked.

"Yes," I whispered in a rough voice. I wasn't extremely good at it, but if someone stayed still and let me focus, I could tell. My she-wolves and I had played many late-night games with that skill after we were trained.

He moved to sit in front of me and asked, "What do I need to do? Ask your questions, Hekla. Pull the truth from me." He rolled his damp tunic up and over his head, tossing it aside. He scooted closer and gazed expectantly at me. Even though I was naked, his eyes were steady on mine. The firelight flickered over us both in the moment of silence. He was serious.

I placed a hand on his chest and stared at his face. "Tell me a lie," I asked and waited.

"The stone in here is pink," he said, and I felt what I needed to feel. I saw what I needed to see.

"Another," I requested.

"I'm wearing frilly, silver underwear," he said, and the dancing firelight suggested a hint of a smile in the corner of a lip, but it was gone in an instant. Once again, I felt and saw what I needed, so I started my reluctant interrogation. Anxiety immediately welled up in my chest.

"Did you… h-h-have sex with… E-E-Eislyn?" I asked, barely able to get my question out as tears sprang into my eyes. My chin wobbled with distress while I waited.

"No," he answered firmly and calmly.

"Did y-you c-cum on… h-her?" I asked and focused everything I could on his body's reactions.

"No."

"Did y-you have a-a-any intimate c-c-contact with her at all?"

"No."

"Did y-you k-kiss her?"

"No."

"Do you c-care about her?"

"No."

I slumped and brought my hands to my face, holding in a confused sob. Everything told me he spoke the truth. How could the truth be so different from what I'd seen?

A banging in the distance startled me, and I sat up straight, listening for the sound again. "What was that?" I whispered, feeling my skin start to crawl. The hairs on my arms and neck rose along with alert goose bumps.

"If I say their name, they'll find us easier. I'd rather they just pass us by while we're doing this," he said quietly and laid a comforting hand on my naked thigh.

"Why are they looking for us?" I asked under my breath and wrapped my arms around myself.

"They're attracted to souls, particularly the dying or brokenhearted," he answered softly, stroking my skin with a thumb. "They'll want to prey on you, but they won't get in. Even if they did, I'd get rid of them with magic. It's safer to wait them out in here. They'll move on."

I brought my knees in tighter, and Belenus said, "Ignore them. We're safe. Ask me more questions."

I placed my hand back on his chest and thought for a moment. So much had happened. I could ask a million questions, but I think most of it boiled down to one.

"Did you do the best you could to keep me safe?"

"Yes," he said. After a moment he added, "Or at least I thought I was doing the best I could."

"Are you really planning on taking over the throne by force?"

"Yes. I have someone trying to sort through the ranks while I'm away."

"And did you really plan on helping me escape the other night?"

"Yes... You and eventually Emer, Bidelia, and Doctor Egres."

I let my hand drop and sighed in emotional exhaustion. All was answered truthfully. "But why are you here, Belenus?" I pressed. "Are you here to drag me back? I'm in the middle of something important."

"I heard," he said. "I spoke to the Moon Goddess yesterday with Koray."

My brows shot up. "Is that where that rapscallion came from? Did she give you a wolf, Belenus? You're not a shifter!" I asked, dying to know what happened there.

Belenus smiled softly and looked into the fire. "My wedding gift to you was me learning how to shape-shift like Emer can. I thought that maybe if you had another wolf to run with, you wouldn't feel so lonely in my realm."

I rubbed tears away crankily, not wanting to be pleased by that. Damnation, that was too sweet of a sentiment!

"However," Belenus said with a small grimace, "I was dreadful at it. Could barely walk straight on all fours. When you learn how to shape-shift, you have to work out the body functions yourself. It doesn't come naturally. Took Emer about three months to learn how to fly properly.

"And then when I mentioned I was going to try to track you, the goddess asked if I was going to use my wolf form, and… well… She thought I'd be more successful if She gave it a soul. So… now I have this inappropriate shit talking to me all the time. I don't know how you shifters stand it…" He shook his head in disbelief.

"So, I suppose that means Escort would have been Eventide's mate as well," I murmured and blinked tiredly at the flames in the fireplace.

"Would have? He is," Belenus said slowly, sounding worried. His hand shot forward, grabbed mine, and smacked it against his hard, gold-dusted chest once more. "Ask me if I'm in love with you, Hekla! Ask me!"

Chapter 17

Hekla

I tried to jerk my hand back out of instinct, but Belenus kept it firmly against his pec. "Please don't run from the truth, Hekla. No matter what, we're still fated, and I've proven myself to be a faithful mate," he said in earnest, swallowing heavily as he stared down at me. His blond brows drew in, and his lips pressed into a thin, worried line. The firelight caressed the elegant curves of his face, outlining his beauty and carving masculine lines along his jaw.

I stared at my hand on his gold-dusted chest, feeling weak under the weight of a hundred thoughts. His request had been a confession on its own, but did I have to love him back right away to accept it?

"Belenus…" I said with a waver in my voice. "Every time I close my eyes, I see… what I saw in your bedroom. I know you've proven it, but…"

"But you're hurt. You're injured. She attacked you, and she will pay severely for her crimes, Hekla. I want to help you heal. Whenever I close my eyes, I see the grief on your face and the moment your heart broke. I hear your screams at night from when they collared you, and it guts me. These were the injuries I mentioned that we may receive. We have to face them as a united force or they win. That… that wretch… managed to make you run from me," he said softly. Compassion ran thick in his voice. "Don't let her win, my female…"

I bit my lip, too exhausted to shed any tears. He was right. If I looked at the entire last week, I could easily imagine the queen and Eislyn pitting us against each other and laughing about it behind our backs. I reminded myself to be furious about it later when I had the energy.

I bit my lip and then spoke the fateful words. "Are you in love with me, Belenus?"

He looked intently at me, like a hawk would a field mouse, and replied, "Yes."

His answer was truthful.

"I…" I choked on my words, but I didn't know what to say.

"I love you so much. Completely and with my entire heart… my entire soul." He paused for a long moment and gazed down at me with tenderness. "Do you want to know the very moment that I fell in love with you?" he asked and palmed my cheek, stroking it softly with a thumb. I closed my eyes and nodded, too overwhelmed to speak. "I'd already felt strongly about you, but I fell in love with you when you ran to my sister after she'd been knocked out and protected her with a set of canines and a pair of clawed hands. You were focused on her survival, demanded doctors, and rebelled against a corrupt queen. Though I was furious and distracted, I still saw everything that was good about you shine in that moment." He leaned in closer, fanning my cheeks with his breath. "You were brilliant and steadfast like the very stars of the gods you serve."

My body was slowly becoming a chemical, hormonal mess as he tilted his head down to brush his nose against mine. It was almost wolfish in the way he nudged me, like he was asking me a question. My eyes were glued to his amber ones that darkened the more his face tilted from the firelight, though nothing diminished their gleam.

His other hand palmed my ear and slid through my hair to cup the back of my head. His heart was racing like mine, but he seemed calmer otherwise… resolute in all actions now. Belenus lowered his head farther until his lips nearly brushed mine. "No matter what, my mate, I dedicate my life to you. If you wish me away, I will go, but I will always protect you from afar. If you wish me to stay, all I have is yours, and all you want will be yours, including my body, my heart, and my very soul."

He closed his eyes, resting his thick, blond lashes on his cheekbones, and slowly touched his soft lips to my trembling ones. My breath caught as he pressed his mouth to mine, moving with agonizing slowness. I was not sure what happened, but the tingles and sparks where our lips touched left me breathless. I felt like his soul was leaning into mine, yearning to push past some invisible threshold to tie itself to me in an everlasting knot. Something was pushing us together, and it was undeniable. It hungered to see destiny fulfilled. I felt it throb in my chest, trying desperately to tug Belenus into me.

His thumb caressed my cheek, and his other hand massaged the back of my head, slowly bobbing my lips into his. He stopped and pulled back a couple inches, opening his eyes to study me. Was he waiting to see if I'd reciprocate?

I was bogged down by a dreamlike trance, unable to believe how quickly he'd raced to right the wrong that'd shattered me. I'd been jolted so immediately out of my heartbreak that I reeled from whiplash. The connection we were made to share lured me back to him, and I leaned forward hesitantly. Terror wrestled with my need to heal, but I tried to break through the fear. Trauma haunted me like a phantom limb, so hard to forget. Still, I fought it and tilted my head up to press my lips to his, like he'd done to me.

His body relaxed further, and he kissed me back, massaging my scalp and running his other hand around to join its brother. Little sparks of excitement peppered inside my belly from our harmonious expression of unity. I slowly opened my mouth when he did, having seen other mates do the same. He sighed into my mouth, obviously relieved that I'd returned the gesture. I took in a quick, deep breath, feeling like I could suddenly pull in the air that I'd forgotten I needed.

A loud clattering, like pots and pans falling, came from the tower next to us, and I started, growing fearful again. I looked over my shoulder and stared at the door that Belenus had locked and barred. Were we safe?

Belenus's rough hands turned me back to face him, and he stared into my eyes. "Don't worry about them. You're safe. Focus on me," he said softly and stroked my cheek again. "You're so beautiful," he whispered, looking at my body without any shame now. He seemed lighter than he had at the castle, like his decision to take over the throne had somehow removed a massive weight from him… from us.

"Thank you," I returned quietly, wiping slightly sweaty palms on my knees.

"I wish I could mark you," he said, stroking my arm now. "But I'll not risk your life if your name is on that contract." He leaned down to peer at my neck and sighed. "That looks so painful, my dear. I'm so sorry. The queen threatened to execute you, and I was so scared… I was so scared that even looking at you would mean your death," he confessed in a thick voice, and I stared at him in shock.

He continued to tell me everything he'd experienced from his perspective as the rain thrashed against the tower, nearly muting the creatures who rambled around the moorland in search of my dissipating heartbreak. I bit my lip at every decision he said he had to weigh, knowing it'd hurt us both but keep me alive.

His story began to have an odd effect on my body, and I found it triggering my heat. Hearing what he'd had to endure for me felt like further proof of his dedication, and my body appreciated that. When he trailed off, done with his story, he cleared his throat and shifted uncomfortably. I was already feeling excessively stimulated and had tried to hide my readiness from him, not wanting to interrupt his venting. I sighed in frustration; I must be filling the room with my pheromones.

"Hekla… ah… do you need to rest? I can go upstairs and let you sleep for a little while until this storm lets up," he offered, trying to be polite about my heat. I knew, deep down, it was because I didn't tell him that I loved him in return. I sensed that he didn't want to overstep. Maybe he wanted to give me time to sort out my feelings and heal from last night's shock. When I froze in my answer, he stood up and turned toward the stairs.

"Does my banishment matter anymore? Sending me back before the month is over?" I asked quickly, worrying at my nails and tucking my lips between my teeth. He slowed and swiveled his head around to stare at me.

"Not if I succeed in becoming king, no," he answered, and I saw several of his rippling back muscles tense from my question. I wiped a bit of sweat from my temples and fanned my face.

"Then we could… you know…" I said in a low, timid voice, "mate?" I bit my lip, anxious for his response.

He cocked his head to one side and crossed his arms. "Do you truly want your first time to be in a grimy, old tower where bloodthirsty goblins used to live?" he asked, looking compassionate but vaguely amused.

I glanced around, grimacing a little at a bucket and a rack of red-stained knives. He did have a point. "I suppose not…"

"How many more days left of your heat?" he asked curiously, not hiding the way he stared at the rest of my naked body.

I furrowed my brows and counted on my fingers, making sure to include the day I was unconscious. "Today should be the last day," I surmised.

Half his mouth quirked into a smile. "I'm not sure whether I'm disappointed or relieved."

"Why would you be disappointed?" I asked. I was certainly glad to be rid of it, being without a partner able to mount me.

He leaned against the stone wall, ruffled his damp hair with his hand, and swept it to the side. "Because then I wouldn't have the perfect excuse to be knuckle-deep inside you," he said with a casual shrug of his shoulders. He was trying to seem unaffected by his own words, but he couldn't hide the subtle blush that filled his cheeks and pointed ears. It certainly made my breath catch.

"You don't need an excuse, but… the perfect one is that you're my mate…" I said, squirming uncomfortably from the ache between my thighs. I sighed and looked anxiously toward the barred door. "Please, don't go upstairs. Stay with me. I'll feel safer…" The creatures of this realm, the unknowns, were scarier than facing a group of lycan rogues.

I turned toward the fire and lay down on my side, not wanting to see the war happening on his face. Steps came closer, and I felt Belenus lie down behind me, scooting his chest to my back. "Don't get me wrong, Hekla," he murmured from behind my head. "I'd gladly take you, but I'd honestly rather do it in a cave or forest than in this filthy place. A tower of death is no place to create life."

I wasn't necessarily prepared to hear that last sentence and desire rippled through me. The words stoked my instinctive need to mate, and I parted my lips to release a silent moan. A small chunk of the hurt that kept my heart from him broke off and dissolved. I wasn't sure why. Maybe the wolf in me continued to appreciate the show of his dedication, that he'd wanted me to create his heir.

My own arousal slicked my thighs, and I trembled from my heat. His rough palm landed on the bone of my hip and slid down between my legs to rub against my throbbing sex. "I'll take care of this for you, though," he said in a voice that was surprisingly loving. "Then you can rest easy while the storm passes, my sweet female."

Belenus

While I rubbed my thumb and forefinger along my mate's suffering sex, I tilted my head down to stare at the deep burns around her neck. All of the black, charred flesh had finally fallen off, and I could see new skin regrowing in the worst sections. It was incredibly lucky that shifters could heal much faster than others, especially if silver could do this much damage. I cringed to think of what that aconite whip would have done to her body. No… no one would touch her again.

I propped myself up on the arm that wasn't tending to her ache and pushed her hair away from her injury. Heat rushed through my own body from her slow pants and moans, but I urged myself to focus on my two goals. I leaned down to kiss her neck, just under her ear, and brought my free hand to her burn, finding a mostly healed spot to start my attempt. Some magical injuries couldn't quite be healed with just a spell, but I supposed I'd find out soon enough. I didn't even know if I'd categorize this as magical. I had to learn more about wolves…

"Do you like that?" I asked in a low voice, trying to distract her while I slowly spread my magic into her neck. I started rubbing her folds with all my fingers except the middle one, choosing to sink my longest one into her drenched channel. She moaned in response, and I glanced over to find her mouth gaping while I gave her pleasure. I smiled—pleased—and allowed my magic to penetrate deeper so I could start with the inner tissue.

I nibbled on her earlobe. "So what does the word 'fuck' mean? We don't have that one here. I've heard it used in so many different ways, though I'm especially curious when you use it in regards to your heat." I curled my plunging finger to rub against the inside of her wall, digging to find the little rough bump that promised to drive my female wild. I let my healing slowly pulse into her neck with every gesture my sunken finger made, trying to disguise and distract whatever pain it may generate.

"I-It's… l-like… any... ahhh… swear word. It c-c-can mean a… uh, ah, ah… a-a lot of things, ah! Use it t-to express a-anger or… frustration… ahhh. It's a-a-also a vulgar w-w-word for s-sex… particularly… oh gods, that's a-amazing," she gasped and tilted partially onto me on her back to spread her legs a little more. I smiled into the side of her head, thrilled I was able to give her a good time while I healed her nasty wound.

"Particularly what?" I asked into her ear, licking it slowly. I glanced down at her neck and found it halfway healed now. I slipped a second finger inside her wet heat and rubbed more firmly into her swollen tissue. She was so hot. Soon… soon I'd have my cock in there, buried and pumping out seed. Tingling pleasure rippled through me at the thought. I couldn't wait.

"P-p-particularly… Oh gods, Belenus!" She writhed, and I perked to find her hands sliding up to grab her own soft, moldable breasts. I nibbled and sucked mindlessly on her ear while I stared intently at how her roaming hands massaged them. "P-particularly," she tried again, gasping and making her breasts press into her hands, "referring to a rawer experience… rougher… s-sometimes…"

"Mmm," I hummed into her cheek, breathing her natural scent in while I could. "Fucking sounds fun. I like how you wolves do things," I murmured and glanced down to find her neck almost completely healed. At this point, I felt like it was safe to speed up the process without her noticing it. I continued rubbing inside her, making her panting accelerate. That noise was like a caress to my own pants, making me harder just to hear it.

Once her neck was completely healed, I nuzzled my nose against her cheekbone and whispered, "I want to touch your breasts. May I, my female?" She whimpered and nodded zealously. I snuck my now-free arm under her waist and pulled her on top of me, keeping her back to my chest with her neck slung over my shoulder. I turned my head to lap at the most sensitive part of her neck and smiled internally, delighted that she probably hadn't even realized I'd healed her.

I slid my free hand up her ribs and molded my hand around her warm, round breast. I groaned in exaltation to finally touch what I'd longed to fondle. She'd teased me for far too long with these two luscious, perfect globes. Tendrils of pleasure spiraled down my abdomen to sink into my groin, and my face heated from my roused vessels. My cock had expanded significantly now, fed eagerly by the same pumping blood.

She arched into my massaging hands, panting harder and displaying a most enjoyable view. She tilted her head for me to offer more of her neck, obviously completely lost to all senses but pleasure. I stared at the spot where'd I'd someday bite and inject my magic, my own signature, into her delicious soul. I licked slowly up that spot—where her shoulder met her neck—and nibbled lightly. She gasped and whined like a hungry wolf, which hardened me to stone, but this was all for her right now. She deserved all my attention for what she'd endured.

I slid my fingers up to gently caress her small, hard nipple, making us both erupt into sounds of pleasure. I rolled the button of textured flesh carefully between my fingers, then pulled a little before pushing down on it. I traced a finger around the taut nib and repeated the pattern. She spread her arms wide and bent one to search for my face. Finding my jaw, she idly caressed the side of my head and traced a finger up my sensitive ear, making me groan through clenched teeth. My cock throbbed in response to the sensations she pulled out of those nerves.

I should probably make her climax before she got herself into trouble… got us into trouble. "Come for me, Hekla… uh… ahhh," I urged into her ear, unable to keep my own guttural sounds of pleasure from my voice. I hissed as she mindlessly rubbed the helix of my ear, and I tried to turn my head away from her roaming digits. "Don't… Don't be touching that, she-wolf," I gritted out and doubled down on my efforts.

"Why?" she gasped faintly as her body began to tense under my ministrations.

"Because it's going to make a blisterin' mess everywhere," I growled and tried to shrug away her hand, but it was now newly inspired. "Damn it, female!"

My hands were already quite busy, and try as I might, I struggled to swat away her free hand that reached up to massage my other ear. I bit my lip and tilted my head back, holding my breath through the pleasurable sensations she stirred along the points of my ears. "Female! Yo—" I growled and moved my other hand to grind against the swollen nub at the apex of her sex.

It felt like a race now. I needed to finish Hekla before I made a damn mess of us. I moved her body up a bit so my knuckles wouldn't brush against the sensitive head of my cock. Perhaps it was time I invested in pants that went up a bit higher.

Hekla began to hyperventilate, then tensed and screamed through her teeth, arching into a beautiful sight beneath my hands. I rubbed along her pulsing sex and channel, panting and believing I was safe from her mischievous, wandering hands.

At least, I thought I was safe. In the midst of her orgasm, her claws came out and stroked fine lines down the rims of my ears. I shouted and moved to grab her wrists, but it was too late.

I arched up against her writhing body and came explosively, tilting my head farther back and crying out in euphoria. I slid my hands down her arms and grabbed her breasts while I went through the pleasurable motions of spending my seed. My hips jerked with each delivery I made, and I eventually felt my own emission drip and pool on my quivering abdomen.

On my last ejaculation, I collapsed beneath her, lifeless on the blanket like a rag doll. My hands slowly massaged her breasts while I caught my breath and tried to wake from the fog our lust had created. I tilted my head to kiss her ear and slid my arms under her breasts to hug her.

"Hekla… female… you made me… make a mess," I mumbled when my breathing slowed enough to talk.

"I think… at this point," I heard her say in between breaths and with a smile in her voice, "I'm allowed to play… by my rules for a while."

I chuckled and closed my eyes for a moment. "You do. I officially and immediately rescind my complaint." I cleared my throat and asked, "I'm guessing I got you with my orgasm… is it a ridiculous mess? It's still raining out, and the creatures seem to be gone. We could rinse off."

She struggled to stand and turned to face me. "You tell me," she said with a laugh, and I grimaced at the sight of my pale seed all over her sex. I wouldn't admit it out loud, but the sight was incredibly erotic, and I'd be fine with losing control again. Although… that would be a dreadful waste of seed that I'd rather spend into my Hekla.

"Oh… well, I'd apologize, but this"—I gestured to the mess I'd made on her—"was absolutely your fault." I shucked off the rest of my clothes to prepare for a good, thorough rinsing.

"I know," she said, sending me a coy look that made my heart flutter. She moved toward the door to listen for movement, and I did the same. I heard no stirring of the soul-stealing sluagh.

"They're gone," I said, nodding in satisfaction and unbarring the door. "Probably scared them away with all the fun we were having." Hekla giggled and pushed past me to run into the pouring rain. "Don't go too far!" I cautioned and dragged her closer to the tower, still worried about the lightning. "And let's be quick about it."

"It's warm!" she exalted, closing her eyes and smiling as she ran her hands all over her body. It was a good thing I'd just finished because now I was able to soberly enjoy what a pretty sight she was. I smiled and ran my hands over myself while I watched her wash. In this moment, she looked… exactly how she should. She was happy, refreshed, and embracing nature. She opened her arms wide and tilted her head back to catch some of the fresh, clean rainwater in her mouth. Unable to hold back my relief, my joy, my gratitude, I stepped into those open arms and tilted her mouth to mine for a kiss.

We stood there for a while, lost in each other, until I pulled back and gazed down at her. "It's so good to see you smiling again, my dear Hekla. I had worried I'd never see it again." My smile faded as my thoughts turned solemn. "Do you think you could ever forgive me? For bringing you here? For not protecting you well enough?"

She rapidly blinked the rain from her eyes as she looked up at me. "If you need to hear it, I forgive you, but I… don't blame you, not anymore." She plopped her head into my chest and hugged me while I guided us back inside to dry ourselves.

Upon closing the door, she shrieked, "Oh my Moon Goddess, my neck is better! What?"

Chapter 18

Belenus

After Hekla was done assaulting me with hugs and kisses for healing her neck, we only had to wait another hour or so for the storm to pass. We stepped out of the dark tower into a sunny day where only a slight misting from the dark, departing clouds gave away the storm that'd been here. Well, I supposed the moorland was soggier, but the warm, deep blue sky should evaporate most of that soon.

I tried to orient myself so I could recall which way we'd been going before the storm halted our progress. The sun hadn't reached its high point yet, so I suspected that we could travel against its path in the sky to head east, at least until I recognized a landmark.

"I'm not sure what to do, Hekla," I said, scratching the back of my neck as we walked in the direction I hoped was east. "I have a takeover to manage, but… I can't leave your side. What is this task you must do?"

Hekla sighed and crossed her arms. I was a little disappointed that she'd dressed, but this realm likely already had her feeling too vulnerable. I shook my head. *Stop getting distracted!*

"The Sky Gods want me to escort Their children home from the... night? They said to follow the Eventide star. Apparently, something happened where They can't see Their children. They don't even know if they're still alive," she said, frowning and scratching her brow. "That last part makes me nervous. I just hope this isn't a big waste of time. It seems to be really dangerous out here."

"Hekla..." I began hesitantly, "the Night Court is... really, really far away, past winter and where the unseelie reside. I only have seven more days to get out of this contract." The stress hit me like a battering ram, and I scrubbed a hand over my face. "Must you do this task now?"

She glanced up at me with a worried look. "They made Their will pretty clear, Belenus. They said the time was now. I can't defy Their orders, and who knows if They'll just take my body over to do it Themselves. I'm still Their vessel, probably until the day I die."

She was right. She could be possessed at any point. "I can't... I can't leave you to do this alone," I said adamantly and furrowed my brows, trying to find some sort of solution for this dilemma. "We need a way to travel faster. Not even wolves will be fast enough to do a round trip in time, and that's without things like storms slowing us down."

Hekla was silent, and I stopped talking as well. The Winter Court would be slow going. The cold reigned eternal and snow fell much of the time, but there were occasional bouts of rain and thaws to melt the frost. The winter fae there would likely attack us on sight, taking us for invaders. The Unseelie Court contained some nasty monsters too. None of this would be easy... or quick.

Hekla sniffed the air and said, "I smell horse dung. Could we be near a road?"

"That's a brilliant observation..." I complimented in awe. "Which way?" Perhaps that would help me verify which direction was east. Roads were somewhat safer too because our traveling patrols deterred creatures from retrying attacks. Hekla pointed slightly toward the right, and I nodded, feeling some relief.

It was a wide dirt road, broad enough for two carriages to pass without any issues. Trees lined the left side of the road for quite some distance, and I was just about to suggest shifting when I froze and grabbed Hekla's arm to stop her. I spied a figure way down the road but couldn't be certain of its nature.

"Hekla, can you scent that over there—I think that's east actually," I asked in a low voice and pointed to the creature. Her lips parted and her nostrils flared as she took a deep breath. Instantly, she wrinkled her nose.

"Well, it's fortunate the storm was moving east to west because the wind is pushing that thing's scent toward us," she said with a grimace. "Gods, that is potent," she added, putting a hand to her nauseated face.

"And what do you smell?" I pressed.

"Rot... it smells dead." Hekla's face drained of blood, her eyes locked on the creature. "How can that thing be moving?"

"Do you have any food on you, Hekla?" I asked, suddenly anxious. If that creature was what I thought it was, I wasn't prepared for it at all.

"I didn't pack any. I always expect to hunt when I travel..." she answered and worried at her hands. The she-wolf's umbral gaze cut to mine worriedly. "Why are you asking?"

Shit. "I need to feed that thing," I stated, edging toward the side of the road. "Hekla, I need you to back up along the road if that gets near you. Stay out of speaking distance. I'll find you!"

I shape-shifted into Escort and gave him full control. *Find anything we can cook, Escort. I don't care if it's the smallest rabbit in the realm. Anything will do.*

Ok, so why did you leave our mate with something dangerous? Escort spat.

I need to keep track of that thing! It could be what we need, I snapped back, irritated with this wolf constantly challenging me. *We're doing this for our mate! Give her strength more credit.*

Escort shut up after that but remained angry. Once he caught the scent of a red grouse, he tracked it and killed it like the expert hunter he was. I supposed that as difficult as the wolf could be, I was at least grateful to be paired up with a competent one.

I let him take us back to Hekla and found she'd retreated a fair distance from the shambling form. It was still following her, or the road. I wasn't sure, but I wasn't going to get hung up on that question. I directed Escort to run past her so we'd have time to start a fire.

Rip this bird open, Escort, I said anxiously. *We don't have time to pluck it. I need to get at that meat now.* The wolf did as ordered, ripping the wings and legs off, then proceeded to tear open the breast to get at the thickest meat. I transformed back, started a quick fire with the fallen branches and twigs, and began roasting small strips of the bird over the fire. I called out to Hekla and gestured her over to help me, then pushed more summer magic into the fire, stoking it into a blaze.

She came running up and ripped easily into the meat with her claws. I made a note to praise her about that later when we weren't in such a rush. We'd had a decent pile of roasted offerings by the time the gaunt corpse veered off the road to approach us. That verified my suspicion.

"It's ok, Hekla," I said soothingly to her. "It won't hurt us. Especially not now. Be kind to it." My poor female waited, jumpier than a spooked hare, and I couldn't imagine how terrifying this must be for her. She hadn't pressed for answers, clearly too afraid to speak.

She scooted to my side and slightly behind me when the fear gorta maneuvered its undead body to a place by our fire. I smiled up at the emaciated dead man that likely originated from the unseelie territory and gestured for it to share a spot by the fire. "Please join us, hungry man. You must have traveled far."

The fear gorta lowered himself to a sitting position, and I kept a grimace off my face at the sound of bones, muscles, and sinew slipping about to make the movements happen. It was not the prettiest faery, this wraith. His sallow, bony fingers held up an alms bowl, tattered clothes shaking under his weak and slippery movements.

"You must be famished," I noted kindly and turned to Hekla. "Would you please offer him some food, my dear?"

She swallowed heavily and sandwiched her lips between her teeth as she scooped up the entirety of what we'd cooked and placed it in the fear gorta's bowl. She wasn't looking well, and I suddenly realized why she wasn't speaking; she was on the verge of vomiting. I had no doubt that opening her mouth would let her taste more than she was already scenting. This corpse must smell a hundred times worse to a wolf… Augh.

The wraith didn't talk. It just ate from the bowl, chewing with decayed teeth as it worked to fill its ever-hungry belly. I didn't think it could have talked if it tried. Eventually, it finished our donation and shambled back to its unsteady feet.

"Don't move, Hekla," I said to her calmly. "Just let it bless you. It's just a quick touch."

She remained silent but froze with all her little arm hairs standing on end. As it passed her, its decaying hand patted her shoulder. My mate's nostrils flared, and her eyes stared straight ahead, wide and unblinking. When it was out of sight, I scooted close and gave her cheek a kiss.

"You did so well. Good job done staying calm. That was a fear gorta," I said and smiled softly when she fell into my chest with a colossal exhale. "If you are unkind or don't give him food when he asks, he's capable of some fairly nasty curses."

"So, what happens now that we fed him?" she mumbled, taking deep breaths and snorting to clear the death from her nose.

"He blessed you with good fortune. I suspect that he gave you luck since we collected no coin. That was what I'd hoped for," I answered and extinguished the campfire. "I don't know how long that blessing lasts, so we need to get going. You should shift and see what luck has in store for you."

I shape-shifted into Escort, and Eventide loped toward the road. *That is disgusting,* Escort said, scenting the remnants of the wraith on the breeze. *I don't know how you tolerated that, Eventide.*

We were moments away from puking, yes, she replied in a strained tone.

Well, I guess we'll see if that luck manifests like Belenus said. I'm hoping to get lucky tonight, personally, he remarked with an edge of lust in his voice.

Behave, Escort, I ordered.

What? You get to finger, grope, and cum all over Hekla, and I can't have an ounce of fun with Eventide? Greedy piece of shit, you are, he retorted nastily. I withered a bit at his point. I'd seen wolf spirits as more of an accessory before I was 'blessed' with mine. Turned out we shared everything. I'd have to give Escort more autonomy, but I also didn't want him to pressure Eventide.

Eventide's an adult wolf capable of consenting and denying, Escort snarled. Had my thoughts been too loud? Shit, this was hard. *I could have forced myself on her a dozen times, but I didn't. I'm a dominant wolf, and I simply know what I want. I make my wants known, and you need to get used to that.*

I regretted not researching wolf-shifters more and more every single day. I was as out of my element sharing a body with Escort as Hekla was with living in my realm. If we could just get through dissolving the contract and taking over the throne, then I could adjust to having a wolf at my own pace.

I stopped making comments after his last outburst and just watched Escort's traveling through his own eyes. He was alert and on guard as he followed Eventide, acting very much like the protective male mate he was. I could tell he wanted to be behind her to keep an eye on her, but I could also tell that he was taking advantage of his spot behind Eventide to enjoy the view found under her tail. Yeah… maybe he wasn't so different from me after all. I was the one afraid of losing control, though. I grudgingly accepted that there might be something to be learned from Escort's confidence.

Eventually, we heard the rushing of a river, and I snapped to attention. *Escort, I think I know where we are now. Yes, we're headed in the right direction, and I recall that soon after this road approaches the river, there's a service for river travelers. I don't think they'll take us all the way to the Winter Court, but... maybe we'll get lucky...*

Escort slinked up to Eventide's side and nudged her playfully. *Hey there, pretty. Belenus says that there's a boat service that might be able to take us upriver to the Winter Court.*

Ok, let's just move parallel to the river then so that we don't miss it, she replied, still on edge with him.

Stunning and smart. A winning combination, he flirted.

J-just go, she stuttered, and we veered off the road to angle toward the river's roar. The air thickened from humidity; the Sun God, radiant today, quickly evaporated the soggy ground. I recalled what Hekla had said a while ago, that I smelled like lemon trees and summer storms. I believed I finally knew what she was talking about. I smelled it now and before the storm hit. I'd just never thought about it, but it was pleasant. It was a fresh, earthy smell.

Yeah, but we probably smell way better than this. We probably flood her mouth with saliva like she does for us. I bet Eventide will get all hot and bothered today on her last day of heat, but what are the odds I'll get time with her? Escort grumbled, half to himself and half to me.

He just would not let this go. *Let's say I allowed you two to... frolic. What the shit am I supposed to do? Watch it?* Also, I had to wonder, wolves didn't... pleasure each other... did they?

Gods, you're so offensive. I'm sorry the thought of me spending time with my mate is so horrifying to you.

That... wasn't entirely what I meant, I grumbled back at him.

I hibernated when you two played around, he said, getting progressively more annoyed with me. *I'd rather you refer to it as giving us privacy. Just tuck your sensitive, scandalized brain back and hibernate. It's not so difficult.*

As much as I didn't want to trust him, I felt like I needed to compromise on something. Who knew what he'd do if I didn't. Could wolf spirits revolt against their 'humans?' I wasn't sure if he heard my thoughts, so I just said, *I'll think... about it...*

Oh, how benevolent of you, he mumbled. We stopped talking about it after that. I was uncomfortable, but he was being downright cantankerous.

Prickly little shit, I thought as quietly as possible.

Smelling damp wood and people, Eventide announced, clearly relieved. Escort hadn't been paying attention, but we scented something too. I supposed it made sense, but I didn't know that us fae had such a distinctive scent. Layered on top was more information, like smells that could help identify what type of fae they might be. They were all folk fae; that was a certainty.

We crested a hill and looked down upon a small dock where several men and a young teenager were tidying up a faery boat. Reclining in the sun by the booth was a... very familiar face. What in the blazing rays was she doing here?

I shape-shifted back into my fae body and marched down the hill to greet her, feeling rather confused. I passed several modest houses and a small inn to reach her and stood by her feet for several seconds before she noticed me.

"Ushka?" I asked, bewildered. What was my mate's previous maid doing here?

Her eyes darted to me and widened, making the scales at her temples flicker in the sunlight. "Oh! Prince Belenus!" she blurted and rolled off the chair to curtsey. She started at the large black wolf next to me.

"Yes, this is Eventide. Hekla's in there," I said but quickly asked, "Why in the blazes are you here? Shouldn't you be in the castle?"

"I quit!" she announced with a tilt of her chin. "Getting kicked out of that room for that... bowfin spring churl of a fae was the last insult!" I wouldn't have been surprised if Ushka was also internally swearing at the queen. She wouldn't dare do that before me, though. It took her a moment to realize that she'd also just insulted my announced "intended," and her eyes nigh bulged in horror. She floundered for something to say, but I dismissed it with a hand.

"Relax, Ushka. The spring princess is an absolute nightmare, and I have no intention of marrying her," I said dryly. Her gaze then moved to Eventide, and her relieved expression turned into one of beaming joy.

"Oh, my lady, you're going to make such a wonderful queen! I'm so happy," she gushed, slouching a bit in her alleviation.

"Hopefully, it'll be sooner than you think," I added sternly. "Do you, Ushka, promise not to repeat any of our current conversation today, previous and future?"

"I promise," she said, and we shook hands. Fae magic bound her to that promise. There'd be no betrayals here.

"Hekla has to get to the Night Court as soon as possible. We're looking to travel upriver, at least to the Winter Court. Is there any string you can pull to help us out? I need to get back to the castle as soon as possible because my people are going to overthrow the queen. I know this is a lot to take in, but it's critical we save as much time as possible, Ushka," I said, watching her face go through a variety of expressions. She was clearly shocked, but I saw the curl of a smile pull at the corners of her mouth. "If you are able to help us out, I'd be glad to offer you a better position at the castle."

"I... I will do better than pull some strings!" she gasped and ran off to speak to an older fae man, who was licking his thumb and rubbing at a smudge on the hull of a boat. He seemed proud of his little business, if that was the owner.

I watched Ushka speak emphatically with him, and I squatted to pet Eventide's head while we waited. I smiled when the wolf leaned into me, occasionally tilting her head up to lick affectionately at my hand. At least she was still fond of me despite Escort's aggressive advances. When I saw Ushka turn back to us, I stood and strode over to her.

"Ok! I can take you! Let's go!" she said, guiding us to a smaller boat. I regarded it skeptically, unsure of how fast we'd be able to go upriver in it. It lacked oars as well. Still, I extended my trust, stepped in, and gestured for Eventide to sit between my legs so I could keep her steady.

"Don't worry," I heard Ushka say from behind. "There's a reason I got this job so quickly!"

I heard mooring ropes slap to the wooden dock and something fell into the water behind the boat, producing a rather sizeable splash. I looked around, frowning. Had she just jumped in?

Woah! Escort yawped as the boat lurched. A mess of long algae bubbled up to the surface of the river, followed by horse ears, a horse neck, and salmon-skinned withers. Eventide started when a huge section of tail rolled across the surface of the water like a dolphin's back.

I patted the wolf's neck, relaxing when I realized Hekla's luck had indeed been blessed. "We're getting towed, Eventide," I said soothingly and scratched under her ear. "That's a kelpie. I had no idea that Ushka was a kelpie, but it would have been in the castle directory of our workers. Looks a bit salmon-like, doesn't she? That bodes quite well for upriver speed. Can't believe our luck..."

I stared in awe as Ushka accelerated, creating larger wakes around herself and the boat. I laughed a bit, high from disbelief, and scrubbed a hand over my mouth. The bank flew by quicker than an eagle. Hekla shifted back into her human body, and I pulled her into my lap, grinning at her sounds of wonder. I wrapped my arms around her, just beneath her breasts, and rested my cheek against her head.

"Your realm... as scary as it is, it's remarkable too," she breathed, turning her head every which way to take in the rocky and grassy landscape. She tilted her nose up and sniffed at the wind, opening her mouth a little to take in the scents that came and went well within a split second. Her little pink tongue rested on her lower teeth as she tasted the air. I nudged her to issue a warning.

"Best close that before a wee faery flies into it," I cautioned jokingly, and she clamped her mouth shut. I brushed her dark hair aside, enjoying how it whipped wildly about in the gale. I leaned down to scent her while I still could, knowing her natural aroma would fade for me once her heat ended.

I grunted in surprise when the boat jumped a little bit and looked ahead to see that Ushka had fallen into a consistent pace. We must be going at her top speed. I gaped at the view, shocked to see the passing landscape blurring. For as long as I've been alive, I'd never seen such a thing.

"She's so fast!" Hekla exclaimed excitedly. "I wonder how long it'll take to get to the Winter Court?"

"I can't be sure, I've never tr—Oof!" The boat skipped again, causing Hekla to bounce on my lap a little. My palms grew sweaty, and I forgot what I was saying when Hekla glanced over her shoulder at me. "Sorry, lost my thoughts…" I admitted, staring down at the pretty eyes gazing up at me through dark eyelashes.

The boat settled into a skipping rhythm from Ushka's speed and wake, which made my mate's naked bottom jump on my lap. I leaned my head back and released a silent groan, trying to decide whether I wanted to move her or not. I could also feel the rounded bottom of her breasts bob against my forearms. I didn't want her first time to be in a nasty old tower, or on a boat being towed by a kelpie, but it'd be so easy to pull my cock out and pierce her soft sex on the next skip. We wouldn't even have to move; the boat would do everything for us.

I tried to be sneaky about lifting her hips so I could slide her away from my erection, but she caught on to what was happening and wiggled her way back to the top of my lap. "Hekla," I warned through my teeth. "If you don't move away, you're going to make me ruin these pants." My cock throbbed after that, echoing my warning.

I really didn't know why I thought she'd ever listen to me. The female was simply incorrigible. She just hooked her feet around my lower legs so I couldn't move her forward again and grinned wickedly over her shoulder. My mate then curled a lip to show off an elongated canine.

You little minx.

I leaned forward, panting slightly as she rode my lap, and said, "You know… my dear… Hekla… If we're playing… by… your rules…" I gasped and groaned, becoming harder than blistering granite. "I still… think you're… cheating…"

I didn't want to disrespect Ushka by getting frisky on her boat, but my hands itched to fondle Hekla's breasts. I just wrapped my arms tighter around her and pushed down to try to keep her bouncing to a minimum. My ridiculously clever mate then started grinding down on me, rolling her hips to tease my length through my pants. I moaned into her hair, feeling a shudder ripple through my body. I was too aroused. She needed to stop.

"You… are… being… very… naughty," I grunted and hissed through my teeth as I started to feel my climax build. "You better stop… my dear, or I'm going to… make you wash… my clothes!"

Unexpectedly, the boat slowed, and I glanced up to find that the river ahead was frozen. There was simply no way that we had already…

"Unbelievable," I whispered.

We were right on the cusp of summer and winter.

I jumped out of the boat as soon as we got close enough, adjusting my pants miserably as I waited for Ushka to make her appearance. Her fae head popped out of the water, and she grinned, looking very pleased with herself.

"Ushka," I began, trying not to talk through my teeth. I felt like my cock would burst if I moved even the smallest amount. "You… have done a great service… to your kingdom. I'll… remember this," I said breathlessly and tossed my fare into the boat for her to collect later. The amount was a hundred times what that trip was worth, and she'd earned every coin.

"Good luck, Prince Belenus!" she said and disappeared after waving a hand.

Exactly. Good luck indeed.

My head snapped over to Hekla, and I snorted out my frustration. Then, I adjusted my pants carefully, trying to calm myself. When my fated mate saw the look in my eyes, she fled, shrieking and giggling like a female who knew she was in trouble.

Chapter 19

Hekla

I ran squealing away from Belenus, who looked like he was one second away from either mounting me or punishing me, and I couldn't say I'd mind if he did both. I ran toward the Winter Court, not needing to look back to know that the fae prince was hot on my trail. I still hazarded a glance and yelped when he was closer than I'd realized. He was faster than I thought! I mean, if he could carry Eventide…

He closed in on me when my bare feet hit snow, and I released a manic shriek, shifting into Eventide midleap. His fingers brushed the tip of her tail, and he grunted in irritation at our escape. Eventide was a cackling disaster in my head, high on a chase that'd get any she-wolf's blood pumping.

We both shrieked when we heard another set of wolf paws barreling through the snow. *Oh gods, oh gods, oh gods, oh gods,* Eventide yapped frantically. *That's Escort! I'm in sooo much trouble!*

As much as she made a show of being uncomfortable around Escort, I could tell she was thrilled, and it was having an effect on whatever was left of our heat cycle. As fast as we were, Escort was larger and had a longer gait than my wolf. She panicked, laughed nervously, and cut across a snowfield toward a frosty stream.

Eventide, if we don't find a way to lose him, he's going to catch up! I shrieked as she pounced onto a thin tree that'd fallen across the stream, allowing her to cross the water in a heartbeat. We heard the thump of larger paws on the tree, but it was followed by a cracking and splashing.

Eventide, you naughty, sexy minx! Get your sweet tail over here! Escort yelled, and she looked back to find him dragging himself out of the cold stream. He shook himself twice, then bounded after her.

Aaah! Our good luck is bad luck! she screeched and accelerated, but he gained on her. *He's mad, he's mad, he's mad, he's mad!*

I felt her feral urge to stop and let him overtake her, but she was too skittish right now. Maybe she needed some encouragement? I certainly wouldn't deny her relief from her heat. She deserved to get to know Escort. He was meant to be with her.

Are you going to let him mount you? I teased her wickedly. *You've been pushing him away. I'm surprised you've lasted this long!*

I... I don't know!

Well, do you want him to?

I mean... he's... insanely... delicious... Yes, it's just... He's just so intimidating! She panted, and I could tell our heat was worsening.

Well, just shift back into me if you don't want to. I'd gladly wrestle with Belenus, I said idly, wondering if that would make her take action.

Well, Belenus may put a stop to it, she said distractedly.

I'll talk to him. I then privately mind-linked my mate. *Belenus, shall we give these two some time together? Let them get to know each other? Do you know how to hibernate?*

Euh... he replied anxiously, *I don't know. As much as I'd like to catch and... punish your wickedness, Escort is really... amorous. I'm about ten seconds away from shape-shifting back.*

It's ok if he's amorous. They haven't spent time together, really. We saved a lot of time today. Maybe let them have some fun? I asked, arguing on my wolf's behalf.

I don't know if I trust this big guy... but if you want me to, I guess... I'll... try to hibernate for thirty minutes? I don't know...

They're meant to be. Don't worry about it! I soothed.

If you say so... he replied and fell silent.

You've got thirty minutes, Eventide, I rallied impishly. *Just call me out if you change your mind.*

O-ok! she said, utterly overtaken by nerves and excitement. Escort immediately pounced on her, which made it seem like Belenus had been trying to restrain him this entire time. They tumbled in the snow, yipping and panting playfully.

My heart swelled knowing that she'd be able to experience a mate's embrace. It'd been my one secret misgiving about having been fated to a fae. I sent a silent prayer to the Moon Goddess, thanking Her for giving my Eventide a wolf to love and protect. I made a quick exit into hibernation when it seemed like things were getting a little serious, and I was as pleased as could be.

I had to peek out a couple times to check if Eventide had gotten untied from Escort yet. On my third foray, they were finally unstuck and sharing a fowl that one of them must have caught. Escort would occasionally give her face a little lick, a tender gesture that would have brought tears to my eyes. Eventide was as happy as she was sore, and she was very, very sore.

How'd it go? I asked her.

I... like Escort very much, she said with a calm, relaxed glow to her voice. *He made a big show of his dominance, but he melted into an adoring pup after. Look at this fat, juicy bird he caught for us!*

I can see that! It looks delicious! I lauded, then spoke openly to Escort. *Hey, nice bird you caught there! Thank you, Escort! You're so sweet.*

My pleasure, he replied, his tone relaxed and content, which was new to me. He must be happy too.

When both finished eating, I shifted back to give Eventide a little rest. When I saw Belenus appear, I grinned; however, my smile faded at his furious scowl.

"Hekla!" he snapped angrily, stomping over to me. "You said it'd just be getting to know each other! I thought you meant to let them run around or lick each other or some shit!"

I balked and stepped back, his words a slap. "They're mates… Belenus… They wanted to mate, and you already mentioned doing it s—"

"Yeah! Us, Hekla! I meant for us to mate! Not the wolves!"

"They are us!" I protested, confusion knotting my stomach.

"You never asked for my consent!" he shouted, and I placed a hand to my furrowed brow. What?

"Consent for what? I'm really confused, Belenus."

"Could you have gotten pregnant?" he asked, not answering my question.

"Well, yeah, w—" I started, but then Belenus snarled and fisted his hands.

"I didn't want him making my heir for me! So, you're fine with letting Escort get to you first?"

"Escort is a part of you, Belenus," I retorted, starting to get angry now… and a little offended.

"He most certainly is not!" he seethed.

My mouth hung open in shock. "So, are you saying that Eventide isn't a part of me?" I growled and leaned toward his face to challenge him. He froze, at a loss.

"Y-you're a shifter, Hekla! You were born with one!"

"Because the Moon Goddess gave me one! She gave you one too! Escort's seed is your seed, Belenus! There's no genetic difference! It's the same! It would be a shifter child from the same person!" I yelled furiously.

"So that was our first time then?" he yelled back, and that was when I finally hit my feral threshold.

"What?" I showed my canines, snarled through my teeth at my stupid, impossible male, and ran. I was furious! My male had dragged me here to his realm, forced this she-wolf into his way of life, and still continued to insult my people! I was fed up with my male's behavior! I wouldn't stand for it!

I hissed out a pained howl through my teeth as I ran. My wolf inside was resting, but fortunately the boost I would have received from her being awake came to me through my rage. The anger fueled me, and I drew from it like a thirsty deer would a stream.

I ran around a hill, knowing I wouldn't be able to climb it fast enough through all the snow. The panting and slushing noises told me that my male was running after me again. I turned my head and issued a warning growl at him, advising him to stop if he valued his life. He scowled, ignored my threat, and followed me to an outcropping where he tackled me into the snow.

"Hekla! Stop!" he said, grabbing at my wrists to prevent me from scratching him.

"You still disrespect my people!" I shouted into his face and fought to get him off me. I pushed his arms up and squeezed out from under him, making a run for it until he grabbed an ankle and sent me falling face-first into snow.

He crawled onto my back and held me down, binding my wrists again with his hands. "I'm sorry!" he hissed, sounding aggravated. "I'm not used to this!"

"I wasn't used to the castle either, my male!" I snarled. "Is it really so repulsive to be like me?" I growled viciously and tried to buck him off, growing angrier by the heartbeat.

"Your wolf isn't a little shit, Hekla!"

"Escort treats Eventide like a queen!" I practically howled, squirming and writhing beneath his weight. As much as wolves generated a little extra body heat, I was getting cold lying in all this snow. "Did you even notice how happy she was? Does that mean nothing?"

My male shifted his weight enough to turn me on my back and crush his lips to mine. I growled into his mouth, punching and scratching, but I couldn't seem to stop kissing him, and that made me furious!

"Of course it means something!" he growled, narrowing his almond-shaped amber eyes at me as his lip curled. "I want to make my mate happy!"

"And you were!" I snapped back, baring my teeth again. "Until you got mad over something beautiful!" I finally heaved him off of me, but his grip stayed firm, and he yanked me on top of him.

"And I said I was sorry! I'm sorry, Hekla!" he repeated, sliding his hand behind my skull to push my lips onto his again. His kiss was forceful, angry, passionate, and made my frozen toes curl. It weakened my resolve to keep running, but I still scratched at him in my indignation. He wasn't fazed for a second!

"And no, that wasn't our first time!" I spat at him. "That was their first time! And they earned it! You and I'd already agreed we'd mate soon! The only difference here is your pride!" I slipped out of his hold, but when he came after me, I took the initiative and wrestled him back down into the snow.

"Shit! This place is so frigid!" he hissed and slapped his hand down through the snow. He must have cast something because all the piled ice within three feet of us melted. The water quickly evaporated, leaving us on a mess of warm leaves under the jutting rocks.

I'd frozen for a moment, shocked by what he'd done. He'd just brought a small patch of summer into the Winter Court! This must have played into his strategy because I was distracted long enough for him to roll on top of me once more.

He settled between my legs and smashed his lips into mine once more, growling but sounding less angry. He pressed into me and caught my wrists, holding them above my head in one large hand. He sank his tongue boldly into my mouth, risking me biting it in my wrath. I accepted its presence grudgingly, giving my male credit for trusting me, even when I was angry.

He drew his mouth away, leaving me whining and angry about the fact I was whining. Leaning down, he took a deep inhale of my upper chest and groaned. "Fine then," he said in a low, gruff voice. "We'll do things your way. Are you ready for me to mount you in the woods here and now like the male you want me to be?" He ground his groin into mine as he moved back up my body. "Are you ready for me to give you what you've been begging for since we met?" He then rolled his hips, showing off the length and heat of his erection. He pressed his lips to my ear and rumbled lowly, "Are you ready for me to fuck you, she-wolf?"

My answer was 'yes,' but I wasn't going to make it easy. A deep frown crinkled my nose. "Of course, fae. But I think the question is," I seethed through my canines, "are you able to earn it?"

He moved his head back, tilting it a little as he gave me a bewildered expression. His grip faltered, and I tipped him over with my thighs. I scrambled away to make him work for it, but he just laughed and tackled me again.

"Oh, no you don't," he said in a deeper voice. "I'm aware of all your little moves now, female. I'm not a general for nothing."

I shuddered in arousal and scrabbled at the warm leaves, still resisting. In that moment, I came to the realization of why I was fighting him so hard. I wanted to *feel* his desire for me. I wanted to know he wanted me. I wanted to see it. I wanted to hear it. I wanted to sense it in every way. I wanted to be wanted so desperately that he'd hunt me to the ends of the earth. After everything I'd been through at the castle, I still needed validation. Deep inside, I was insecure now and craved something to help me heal. I needed proof. I needed much more proof.

"Prove it!" I snarled, continuing where my thoughts had ended. "Prove you want me! Prove you need me!" My breath sent smaller leaves skittering across the pile.

"You needn't worry about that, female," he said and removed my bag from my back while keeping me pinned to the forest floor. "I'll make my needs loud and clear..."

I heard the shuffling of him removing his own gear and clothing. When he shifted his weight to yank his pants off, I squeezed out from under him, but he caught me and shoved me aggressively toward the rock wall. I stumbled, caught myself with my palms and made to turn, but he was behind me in a blur and caught my hips in an unbreakable grip.

My breaths became light pants when he leaned over my braced body. I stiffened but excitement replaced anxiety when he tilted my hips up to nudge his dry, erect cock between my thighs. A shudder rippled down my body, and when it reached my core, the throb forced moisture down my thighs. I hung my head and whimpered, almost painfully aroused.

"Ohhh, she-wolf," the fae male behind me purred, "perhaps you're not as mad at me as I thought..." I felt a finger slide up my inner thigh to collect some arousal. I heard a sucking sound from behind me, followed by an appreciative hum. "Mmm, ripe in every season."

Just to see what he'd do, I struggled angrily again. His wet hand gripped my hip again and fingers dug in warningly. He chuckled darkly and angled to brush the head of his cock along my sex, sending more of my arousal dripping down his length. It was his turn to shudder, making his hair-dusted thighs vibrate against my legs.

"Oh, you are positively weeping, she-wolf," he said in a quiet, lustful voice. "Imagine if the court walked in on us doing this but couldn't do anything about it?" He released a long, tortured groan as he began to slide his erection along my sex and between my thighs. He teased me by only slightly brushing against the throbbing, swollen flesh just above my opening. The wolf in me found that unacceptable, and I growled lowly at his tormenting. He was unbothered. "Just imagine me risking everything to show them that you came first. I should have fucked you at the banquet. It wasn't like it hadn't crossed my mind," he gnarled. He bucked into me several times to illustrate his thoughts. "Should have just spread you out on the table with the rest of the feast and parted your legs for my tongue. You make for a fine appetizer," he remarked lasciviously.

I felt his feet nudge between mine to splay them. I tried to dig my feet in, but he grunted, wrapped his arms around my thighs and yanked them wide to get better access to me. He sighed in satisfaction as his hands moved to massage my rump. "I've been such a fool, my wild female. I could have had this pretty flower so much sooner. I should have fucked and marked you the moment I saw your exquisite naked body."

I moaned from his words, drinking in his compliments and possessive thoughts. I whined again, arching my back and bracing myself with my legs. I looked down to watch his hard, veined sex slide along my folds, and I whimpered pathetically when it dripped a bead of precum.

I felt him pull back and angle his lubricated cock to push against my entrance. Wild with impatience, I dug my claws into the rock face and let out a howling, desperate keen. The fae male wrapped his bulging arms around my waist as he prodded rhythmically, pressing harder with every nudge.

"You… were… such… a… tease… you… minx!" he grunted with each pump. I hissed in pain because, despite his force, he wasn't going in any deeper. He was hitting my virgin threshold, and sex no longer seemed possible. I shuffled forward to get away from him, but he just dragged me back toward his cock. "No, there's no getting out of this," he growled and pressed into my slick entrance again. "Don't forget the Moon Goddess made us compatible, female. Have a little faith."

Though he sounded angry, he pushed slower this time, creating a burning pain as my skin stretched to let his heavy erection discover my channel. I yelped as he jerked forward a couple times, pushing in deeper, and didn't stop until I felt his groin pressed against my backside. He held me still, letting me get used to the almost unbearable fullness I felt. My skin was so irritated around my entrance, and I squeezed my eyes shut, whimpering as quietly as possible.

"That's a good female," he crooned lowly into my ear. "Just get used to having me in there." He swelled within my channel, like he was becoming more excited just being there.

"It hurts," I panted, and a pathetic whine escaped my chest.

"I know…" the fae murmured, sliding his hands up my back to rub my shoulders. "I'm trying to be gentle."

No… I didn't want him to hold back because I still needed to see his need. I wanted his desperation, even if it'd hurt. "Prove your need for me!" I snarled to provoke him. "I'm ready!"

"Oh, I think I've been proving it." He chuckled coldly. "But fine, I'll take you how I want to."

He rolled his hips a couple times, pulled out completely, then pushed back in again. He fed his length through my channel, and I could feel the head of his cock slide along my shape, parting my inner walls. It was like he was trying to memorize every internal inch.

I licked my lips and released a soft moan at the first sensation of pleasure. Through the pain, the filling of my empty space with hot flesh very much agreed with me.

The fae behind me hummed excitedly and sped up his strokes. "Oh, Hekla," he groaned. "No one compares to you. Not even a little." He released an enthusiastic cry and slapped his hips into my bottom and thighs, sending his stone-hard length into my depths. I whimpered and bit my lip, feeling myself continue to lubricate him with my desire. His strokes became wet and smoothed, making it easier for me to receive him.

He groaned and accelerated, slamming into me now and forcing a wail out of my throat. "Do… I… really… have to… leave… this… fine… flower?" he gasped, gripping my hips and yanking me back to collide with his thrusts. I felt my core clench at his erotic compliment, and he moaned loudly in response. "Do… that… again!" he gasped.

"Make me!" I retorted breathlessly, panting too hard to growl.

He slapped my butt cheek. "Don't… talk back... to your… prince!" he grunted. "Oh, Moon Goddess… you're… gripping me so… tight…" He moaned louder as he continued to slam our bodies together, sinking his length deeper. I shuddered and clenched around him again, making him release a guttural groan. "Oh sh-shit!" he swore, and I swore he hardened further. The tip of his cock tapped at something in my depths, and I gritted my teeth through an overwhelming wave of arousal. I clenched around him again, making his panting deepen.

"Do you… feel that?" He moaned, his sentences jostled by his panting and thrusting. "That's what… I'm going… to feed… the mouth… of… your… womb."

He jerked out of me, unstoppering my core and allowing some of my desire to run down my leg. "Shit!" the fae said breathlessly and pushed me down to the ground, wrestling me onto my hands and knees. "You want me to treat you like a wolf, I'm going to fuck you like one," he growled, gripping my hips again to squeeze back into my heat. It was more difficult this time, as my entrance had tightened, and his heavy erection had swollen larger than when he'd originally entered. "And you're going to howl for your dinner, filthy she-wolf!"

He plunged in wetly, going deeper than before, his grunting turned into wild, rhythmic sounds of bliss. I whimpered and occasionally yelped with each hard thrust, feeling my spine bend under the force of his penetrations. The tapping against my back wall turned into thumping as he stretched my limit. I reveled in the pain, I loved it, too aroused by the thought of him delivering his seed straight through my inner threshold.

"Gods, you're so wet. You're just drooling for me to feed your womb, aren't you? You little minx." His slamming turned bruising. "You want golden fae pups, female? Want me to…

impregnate… the fuck… out of you?" he gritted out in a desperate, hushed voice closer to my ear as he wrapped his arms around my waist.

I whimpered, whined, and moaned at his erotic question, then nodded fervently, wiggling my bottom in response. My own words wouldn't come out; I was too lost to excitement, too embraced by my ravenous inner wolf.

"Then howl for me, female, and I'll feed you," he grunted, his heavy panting sounding more from arousal than exertion. "I don't… give a shit… who hears us…"

He raised his hips and angled downward, sending the bulky head of his shaft along my front wall. I wailed. He dug into and along the sensitive patch within me, stroking heavily until I tightened up and endured the approach of an unavoidable storm. The hairs on the back of my neck stood on end as I anticipated a lightning strike.

"Howl for me, Hekla," the fae male urged in a tight, deep voice, stroking harder into my wall. "Howl at the fucking sky. Tell the Sky Gods who pleases you most!"

My arms trembled, and my entire body began to clench, including my core, which made him hiss through his teeth. "So tight! So hot! So fucking wet! Shit, Hekla! Sh-shit! Howl for me! Howl!"

The storm clouds within me swirled, and the heat broiled in my sex. I braced myself, arched farther, and released a throat-rending howl. My walls clamped down on my mate in a fierce, feral grip, trying to trap him in me, but he managed to increase his pace for several more thrusts and slammed fully into me.

"Yesss!" he yelled out, screaming his pleasure through his teeth. "Milk me, Hekla! Shit! Suck me dry!"

My sex rubbed his seed out and welcomed it eagerly, milking his cock in waves as he'd begged of me. His head nudged rhythmically into my back wall, pushing into it, desperate to fill me with his young. He squeezed his muscular arms tighter, flexing his groin with each ejaculation and moaning in euphoria.

I wept from the pleasure as hot summer lightning coursed through my core. Combined with him filling every ounce of space and the arousal I felt from him feeding my womb, I was wrapped in ecstasy. I clawed at the ground, overwhelmed by finally having my male mate with me. We pulsed sensually together, drunk on each other and the enhancement of the mate touch. He reached to massage my sweaty breasts, sighing and shuddering as he delivered his last spurt of seed. Then, he placed several kisses on my back, and I melted beneath him. He caught me before I hit the ground and slowly slipped out his spent cock, unstoppering his seed this time.

"And now... for dessert..." my mate murmured breathlessly. He laid me gently down on the warm leaves to hold me, and I finally got my first good look at him since we'd fought.

It brutally woke me from the hazy dream. I gasped at the sight, putting my hands to my mouth in shock and dismay. He smiled at my realization and stroked my hair, tucking a strand back behind my ear. Gesturing to his bruised, battered, and bleeding body, he said, "You wanted proof? Here's your proof." I'd given him so many deep gashes with my claws, but I'd never once heard him cry out in pain.

My eyes watered, and I cursed myself for taking my rage out on him. He'd been rough with me and spanked me a little, lightly, but he'd never struck me. He'd never drawn blood—ever. "I'm so sorry," I whispered, gaping at a particularly deep cut between his collarbone and chest.

His face sobered as he stroked my cheek with a thumb. "I value you over my own health, Hekla. That's how much I need you. I'm willing to take your hurt," he whispered back, staring at me from under his tousled sunny hair. "I don't think you truly realize how much you mean to me. I hope this helps you see that." His face contorted. "That wasn't meant to guilt tri—"

My chin wobbled, and I interrupted him, crying. "I'm s-so s-sorry!" I sobbed, placing my face in my hands. Belenus pulled me up against him and kissed the top of my head.

"It's ok, my dear one," he murmured, stroking the back of my head. "You've had a lot of hurt buried deep. I'm glad you were able to let it out, especially since so much of it was my fault." He kissed my head again and took a deep breath of my scent. "I'll do better. I'll be more open-minded for you. I've made a lot of mistakes…"

I cried into his arms and felt more of my pain drain out of my heart.

"I love you, Hekla. Never forget that because it's forever."

I nodded into his chest, then leaned back to study his cuts.

"C-can you heal th-those?" I asked through a quivering jaw. I rubbed the tears from my eyes, and his gaze dropped to himself with a chuckle. He placed his fingers on each gash, and they healed, though much slower this time.

"My magic isn't as potent in the Winter Court, but it'll still work. It's just a slower process now," he explained. I watched him work on healing himself, and when he was done, he grinned his flirty grin at me. "See? Nothing to worry about, Hekla." He tilted my chin up to lay a soft, affectionate kiss on my lips. He wiped another one of my tears away with a thumb and released my lips to nuzzle my nose.

I felt something cold land on my cheek, and Belenus hummed happily, poking my cheek to garner my attention. I aimed my eyes skyward to find a gentle snowfall. Snowflakes drifted to meet us as we lay in each other's arms.

Chapter 20

Hekla

Belenus kissed the cheek that had melted the first snowflake. I hummed in delight and stared at my beautiful fae mate whose pointy ears and nose were starting to turn a little flushed from the cold.

He moved into a crouch and spread my legs to regard my sex. “Let’s see what the damage is…” he murmured, and I felt warmth bloom in my chest from his attentiveness. He was still sweet even after I’d cut the poor man to ribbons. “Just looks irritated from being stretched, my dear, but I’ll take care of that. You got lucky. No tears.”

Thank you, fear gorta?

I spread my legs to give him more room, and he placed his warm hands on the sore threshold of my sex. I sighed in relief as the pain faded but started and yelped when he replaced his hands with his lips, giving my entrance a kiss. I had not expected that! My heart raced, and he chuckled from my reaction before helping me off the ground.

"We should probably get going," I said, regarding the surroundings. "Days are shorter in winter, and I have a feeling that above this cloud cover the Sun God will be going to sleep soon. That… confuses me so much, I don't even want to begin to try to figure out how that works here." I placed my hands on my cheeks. How could the Sun God possibly retire at different times?

Belenus, done dressing, threw on his gear. "Well, we did save several days of traveling already. We should find shelter at the very least."

I dressed swiftly too, shivering even in the small patch of summer Belenus had created. I wished I could shift into Eventide; she could handle this winter without a problem, but she still needed rest. Rakel could probably handle this without even shifting, being from a colder climate.

"How are we going to know which way is north if the sky doesn't clear?" I asked, looking up only to catch several snowflakes on my eyelashes. I brushed them off and tried again.

"We'll worry about that after we've found shelter. I'll try to think of a sol—" he said but paused and stared ahead at a log cabin we'd almost stumbled into from a sharp descent down a hill. Surrounded by a thicket and taller redwoods, it would have been harder to spot from any other angle. Since it was also made of birch, it was nigh impossible to detect amongst the snow.

"Should we knock?" I whispered, wondering about Belenus's thoughtful expression.

"I'd normally say no, but if your luck is still going strong, this could be what we need…" He put a finger to his lips and tilted his head. With a shrug, he strolled down to rap his knuckles on the wooden door. I took a cursory glance into one of the cabin's windows, but the off-white curtains were drawn tightly. The glow of a hearth and smoke coming from the chimney suggested that someone must be home.

"Someone's coming," I warned, hearing hasty steps on a wooden floor. The door opened, and my mouth hung open in astonishment.

"Talam?" Belenus sputtered and released a disbelieving laugh.

"Prince Belenus?" the fae who used to be my maid exclaimed. She looked at me, and her hands flew to her mouth. "Lady Hekla! What are ye both doing here? What happened to the engage— I'm so sorry, where are my manners? Please come in! Come in, come in!"

We followed Talam to some cushions by the hearth where we settled. Snow didn't often come to my old pack's territory, so it was easy to forget how intensely and easily its cold sank beneath flesh. I worked to shudder the chill from my body and allowed the heat from the fire to seep into my clothes and skin. When I could think of anything other than finally getting warm, I glanced up and found Talam waiting patiently. She scratched at the base of an antler while she waited for the entire story.

Once again, Belenus swore her to secrecy and caught her up on current events. She nodded along as she listened, occasionally gasping or muttering curses. She rose to fetch some refreshments, all the while shaking her head like a disappointed teacher.

"To think our queen has sunk so low. Seems as though my sisters and I left just in time…" she muttered, returning with some cider, a plate of cheese, and a loaf of freshly baked bread.

"Are you talking about Ushka and Spayr?" Belenus asked, a puzzled expression on his face. "I had no idea you were siblings. You look nothing alike."

Talam's grin spread, and for just a moment, I saw a flash of consideration in her knowing look. Something also shifted in her demeanor, and her presence seemed… bigger now. "Well, that is because we're godlings, my dear Prince Belenus."

I choked on my sweet cider until tears ran down my face.

"Oh dear," Talam said, worrying over me and patting my back. "I should have said that after ye took a sip."

I sputtered for a minute as I tried to clear the liquid from where it shouldn't be. It took forcing several more coughs until I was mostly better, then I looked over to Belenus who was also patting me. He frowned after I gestured that I was fine, and he turned his attention back to our host. "Why… Talam, why would you three work as maids? Of all things? Especially under a queen who wasn't doing you any favors…"

"Hardly a better place to keep an eye on the Summer Court during its time of need, don't you think?" she asked seriously, sitting tall and confidently. "All those who live in the water, on the land, and in the air… don't deserve to suffer another wretched queen."

"If you're godlings and feel so strongly about it, why did you leave?" Belenus asked, his question more curious than accusatory.

"Because we had to be here!" she said with another grin and spread her arms. "Er, I had to be, that is."

I rubbed my temples, trying to wrap my head around everything that was being said. "Talam… you knew we were going to be here? Does that mean you're Fate's godlings?" I asked, furrowing my brows. I had so many questions… I thought that only Fate and the Moon Goddess knew what would come to pass.

"It's possible," she said with a shrug and didn't seem to want to divulge more than that. I looked over to Belenus for his thoughts, growing more overwhelmed and tired by the heartbeat. He leaned into me, deep in thought, and grabbed both my hands to warm them. Talam just sat there patiently, nibbling on some cheese and bread.

"Is there a quicker way to the Night Court than walking, Talam?" I finally asked, nervous that there wouldn't be. I was still so worried about Belenus's situation. If we couldn't get back in time… My task and the contract threatened to tear me in two. "And… do you know if there's a way to break Belenus's marriage contract?"

"Oh, I can't help ye with the contract, but I can help ye get to the Unseelie Court in a couple hours," she said.

"A couple hours?" Belenus exclaimed, blowing out a held breath and raking his hands through his hair. "That's… blisterin' quick."

I nodded wearily. That was obviously phenomenal news, but I was also so very tired. "I suppose we should take you up on your offer…" I said, trying not to slur my words. "When would you like to take us?"

"Probably now. Take advantage of yer luck while you have it," she answered and cleared the food tray from the floor. I shouldn't be surprised that she knew about the fear gorta. Talam returned and squatted before me with a cold, wet towel. She dabbed at my face and murmured, "I know yer tired. I'll take ye straight to Spayr, ok? She'll have a bed for ye."

I smiled into the towel, appreciating her trying to perk me up like she would've as my maid. "I am wiped, Talam," I agreed with a yawn, trying not to thank her. Belenus and I gathered our things and left the cabin with her. The godling seemed to have much more energy now, and I wondered how much of herself she'd had to suppress while she was playing maid. Had she felt like me when we both couldn't be ourselves?

A swirl of light rushed about her, and Talam turned into a huge white hind. I balked and took a step back, not expecting something so large to appear so close to me. Belenus caught me, gave the deer a dubious look, and lifted me onto it.

I clutched at the short, bristly hair and hard, lean flesh. There was something very wrong with this picture; a wolf did not belong on a deer. This was the very picture of absurdity. It was also terrifying. It was one thing to have Eventide control any of our movements but to rely on an animal to carry me... that was a lot of trust to place in Talam. I swallowed hard and looked over the deer's shoulder. I wasn't afraid of heights, but... from atop a deer, my feet seemed too far from the ground. At least in a carriage the ground was hidden. I felt very, very vulnerable.

I waited for Belenus to adjust some of his gear and climb up behind me. At first, I didn't know how he was going to get up, but he vaulted effortlessly onto the white deer like the strong, nimble fae he was. I had a very capable mate... virile and athletic. However, I was much too tired to be turned on.

"I have no idea how this is going to work," Belenus grumbled as Talam started walking. "Deer cannot be ridden by ones such as us… their leaps are too jarring, and their spines are not meant to carry riders, not like how we've bred horses to carry us. Dig your heels in the best you can, my dear," he said while wrapping his arms around my waist.

"Just trust in the godling," I replied sluggishly, too fatigued to laugh stupidly about him saying dear while we were on a deer. I already couldn't wait to get off Talam and sleep. I leaned forward to try to find some sort of grip on her back and made a silent prayer to the Sky Gods. *Please don't let me break my neck today.*

Talam began trotting through the snow and evergreens, which was a little bumpy, and I was starting to realize what Belenus meant. I'd never ridden a horse before since they didn't like shifters, but I could tell there was a lot more spring in a deer's gait than there was in a horse's. His arms tightened around me when the hind finally broke into a gallop, exposing his own nervousness.

Very quickly though, I felt my seating grow more secure, and the ride felt less jolting. I blew out a breath I hadn't realized I'd been holding and felt Belenus's lips bob against my ear. "I think she's smoothed out her gait for us, somehow, which is good because I don't think I could have handled several hours of lurching about," he said lowly. "On a deer, that is," he amended with a chuckle.

"Are you going to be ok back there?" I whispered with a lazy huff of laughter.

"Bouncing into your fine, round rump for hours? Absolutely not. This promises to be the worst several hours of my life," he grumbled into my ear.

"I have no control over that on this ride." I snorted. "We could stop and switch spots?" I offered.

"No," he said grumpily, wrapping one arm tighter around me while sliding his other hand up in a futile search of a way into my dress. "Because then I won't have your breasts to keep me company," he mumbled, sounding much crabbier than I knew he was.

I snorted in amusement, glad for the warmth at my back while the snowfall around us became a beautiful, speeding tunnel.

Belenus

Hekla was nearly limp in my arms as the third hour neared. More than anything else, I worried about getting her to a place she could rest. It wasn't like she was in danger; I just didn't like seeing my mate so exhausted. Her head drooped a little, and I squeezed her tighter to keep her secure. My heart clenched; I just wanted to take care of her right now. She'd needed care so many times since arriving here, and I couldn't fail her ever again.

Due to the speed of the godling, the snow now traveled horizontally, and the forest on each side blurred with green and white. I had to wonder how much of meeting the three godlings was from the fear gorta's influence and how much was from Fate's influence. Then again, Fate was superior to the fear gorta and likely put it in our path. I snorted and stopped thinking about things that would give me a headache. I'd leave that mystery to our philosophers.

Talam slowed as the pale grey clouds above stopped along an invisible barrier. We must be leaving the Winter Court now. Its weather could no longer follow us. Good. Neither Hekla nor I would miss its pervasive freeze.

And ahead of us? The Unseelie Court was a place I'd never stepped foot, and my very presence here felt unnatural. It was like I'd invaded an intimate, sacred space. My kind did not belong here and were not welcome.

As Talam moved deeper into the court, I noticed it was as gloomy as the Seelie Court was lively. Having Hekla as my mate, however, forced me into seeing this place differently than

I would have months ago. My summer and seelie kin would find this place horrifying, but I tried to focus on the details, see what made this place normal for the unseelie. What was it about this place that felt like their version of home?

The sky was a little hazy, a little dark wherever the dull sun couldn't touch, but the temperature was perfectly comfortable. The ground was dark and the mud was caked, but I did spy animal prints that proved wildlife thrived here. The trees, though twisted into gnarled shapes, still created life. They sprouted humble leaves, and some produced fruit. Strange and shadowy creatures roosted in their eaves just like our birds.

Whatever animals I did catch before they disappeared were bizarre in their form and movement. They would be considered far more 'nightmarish' than anything one would find in the other courts. A creature resembling a featherless, wingless crow with pincers and tarantula legs stalked through the underbrush, ignoring our passing entirely. A six-legged lizard clung to a particularly tangled spot on a large bramble, its face a blank, humanlike mask. The small faeries here appeared chaotic and mutated, and many were emaciated with wings so shredded that I wondered how they stayed in the air.

Yes, the strange invoked fear, but the strange was simply another form of diversity. I remained vigilant but became less stressed as I digested the new environment. I must look odd to them. Hekla entering my life, bringing new experiences and change, was a larger blessing than I could have ever imagined. My eyes were open, and the goddess's words made more sense by the encounter.

Talam trotted through the bizarre, curling woods, occasionally disturbing the quiet sleep of witch's hair lichen that hung from nearby branches. They swayed slowly, almost as if they moved in a different time than the rest of us. She eventually landed on a road and continued following it, putting us on a path southeast.

The trees thinned, and we entered an expansive pasture that contained a large herd of cattle. I was surprised to find that the bovine looked perfectly normal. There was nothing I'd consider 'unseelie' about them at all. A muzzled cù-sìth guarded the herd. It sat silently in its watch, but its eyes were fixated on our approach.

Talam turned and headed toward the top of the hill where a figure stood waiting. Under the dim light of the setting sun, I could see it was Spayr. "Oh, thank the Sun God," I muttered and rubbed Hekla's arms to perk her up a bit. "We're here."

"We are?" she asked drowsily and wiggled to sit a little taller. I pointed over to where Spayr waited, and she was now waving at us. Once Talam came to a stop, I jumped off and helped Hekla dismount. She slid down with her arms wrapped around me and wouldn't let go, so I just decided to carry her and save my tired mate some energy, despite my own fatigue.

Talam returned to her folk fae form and embraced her sister. I strode up to her and smiled in greeting. "You really left the castle, didn't you?" I asked Spayr with a chuckle. "You quit your job all the way to the Unseelie Court."

"Well, I'm sure my sisters have said the same thing about it as I would. Not another wretch— Oh, you told them about us, Tri?" Spayr asked, looking over at her sister who'd nudged her.

"Yes. Let's get them a place to rest. I'll update ye on what they've told me. I'm sure they don't care to repeat it for the third time," Talam said, smiling over at me and Hekla.

"Tri?" I asked.

"Oh, Talam is not my real name," Tri said. It dawned on me who they were, and I tilted my head skyward, parting my lips in thought. I nodded slowly, needing to be a little more awake to completely process this disclosure. How had I not guessed this before?

"Belenus?" Hekla asked drowsily. I didn't know if she was sensing my stupefaction or if she just wanted to get to a bed.

I looked over at "Spayr" and said, guessing her true name, "Understood. Might you have a place we could spend the night... Lion?"

Lion grinned and gestured for us to follow. Yes… Spayr was Lion. That could only mean one thing for their other sister.

We marched over the hill toward a ranch sitting adjacent to an inn. A few other homes populated the small community, but it was fairly quiet, and no one was in sight. Instead of taking us to the ranch or inn, Lion turned onto another path and brought us to a small blue house with a thatched roof. Dozens of bird feeders hung from overhangs, and tiny wood houses were scattered about the eaves, tucked away in dark corners. It seemed like the garden was a sanctuary for all types of flying creatures. That made sense to me now.

Lion welcomed us in and showed us to a cozy little guest room. "Make yourselves at home," Lion said. "There's water and cups in the kitchen, help yourself to the pantry as you need, but let me know if you require anything else. Hekla, my dear lady, you look about ready to pass out. Get your mate to bed, Prince Belenus," she said and curtseyed. She looked as her sister did now; Lion's very presence swelled grander than her size dictated.

"Oh, by the Sun God, please don't curtsey. You're a godling!" Hekla protested, perking up a little in dismay. Hekla's words echoed my thoughts. It didn't feel right for them to show us deference.

"And godlings do what they want," Tri said, popping her head in the doorway. "Good night. I'm off to discuss matters with my sister." The two godlings walked out, closing the door behind them.

I placed Hekla on the bed and took her bag from her. She immediately tossed her shoes off and crawled under the thick cotton blankets, groaning in satisfaction. After I fetched some water and snacks for my mate, I relieved myself of my gear and most of my clothes and followed my mate under the sheets. She whined wolfishly once she finished eating and settled her head on my chest.

"Long day…" I said quietly and stroked her hair. It'd felt like a blistering week.

"I have hundreds of questions," she mumbled.

"I'll answer them tomorrow so you'll actually remember the answers," I murmured, chuckling lightly. My heart swelled with warmth, with love, as she wrapped her arm over me and nuzzled sweetly. I whispered, "I wish you the most beautiful of dreams, my mate. Ones as beautiful as you."

Lion woke us to break our fast, and after eating, we readied ourselves for the trek to the Night Court. "Where's Talam?" Hekla asked, yawning and downing the last of her tea.

"Her name is actually Tri, Hekla. And Spayr is Lion," I corrected. She probably didn't recall much of last night, having been nigh dead to the world upon our arrival.

Lion passed her a roll of parchment. "She departed earlier this morning but left this for you."

Hekla licked her lips and unrolled the paper. I leaned over to discover that it was actually a map of the fae realm—an odd version of it. There were no location names, only spiral symbols that had been drawn with heavier lines, and I assumed these were noteworthy destinations.

"What are these swirls, Lion?" I asked, furrowing my brows as I studied the map over my she-wolf's shoulder.

"They're connected doors that only fae can use. It's the only way to enter the Night Court," she answered, picking at a stick of spiced beef jerky.

Hekla traced her finger along the border of the Night Court. "What are they trying to keep out of there? Maybe that's the threat to the Sky Gods' children…"

"It's what they're trying to keep in there," Lion said, ripping into a piece of jerky. Hekla hummed and tapped on several swirls as she pondered.

"How do these doors work? Do they go to the ones you target? Do they go to one that's adjacent? Do they go back to the human realm, and you have to find the corresponding one from the human realm?" I asked.

Lion leaned forward and gestured. "They're connected. Look closer at the spirals."

Hekla saw it first, the subtle, matching symbols that indicated which doors were connected.

"So these are kind of like shortcuts too…" I murmured, already trying to sort out the fastest way back to the Summer Court's castle.

"There are more in the sky and in the water, but you only require Tri's map. The winter fae and unseelie only know about the ones by the Night Court." The godling held out a hand and grinned. "If anyone else looks at this map, it'll be blank, so if you lose it, the locations will remain secret. Do you promise to not share these locations with anyone else, Belenus and Hekla?"

I accepted her hand and shook it. "I promise to not disclose the locations of these doors." Hekla repeated my words and actions, fully satisfying Lion's demand.

"Then let's get going, shall we?" the godling suggested and gestured to the front door. We filed out and let her lead us to a quiet section of the pasture, away from all the cattle. I could only wonder how Lion was going to take us to the border, and I prayed for anything but another deer.

The peace of the moment shattered. A colossal crashing, as startling as a thunderclap, came from about a mile away, buried in the woods, but once it sounded, it did not cease. The cracking and rustling loudened and headed in our direction.

Lion's eyes widened, she whirled to us, and waved frantically. "Get on, get on, get on, get on!" she yelled and shape-shifted into a colossal black-and-white bird with enormous webbed claws. Well, that was the largest boobrie I'd ever seen in my life.

She crouched as low as possible and spread a black cormorant's wing, inviting us up the feathered ramp and onto her back. I hauled Hekla over my shoulder to save time, bound up onto the bird's back, and settled my mate between my legs.

I prayed to the Sky Gods as I panicked, not knowing how Hekla and I were going to stay on this creature. All I could do was gather a handful of coal-black feathers in each hand and accepted it wasn't the time to be gentle.

"Go, go, go!" I shouted as I dug my heels in and sandwiched Hekla tight between Lion and me, knowing we had a very steep launch ahead of us. Lion scuttled into a run and flapped desperately to become skyborne, the muscles beneath Hekla and me flexing monstrously, fed by the godling's might. The cattle parted ahead of us, startled by the noise and the colossal bird headed in their direction.

Over the din of trees getting trampled, I could make out the sound of four massive hooves and two sweeping limbs, like hands parting the woods. The thundering came right behind us now, and I wasn't sure if I could bring myself to look.

I knew what it was, and it was something no fae ever hoped to see in their lifetime.

Lion was jolted violently and roared the boobrie's horrifying, bull-like bellow out of pain. I had to look back to check, and I knew I'd have nightmares for years, but I was the only one here who could help.

As feared, the monstrous nuckelavee was there, in all its horror, towering larger than a barn—a demon of muscles, bones, and every other tissue but skin. It was a disturbing union of horse and rider, combined as one. The flayed rider's torso came straight out of the horse's back, the rider's arms long enough to drag on the ground, a reach lethal even for sky creatures.

Like the one we were on.

It'd tried to snatch Lion but had only managed to pluck several large tail feathers. Hekla tried to turn and look, but I snapped, "Don't look, Hekla! Eyes ahead!" I didn't want her seeing it. I wouldn't allow her to have any more nightmares than she already had.

Once she complied, I searched inward to find my pure summer essence. Of all the courts, the nuckelavee could not enter the Summer Court, and I had to take advantage of that weakness, even if it would drain me. I wound up as much of my summer magic as I could and waited for the right moment. The nuckelavee swiped violently to knock us out of the air, but I released a concentrated blast of broiling sunlight and knocked its hand away from Lion. It recoiled in rage and glared up at us as we escaped east toward the Night Court. Two horse eyes, two rider eyes—radiating hate as scalding as my magic.

I patted Lion and yelled over the wind, "We're clear!" She bobbed her head in acknowledgment, and I wrapped my arms around Hekla to steady us both. I leaned into her slightly, growing more ill by the second from losing so much of my natural magic. It'd be hard to regenerate out of the Summer Court. I closed my eyes and took a deep breath, trying to accept that Hekla's good luck had finally run its course. We were now being hunted by a nuckelavee.

Chapter 21

Hekla

I wasn't sure what had attacked us. Belenus had snapped pretty aggressively at me, so I trusted him and kept my eyes on the horizon. He was leaning into me now and breathing a little heavier than normal.

"Belenus?" I asked, trying to speak above the wind. "Are you ok?" My ears popped as Lion climbed higher, and I grimaced in pain, wishing I could do something about the pressure in my head.

"I used a lot of my magic…" he murmured tiredly, and I had to strain to hear him, "to fend off that nuckelavee…"

My fae man sounded awful, and I chose to focus all my attention on him. I had multiple reasons for that. Caring about him was one. Critically needing a distraction was two. Clutching to a flying creature was considerably worse than riding a deer. If I thought about how far off the ground we were, I'd start screaming and never stop. *Just talk to Belenus, just talk to Belenus, just talk to Belenus. Oh gods, wolves don't belong on birds!*

Or on deer! Eventide lamented. *Please don't look down!*

Not planning on it!

"Can I do anything?" I asked Belenus over my shoulder and placed one of my hands over his. He sighed ever so slightly in relief. Maybe the mate bond would help?

"I... don't think so. My magic will take a long while to regenerate outside of the Summer Court," he explained. "I'm just drained."

"Lean on me, mate," I ordered, sitting straighter. "I'm strong." I sensed his hesitation, but he put more of his weight against my back, and I patted his hand. "Good. Trust your female," I said in approval. I was not as powerful as Belenus, but I was still a she-wolf and a strong one at that.

I spent the morning's flight on Lion simply watching the horizon. I was wondering how obvious the border of the Night Court would appear. The thought of going from daytime to nighttime in a single step was impossible for me to imagine. Most everything I'd seen since arriving in this realm was just as mind-boggling. How strange it would be to think of this all as normal. I wondered how the fae would fare in my old realm, experiencing the seasons as they approach instead.

Finally, we saw it, the hazy unseelie sky ending in a sharp line, pressed tight against the black of night and brilliant, glittering stars. The divide rose as high as the eye could see, blurring together in the embrace of the Sky Gods. As we drew near, Lion descended, and she landed—albeit a little roughly—at the threshold of the Night Court. A stygian woodland waited before us; the spindly unseelie wilds watched our backs.

We're here... Eventide whispered. We both couldn't believe it—the impossible manifestation of luck.

I wondered if we could give that fear gorta a medal for its service to the Sky Gods. Perhaps he'd rather have an endless supply of food. I snorted a laugh at the mental pictures and Eventide's cackles joined my mirth.

Make him a court advisor, she added, and I nearly erupted into laughter as Belenus helped me off Lion. Oh, great Sky Gods, dealing with this realm was making us lose our minds.

I removed my bag from my shoulders and pulled out the map. There had to be something to orient us, and I twisted my lips in thought. Landmarks? Tracks maybe? If the fae knew about this door, then it should be heavily trafficked, right? Well, maybe not heavily.

"I'll leave you here," Lion said, frowning westward. "I'm worried about the ranch. That nuckelavee could have destroyed, sickened, and wilted everything by now."

"Go," Belenus encouraged with a grim look on his face. "I'm sorry if we drew it there, though I'm not sure how."

Lion nodded, crouched, and transformed midleap into the giant… seabird thing. I watched her depart with a guilty heart, hoping we hadn't been the cause of luring the nuckelavee.

Belenus heaved a sigh and glanced around him. "I feel the door nearby," he said and beckoned me with several fingers toward him. Perking up, I grabbed his offered hand and followed his prowl. I sniffed the air, wondering if maybe the door gave away any scents to its whereabouts, though, I doubted it.

Belenus finally froze and reached out with his other hand. "It's here," he announced, nodding as his eyes searched the ground.

I sniffed once more, positioned myself next to him, and frowned. "I don't scent anything. You were the only one who could find it," I said, feeling a little disappointed. I paused then, wondering if perhaps Belenus had been destined to come with me as well. That was…

He sighed, "I figured. I just feel its magic. Are you ready to go through, Hekla?" He turned to look back at me with the smallest amount of worry in his amber eyes.

He's tired, Eventide noted. *Escort says Belenus is worried he won't be able to protect us as well as he could.*

I gave my mate a little smile while I chatted with my wolf. *Tell Escort that he needs to be Belenus's support right now. He'll need him more than ever.*

On it…

"I'm ready, my mate," I said and lengthened my canines to give him a feral grin. I would protect the both of us.

His gaze softened, and he leaned over to press his lips to mine in a gentle, loving kiss. I wrapped my arms around his neck and returned his sweet gesture. His hands found my waist, and his fingers dug in. Soft lips massaged mine for several minutes, then released so Belenus could lean his forehead against my own.

We stood in comfortable silence for a minute before he asked, "If anything goes wrong, Hekla, you need to leave me behind, ok?"

"No," I said calmly. "If anything goes wrong, I will make it go right."

He laughed weakly and tilted his face to press our noses together. "I have no doubt you would. There's no arguing this one, is there?"

"Nope."

"Alright... let's go find the Sky Gods' children," he said without letting me go.

In a heartbeat, we appeared on the other side of the threshold, standing under starlight and shade. Indeed, though I could look behind us and spy the daylit unseelie court, the night here took none of its illumination.

Drawing a steadying breath, I stepped ahead of Belenus, and we marched onward with held hands. I decided to continue following the Eventide star until I found any signs of the ones the Sky Gods wanted us to bring home. At least, I followed it when I could find it through the trees.

The nature here was lusher, but I had no idea how the plants and short trees grew without a sun to nourish them. The starlight itself couldn't possibly be enough. I did notice that their roots spread farther, as if the soil gave them all their sustenance. Vines fought them for space, and the underbrush spread as aggressively. Strange ferns glowed from beneath their fronds, their sori creating a dim mint glow. Rodents darted from us, and the briefest glimpse showed a dusting of glowing spore clinging to their fur.

They'd better beware of predators noticing that… Or perhaps it tasted bad. I had so many questions.

We discovered a trail that meandered deeper into the woods, and my eyes had to readjust upon encountering small fruit and plants that glowed a touch brighter. Small gourds, radiating a creamy orange light, hung loosely from trees, making me wonder if they were edible. I certainly wasn't going to risk it, but I continued to be curious.

I slashed away the obnoxious vines blocking our path to save Belenus some trouble. I didn't want him swinging his sword about unnecessarily. Eventide giggled, which made me snort with amusement.

Speaking of mates. Escort isn't sure he can come out if Belenus's magic is so low. He still has to use some to shape-shift, Eventide informed me, sobering. *I think that kind of verifies that they use magic to mind-link too... so that mystery is solved. Maybe.*

Ok, good to know. We will protect them, I said firmly.

We will! Any finger that touches Belenus is a dead finger!

I paused when I scented approaching strangers. "Belenus, I smell people," I whispered and put a hand behind me to make him stop. I elongated my canines again and used all my senses to try to figure out how they'd approach. "They're circling." I lowered my voice more and moved closer to Belenus. Which body was closest? They were so quiet!

I decided I didn't want them making the first move. "Reveal yourselves!" I shouted. "I've come to help the children of the Sky Gods! You'd be smart not to bite the hand that feeds!"

A brunet male with skin almost as white as bleached bone jumped down from a tree twenty feet ahead and was followed by nine other individuals. The figure replied quietly, "What if we were born to bite those hands?" He didn't move an inch. His dark red eyes held a combined gleam of wariness and curiosity.

"The first thing I'll teach you is that wolf-shifters care not for indirectness. My name is Hekla Himinn, and I've been sent by the Sky Gods to bring Their children home," I announced.

"The male behind me is my mate. To harm him is to die, just so we're clear."

The male simply looked to his right, at a cluster of his comrades, and nodded. "Bind them and bring them back."

I growled loudly and yelled, "Do not do this! You're making a mistake! I don't want to hurt anyone!"

The male simply stared at me while his people converged on us.

"Stop!" I growled louder, feeling my rib cage vibrate from the force. Their defiance infuriated me. How dare they try to ignore the will of their very own gods? These had to be Their children!

Tell them! Eventide snapped.

"Stop!" I snarled, backing up with Belenus who'd just drawn his sword. My nostrils flared, and my claws and canines extended as far as they'd go. The rumbling in my chest grew louder, as though my body told me we were capable of so much more.

SHOW THEM WHO WE ARE!

Feeling a swell of conviction that couldn't have been from my feral mind, I howled, stamped a foot down, and leaned toward the stalking attackers. "HOW DARE YOU IGNORE THE VESSEL OF THE SKY GODS! SUBMIT! SUMBIT! SUBMIT!" Certainty, power, and sovereignty rolled within my lungs and throat.

To my disbelief, they fell like omegas to the ground, pressing their faces into the dirt and shuddering. Some were crying, and others groaned from pain or frustration. I stared while I tried to catch my breath, fighting shock to regain my wits. The muscles on my face pulled into a surprised scowl when I realized what I'd just done.

That was an alpha command. I'd just commanded complete strangers into submission. Was this the Moon Goddess's blessing? Had it finally shown itself? Eventide was in such a daze that she didn't seem capable of speaking. I felt an urge to take a frightened step back but held firm, not wanting to show any weakness to these people. I looked ahead to find their representative submitting as well. They had all fallen to the authority of an alpha's voice.

"Shit," Belenus whispered from behind in a hoarse voice. I didn't want to take a step back, but I wanted Belenus. I floundered blindly for his hand, and he took it immediately, squeezing it tightly to show his support.

I took a deep breath and pointed my finger. "You, the one who spoke for these people. What is your name?"

The submitting male, hidden behind dark locks, answered, "Nofre Alcon."

"Are there more of you in this court?" I asked, trying to be calm and not come across as too interrogative. If I was in power here, there was no need to scare or abuse.

"Yes."

"How many?"

"Four hundred and twenty-four." He sounded more beaten down upon every answer.

"And there are no other kinds of people here? That must make you the ones the Sky Gods sent me to collect?"

"We are the only ones," he answered truthfully… but tiredly. He stopped fighting my commands and seemed to just give up, body and soul, kneeling with his face in his arms.

I looked around and tried to steady myself for my next command. Inside of both Eventide and me was something like a gift that had opened, releasing an alpha-like power that settled in my chest with the unwavering permanence of a star in the sky. Once I'd found it… once Eventide and I had found it, it was so easy to wield.

Congratulations, Alpha Eventide, I whispered to her, feeling like I was in a dream. In her shock, she continued her silence. Just like wolf males, female alphas were born, not made.

"Please return to your feet," I said, stepping back to give everyone more space. The children of the Sky Gods stood, and the mood had completely changed. Everyone had a different expression on their face; some looked worried while others appeared excited or even furious. "Take me to the rest of your people. I have a message from your gods that must be announced,"

I requested, only using the smallest amount of command in my voice. Belenus's safety was still my priority.

I followed Nofre and his comrades through the woods to a village that glowed in the dark. Stopping in awe for a moment, I soaked in how they used nature for their light sources. I could tell that these people have been in the same spot for a very, very long time. The homes had been rebuilt time and time again, renovated with materials old and new, and made from all the resources the forest had to offer. Many of the plants I'd seen glowing in the forest were planted here to light up the area. For higher trafficked areas, torches were used to brighten and heat up the space. They didn't seem as advanced as the other fae courts, but I had to assume their isolation had made growth a little bit of a challenge.

I was also concerned to see that every single face, though a bit fair like the fae, was hungry. Looking at thin limbs and gaunt faces, I realized these people were starving. No offspring were to be found either. I was starting to collect a lot of questions.

Nofre led us to a large tent and ducked in first, expecting us to follow. I entered cautiously, flexing my claws and hoping we'd be met with peacefully. A large, round table took up most of the space, but no one was in the tent.

"I will return with our..." Nofre began, then frowned. It was like he didn't have a word for what he wanted to say. "I... will return with our more important... people..." He sighed and left.

Belenus adopted a thoughtful expression as he meandered around the room. "They don't have a name for their representatives. They must have zero outside interaction. This must be the most tight-knit community I've ever seen. Isolated."

"And the hungriest..." I added worriedly. "They don't look so good, Belenus. Will they be able to travel?"

"Let's get all the facts first, my female," he said softly, wrapping an arm around me. I leaned my head on his arm while we waited and went through everything I wanted to say. Nofre returned with six other individuals who bowed to Belenus and me.

We returned the greeting, and I added, "Starlight preserve you," before joining them at the table.

Nofre then introduced us to the six individuals, and I knew I'd have a hard time remembering the names, just like the fae delicacies. Nofre, Ferrer, Luzia… Ah, I couldn't keep up.

It was my turn to make introductions. "It is good to see you've taken the time to meet with me. My name is Hekla Himinn, and I'm the vessel of the Sky Gods. This male with me is the crown prince of the fae's Summer Court, Prince Belenus."

There was a great deal of murmuring at the table, and a fae of indeterminable age brushed his dusty brown hair from his black eyes and said, "Prove it."

Sounds of both disapproval and approval erupted at the table, and Nofre sighed. "I told you what I saw, Ettor. Why are you risking her wrath?" he chided, blinking slowly from his lethargy.

I licked my lips and said, "As a wolf-shifter, I speak plainly, Ettor. I really don't want to humiliate you in front of your peers."

Ettor looked uncertain, but he set his jaw and stared at me. I took that as a challenge and said, "SUBMIT, ETTOR." I didn't put a lot of strength into it, just enough to show him that I could overpower him at any moment. Ettor leaned forward and, as ordered, unwillingly showed the back of his neck in submission. "I've been blessed by the Moon Goddess. I am an alpha. I hope this is sufficient evidence?" I asked, looking around the table while releasing Ettor from his humiliation. I had not enjoyed that, but apparently it was necessary.

There were nods at the table, and I moved on to the only item on my agenda. "My reason for coming is very simple. As I am the vessel of the Sky Gods, They have spoken to me and tasked me with returning you back to your original realm. I am here to offer my services as your escort back to where your people originated, the Realm of the Humans. I have connections with royalty over there who I'd work with to aid you in your rehabilitation and relocation. Since it seems like you have a potential famine here, I'm sure we can provide you with food until you're self-reliant."

The table burst into laughter at my last sentence, and I waited until the chuckling died down before another person spoke. It was a female of… indeterminable age as well. Actually, I couldn't tell how old any of them were. It didn't help with how sickly they appeared.

"You can provide fresh blood for over four hundred of us?" she asked bitterly, pressing her lips into a thin, grim line.

"Interesting," Belenus said from next to me. "Hematophagy. What kind of blood are we talking about? Cattle?"

The table fell quiet at his question, and no one would make eye contact with us. "People?" I hazarded from their reaction. I must have guessed right because the mood at the table plummeted.

"We would… accept cattle," the female said darkly. "It is not as nourishing, but… I can't imagine us being welcome if we started feeding on our neighbors. There are little of us left as is. Prey animals hardly cross into this court these days." She looked away. "We're starving to death. The strongest of us have been donating their own blood to keep the dying alive."

Belenus set his elbows on the table and scrubbed his hands over his face several times. He left a hand on his chin in contemplation. "I have several ideas, but let me think on it before we discuss them," he finally said.

I was incredibly surprised with how open-minded Belenus was being with these cannibals. No, perhaps cannibals wasn't the right word. They certainly didn't act proud of their nature. If anything, they seemed ashamed of it. That was something I didn't quite understand.

"I don't know why we're even continuing this conversation. We can't leave the Night Court anyway," another female said.

"Why's that?" I asked.

"Only the pure fae can come and go. We've been trapped here," she replied, scratching the back of her head. "Trapped here forever…"

Right… I looked at Belenus for the answer to this one, and he wasn't deterred in the least. He said, "I can take people with me. It'd take a while, but once we get a good group on the other side, you can use the time to hunt and feed yourselves. Get some of your strength back for the journey home."

The people at the table began to look at each other, seeming to take our idea seriously. "We're dying here," one of them said adamantly. "We could return to where we were born, where there's food. We could have fated mates again."

"Again?" I asked curiously, tilting my head as I regarded him.

He raised his hands. "We're almost all related now," he explained. "We stopped getting fated mates long, long ago. We're only still alive because of our long lifespan. We don't mate anymore. We have no pups here."

These people were on the verge of extinction. These people… what were they, though? I pressed for an answer. "I'm a wolf-shifter, and my mate is fae. You are not human, I am assuming. Are you shifters?"

Nofre picked at one of his nails and heaved a deep sigh. "We are. I suppose I should summarize our history, but it's not simple," he said. Belenus and I leaned forward a little, giving him our full attention. "Our history was passed down through stories, so we have nothing written from that time. We've been told that our gods birthed us as sky-shifters. We came in all different kinds of forms, all capable of flight to celebrate the sky as our gods desired. Birds, hardy insects, and other odd things.

"Some time later, the gods became displeased with some people in this realm. These people, so-called witches of rot, migrated over and were trying to corrupt the unseelie into their way of life, or use them to take over more fae territory because the magic was stronger here. That part of our history is a little unclear. What we do know is that the witches were sent back to their original realm—our original realm—by the Sky Gods, who'd volunteered for the task. Needless to say, the witches were outraged at being banished from the fae's realm.

He heaved a sigh and continued, "All they could do was get revenge, so they hunted down the Sky God's first children, cursed us, and performed something called a counter spell to whatever method the Sky Gods used to banish them. That spell locked us in the Night Court, where they'd been living before their banishment. They took away our original… shifter forms and replaced them with another creature that gave us bloodthirst in hopes we'd drink each other into extinction. The curse was a slow, cruel torture for our people. I… suppose you'd call us bat-shifters now.

"Over time, we began to run out of food and couldn't reach out for help. We'd done the best we could to not give in to our instincts and tried to survive on wildlife, but it wasn't nourishing enough. We couldn't follow the game that migrated from the court, and some of us fell to the cravings, preying upon their own people to survive. Our numbers dwindled from hundreds of thousands to… this…" Nofre gestured around him grimly. The other shifters at the table didn't look mentally present. Instead, something haunted their faces—memories. It had them all.

I didn't think I'd ever heard a more depressing story. That was all I could think about for a moment, but I couldn't utter the words. They didn't need to feel any weaker or more pathetic than they already did. It infuriated me too. These people had never received justice. They'd been caught in the middle of an impossible conflict. My heart clenched with hot pain.

A thought occurred to me, and I turned to Belenus. "I recall that the witches had blocked the Earth Gods' ability to communicate during Eisteinn's attempts to take Ragna. I suspect that's why the Sky Gods have not been able to see Their children this entire time." I turned to the bat-shifters at the table and said, "Your parents, the Sky Gods, haven't been able to see you. They didn't even know if you were still alive, which was why I was sent."

"I suppose that explains these then," a male with white streaks in his brown hair said, sliding a rock the size of my fist across the table to me. "We've been receiving these over the last month. We've collected a dozen of them after they fell from the sky."

I picked up the rock and brushed my fingers over the pockmarks that reminded me of Ragna's lunaite. I turned it over in my hands and found an inlaid silhouette of a black wolf. My pulse jumped upon a realization; the Sky Gods had sent a message down in hopes Their children would be prepared for my arrival.

"This is Eventide," I said softly, tracing the shape. "She's my wolf. As black as this image." Rather than waiting to be challenged, I removed my clothes and shifted into Eventide before their eyes. She jumped into my seat and glanced around the table. She felt an urge to scratch behind her ear but tried to keep her stoic pose, suffering greatly for it. I found that mildly amusing and supposed it was a good call to keep up appearances.

They stared and slowly woke from their hopeless demeanors. "I vote we leave," Nofre said after taking in Eventide's presence. "We're starving here. At this rate, we will go extinct. Our people deserve a chance to go home. They deserve a chance to thrive."

The table murmured an agreement, and Belenus said, "Take your time deliberating. Talk to your people, and if this is what you want, we can leave. Is tomorrow morning enough time to get things in order here? You obviously need to eat, so we have to get you into the Unseelie Court to find game before we start traveling. It won't be safe; you'll need to help protect each other. We two can only do so much."

"I think that's acceptable," Nofre responded, and the rest of the table made their agreements known. Ettor was still sullen, but I had to assume he was just as hungry as everyone else. Starvation did nothing for the mood.

I shifted back and clothed myself to address the group. "Do you have a place we could rest until then?" I asked. One of the females nodded and gestured for us to follow. Before leaving the tent, I turned one last time and said, "Please don't be afraid to come to me for more questions. Your survival is paramount." They didn't seem to know that word, so I hastily added, "Critical. Your survival is very important. We are like kin." I tapped my fist on my chest and left the tent with Belenus's supportive hand in mine.

Chapter 22

Hekla

We followed the bat-shifter to a guest room in a small house. Opening a door, she said, "We used this for the occasional fae who'd wander into our territory. They'd be able to stay here as a place to rest safely so no one could prey upon them in their sleep. We kept it in decent condition out of nostalgia and… in hopes we'd have more visitors someday who could help us." She looked sadly around the room, and I had to wonder if she'd ever seen it used in her lifetime. I didn't have the heart to ask.

"Soon you'll see all sorts of people," I said softly, moving to put a hand on her arm. She wrinkled her nose and stepped away from me.

"Please… don't come any closer. You and your mate smell… well, you are tempting to put it mildly, and I am hungry. I will leave now." She wandered out then, looking lost in a haze.

I closed the door and finally allowed myself to cry. Seeing so many innocents suffering tortured me. I needed them out of here as soon as possible. Belenus led me to the bed, tucked us in, and let me vent my despair and anger for these people.

"It's hard to accept what's happened to them," he said quietly and squeezed me. His thumb found my wet cheeks to wipe away the tears. "Just remember you're saving them. Take solace in the reality that you got here in time. I'm so… honored to be your mate. I don't deserve you, but I'm grateful for it."

"Don't talk like that," I whispered hoarsely. He nodded, sighed, and buried his face in my hair. Worried about him as well, I asked, "How are you feeling?"

"Drained… I'm barely making progress. Tomorrow will be a struggle to move everyone."

"Does my mate touch really not do anything?" I reached up to palm his cheek, stroking his scruff with a thumb. He leaned into it and didn't respond immediately.

"Now that I can pay attention, I think it does. I know it speeds up healing, but maybe it helps me absorb magic faster? Hard to say…" he murmured and placed a large gold-dusted hand over mine, holding my palm in place. "Feels amazing either way."

I sat up, loosened my dress, and slipped it over my head. Belenus swallowed heavily when I removed my undergarments and placed them in a neat pile by the bed. Then, I crawled up next to him and ordered, "Lean up." He allowed me to slip his tunic over his head and untie his pants.

"What… are you doing?" he asked curiously but sluggishly.

"Giving you as much of the mate touch as I can," I said, slipping off his pants and undergarment to be greeted by his swelling erection. *Oh hi.* I hadn't expected seeing that considering how tired he was.

"I-ignore that. That just happens often around you," he admitted, smirking weakly in good humor. I beamed from such a pleasing compliment and lay down on top of him, straddling his hips and nuzzling into his hard chest. The mate touch tingled everywhere we met, and I basked in it, holding back a sigh of pleasure. It also worked to distract my grief.

"How's this?" I asked him. "Better?"

"Yes and no," he replied, chuckling lightly. I felt that his cock had swollen against a butt cheek, throbbing and wet with precum. I didn't have to ask what he meant by 'no.'

I traced a finger along his chest, dipping it into the tight creases between his muscles. The room was lit by several potted plants, casting an orange glow that made his skin look all the more golden. "You're beautiful, Belenus," I murmured, staring at his fascinating skin. "Did you know that?"

"Yes," was his simple reply, a grin in his voice. He definitely knew he was attractive. I restrained a derisive snort and continued to caress him, enjoying the little sparks and tingles.

The fae were a radiant people, and even the oddest of the folk fae had their otherworldly charm. This realm had truly shattered my expectations. Nothing, truly, could have prepared me for moving here.

Belenus broke through my quiet thoughts, softly adding, "But not as dazzling as you, my dear. Like I told you before, you're the most beautiful female in history."

"You're sweet…"

"Not as sweet as what's between your legs."

I glanced up at him, and though his eyes were closed, one corner of his lip was curled into the tiniest smile. Was he delirious? He wrapped his arms around me and sighed in contentment. "I always feel like I can't get close enough to you," he said while flexing his arms. "Perhaps that's the instinct to mark."

"Perhaps," I echoed thoughtfully, wishing we could mark each other without the threat of death looming over our heads. "I can't wait to do it," I said.

He hummed in agreement, slid a hand down to cup my bottom, and patted it. "Can't wait to make this mine for all eternity," he mumbled.

I failed to hold back a chuckle. He was so bold when he was tired. It was also, unfortunately, arousing me quite a bit, and I prayed to the Moon Goddess that I wouldn't drip on him. This position may have been a mistake.

Or maybe it was just what Belenus needed. Curious to see if it'd make a difference, I lifted my hips, aligned his prodding length with my core, and sat down on his lap, squeezing him into my channel with one smooth move.

Belenus's breath caught, and he peered up at me through one eye. Without saying anything, I lay down on him and kept him firmly nestled inside me. I held back a satisfied moan, wanting to focus completely on him. "Does this help more?" I asked and delivered a soft kiss to one of his pecs.

"If I said yes, can you do this every time I use magic?" he asked weakly, and I laughed silently into his chest. Oh, how I loved this male.

I froze, shocked by my own thought, and tried to recover quickly lest he thought there was something wrong. My face heated, and my heart pounded beneath my breasts, but I just nuzzled into his chest, trying to come back to the moment.

I decided not to leave my male unattended, so I sat up on his lap and lifted my hips, experimenting with this position. Belenus heaved a deep sigh and swallowed hard again. He rested his hands under his head to prop it up and watched my movements. I caressed his carved abdomen with my fingertips, admiring his physique, as I settled back down onto his lap and buried him down to the hilt. His stomach clenched from either the touch of my hands or how I stroked him with my sex.

"What do you feel?" I asked quietly, raising myself so that his tip was barely gripped by my threshold. I had to push myself up pretty high to do that as my mate was quite long, but I loved its shape, the rounded tip that massaged me so well. I sank back down to his lap, reveling in the wholeness I felt when his girth stretched my channel.

Belenus licked his lips and said, "I feel like I'm drawing something from you, but I don't know if it's energy or…" He trailed off, staring at me while I slid up and down his length. "That is such a sight…"

"I wonder if it's because the alpha in me is awake now." I moved my hands to stroke his waist, loving to touch my Belenus. "Alphas give more energy. You mentioned not noticing anything on the flight here."

"Right..." he said in a strained voice. His fingers twitched, and he closed his eyes.

"Are you alright?"

"Y-yes, you just feel very, very, very good."

I leaned forward and pressed my lips to his, taking shallower strokes to do so. He groaned into my mouth and thrust his tongue inside. I shuddered like a wolf shaking off water and moaned in response, feeling heat wash down my body. Lemons and summer rain filled my veins as the heat settled into my core, slicking a cock that continued to harden within me. He stretched me almost uncomfortably wide, but the extra lubrication helped, and I was given some relief. Gods, I loved our perfect fit.

Belenus buried his fingers in my hair, massaging the back of my head while he explored my mouth. His smooth tongue slid across mine, continuing to show how he couldn't get close enough to me. Every lick twisted sensually and stirred my ardor. Out of absolutely nowhere, though, he released my lips, tilted his head back, and cried out as he began bucking his hips, burying his cock into me with quick thrusts.

"B-Belenus!" I gasped in shock and braced myself against his sudden attack. "I-if you w-wanted it th-this h-hard, l-let me d-do it!" His pounding was making it hard to talk. "You're d-drained!"

He merely grunted and shook his head, not breaking stride with his thrusts. "Oh gods," I whimpered, white-knuckling the sheets to keep me in place while his hips slapped wetly against my bottom. What happened? What had come over him? Him storming my sex excited me by the heartbeat, and I thanked my core—from the bottom of my heart—for keeping me lubricated.

"Uh!" Belenus moaned and slapped both hands down on my bottom to cup my cheeks while he ravaged me. I dug my claws into the bed and buried my face in Belenus's neck, unable to do anything but take what he gave. Each fervid pump into my depths sent a surge of arousal through me, and it wasn't long before I was panting and whining from the sheer thrill of his taking. The alpha in me took a step aside, allowing me to enjoy my male taking over for now, though I had no idea how he'd gotten so energized.

"Be—le—nus!" I cried, biting his shoulder to muffle my screams. There were no windows in here, and the room was locked, but I was still self-conscious of enjoying myself while everyone outside was suffering.

Saying Belenus's name only seemed to spur him on, and his wildness was bringing out my wolf. His fingers massaged my bottom, then gripped tight and yanked my hips down to meet his ravenous thrusts. I screamed into his flesh, sinking my canines in to stay secure, and I had just enough of my mind left to avoid the marking spot.

"Gods, yes!" he cried after grunting. "Bite me, filthy she-wolf!"

I growled into my male's shoulder, warning him not to provoke me any further lest I lose all control. Nothing could stop my eagerness, though, and my channel clenched fiercely around him. He gasped and gave a guttural cry of pleasure, breaking his rhythm for just a second. He resumed with a fierce intensity, bucking with abandon and slamming as hard as he could. I placed my hands out farther with my claws, trying to keep myself from being pushed over Belenus's head.

Belenus released my hips, removed my jaws from his shoulder, and pulled me up a little so he could wrap his sucking lips around one of my jostling nipples. I gasped and shouted through clenched teeth, feeling bursts of pleasure shoot from where his mouth suckled to deep within my breast. I had to hold on to his shoulders now as he made me arch into him, still wildly pumping his hips.

Between the new sensation of his lips pulling on my breast and his vigorous charging into my channel, I felt a lightning storm brew in my heated core. I whimpered, whined, and pawed at my male, desperate for him to finish and make me his. This she-wolf had waited too long, far too long for him to make a move. Didn't my mate want me?

"Oh blisterin' sun, the wild sounds my female makes!" my male snarled, releasing my breasts to thrust my hips into his brutal strokes once more. I tilted my head—still whining—and lapped at his ear, licking up to the tip to soak it in my saliva.

"Shit! Fuck!" he roared and slammed my hips down hard to bottom out inside me. He arched his back as he came, gritting his pleasure out through his teeth as he spurted against my back wall. The fae grabbed my head, tilted it to the side, and sank his teeth into my marking spot.

I froze and screamed soundlessly, too wrought with euphoria to release any noise. I was struck by summer lightning from within, and the rays of sunlight that were bursting in through my shoulder violently pushed out my orgasm. My eyes shut tight, and I leaned into his iron grip, convulsing with the gifts he'd just given me. My channel clenched to keep my mate in there as he spent his seed, which made him moan deliriously into my shoulder.

When he pulled his teeth from me, I gripped his shoulder and dug my canines into his marking spot, finally claiming this strong, virile, male fae as my own. I let my mark sink deep past flesh and bone. I pushed it so far in that it touched his soul. It branded itself there, as permanent as any constellation in the sky. My unbreakable tether was there to protect and support him for the rest of our days. We were always meant to rule together.

The male screamed through his teeth, his call vibrating into me, and came a last time, his jerking nearly bucking me off. Fae fingers—large, rough, hot—dug into my back with bruising pressure, but I kept my canines buried deep as he unloaded against my cervix. My walls massaged him with the longest orgasm I'd ever had, hoping to herd his seed deeper to make a golden pup. My womb wanted it all. It wanted to make him an heir.

An heir?

For who? For a king? No, that wasn't right… A prince? Prince. Prince Belenus. Belenus!

Clawing out of my feral mind, I released my canines from Belenus's shoulders and put a hand to my bloody mouth, gaping at the permanent mark I'd given him.

It came out choked. "What have we done?"

Belenus

I stared blankly at Hekla, who stared blankly at her bloody hand, a hand covered in both our blood. I sat up, still breathless, and brushed her hair away from her neck. I paled at the mark I'd left on her during our wild mating frenzy.

"What have we done?" she repeated, shaking her head in disbelief.

"I don't know what came over me, Hekla," I confessed in a thick voice. "I just… felt something take over. I've never experienced anything like that before."

"What did it feel like?" she asked, her expression still locked, stunned, as she traced the mark she'd left on my neck. I could feel her shock through our new bond, and it only compounded my distress.

"It felt savage, like I was a beast that needed to claim you. It's like you didn't even have a name anymore. You were just… my female. Everything else was forgotten," I answered, tracing a thumb over the bite mark that was already scabbing on her neck. She healed so fast… but I could still feel my magic there, permanently nestled inside her. If it was any other time, I'd be aroused by it. It was as erotic as the thought of impregnating her.

"That sounds an awful lot like your wolf's instinct. That's what I felt when I marked you. That's actually what I feel when I'm the most aroused. The wolf takes over my mind," she said, tapping her head and looking away from me. "I must have provoked him too much. Perhaps he didn't like an alpha on top of him and needed to assert his dominance… Oh gods, this could be all my fault!" She covered her face with her hands.

"No… no, no. Stop that, mate," I ordered, pulling her hands away from her pretty face. "I marked you first. I'm the one who lost control, and now we both will have to accept the truth and repercussions." I'd broken the marriage contract. I'd no longer have extra time in public if we got home before the two-week deadline. I'd have to do everything from the shadows and stay far away from the queen and that document. It would lure me in to sign my failure. Then…

"I'm still sorry." She didn't seem comforted in the least.

"I'm not. I liked you on top," I said with a weary chuckle, trying to make her smile a little. When she didn't, I decided to use her own words against her. "When we get back, if anything goes wrong, I will make it go right, ok? We will survive this. I don't care what I have to do. They won't win. They won't destroy our long life of love together." I tipped her chin up to meet my gaze. "Is that understood, my mate?"

She nodded and sighed. I sensed her anxiety and fear of loss. "It's just… as soon as we get back, if they see you, they'll know the contract was broken. They could execute you on the spot."

"I'll make sure nothing bad happens. I promise," I said and lifted her off me to tuck her in at my side. "I'll fight with everything in me."

She leaned her forehead into mine, and we embraced under the sheets. "I guess it doesn't matter how long it takes for us to get back now," she said with a sigh.

"That's… a very good point. I still need to get back to my soldiers for the takeover, but yes… you made a good observation." I blew out a breath, somewhat relieved. A weight lifted, a small one, but now it felt easier to focus on the takeover. My mind… cleared.

Hekla closed her eyes and sleepily said, "All things aside… I don't regret marking you, Belenus. You'll always be the one."

I gave her a soft kiss on the lips and pulled her into my chest, taking this moment to treasure my fated mate. "I don't either, my female. It's you. It's only ever you."

We were woken in... the morning? How did one tell time in a place such as this? Hekla and I threw our clothes on and geared up for the road again. This time we'd be responsible for over four hundred hungry bat-shifters.

"We're going to draw a lot of attention if we're not careful," I warned Nofre, who appeared to have taken charge of the migration. "We'll have to stay clear of fae settlements and scouts. I doubt we'll be leaving the Unseelie Court without the unseelie on our tails."

Nofre's expression hardened. "We were held unjustly for too long, Prince Belenus. I guarantee you that my people won't fall easily once they get some food in their system. We will fight for our freedom."

Hekla then introduced her plan for feeding everyone. "I'll be taking small teams to hunt and bring back as much game as we can while Belenus works on transporting your people. You'll have to ration and share at first, but we'll keep hunting as we travel until everyone is in good shape and can assist in providing for themselves and others. I'd recommend bringing a mix of the strongest and weakest out first, so we can hunt and tend to the ones who are most at risk."

"A good idea," Nofre agreed. "I'll make sure we prioritize as recommended."

I asserted, "And get some reliable people to watch over the ones I send over. Let's keep people from wandering. I know it will be tempting for them to go off and hunt, but we can't risk getting separated and leaving someone behind. We need to stay organized."

Nofre nodded again, surveying the crowd that had gathered at the border. "Understood."

"Is this everyone?" I asked, feeling my heart tug at the sight of so many gaunt, starving faces.

"Yes, but we'll do a head count at the end. If anyone is missing, we'll come back and do a search, but this should be it. We've asked for individuals to partner up and make sure their partner isn't left behind."

"Good." I scrubbed a hand over my chin, checking the list off in my head. "Ok, well, I'll try to take ten people at a time, so this will be more than forty trips. You're going to have to bear with me."

"We're traveling with a bear?" Nofre asked, his eyes squinting in confusion.

"Never mind. Just be patient. It'll take a while," I said, waving a hand to dismiss the misunderstanding. It was a miracle we'd been able to communicate as well as we had so far. No doubt fae visitors must have helped modernize their language once in a while.

Nofre summoned ten individuals, and once I rolled up my sleeves, I instructed them to hang onto my arms. They eyed my veins hungrily, and I did my best to ignore it, but I'd be lying if I said it didn't make my skin crawl just a bit. I glanced over at Hekla, who seemed displeased to see females touching me, but I knew that reaction was the possessive wolf in her. I could feel both her jealousy and shame through our bond.

In the first batch, I dropped off the female who'd taken us to our guest room, Luzia, and the male with the white streaks in his hair, Ferrer. They were in charge of herding their people and keeping them together as I delivered them across the border.

When I dropped them off, the shifters covered their eyes, and the air was full of moans and hissing. Ferrer stumbled blindly over to me and braced himself on my shoulder. "Prince, it is too bright. It burns out here! This is the sun? It's so hot! How do you stand it?" he asked through gritted teeth. His heart panicked, his breaths quickened, and his body had gone rigid.

Sun God's fire! These people had evolved under starlight!

"Shit! I should have foreseen this! Follow me. Link hands everyone!" I shouted and gripped Ferrer by his wrist. We got a train of shifters going, and I guided them to the protection of the forest. It was shaded, and likely not enough to ease their distress, but it would have to do. Some had fallen behind and released strange clicks in their blind rush to catch up. I was about to ask but Ferrer interrupted my thoughts.

"Bloody clots," he swore, blinking rapidly and trying to get his eyes to adjust. "I don't know how we're going to hunt in these conditions. This sun our ancestors spoke of is more brutal than I had imagined." His reddish-brown eyes were so dark, I almost couldn't tell how dilated his pupils were. They weren't very small, and if that was his limit, these people would be better off traveling at nighttime. Their pale skin would burn easily too.

This complicated matters, but I believed it wasn't anything we couldn't work with. I placed a hand on his shoulder to comfort. "Get your people resting, Ferrer. I'll see what we can do about food when I'm done moving people out. Hekla can get a start on finding game. Hang in there."

"Hang in where? Oh, the trees? No, more shade at the bottom." He turned before I could ask what he meant.

After ten trips, I called for a break and went to go see how Luzia and Ferrer fared with their group of one hundred. I was pleased to see some of the more emaciated shifters sharing game that Hekla had caught. She wasn't around, so I had to assume that she was on another hunt. She had to be working hard, and I felt a surge of pride for my mate. When we returned, after we claimed the throne, I was going to spoil her beyond rotten. Mercilessly.

By noon, I'd finally finished moving everyone across the border. We agreed to let the bat-shifters rest so we could travel at night, and I shape-shifted into Escort to see if we could find something bigger for them to eat.

Long damn day. Going to be a long damn night too, Escort commented idly, sniffing the air as he loped west toward some plains we'd seen on the flight here.

It's just a short while. We might be able to squeeze in a nap if we bring back enough for the weakest to share, I replied, helping him keep an eye out for larger prey. Escort had been much less of a little shit since he'd mated with Eventide. Curiosity about Hekla's theory had me asking, *Tell me how you feel about having an alpha for a mate. Was that why we lost control?*

I'm too dominant to feel threatened by anyone. Escort snorted.

What an ego on this wolf, I thought to myself. *Escort is nothing like me.*

Ego? Excuse me, Mister I-know-I'm-beautiful, Escort retorted. Shit, he'd heard me.

So why'd we lose control? I asked, hastily returning to the previous subject.

Our beloved alpha revitalized us and triggered the fuck out of our feral lust, he answered. *Our instincts demanded we claim our mate immediately because she is a powerful female. If she keeps us strong, we can keep her safe. Our pups will be invincible.*

He seemed so cocksure. As much as I doubted the invincibility claim, I admired his conviction. I was about to ask another question when we caught the sound of thundering hooves. Fear invaded both Escort and me when we realized the nuckelavee had finally caught up to us. Had it just sped east at a dead run this entire time?

Hekla! Eventide! Escort screamed through our bond, hoping we were within range of her to send a warning. We were met with silence, and the terror became overwhelming, crawling and penetrating like brambles. What if it was tracking her instead of me? I'd clearly shown I had summer in my veins, so it'd probably avoid me.

Oh gods, run Escort! We have to find her! I shouted. My blond wolf bolted back the way we'd come. He ran faster than I thought any creature could, and I was once again grateful for being paired with a superior beast. I'd admit it at this point. Escort was a superior wolf.

The nuckelavee was finally visible over the southern tree line, its rider's skinless head bobbing like a corpse's. It moved parallel to my wolf, escalating this into a lethal race. Escort continued to scream for our mate over our bond, hoping she'd finally come within range of us.

Energy... Escort panted. *Belenus, give me some energy so I can go faster!*

I had no idea how in the shit to do that, but I fumbled around in my mind, trying to push what I could toward the wolf. After several panicky attempts, my efforts seem to have paid off, and Escort flew like a hurricane. He sure as shit was as mad as one.

Escort? What's wrong? Eventide's voice popped into our head. She'd finally heard us!

Are you out hunting? The nuckelavee is coming! Eventide you have to run! Escort shouted in desperation, terrified of losing her. His tone—he was as in love with Eventide as I was with Hekla, wasn't he?

No! Oh no! I have to drive it away from the shifters! Eventide replied.

No, you have to run! we both screamed at the same time. Our mate had gone silent, and we veered toward where we'd left the shifters. Was she there? Had she left already?

We came to a stop by Nofre, scattering dirt everywhere and startling the shit out of him. I shape-shifted back, looking frantically around for Hekla while grabbing his arm.

"What's going on?" he asked, alarmed.

"A nuckelavee is coming! It'll be nearby any second! I have to find Hekla! It might be hunting her! Which way did she go?" I asked him, hoping to every single god that he'd seen her leave.

"How big is this knuckle lovey?" he asked, tilting his head and narrowing his eyes. Curiosity flickered in his sharp red gaze.

"Monstrous. Bigger than a barn. I don't have time for th—"

Nofre interrupted me by turning to his people, cupping his hands around his mouth and shouting, "Everyone up! Lunch is here!"

Chapter 23

Belenus

I gawked as the majority of the bat-shifters jumped to their feet in the blink of an eye. Their eyes became as sharp as Nofre's, and it seemed that they all had just enough adrenaline left in their system to make one last fight for food. Not only would they have to take down the colossal, violent nuckelavee, they'd have to face the disabling embrace of the sun. Perhaps once it was taken down, it could be dragged to a tree line if it didn't end up falling in the woods.

Nofre and Ferrer took the lead while Luzia stayed behind to watch over the ones too weak to hunt; I was happy to see that being only twelve shifters. I'd gladly help carry them to the carcass once the nuckelavee's thrashes stilled.

Eventide! Hekla! Guide the nuckelavee toward the shifters! Trust me on this one, Escort shouted over the bond.

What? Eventide replied. *They'll be slaughtered!*

Mate, do you trust me? I asked firmly.

... *Yes,* she said.

What's your plan? Hekla asked, her voice thick with worry.

The bat-shifters are hungry. I have about four hundred waiting to ambush it. Bring their food, mate, Escort directed. I grunted in agreement.

A-alright... Eventide replied, then we heard her shriek.

Mate! Escort cried. *Where are you?*

W-we're coming! Oh my Moon Goddess, it's faaast! Eventide sobbed frantically. *This thing is the scariest thing I've ever seen in my life! I may pee myself!* she shrieked.

I'd tried to save her the horror of seeing it when we were attacked for the first time, but unfortunately, Fate had other ideas, I supposed.

Don't look at it, just run! I urged.

We waited anxiously to scent our mate, but we heard the nuckelavee's approach before anything else. The cracking of trees and the thrashing of shrubbery made for a terrifying introduction.

"It's coming!" I yelled to Nofre and Ferrer as we ran south to meet it. They both shouted orders to their people and separated into groups. Eventide burst out of the brambles, screaming through the bond in terror, and shot past the shifters, unable to stop.

The nuckelavee became visible over the treetops and crashed through the trees, easily swiping away anything that dared slow it. It was so much worse close up like this. Not only did it look much larger than I recalled, a living tower, I could better see the workings of its skinless, gruesome form. Its slippery yellow veins were visible all throughout its body, wrapped around waxen sinew and quaking muscles. The rider's head continued to loll in all movements, like it was drunk or balancing upon a weak neck. The horse's head, having only one eye, seemed slightly more alert. The air rippled with its every exhale, and I recalled that those fumes were toxic. Seeing this creature once in my life was enough. Twice was almost more than I could handle.

The bat-shifters, however, had a completely different reaction. There were exclamations and murmurs of excitement among the four hundred. Not one of them seemed afraid at all. They did have the numbers... and the appetite.

"Shittin' stars! You don't have to search for veins!"

"It's a bleedin' buffet..."

"It's like it's begging to be sucked dry."

"No skin. I want to cut an artery and shove my face in it."

"That thing makes me aroused as h—Ahhh!"

The nuckelavee reared when it encountered the army of bat-shifters, but I couldn't tell if it was in surprise, fear, or anger. Perhaps the nuckelavee wasn't capable of feeling any emotion; it was just a heartless monster of death and sickness. When the colossus landed back down on all fours, quaking the earth beneath our feet, it swept down with its horrifically long arms to scoop up some shifters.

Unfortunately for the nuckelavee, such an action with these people was like scooping up swarming ants. The shifters shot out of its grip before the hands even started tightening and raced up its arms. Throngs of shifters ran ahead, closing the distance in a blink, and jumped onto the monstrosity. In less than several minutes, all the shifters we'd brought with us were latched onto the nuckelavee, feeding like ravenous ticks.

The nuckelavee tried to swipe off the hungry bat-shifters, but they simply jumped to a new spot when they risked getting crushed.

They are so bloody fast, Escort said in awe. *Look how high they can jump.*

I'm going to read up on bats when all the dust settles. I'm curious about the species now, I mused.

I had Escort run back to instruct Luzia to herd the remaining shifters over to the nuckelavee. It was only a matter of time now until it lost consciousness. I had no doubt there'd be more than enough food for everyone. I picked up the weakest shifter and walked back to where the feast was taking place. A thought occurred to me, and I had to wonder if it had been the fear gorta's influence that got this monster stalking us at all. I couldn't have imagined a better way to feed this many hematophages.

I took a deep, deep breath and sighed it all out, feeling relief roll more weight off my shoulders. With everything Hekla and I had been through, this shift in outcome had been desperately needed. There was nothing like the occasional win to keep one fighting as hard as possible.

When I returned to where everyone was feeding, I was pleased to see they'd now gotten the nuckelavee lying on its side. Its hooves kicked sporadically, and it swiped with its arms, but it was clearly dying. Bat-shifters completely covered it from heads to tail, and the air was thick with the sounds of four hundred individuals sucking, swallowing, and moaning. I settled the fragile shifter down in a safe spot—but close enough for them to hobble over once the nuckelavee was dead—and went back to grab the next person. Luzia and I worked for a little bit longer to carry people over, and I set about looking for my mate, who I hadn't seen since she'd run past me.

With Escort's help, I followed her scent a little farther north where Eventide hid with her face buried into the corner of a rock face. I squatted by her and petted her back gently, stroking her without saying a word and letting her know I was here for her. After about five minutes, she shifted back into Hekla, who crawled naked into my arms without a word. Slowly, knowing her inner wolf was very much at the surface and very spooked, I picked her up and brought her back. We couldn't leave the shifters alone for too long.

I kissed the top of her head and spoke softly, "You're so brave. You're the strongest female I've ever met, and I'm so proud of you. You just fed an entire endangered species today; did you know that? No one else could ever make that claim."

"I did, didn't I?" she replied faintly, staring blankly at the scenery. She blinked her long, dark eyelashes, fighting to come out of shock.

"Yes, you did. You should have heard what they were saying when they saw their lunch for the first time. They were practically drooling with excitement!" I shared with a grin. "You made a lot of people happy and healthy. Be proud of yourself, my sweet alpha." I stroked her hair from her face and grabbed her bag on the way to the shifters' current location.

"I'm going to have nightmares," she murmured when I set her down near the feeding shifters.

"No one who sees the nuckelavee doesn't get nightmares. I'll get them too, but we'll both be stronger for it." I squeezed her hand. "Face your fears and be stronger for it."

Shifters finished their meal and dropped lazily from the dead nuckelavee's body. Some went to help the weak feed, but the majority wandered off into the woods. Each shifter split off, none staying with a partner. I stood and was about to shout for everyone to stick together, but Nofre approached and waved to stay me.

He shook his head. "Let them go. They need to… do this."

"What is happening?" I asked, eyeing the woods. I was starting to hear some very telling noises.

Nofre sighed and looked toward the source of the sounds, frowning. "I don't know if this is something we should be embarrassed about or not," he said, scratching the back of his neck. "Once we feed, and our body recognizes we're healthy enough, we have a strong impulse to breed. Since we're all related, we must go off and… tend to ourselves individually. Ease the torture of not being able to mate. It's how we've evolved to try to make up for our dwindling population."

The fae at court would find it base, but nothing these people have endured was of their own making. "The instinct makes sense, Nofre," I said with a sigh. "You will have to rebuild your population. I would love to hear reports from your people on how they're faring once you've settled. I will pray for many fated mates to come your people's way."

"That is kind of you," he said shortly. "We will have to repay you for what you've done. In the meantime, though, I must go or I will ruin these pants. Please excuse me." He strode off into the woods to find a quiet place to… not ruin his pants. "Blood clots, I'd kill for an unrelated female right now," was the last thing I heard him mutter before he left my sight.

I clamped a hand over my mouth to hold in a rude laugh and walked back to my mate. I sat next to her, feeling a little awkward as the forest became full of moaning, grunting, and panting. Hekla, still naked, had all her claws out and was tapping them anxiously on her knees. I could feel her discomfort through our bond, but it was slowly turning into arousal. I couldn't say that the symphony of pleasure wasn't affecting me. I was already at half-mast.

I slid a hand under her arm to palm her breast, and she stiffened, her heart rate accelerating exponentially. I molded my hand around her curves and pushed up to enjoy the weight of her flesh in my palms. Her breast was so soft and so perky. I leaned my head on her shoulder and stared down at her full globes, running my thumb over a tight little nipple. She released a tiny whimper and pressed her thighs together.

Oh, thank the Sun God, Escort grunted in relief and disappeared to give us privacy.

"I remember when I couldn't wait to touch these," I murmured into her ear. "Fondle them, lick them, suck them." I pinched her nipple lightly between my thumb and forefinger. "I especially can't wait to play with them when they're full of milk for our young."

"Belenus…" she whispered helplessly, leaning her cheek against my head while I stared at her breasts.

"You're so beautiful," I whispered back to her and slid my hand to grab as much of her breast as I could, squeezing gently to watch her brown flesh swell between my fingers. I lifted her in my arms and cradled her high enough to take as much of a breast as I could into my wide-open mouth.

A shudder raked through her, and I felt her desire ignite. "B-Belenus… they could come back any m- Ahhh… any m-moment," she moaned quietly, digging her claws into my back and shoulder.

I slid my lips off her breast and said, "They've all fallen asleep. You know what happens after a big meal and masturbation. They'll be out for a long while..."

I laid my mate down on the grass and nearly ripped my clothes off so I could get to her as quickly as possible. I stopped, though, when I got a good look at my fated mate and studied her for a moment while she peered up at me. Her shiny dark hair had fanned around her head, making her look like a forest nymph.

The most beautiful nymph these woods have ever seen, to be sure.

I loved that my mate was a wolf. She brought something out of me that I never knew I needed, at least not until Zorian had lectured me. Her fair forthrightness had planted a seed in me, and I believed it had been the catalyst to me finally maturing, though I was much older than her. She kept my eyes honest too. It was refreshing to see the world as she did. The fae at court lived through such a judgmental filter, and Hekla was a fresh wind that blew away all that stale air.

Her face was expressionless as her midnight eyes stared at me, but I could feel her arousal and affection through the bond. I felt something else too, and my heart nearly stopped once I realized what it was. It couldn't be... but it was.

I felt love from her.

Hekla loved me.

I sucked my lips between my teeth and swallowed heavily, trying to keep tears from my eyes and words off my tongue. She'd tell me when she was ready. I had to be patient and remember the torture she'd undergone at the palace. I must continue to prove myself trustworthy.

The sensation of feeling her love toward me was overwhelming, though, and I fell to my knees between her legs. I leaned over her, looked her square in the eyes, and said, "I may worship many gods, but you, Hekla, are my true goddess, and I love you more than I could ever begin to describe." I needed her to know that whether she told me or not, my love for her was indestructible.

It didn't rely on anything but how I perceived her. I pressed my lips to hers, wrapped my arms around her back and neck, and brought her up to my chest, unable to get close enough to her.

She whimpered against my mouth, and I groaned a lustful reply, slipping my tongue between her full lips to dive into her mouth. The feral sounds she made possessed me. They unleashed the wolf inside of me, the part of Escort's instincts that was always around, whether he was asleep or awake.

My heart thrummed in its cage, awakened by carnal excitement. My blood sang for her body, and it rushed into my cock until I thought I would burst. I reached down with a hand to massage it, moaning at how hard I'd become. Only Hekla had ever made me this long and unyielding. Perhaps it was a fated mate trait.

I longed to return the favor. I wanted to set her body on fire the way only a fae mate could. I massaged her lips with mine, pressing harder in my growing passion. I felt inside for my hot summer magic, my raw essence, and infused the smallest amount in my hands. I palmed the sides of her face first while I devoured her mouth and let her feel my summer heat. I was turning myself inside out for her, showing her my rawness and how everything I was belonged to her.

She gasped into my mouth. Only I could give her this. Now she'd feel summer warmth and the erotic thrill of my essence on top of the mate touch's pleasure. I slid my hands down her slender neck and massaged where they met her shoulders, taking care to add extra pressure to the mark I'd given her. Hekla arched sharply and groaned into my mouth. My breath caught at her noise, and I continued, sliding my hands to her shoulders and down her firm, strong arms.

"Why," she gasped, breathless from how I pleasured her with only simple touches. "Why does that feel so good?"

"It's an intimate act," I murmured and buried my lips into her neck to kiss it. "I'm spreading my raw, personal magic essence all over your body. It's the most aphrodisiacal experience a marked fae can offer their marked mate." I lapped at her mark, making her convulse as I slid my hands down hers to intertwine our fingers. "It's as close as we get to further marking our territory, I suppose. More erotic than ejaculating on a partner."

She tilted her head back, showing her lengthened canines as she released a howling cry. I could feel her arousal spike at my words, and I continued to drag my hands along her newly formed goose bumps, releasing magic as I moved. My hands glided down her warm sides, and I moaned in appreciation of her curves. She was in beautiful shape and as healthy as could be. Primed for mating.

I laid her down and lifted both her legs over my shoulders. I couldn't help but stare down at the glistening dark curls around her sex as I massaged her legs all the way to her feet. I wanted to dive in there with my throbbing, aching cock, but first, I wanted to drive her as crazy as she made me. I gripped her ankles and leaned down to kiss her, bringing her thighs up to her torso. I slid my palms down the backs of her legs and grabbed her butt cheeks firmly. She jolted again, unable to buck in her position, and released a long, agonized whine.

"Please, my male!" she begged, panting heavily. I loved how her breasts pressed against my chest. I loved feeling her tight, hard nipples nestled in the center of her softness. I massaged her buttocks, but I couldn't resist any longer and slid my hands between us to grope her excited globes. Everywhere my hands touched, heat followed, encouraging circulation and blood flow. Her breasts were sweaty and swollen now, just how I liked them.

"Please what?" I whispered into her ear as I played with her hard nipples, gently twisting and pinching.

"I need… I need you!" She whimpered, and I could just barely make out her elongated canines as she spoke and panted. That was incredibly hot. I loved her canines.

"Need me to what?" I teased and slid a hand down between us to cup her sex, very excited to try this next part. I slathered my magic along her wet folds, letting my essence settle on her intimate skin. I traced a line around her sensitive clit, and Hekla bit her lip to try to contain a screech of pleasure. I drew a tiny bit more of my essence out, focused it onto my fingertips, and plunged two fingers into her dripping core, displacing some of her natural lubrication. Gods, no woman had ever been so sopping wet. This female provided a sexual experience I simply did not deserve. My cock begged for a dive.

Hekla's head tilted back as far as it could go, and her claws ripped at my back. I grunted and grinned at the reaction I got, pleased as shit to have her right where I wanted her. I slid a third finger into her channel and swirled my fingers in a small, gentle circle. I pumped them several times to fill her with the rest of my essence and repeated my earlier question. "Need me to what, she-wolf?" I growled and nipped her ear.

"Fuck me, fuck me, fuck me, mount me!" she chanted, getting progressively wilder. She dug her claws deeper into my back, holding on without displaying any intention of letting go. I licked my lips, smiled savagely into her hair, and pulled out my fingers to rub her slick on my desperate cock.

I leaned forward and pressed the head of my cock against her threshold. She felt more exquisite than ever, and I looked forward to giving her the best orgasm of her life. I eagerly pushed past her swollen entry and squeezed myself into her snug channel. Tingling heat gripped me, nearly taking my breath away.

Hekla pulled herself up to howl her pleasure into my chest. As much as she wanted to muffle it, there really wasn't any point. I could still hear the stragglers among the bat-shifters moan from their own activities. Not everyone had fallen asleep yet. I could guarantee that no one cared.

I was already as hard as could be and felt myself press against her back wall, shuddering in delight from filling her to the brim. She stretched so deliciously for me, locked so perfectly, that we couldn't be anything but meant to be.

"You got your wish, female," I growled down at her, bracing myself for faster movement. I dragged my cock backward and threatened to leave her entirely, but she released a little growl and sank her claws deeper, issuing her own threat. My abdomen cramped in arousal, and I slammed my hips forward, bottoming out roughly. "Do you feel my magic on your skin?" I asked heatedly and began to drag my cock back out again despite her attempts to clench her walls and trap me. "Do you feel it," I moaned and slammed my hips forward again, making her cry and thrash her head, "inside you?"

I grinded my hips against her swollen sex and licked a short line up her calf, enjoying her flexibility. I rolled my groin into her, patiently building her climax. She was squirming and thrashing and completely at my mercy in this position. Her whimpering punctuated every pant, and I felt her muscles tremble. "I feel it! I feel it! Ah! Ah! Ah!" She moaned, kicking her feet. "It's so hot! It's melting me!"

"That's me, she-wolf," I snarled down into her ear and started rocking my hips, wetly sliding in and out of her sex. I felt her slick drip down my length as proof of her intoxication. "That's my very essence. It's what I injected into your mark, and it's what I slathered all over you so no one will ever mistake who your fated is! You are my mate. Mine! Tell me who your mate is!"

"Y-you!" she yelped, hanging on for dear life when I started pummeling her core with my hips, smacking her with a taut sack. "Ah! Uh, uh!" She yowled, forgetting about the shifters in the woods that'd made her act so reserved earlier.

"That's right. You belong to the prince of the Summer Court, she-wolf! Now watch him worship you," I hissed, speeding up and angling to rub along her sensitive, swollen spots of pleasure. I gathered the tiniest bit of magic on my forefinger, reached between us, and tapped on her clit.

She seized, opened her mouth in a soundless scream, and tossed her head back as the orgasm hit her. I cried out through my teeth as she clamped down on my cock like a coiled snake's death grip. I couldn't thrust anymore, which ended up being more than fine as her pulsing channel squeezed my orgasm out of me. I shook violently as I unloaded into her, crying up toward the forest's canopy in my ecstasy. Her channel throbbed unapologetically along my cock, milking every rope.

"Take my seed, she-wolf," I grunted, straining in our long release. "Take it. Suck it all up!" I ordered through a clenched jaw, jerking my hips to punctuate my feral thoughts. Tears streamed down Hekla's cheeks as she pulsed beneath me. She finally released a weak howl, overwhelmed and overstimulated by euphoria.

We both came to a shuddering halt, gasping to pull oxygen back into our lungs. I slowly lowered her legs from my shoulders, knowing her hips would probably be stiff. Then, I slid my sated cock from her and collapsed to the side, rolling her with me in an exhausted embrace. After a couple minutes of indecision, I forced myself to get dressed and helped her with her own clothes.

"There," I said tiredly, collapsing to the ground once more and wrapping her in my arms. "Now we can rest and be ready to go when night falls," I mumbled, finally feeling like I could relax after our intense joining.

"You... you... " Hekla mumbled, shuddering, "are... very skilled... my prince."

"Only for you," I mumbled back, cradling her as closely as I could. "You make me so happy."

I felt her emotions swell with joy, peace, and satisfaction. Her love for me emanated once more, and I nearly groaned from how wonderful it felt. That in itself was the best reward this fae could ever receive.

Chapter 24

Arse

I'd been working on my tunnel for a good handful of days now because I'd nothing else to do. I'd always made sure to return to Hekla's room before Bidelia got there so I could greet her and she could let me in to sleep. Bidelia never went back to her room, choosing only to stay where Hekla used to sleep. I figured it was a grief thing. I too felt Hekla's absence. I hated that I'd left my first decent owner, but I felt that Bidelia needed someone… and I was afraid of the wild. I was too disabled to survive in the open if something happened to Hekla.

Curse my deformity. Curse my very existence. I was pathetic and unworthy of the good in my life.

Tonight would be the night, though. I had my plan. It was an elaborate strategy to get justice for my owner. It would disable her at court, that evil spring whore. Once my plan was complete, she'd rue the day she came here. Once I'd weakened her, it was only a matter of time before the others finished her off for me. I was not evil, but today might make me question that. I was willing to carry that burden.

I walked confidently down the corridors to Hekla's old suite, now the place of overripe villainy. Instead of turning left toward the suite, I continued down the hall and nudged open a broom closet that Bidelia had left just the tiniest bit ajar. No one had noticed the way it was cracked. Once I was inside, I left the door how I'd found it, hoping no one would shut it. It was my way out, but if I didn't return tonight, Bidelia would come find me. I trusted the wee thing.

I pushed a box aside with my chiseled arms and entered a tunnel I'd painstakingly crafted. Loosening stone bricks was as hard as shite, but I was a male in my prime! I made it happen. When I'd realized that my wings were never going to grow, I'd built up the rest of my body. If only the females were into muscular mac-tallas. No, it was all about the wings… Big, beautiful, dusty mac-talla wings meant more to them than a strong male's giant banger.

I snapped myself out of my self-pity and crawled through the tunnel, making sure the box was back in place. I stalked through the walls and crept around support beams to get to my destination. Yes, deformity aside, I was not only strong and virile but also stealthy.

I reached the end where I pushed against a loose stone and lowered it gently to the floor on the other side. The whore princess would not be here; I knew her schedule. She'd likely be at dinner still. I returned the loose stone to the wall once I was out and surveyed my battleground. Oh yes, this would do just fine.

Plenty of clothes to destroy.

The silks, cottons, and satins were mine to chew. They'd be riddled with holes by the time she returned, and she'd know the true meaning of no mercy. I'd have to be strategic, though. I needed to isolate and sabotage the parts of each clothing item that would be the hardest to repair. So I set about my labors and ravaged the clothes in the closet, showing no kindness or compassion. Revenge had never tasted so good.

Once I was satisfied with my revolution, I crept out of the closet to see what else I could destroy. I'd already moved faster than anticipated, and I believed I had more time to destroy all she held dear. I was about to jump onto the bed to see if there was any jewelry I could chew on when I heard heels clicking outside the door.

My very life flashed before my eyes.

I clambered under the bed, rolling like a warrior avoiding a falling claymore, and pressed myself against the wall. I eyed the closet door, but there was no getting over there in time. I'd eaten the bed, and now I had to lie in it. Whatever happened this fateful night, I'd face my destiny with pride.

The whore princess walked in and sat at her desk. She hadn't noticed the closet yet. That was good. A knock on the door made her shuffle the papers, like she was hiding them. She let in another fae woman, one that I had scented before at the banquet. The blonde who'd been leering at the two-timing prince.

"To what do I owe the… pleasure?" the whore princess asked, sounding less pleasant than she usually did, though it wasn't much to begin with, was it?

The door closed and the blonde said, "I just wanted to concede to your victory in obtaining the prince's hand."

"It was never a competition," the princess sneered.

"I just thought we could have worked together," the blonde stated resolutely. "I poisoned his mate. I tried to get her out of the picture, which helped you, did it not?"

"No, I got rid of her all by myself. You can thank your prince for how much he masturbates into the trash." The princess snorted in an unladylike fashion. She strolled slowly to the glass balcony door by the bed, so I shuffled back silently to put some distance between us.

Wait… she got rid of Hekla? Was the prince truly framed?

"Though now he's run off because of your little games," the blonde said through her teeth, clearly irritated.

"He'll be back. He won't want to risk an execution."

Execution?

"I've also come to make a request. I wanted to get your blessing first. It's not in my nature to step on toes." Hesitantly, the visitor paced over to the whore princess.

Oh, I had to keep myself from laughing at that one. Not in her nature, my arse!

"Spit it out," the princess snapped.

"I'd like to be appointed as a mistress. I think that if we were to team up, we co—"

My eyes nearly popped from my head when flowering vines sprouted all about the princess and wrapped around the blonde. From my limited vantage, I noticed she had seeds sewn into her clothes, which was where the vines originated. Tricky whore, this one!

"Don't touch my shit," the princess hissed and slammed the blonde through the glass door with the vines.

Holy shite!

I couldn't see the blonde. I had no idea if she was even on the balcony. There was another knock on the door, making me jolt in surprise.

"Your Majesty," the princess said, and I saw her curtsey.

"Quit the act. It's just me," the queen snapped. "What have you done?" I had to assume she was referring to the giant pile of glass and puddles of blood.

"She was conspiring against the throne," the princess replied lightly.

Pffft!

The queen was silent for a while, then she said, "I'm asking once more. When will he be delivered after the contract is fulfilled? I'm not making this sacrifice for nothing."

"You are such a paranoid thing, aren't you?" the princess remarked snidely and waltzed over to the office, which was next to the closet. I waited for the queen to follow her, but she stayed out of the room, hovering in front of my escape route. Shite! I turned to face the balcony. It was now or never if they discovered my assault on the closet. I thought that the worst-case scenario would be the princess standing on a stool and screaming if she discovered me. Now, I was certain she'd make mac-talla soup out of my fine arse.

I launched through the hole in the balcony door, taking care to avoid the broken glass. The blonde wasn't out here. Had she fallen? I climbed to the edge of the balcony and took a deep breath. If I landed on the hedge below I might not die. I might get skewered, but I might not die.

For my prince and court, I said nobly and jumped off the balcony—right into the arms of the prince's sister, who was spying just under the eaves.

Before she could say a thing, the shriek of ten thousand ban-sìths erupted from the whore princess's room. "MY CLOTHES!"

Mission accomplished.

Mella

I stirred from a kiss on my cheek but tiredness had me growling and rolling over. It wasn't even dawn yet. Who woke before dawn? A deep chuckle caressed my ear, a handsome noise that went straight to my sex, but I still wasn't moving a damn inch. Another kiss landed on my cheek, then another, then another…

"Ahh!" I sat up, growling louder and looking around wildly. I finally recognized the laugh and turned to see my fae mate grinning down at me. My brain caught up with my body, and I joined in on Belenus's laughing as he helped me to my feet.

"The bats are taking one last pass at the nuckelavee, and then we'll leave," he said, nodding in the direction of the creature's body.

"Are they going to be good to go after…" I asked quietly and tactfully while executing an explicit hand gesture to make my meaning clear. Belenus released another burst of laughter and quickly covered his mouth.

"Nofre says they'll just have to deal with it. It won't be as bad since they ate their fill earlier. They're just unwilling to leave good blood behind after starving for so long," he explained, grabbing the rest of his gear. He winced and added, "Though I have to say, the blood doesn't look that good. That thing's full of black blood. Eugh." He shuddered.

I grimaced myself, praying it also wouldn't make the bats sick. "Hopefully it tastes like licorice."

"Now I will never be able to eat licorice again. Thank you, my alpha," Belenus said with a snort as we wandered to where the shifters planned to meet us. An unexpected scent—a putrid one—wafted to me, and I gagged before I could even start in surprise. I'd know that smell anywhere now.

"Fear gorta!" I hissed to Belenus and whirled to chase the scent.

"Shit!" Belenus said and followed me. The closer I got to the fear gorta, the more I could smell someone else nearby—Ferrer. In a clearing, the bat-shifter was pointing away from the forest while aggressively shooing off the undead faery, who finally turned to leave. There was no way he would have known what it was.

"FERRER, COME HERE!" I commanded and waved him over in a panic.

"The fear gorta is leaving, and it doesn't look happy," Belenus said through gritted teeth. "Ferrer is cursed now. I have no idea what to do about this."

I looked at the departing corpse but couldn't verify his observation for the life of me. How could a fear gorta look anything other than unhappy? Ferrer then sped over to me in a blink, and I took a step back in surprise.

"Ferrer, what did you do to that thing? Did you feed it?" Belenus rubbed his temple with his fingers and asked in a lower voice, "Were you polite to it?"

The male frowned and tilted his head in confusion. "It came toward my people, but when I approached it, it shoved a bowl in my face, so I told it to leave. We don't have food to spare, and I didn't like the look of it. Wasn't edible either."

I resisted copying Belenus's temple rubbing. "Did it touch you, Ferrer?" I asked with a light growl.

"Yeah, patted me on the shoulder. Took rejection rather well, but I still told it to leave my people alone," he answered, brushing his hair from his red-brown eyes, the color of dried blood.

"Well, you just got cursed," Belenus said with a frustrated sigh, moving his fingers to squeeze the bridge of his nose. Ferrer gave him a skeptical look and crossed his arms.

Is it just me or has he bulked up since eating? Eventide asked.

No, I guess they recover pretty quickly? Maybe as fast as wolves? Maybe faster? I replied, and she hummed thoughtfully. Speed seemed to be a boon for these folk; they definitely moved faster than wolves. I wouldn't be surprised if they healed just as swiftly.

"What is the fear gorta's curse?" I asked Belenus since Ferrer didn't seem concerned in the slightest.

"Well, Ferrer here is going to experience some pretty bad luck and never-ending hunger until we get that curse lifted. Shit, I wish I had known there was one nearby! I should bring some game back for us, mate, and use the leftovers for any other encounter."

"If you say so." Ferrer shrugged and started strolling off with his hands in his pockets.

"You're not hungry, Ferrer?" Belenus called out to him. Ferrer laughed and waved him off, disappearing into the trees to return to his people.

"Maybe it's because he just ate?" I pondered out loud. "Will he survive the trip back to the castle, Belenus?"

"I'll make sure he does, but it'll be a challenge. We'll get him extra meals and make a litter if he gets too weak. The bad luck will be a problem. Shit, I wish we'd gotten here in time!" he snapped, furious with himself.

"Should I go feed that fear gorta? Get us some good luck again?" I offered, patting him on his arm. He shook his head aggressively.

"Do *not* go near that thing now. It's going to be cranky as shit. Let's… just get people going. We can only march til dawn, and we'll have to find them cover by sunrise."

I kept an eye on Ferrer while we traveled with Eventide at our backs, but he seemed to be doing just fine. If anything, he appeared to be thriving. The sickly pallor had left his flesh, leaving him with the healthy light skin you'd expect from a people who never saw the light of day. His eyes were vibrant, and he moved with purpose, confidence, and grace. He was a rather good-looking male. They all were actually.

I pondered their ears and directed a question to the other leader, "Nofre, have your people always had pointed ears? All the shifters I know have rounded ones, like humans."

The bat-shifter, strolling next to me as healthy as Ferrer, said, "Humans? We have so few references to them… Per your question, over the hundreds of years, fae from the Autumn and Winter Courts would find themselves in the Night Court for one reason or another. They'd either been exploring or entering the door on a dare but were almost always fated mates with one of us. We treated them like royalty so they'd stay, but that usually wasn't necessary. Most volunteered to stay, thinking we couldn't go back with them. If only we'd known…" He looked thoughtful, but not regretful.

"So they bred heavily into your line. I guess it makes sense that you look a little like fae," I replied.

"We had hoped our pups would escape the curse of our colony, but they were all born as bat-shifters. They were never born pure fae."

"Well, now you're not alone in the world, Nofre. You have kingdoms that will help, I know it." I didn't need to force confidence into my voice. It simply was the truth.

A hissing, demonic growl came from behind, and I turned to see a shifter returning with a prize from a hunt. I paled when I saw her quarry and blurted, "I will give you much larger, juicier prey if you hand that over to me! I will go hunt right now! Can we trade?"

"What's happening?" Belenus turned around and said, "Oh. Yes, you'd better hand that over before she goes feral."

The shifter frowned and eyed what she intended to drink dry. "Is this a sacred animal?"

I grimaced, not sure if I could put it in a way they'd find acceptable. These people were forced to drink their own kind. I had to assume that pets wouldn't mean a thing to them.

"Not exactly, but the species is… unique. Please, let me get you better prey. Let's trade."

She shrugged and handed the mac-talla over to me. I gripped the fussing creature and let it throw its tantrum while I heaved a colossal sigh of relief. I gave Belenus a pleading look and held out the mac-talla so I could go hunt. He shook his head and kissed me. "I will get the kill," he insisted and shifted into Escort. The blond wolf loped off to find something more substantial for the shifter, and I nearly wept from his sweetness.

He is so good to us! Eventide sobbed.

I nodded silently, a touch emotional now, and directed all my attention to the stressed-out creature in my arms. It had chomped down on my wrist and froze, not understanding why I wasn't letting go of it. "I'm not going to hurt you. I just kept you from getting eaten, little mac-talla. My name's Hekla."

The little mac-talla didn't even blink and I sighed, resigned to my next idea. I brought it up to my unbitten ear and tried to get it to bite that instead of my wrist. Maybe I could get it to bond and talk to me, build a little trust here. I shook the creature a little in encouragement, but it merely opened and erratically fluttered its wings.

"Come on, bite my ear so we can talk," I said, nudging its mouth toward my ear. Feeling eyes on me, I glanced over at

Nofre, who was giving me a very strange look. "No, I'm not crazy, Nofre. Stop staring at me like that," I growled. "These creatures create mind-links with their… 'owners.'"

At the mention of owners, the mac-talla bit my ear and then decided not to let go. I took a deep breath and managed to keep walking with the colony. I didn't want to make any sudden movements or it could take some of my ear with it. I could only imagine how stupid this looked to the shifters behind me.

"Fine, mac-talla, you can hang on all you like. I'm not going to hurt you, and you're going to realize that this is all very silly."

Are wild mac-tallas like the domesticated ones, though? Eventide asked.

That's a good point, and now I'm a little worried, I replied.

Luzia ended up on my other side. "Do you need help with your lunch?"

I sighed and pressed my lips together in a line. I was about to say no when a large group of armored fae warriors on horseback, perhaps fifty, stopped to block our progress.

"HALT!" I ordered the colony and studied the fae in the front, the one with a subtle glow much like Queen Fedelm's, except his light shone in a shivering silver. His hair fell over his shoulders in an inky waterfall, draping well past a silver-dusted face, one almost as pale as the bat-shifters. His eyes were like the cool branches of a blue spruce, but his scrutiny was colder.

He snapped something in fae, but when I gave him a confused look, he promptly switched languages. "State your business in the Unseelie Court!" he commanded, issuing his challenge in a loud, kingly voice.

"My name is Hekla Himinn, vessel of the Sky Gods!" I returned with as much dominance as I could muster. "I have been tasked by the Sky Gods to return Their first children to the Realm of the Humans. We are passing through the Unseelie Court and Winter Court in order to achieve this!" I couldn't imagine I looked very imposing with a living mac-talla earring, but I did my best. "We mean you and your people no harm. We are merely travelers."

Escort, Eventide said, mind-linking our mate. *We've been stopped by authorities. Maybe around fifty soldiers.*

Almost there, Escort replied, angry.

The fae surveyed the colony. "We were under the assumption they were locked in there," he said. "They've not wandered for centuries. Why now?"

"I've not been given that answer," I replied and raised my chin. "I simply must do as the gods dictate. My mission is one of peace. I'm saving them from extinction. They were starving to death because all the game migrated. They will not be on your lands again after we've left."

Escort ran over the hill, dumped a fat, dead fowl at the she-bat's feet, and shape-shifted into Belenus to return to my side.

The man scowled in surprise. "A Summer Fa— Is that the prince of the Summer Court? Why would you be involved? You understand how bad this looks, don't you?" the fae snapped and climbed off his horse. "Why didn't you reach out for permission and an escort?"

"King Nechtan," Belenus acknowledged sternly and strode forward to grasp his arm in greeting. "The vessel of the Sky Gods is my mate. We left in kind of a last-minute emergency situation. There was no time to go through the proper channels."

That wasn't quite true, but this king didn't need to know about our personal issues. Though, the issue with the summer queen did put us in a hurry. I adjusted the weight of the mac-talla on my forearm, which was starting to ache from the odd position. Belenus cast a quick look at my situation, and my face burned in embarrassment.

I'll explain later, I growled in a mind-link.

The king scrutinized him. "If I didn't think you much better than the summer queen, perhaps I'd be less inclined to believe you. This is still highly unusual. I can't let you pass without an escort, but I do need to have more details for my report," he said while adjusting his black cuirass, a dark warning in his tone. He turned to another warrior who had a countenance as grim as his king's. "Slaine, keep an eye on things here. Leave the travelers alone." Slaine nodded and didn't utter a word as he dismounted with the rest of his men.

I looked to Nofre and gestured to his colony. "I sense the king wishes a private discussion. I'll trust you to keep things peaceful here until we return," I ordered, and Nofre nodded much like Slaine had.

"I'm… honored," Nofre stated, but he continued to stare at the mac-talla, and his lips twitched ever so slightly. Eventide gave a withering sigh in my head, and I silently echoed her.

Belenus, King Nechtan, and I wandered out of earshot of our parties. "What is the winter king doing in the Unseelie Court anyway?" Belenus asked curiously. "Though I do understand winter is overseen by them."

King Nechtan sighed, "The unseelie are putting more resources into the Autumn Court right now." He pinched the bridge of his nose, a habit that reminded me of Belenus, and added, "They're investigating suspicious activity between autumn and spring." His frown deepened. "It'd be nice if things just stayed peaceful. We're all quite tired of dying over nothing." He then gestured to us with an irritated expression. "And once the unseelie received reports of unknown travelers and hundreds of individuals appearing out of nowhere—*you*—they requested I divert my men. I just happened to be in a meeting here, getting updates on the Autumn Court."

Belenus scrubbed a hand over his stubble and nodded, deep in thought. "The activity in the Spring Court, that doesn't happen to involve their royal family, does it?"

"Why do you wish to know?" the king asked, narrowing his eyes. Before Belenus could reply, understanding lit up the king's expression. "Ah, your… intended. We heard. Now I am very confused." He gestured to us both. "You both are mated, but…" King Nechtan began, then turned to me. "How is it that you're mated and not the princess? You are not one of their princesses."

"We're fated," Belenus growled out before I could say anything. "I'm not marrying that spring wretch."

King Nechtan snorted dourly. "Runaway lovers? Good luck with whatever marriage contract you had."

"Not runaways," I snarled, offended. Granted, I'd run from Belenus, but that was when I thought he'd betrayed our future together. "We're returning to put Belenus on the throne." Belenus shot me a warning look, but I showed him a canine.

"That wasn't wise to divulge to another court, Hekla," he scolded.

"I'm not playing by your broken fae rules anymore," I spat back, then I sent a challenging glare to King Nechtan.

The king gave me an assessing look. "I take back what I said about the contract, Prince Belenus. Good luck with your mate. Might be she outshines you on the throne." He pressed his lips together, almost like he was suppressing a smile, but with his grim countenance, it was hard to tell.

"Back to the Spring Court…" Belenus prompted, sending me a look that told me I was due for punishment.

Bring it on, Eventide dared. *I'll let Escort punish me any day.*

I cleared my throat and tried hard not to laugh. She must have said it loud enough for Belenus to hear because his ears turned ruddy.

Can't take that back, Escort retorted—severely.

The king returned to the prior topic. "As you know, the Autumn Court married into the Spring Court. Now that the Spring Court is trying to marry into the Summer Court, there's concern that there will be an imbalance of power. Even though both the Autumn and the Winter Courts fall under the unseelie's jurisdiction, it doesn't mean that we can ignore this instability."

"What makes you think there's a power change? It's marriage, yes, but is there evidence of conspiracy?" I asked, adjusting the mac-talla's weight again, which earned me a threatening growl from the creature. Its dusty wings fluttered again out of stress.

Someone just kill me, I groaned to myself. *A fine representation of a future queen I am.*

"I cannot ignore this any longer. Pray tell me why there is a pregnant mac-talla hanging from your ear. Is this a Sky Gods… task?" the king asked skeptically, bewilderment subtly breaking through his dark expression.

"Pregnant?" I blurted and glanced in the direction of the angry thing. "Is that why you're so wild right now?" I asked her. It didn't reply.

"Her pouch is full," the king pointed out.

Oh. Indeed, I had not noticed, and I made a note to be much more gentle with her.

I muttered my explanation. "Well, a child of the Sky Gods was going to eat her, so I traded her for better game. I have a mac-talla back at the castle, and I couldn't bear to see one get devoured. I tried to get her to bond with me, but she never let go."

"I used to breed them," the king said, looking nostalgic.

"By all means, keep her if you want. Just don't kill her. Look, you don't even need to breed her. That's half your job done right there," I said, trying to sell him on the idea. My arm was getting really tired, and my ear throbbed.

"Perhaps I will make sure she develops them safely and release her," King Nechtan agreed. I breathed a sigh of relief when he pressed on her jaw to release me, keeping her in an expert hold. Something softened in his bearing as he regarded his new charge.

I touched my ear and found the blood I could smell. I wasn't sure if she bonded with me or not, but I highly doubted it.

Belenus sighed, rubbed a hand across his forehead, and said, "Back to Hekla's question about the power balance…" He leaned over to press a finger to my ear, healing it in a blink. I smiled gratefully at him.

"Right," the king replied, returning to his stern demeanor. "Belenus, I don't know if you're aware of our own history with the Sky Gods. The unseelie and winter fae wanted nothing to do with the witches that used to be here. To make the story as brief as possible, they caused trouble, and the gods returned them to their original realm—forcefully. With sightings of them trickling back in over time, we weren't about to risk the gods' wrath by welcoming them after their banishment."

"Their children just recounted this story..." Belenus said with a furrowed brow. "The timing of this subject is unexpected."

"We've detected signs of witchwork along our borders, especially between autumn and winter, and some of our diplomats have returned with disturbing stories. Sightings of rot-witches, mostly," the king expounded. "Either the Autumn Court is remiss about removing them or they're working with them. This is what the unseelie are investigating."

"We haven't seen any on our borders... but perhaps it's a matter of time." Belenus looked anxiously at where the colony was waiting. "We need to get a move on. I have to return to my people and kick that spring princess out of our territory."

King Nechtan's frown turned thoughtful, and he tapped his fingers on his thigh while shifting his weight. "I think I will call her Skye," he said, staring down at the now-calm mac-talla and petting her. He paused for several more moments, clearly ruminating, before he calmly stated, "I will have to escort you out, but perhaps you'd like further assistance with your endeavor? The removal of spring from summer would ease the Winter Court's fears."

Belenus's jaw didn't drop, but I could easily imagine it through his serious mask.

Chapter 25

Belenus

I wasn't quite sure I'd heard King Nechtan correctly. Had he just offered me assistance in usurping the summer throne? I studied him for a minute while I considered his offer.

"Is the Winter Court so worried about autumn that they'd offer help to a neighbor they share a fragile treaty with? Our war is not as old as that… or as forgotten among our people as you might think," I said cautiously.

The king maintained his cool composure and continued to stroke the tired, pregnant mac-talla. "Simply put, yes. I would say so. I have not been king for as long as my father, but I can tell you that I'd rather establish balance than risk more bloodshed in the long game," he answered grimly.

"You break the pattern of your brutal ancestors," I mused but was taken aback by his scowl.

"We were never as barbaric as you perceived," he retorted icily.

I placed my hands up in supplication. "Forgive me, King Nechtan. An insult was not my intent." He seemed somewhat mollified for now, but his jaw clenched. I needed to be more careful with my wording. I glanced at Hekla, who was also giving me a disapproving look.

Shit.

Great job, Escort growled.

"When are you executing your attack on the throne?" the king asked, calming as he stroked the creature who'd fallen asleep on his arm.

"As soon as I return. There is not much time. I had planned on being back…" I answered, trailing off and counting the days in my head. I grimaced at how little time was left. "After dawn, I will have three more days before the wedding. Not that I haven't already broken the contract. They won't know that until they see me, though. I need that time! I need to find a way out of that contract."

"There is no way you will be able to march to the Summer Court within three days' time," King Nechtan informed with a shake of his head. I hesitated, not exactly wanting to divulge that I had a map with connecting doors. How did I want to navigate this?

"There may be a way," I replied evasively, "but I must think on it before I run it by you." I needed to peruse the map and consult with my mate on our next course of action. In the meantime, they could march us west.

"Then I suppose we should get going." King Nechtan nodded curtly and turned to where he'd left his warriors. I glanced up at the sky, knowing we only had several more hours before we had to find enough shelter for the bat-shifters. The gods knew I was exhausted too.

The Sun God spilled his rays into the horizon, but we discovered that the nearby spindly woods were too sparse to offer decent coverage. Fortunately, King Nechtan worked with his men to erect shelters made of snow. I imagined that being outside of their court must have cost them quite a bit of magic. I was not only appreciative of their efforts, but I was also surprised by how dedicated they were in their assistance. I would keep an eye on them, but my gut told me that King Nechtan and I were on the same page. I also… trusted Hekla's judgment too.

Hekla and I poured over the map in private and isolated the best door to the Winter Court. Nothing went straight to summer. "We may have to blindfold the king and their men, and I have a feeling they will not cooperate. Like an alpha, the king would want to know about any doors to his court," Hekla murmured, tracing a finger idly on the paper. "It's a vulnerability."

"I know that I'd want to know if there was a hidden door to my court," I sighed while rubbing my temples. I was damn tired and ready to sleep with the rest of the shifters. "Fortunately, I do know now because of this map, but I'd understand his fears about it."

"Would mentioning the godlings help?" Hekla asked, looking up at me with her gorgeous, sparkling eyes. I was momentarily distracted by them, but I shrugged and twisted my lips in thought.

"Let's sleep and speak to him when the Sun God goes to rest," I replied, folded the map, and led my mate back to the shifters to retire.

I was woken just before nightfall by King Nechtan, who held up a letter that he seemed to want to discuss. I looked over at my mate, so sweet in her sleep, and hesitated in my decision to wake her. I was torn between wanting to make sure she got enough rest and including her in all important discussions. I also had to wonder if she was already with pup… or fae.

Grow up, I reminded myself with some irritation. *Hekla can handle it. She's already a queen by nature alone.*

She'd kick your ass for letting her sleep through anything important, Escort remarked dryly. I grudgingly acknowledged his point and gently roused her.

"I received a report from my scouts in the Winter Court that a woman claiming to be your sister was apprehended in our territory and held for questioning," he said, handing the letter to me.

"Emer?" I fumbled with the letter and read it thoroughly. "What the shit? She was looking for me?" I asked no one in particular.

"Do you think something happened at the castle?" Hekla asked, putting a hand on my shoulder.

"It must have if it drove her into the Winter Court all by herself," I muttered in shock. I looked up at the king and asked, "Can we request a rendezvous on our way west so we can talk to her?"

"Considering she didn't seem to be spying or attacking anyone, I think we can arrange that," the king said, studying my expression. I knew he was going out on more than one limb for me, and I was grateful for his flexibility. He might have a grim and cold countenance, but I think he held out for more hope than he was willing to admit.

I wanted to ask if my sister had been tortured or beaten for information, but I had a feeling that would be a terribly stupid and offensive question. I had to show some trust as well. I would get Emer's retelling of it too, of course.

"On my idea for shortening our travel time," I said, wording my idea cautiously, "I've been told there is a direct fae door from the Unseelie Court to the Winter Court." I stopped to assess his reaction to that bit of news.

Aside from his nostrils flaring, the king didn't betray any of his surprise, and replied, "Continue…"

"I have been sworn to secrecy about its location and the one from the Winter Realm to the Summer Realm. I am… uncertain how to proceed without disclosing the location to you and your warriors." I tried not to hold my breath, but I was anxious to get this talk behind us.

"How did you get this information?" the king demanded harshly, drawing his brows and pursing his lips in ire. The disclosure of an unknown door from winter to summer had fractured his demeanor.

"Triskelion," I confessed with a sigh. "Triskelion divulged it to speed up our trip to the Night Court. Hekla fed a fear gorta, and things lined up for us immediately." I shrugged helplessly, not able to prove it and unwilling to tell him of the map's existence. "I realize this all sounds outlandish, but the Sky Gods and godlings are motivated to help the children of the Sky Gods and dethrone the summer queen."

"Triskelion has been quiet for hundreds of years," King Nechtan said in a low voice and regarded me with a degree of suspicion. I threw up my hands and looked at Hekla.

"We promised Lion," Hekla said, worrying at her claws. "That's magically binding, isn't it?"

"Yes," I growled and paced.

"You are really testing my trust here, Prince Belenus," the king warned, crossing his battle-hardened arms. "The existence of these doors leaves my court vulnerable."

"Only my mate and I know of their existence—except for Triskelion, of course," I replied, trying to reassure him.

"Let's make a promise, then," Hekla said firmly. "A promise to not use the doors in a way that would threaten the peace and safety of your court. Then we'll blindfold you and pass through the door."

I bit my tongue at Hekla's bold offer. Once again, she laid everything out on the table.

She's a wolf, Escort reminded me. *She won't play fae games, Belenus. She's aiming to get shit done.*

I scratched the back of my neck and didn't reply to my wolf, but he was right. We were playing by her rules now, and they'd worked well so far.

"I must express that I am very unhappy about this." The fae king glowered. "I insist we detail the promise, and once you take the throne, Prince Belenus, we will need to discuss how you plan to safeguard the summer door to our court."

"I think that's reasonable," I said, letting my shoulders drop in relief.

Once we established detailed terms of the promise, both Hekla and I bound ourselves to it, shaking the king's hand to magically finalize the agreement. As we neared the location of the unseelie door, I reminded King Nechtan of the plan. "We'll blindfold you a mile from the unseelie door and remove the blindfold a mile after we've left the winter door."

The king and his warriors grudgingly allowed themselves to be blindfolded, and Hekla ordered the shifters with an alpha command to link hands and close their eyes. We led them carefully through the door over several hours and trudged through the frigid snow to a place where I was comfortable removing their blindfolds.

I held no illusions about that door remaining a secret. I was sure there were a number of ways the king could try to track his way back to it, even if I could remove the snow tracks. I was more concerned about the door from winter to summer, but that was nowhere near the top of my list of priorities.

The king took in the scenery when he pulled the blindfold from his steely gaze. "Remarkable," he said. "There was a door under our very own noses." Snow drifted down, and he adjusted his cape over the mac-talla.

"How shall we rendezvous with Emer and your guards?" I asked, motioning for the warriors and shivering shifters to continue our westward trek. The king unfolded a map and leaned over to discuss our current location with Slaine. Once they sorted out where we were, King Nechtan pointed northwest.

"We have a half a day's ride to the rendezvous point. They've already left the castle and should be there first," he said. I turned around to see how the bat-shifters were doing, and they appeared as miserable as Hekla. I could sense her temptation to shift into a wolf far more equipped for this weather.

I held a hand out to her and said, "I want to carry you. I am very cold." I tried not to let a rakish grin destroy my serious mask, but she saw through me anyway. She was too smart to fall for it. She shook her head but beamed at my attempt to warm her. I knew she didn't want to appear weak. The things we did for our image... I supposed the wolves must have that same dilemma.

We marched on, and once I saw Emer's strawberry-blonde hair among a bevy of winter warriors, I ran ahead and enveloped her in a hug. I'd never been so happy to see her, and I suspected she felt the same, now sobbing in relief. "B-Belenus! I'm so sorry! I d-didn't know where to find you!" she cried, rubbing her puffy eyes.

"It's ok. I've got you now, Emer," I consoled. "But why in the shit are you here? Did something happen?"

Hekla and King Nechtan caught up with us and waited for her explanation. Such was Emer's distress that she only spoke after Hekla encased her in a comforting hug. "Belenus, I… I overheard Mother say that…" She stopped in the middle of her sentence and froze as though the Winter Court had wrapped her in ice. Beneath her pinkened, frozen nose and cheeks, her skin paled. She was staring at something behind me, and I turned sharply to see what had shocked her.

Nofre was being held back by a surprised Ferrer and Luzia. His nostrils flared, and his knuckles blanched as he fought some kind of internal battle. I didn't know what happened to his shirt, but it was gone and large, charcoal bat wings were spread wide, twitching and flapping in his agitation. His chest heaved and his fangs lengthened, but then he slammed his eyes shut as though he had suffered some agonizing injury. When he tried to turn from us, Ferrer and Luzia helped him stumble away, both looking back worriedly but offering no explanation.

I returned my gaze to Emer to find her trembling lips trying to form words. Her eyes followed Nofre's departure with a look of horror, and she quietly uttered one word.

"Mate."

I gawked at Emer, who was huddled against me. "Nofre's your mate?" I blurted in surprise and gawked at Belenus. He appeared just as stunned, but I could feel a flurry of emotions through our bond. He went from shock, to disbelief, to a very brief flash of gladness that was quickly drowned out by disapproval and shame.

I reached out and grabbed his hand. *It's ok to feel confused. This is all very overwhelming. I will go talk to Nofre if you take care of your sister,* I said to him. *We must address recognition before anything negative escalates.*

I don't think Nofre would hurt her, mate, Eventide murmured in an attempt to comfort him.

Escort was, I believed, purposely silent. I could imagine him telling Belenus not to be prejudiced against the bat-shifter who was mated to his sister, and I think he ultimately didn't trust himself to speak. As assertive as Escort could be, I believed he knew when to stay quiet.

"Let's continue westward, shall we?" I prompted King Nechtan. He pressed his lips together in impatience, and he obviously wanted to know what Emer had to say, but she didn't look like she was going to talk anytime soon. She just stared off to where Nofre had disappeared, lost in dissociation. She didn't look happy, and I very much remembered that she mentioned not ever wanting a mate—a husband. I hoped she meant a fae one.

After the king got his warriors moving again, I gently moved Emer to Belenus, who brought her out of the way of the marching warriors and shambling shifters. Taking in the entire group, I realized we'd have to stop soon and hunt. I had no idea what their metabolism was like, and I was certainly famished.

I followed Nofre's scent to the end of the four hundred and twenty-four shifters, where Ferrer and Luzia were arguing with him. "Nofre," I said gently, trying to get his attention, "what happened back there, aside from recognizing Emer?"

"Emer?" he echoed and glanced up at me with weary red eyes. He looked like he'd shed several tears since leaving the front of the colony. "Her name's Emer." He gritted his teeth and squeezed his eyes tight. "Did you see how she looked at me? Like I was a monster?"

"Well, to be fair, you did look like you were about to attack her," I said. I knew it was blunt, but I wanted to get to the heart of the issue. I wanted to see how I could help. Emer would soon be the king's sister and needed some stability in her life to handle any given responsibilities.

"I didn't want to attack her… I wanted to claim her," he said, looking away in shame. "The next time we feed, the males may fight over her since she's the first unmarked, unrelated female we've encountered."

"Fuck," I cursed. "I hadn't thought of that. That is a problem…" I stared down at the snow while we trudged behind the colony. For a little while, as I pondered, all that filled the air was the crunching of snow underfoot. "I don't know how many males we have with us, but that would be too many to handle if it turns into a fight. I don't want to see any injuries or deaths over something like this. There are already too few of you as it is."

"Perhaps you or Belenus should try to get ahead of us. Distance might solve the issue if you're far enough away," Luzia suggested.

"No! I don—" Nofre began but then shut his mouth tight. I knew what he was going to say. He didn't want to be separated from his mate, a common sentiment among shifter males.

"We haven't had a fated mate join our colony for… probably well over a hundred years?" Ferrer said, looking to Luzia for verification. She shrugged with a pout, seeming not to know either. "I'd say that at least ninety-five percent of us have never had sex."

"Fuck!" I cursed again, flinging Zorian's favorite swear word about willy-nilly due to how extreme this all was. They've been really missing out, and I couldn't imagine how pent up they must be. "Emer must be especially precious to you then, being the first fated mate in forever for a colony member. Don't you think that announcing that fact to your colony would inspire them to protect her instead of claim her?"

Nofre looked skeptically over to Ferrer, who sighed and ran his fingers through his hair. "I don't know. It's hard enough to think of anything but breeding after eating. It's possible. I suppose if she were mine, I'd probably announce it t—" Ferrer didn't finish before Nofre crinkled his nose and snarled at him. "Blood clots! Back off, Nofre," Ferrer snapped, stepping away from him. Luzia put some distance between them as well.

"That's normal, Ferrer," I said with a sigh. "He's going to be territorial. Best to word things with care. You all have a lot to learn about having fated mates. I'm tempted to throw a class together." I muttered that last part to myself.

"I'm utterly terrified of something happening to her," Nofre admitted with a strained expression. I could already see that by how taut the cords in his neck were, practically pulled bowstring. "I'm going mad with anxiety being so far from her already."

I took a deep breath, letting the crisp scent of pine fill my lungs while I thought. "Belenus isn't a general for nothing. He will keep his sister safe, but you're going to have to talk to her," I counseled.

"The prince's sister?" Nofre exclaimed and halted. He folded his hands over his nose and mouth, looking overwhelmed. The pressure he was under must be crushing. "I… I can't talk to her. She looked so horrified. She smelled so good, though! What if I bite her?"

I had an urge to joke about her potentially enjoying that but held my tongue. Luzia crossed her arms and said, "You might have to fast, Nofre."

"That's a good idea," he said and pointed at her, immediately agreeing. "I will do that. It will keep my mind clear."

"And your cock calm," Ferrer said casually. I held a snort of laughter back and begrudgingly agreed.

"That will weaken you, though, Nofre. Keep that in mind," Luzia added.

He started walking again, returned his hands to his face, and muttered, "This bloody sucks. Vessel, I'm truly relying on your guidance here."

"And you will have it," I replied simply, placing my hands in my pockets. "I know you are a good male, Nofre. I can sense that. What do you want me to do? Speak with Emer or arrange for you two to talk with supervision?"

"If you could convince her that I'm not a monster first, that would be preferable," he mumbled.

"If that's what she thinks, she won't truly believe that until you both get to know each other, but I will do my best to allay her fears."

"Thank you..."

I jogged awkwardly in the snow back to where Belenus quietly chatted with Emer. It was a relief to find her talking again, though she seemed depleted. Catching up, I held her hand without saying anything and glanced over at Belenus.

How is she doing? I asked my mate.

She's still in shock. She found his behavior monstrous and frightening.

Did you explain his nature?

I went over their history, yes. She's a little calmer. More sympathetic, he answered, *but she's still scared of him.*

Nofre did point out a serious problem, though. She might be approached by many males after the shifters eat. She's the first unmated, unrelated female they've encountered.

Fuck, Belenus cursed. He was on the same profanity page as me, apparently.

They recommend taking her ahead of the group if possible, I added.

We do have the horse she arrived on, he said in realization.

I don't think Nofre can be separated from her, though, my mate, I disclosed and proceeded to tell him everything I discussed with the three bat-shifters.

This is very problematic, he uttered in frustration.

Can't we just use an alpha command on them to keep her safe? Eventide chirped.

I stopped in my tracks and smacked a hand to my forehead. Someone bumped into me from behind and apologized profusely. That was my fault, though, and I swiftly returned the apology.

I am the dumbest she-wolf in the world, I moaned. I caught up to my mate and Emer, feeling like a complete idiot. My brain must still be processing the Moon Goddess's blessing. To think I forgot I was an alpha!

Over our bond, I felt a mixture of amusement and relief from Belenus. *I didn't think of it either...* he consoled and chuckled out loud. Emer's lost gaze darted to him, but he dismissed the unspoken question with a shake of his head.

"Emer," I said softly, wrapping an arm around her shoulder. "Can we talk?"

Belenus marched ahead to give us some space and Emer sighed. "Is this about… him?"

"Oh yes, it absolutely is. Did you know that he's freaking out back there, worried to pieces that he scared you and that you think he must be a monster?" I asked, knowing that she communicated as bluntly as I did. My goal was to 'humanize' him.

"No…" she admitted, a small guilty pout pulling at her lips.

"When he saw you, he had this massive urge to protect you. You know how territorial these dumb males get." I smiled and nudged her in the ribs. The corner of her lips twitched a little.

Ooh! We almost got a smile out of her. Keep going! Eventide cheered.

In a lower voice, like I was gossiping about something juicy, I asked, "Did Belenus tell you about their crazy post-eating instinct?" She shook her head and her eyes lit with curiosity, locking onto mine. "They get crazy horny after eating," I shared, giggling quietly. "It's an urge they developed because they're at risk of going extinct. The first time they ate, they all went off to masturbate!"

She released a bark of laughter and then covered her mouth, glancing back at the colony of shifters. "No… Really?"

I nodded with wide eyes, smiling wickedly. She snorted again but blushed this time, cheeks growing rosier than they'd been from the chill.

"Anyway, I just wanted to comfort you by letting you know that Nofre's decided to fast. He won't eat for now because he doesn't want to pressure you on accident. Instincts are a nightmare, aren't they?" I patted her shoulder, moving into the guilt-trip phase of my plan.

She gaped, stricken. "He's going to starve himself?"

"Yupper puppers," I verified calmly, like I was talking about the snowfall.

"Because he doesn't want to pressure me into sex?" She seemed to be having a hard time accepting that.

Excellent. Monsters don't sacrifice their well-being for others. Nicely spun, Eventide complimented.

Thank you, I replied smugly.

"He's used to starving. He'll be ok." I rubbed her arm in comfort, laying it on thick.

Now she simply looked aghast. "Where is he? I think this warrants a conversation…"

I twisted my lips in a grimace and replied, "He's afraid of scaring you again. Maybe wait a day or two to talk?"

"No!" she snapped and stalked off into the colony to find her fated mate. Had Emer not been so vulnerable, she would have seen right through my little strategy. Honestly, I was surprised this worked at all.

I broke into a broad grin and Eventide released a proud howl of victory. Belenus fell back to return to my side and held my hand. "I can feel that you are very pleased with yourself," he murmured into my ear. His breath made me shudder, and I sent a feral grin his way.

"She went off to confront Nofre about his self-starvation plan," I reported proudly.

"Let's hope that doesn't turn into a fight," Belenus drawled.

"Our fights always seem to turn out well," I whispered suggestively, and his pulse quickened.

"Well, if it turns out well for them, I may have to see what happens when I give you a reward."

Ok, stop, I ordered him. *You are making my panties wet.*

Uh, no. This is revenge for teasing my cock so mercilessly. Next time I get you alone, I'm going to reward you so well, you won't be able to walk for a week. I've got a beautiful golden trophy right here for your display case.

Belenus, stop!

No.

Chapter 26

Hekla

Belenus was only able to tease me for about twenty minutes before Emer came stomping up from behind the trudging colony. My mate raised his eyebrows at her stormy expression and clasped his hands behind his back.

"How did it go, Emer?" I asked, having a feeling it didn't go as well as I'd hoped.

"The man is infuriating! He is so stubborn! H—" she ranted, swinging her fingers up like she was pretending she had claws.

"Male," I reminded her.

She was thrown for a second, breathless. "What?"

"It's a shifter thing." Belenus sent an attractive, cocky grin my way. "They don't use man or woman. Just male or female."

Good boy, Eventide praised happily.

I am also, on occasion, a good boy, Escort reminded her, hungry for attention. We'd have to give them time together soon.

Emer waved her hands about and snapped, "Whatever! The point is, that male will not listen to reason! He's simply not going to eat!"

"Oh, that's unfortunate," my mate said with a sigh.

"Guess he truly cares about you," I said, shaking my head. That seemed to calm her a little bit. "A love worth starving for, what a romantic notion," I murmured loud enough for her to overhear. If Emer ever caught on to my little game, I was going to be in a lot of trouble. I glanced covertly over and nearly burst into laughter at the sour expression on her face.

She did seem relatively back to normal, though. Maybe she was capable of discussing what happened now. I looked ahead and called out to King Nechtan, who turned and relinquished his reins to Slaine. When we caught up to him, I turned to Emer and asked, "Are you able to tell us what happened now? It's ok for King Nechtan to be here. He'll be helping us, Emer."

"I see…" she said, calmer now, though her brows had drawn in worry. Belenus wrapped an arm around her shoulder, and we waited patiently for her to talk. "Things went really quiet after you both left without a word. I found out what actually occurred from your human, Hekla. Koray told me everything he knew, and I wasn't comfortable staying uninvolved anymore. Especially after…

"I finally unearthed who'd poisoned you, Hekla," Emer said to me, breaking from a pained expression and pressing her lips together in a thin line. A short, surprised growl burst through my lips, and I covered my mouth to not interrupt her further. "I discovered it was Lynet and told her that if she didn't help me, I'd get her sent to the dungeon. I forced her to go to Eislyn's room to try to either get information out of her or form an alliance to collude if there was an opportunity for it. I wanted to listen from outside her balcony and find out if there was more to Eislyn than I suspected." Emer kicked her boots particularly hard through the snow, and her eyes pinkened. She sniffed, sending several tears down her cheeks.

"Turns out that Lynet was either a really bad actress or Eislyn was crazy as shit. I guess it's probably both," she said that last part with a laugh and rubbed her weeping eyes. "Eislyn killed her, Belenus. She threw her off the balcony, bound in vines with nothing to break her fall but her neck. It happened so fast I didn't expect… I didn't think…"

I stilled in horror. The casual death had me reeling. Wolves were relatively violent but outright murder was rare and usually not without serious reason.

"Gods…" Belenus whispered.

"Then, Hekla, I heard a scrabbling, and the next thing I knew, your mac-talla was jumping off the balcony too! I barely caught him in time." She chuckled again and wiped mucus from her upper lip while I continued to gape at her.

"What was Arse doing in there?" I asked, aghast. "What was he thinking?"

"He," Emer began, outright laughing now, "ate holes through all her clothes in revenge!"

The laughter I was most surprised to hear came from King Nechtan. It was a deep, handsome laugh that made him seem a little younger. He just shook his head, laughing while keeping a shoulder bag close to him. I could barely see the pregnant mac-talla's breathing swell the fabric. I imagined he had a lot of experience with ruined wardrobes, and I wondered how many socks he'd lost to a hungry mac-talla.

"And then? Emer, you mentioned something about the queen," Belenus prompted, deeply focused now. I sobered a bit myself, processing that the woman who'd poisoned me was dead. Though she did me wrong, her actions weren't enough to justify a death sentence. It had me feeling a bit ill.

Emer nodded and bit her lip. "Our… our queen came in right after and asked when someone was going to be delivered. Apparently, part of the marriage contract was for the return of an individual from the Spring Court."

Belenus narrowed his eyes and asked, "Did she mention a name?"

Emer sandwiched her lips between her teeth but couldn't hold back her sob. Movement caught my eye, and I looked over my shoulder to see Nofre several rows back, staring worriedly at Emer with a shadowed brow and a restless stance. He looked very much like he could sense her pain and didn't want to keep his distance. The restraint impressed me, though, the context was sad.

"Emer?" Belenus pressed.

"I heard the queen say the name Ailill!" she blurted out and hugged herself. Belenus's face dropped all expression, and King Nechtan finally acted like he'd heard something important.

"Belenus," the king asked, "did they ever recover the body of your father?"

This part of his family history was news to me, and I moved closer to my mate, worried about his state of mind. "Was that your father's name? Ailill?" I asked, experiencing the mess, the buzzing, of his numbness, shock, and confusion.

Belenus stared ahead and cupped his mouth. Emer released another reluctant sob, as lost as her brother. I gestured for Nofre to come closer as he stalked us. He had to be Emer's support if Belenus was going to need me. The bat-shifter furrowed his brows, not understanding what I wanted but approached me regardless. In a decisive move not to be argued with, I grabbed his hand and placed it on Emer's shoulder. They both stiffened from their very first contact, but after a moment of adjusting, Nofre broke through it first and gently squeezed her shoulder. She gradually relaxed, so I gave Nofre a meaningful look and allowed him to take my place while I swung over to stand by Belenus. At least Nofre had managed to find a shirt, and his wings seemed to have disappeared for now.

I linked arms with my mate and looked up at him. His face was drawn, and he seemed lost in thought. "I have no proof that his body was recovered," Belenus replied to the king when I moved to hold his large hand in mine. "The queen said that he'd been cremated, but I wasn't there to bear witness."

"So very likely the summer queen lied, and your father never returned from the Spring Court," King Nechtan said, scratching at his argentine chin. The winter fae seemed as silvery as the summer fae were golden.

Belenus's breath caught when he realized I'd asked something as well. "And yes… that was my father's name." He squeezed my hand, and I leaned my head against his shoulder, hating the pain I felt from him. He was shocked and confused, but there was also a sense of clarity. Maybe this would explain a great many things.

"But why lie about it?" King Nechtan wondered. "If he was captured, why keep that a secret? Why not attempt a rescue? That seems worthy of waging war for any court. If I had a queen, I'd stop at nothing to bring her back, even if it was a marriage of convenience."

"I don't know," Belenus said blankly. "He'd been gone for the majority of my life. I barely even remember him bringing Emer home."

King Nechtan leaned over to patently study Belenus's sister. "Where did Emer come from? You said she's adopted, yes?"

My mate shrugged. "He just brought Emer home. Found her on one of his trips. The queen didn't want any more children after me, but I guess Father wanted a daughter."

"Wonder where he found her. She's more an autumn fae than summer with that red in her hair," the king mused. Emer had stopped volunteering information and stared straight ahead. Nofre still looked uncomfortable, but I heard him quietly whisper that he liked her red hair. Emer's lips twitched, and her cheeks blossomed from the compliment.

"Our orphanages often have fae from other courts. Families get separated from wartime," Belenus replied.

"The timing is unusual, but I suppose that's possible." The king didn't sound particularly sold on Belenus's explanation.

"So what do we do with this information?" I asked. "If we dissolve the contract, this person, who may or may not be your father, won't be handed over."

"No, they won't be, and I'm starting to understand why the queen was so fixated on this marriage. If the only thing the

Spring Court wanted was a spring princess on our throne, then the queen was willing to marry me away in exchange for this mystery person. It has to be Father. It simply has to be him. I can't imagine anyone else she'd sell her son for. But she hated him, though." Belenus placed his hand over his face and snapped, "I'm so blisterin' confused!"

"There must be more to this," King Nechtan stated confidently. His confident observations and focus on results reminded me a little of Zorian. If Belenus and I took the throne, I honestly believed he'd make a good ally, and I could see us developing an advantageous relationship with his court. I'd have to keep an eye open for how we could all best benefit with improved communication.

When we take the throne, Eventide corrected. Yes, we had to stay optimistic.

"We need more information," Belenus agreed. "In the meantime, we may have a little over a day until we reach the next door. We'll need to stop a little sooner than normal to give the shifters time to hunt. We don't exactly have a nuckelavee for them to split this time."

"Did you say nuckelavee?" the king inquired sharply.

I explained what had happened, and he raised his thick black brows, suitably impressed. "I wouldn't mind hiring them for problematic predators and demonic fae," he said thoughtfully. That proposal intrigued me, and I filed it away for later. The bat-shifters would need to build their economy, to develop something of value to trade for blood rations. I sensed I had a lot of work ahead of me, but I was more optimistic about their future than I was several days ago.

We eventually released the exhausted bat-shifters to hunt for food. Fortunately, some of the game like deer and boar were large enough to share, but there were almost too many bellies to fill; hours passed before everyone received their meal. The winter fae warriors shared some of their rations with Belenus,

Emer, and me, since none of us wanted to take game away from the blood drinkers.

In dire need of distraction, Emer wandered off, lifting her skirts and stomping purposefully through the snow to see if anyone needed wounds tended to. I kept an eye on her, not trusting any lustful shifter who might try to take advantage. The wary thought had me sighing; it wasn't their fault, and it was atrocious that their curse manipulated so many facets of their lives. If I couldn't tolerate over twenty-five years of no sex, I didn't know how some of them stayed sane after a hundred years—or however long they lived. I hadn't thought to ask.

Belenus and I huddled over our campfire, warming each other as the cold bit our backs. Sleeping outside in winter, even with the Sun God's rise, promised to be miserable. I was about to ask Belenus what he thought of shifting before sleeping, but was interrupted by Emer's bird form. She darted out of nowhere, and circled frantically before finally squeezing into the gap between my neck and my hair.

"Ah!" I shouted in surprise, then flinched and ducked as a large bat swooped past me and banked to avoid crashing. That scented like Nofre! What I feared had come to pass—or so I suspected.

"NOFRE!" I commanded in a harsh alpha tone to get his attention. "STOP HUNTING EMER! GO MASTURBATE!"

The bat faltered in his flight, and I'd swear to my dying day that I saw deep shame in his little black eyes. In half a heartbeat, he flew off, hopefully to do what I'd ordered.

Emer jumped from her sanctuary under my hair and changed back to her fae form, cackling wildly from the adrenaline rush of a close call. Belenus could have been enraged at Nofre's attempt to mate with her, but he just started laughing too. I buried my face in my hands, unable to believe the words that had come out of my mouth. It promised to be the most utterly ridiculous thing I've ever said, and will ever say, in my lifetime. Deep chuckling from the winter warriors hit my ears, provoking further embarrassment. Trail was going to die over this story.

"You just"—Belenus roared with laughter—"ordered someone to go masturbate."

"Just practicing being queen," I mumbled into my palms.

Maybe it'll work on Belenus, Eventide pondered.

"Don't even joke about that!" he protested out loud.

"You weren't kidding!" Emer continued, cackling with tears in her eyes. "I yelled at him to eat and shoved a rabbit in his face. He crumbled at the sight, sucked it dry, and looked at me like I was dessert! Oh, someone needs to break this curse. These poor shifters."

I just kept my face buried in my palms, truly wondering what my life had become.

I wandered through the woods because I hadn't seen Belenus for a while. He wasn't answering my mind-links, and Escort had fallen silent too. I couldn't even get Eventide to talk to me. A deep dread filled my belly, painfully tangling my guts as I stumbled through the underbrush. I'd occasionally catch the briefest scent of Belenus, and though it wasn't potent, it helped me track him to a moonlit clearing. I didn't know why I hadn't heard anything. The view before me crushed my heart—shattered it to bloody shards.

Belenus and Eislyn were wrapped in a passionate embrace, writhing naked and joined at the hips. I fell to my knees and screamed, but neither of them heard me over their lovemaking. I asked him why he was doing this. I begged him to explain and tried to convince him he was bewitched. From the look on their faces though, I could see the fierce love they had for each other. Eislyn didn't even take a second to gloat, to sneer at me. They were completely focused on their joining.

Once Belenus leaned down to mark her, I screeched until I woke, drenched in sweat. The nightmare had wrecked me, and I sobbed. I searched for Belenus in the darkness, but once again, I couldn't find him. Had it been a dream? It must have been!

Like I'd dreamed, I picked up his scent... which led me to the woods. I prayed to every single god that he'd be alone this time, but it was not so. Belenus's face was between her legs this time, worshiping her core as he used to mine. Another piece of myself died as the agony of betrayal ripped through me. The crimson shards that had been my heart crumbled into red ashes. I screeched until I woke anew.

Belenus was gone, so I wandered back to the meadow to find Eislyn's lips around Belenus's cock. Another piece of myself died, and I woke again. Each time I stood from the cold ground, I knew I'd find them locked together in bliss. Each time I became a throwaway, I died a little more until all that was left was a husk.

I had no idea how many times the experience repeated, but I had lost hope that it'd ever stop. I had no idea if the current iteration was real until I'd wake, and I wished for death with each foray into the woods. The shadowed ground offered no alternate routes. The only way out was forward, but it was never a true escape.

After the trauma ate at my husk, my feral mind escaped. I repeatedly fell into my wolf form and ripped my mate to shreds. Somehow, they never noticed my attacks and continued fucking until they were dead, torn to pieces. Then I'd utterly lose my mind to grief and wake. There was no knowing how long the cycle clutched me, but at one point, I'd finally woken to a different space.

Above me, the Sun God cut into my vision. He was awake this time.

Then I remembered it all. I shrieked and jumped to my feet, unbalanced and wild. I wasn't alone this time. Belenus woke with a startled expression, his amber eyes darting to me. His form blurred as tears took my vision and streamed down my face. Still, I could see movement, and I recoiled when my ex-mate reached for me.

"No!" I screamed in his face and slashed, raking my claws into his forearms. Knowing he was just as dangerous, I immediately lunged to kill him, but he side-stepped and attempted to grapple me. I scrambled from his grasping hands and snarled at the approaching soldiers and shifters. Their faithless eyes covered me, suffocated me.

"Traitors! You're all traitors!" I screeched at the top of my lungs. "You betrayed me!"

Too many enemies. Too many wicked fae attempting to catch me. I had to escape his army of turncoats. I spun on a heel and left the swarming commotion behind me, unable to absorb what people yelled. It didn't matter. They'd all betrayed me and supported the man who'd killed me.

I tried to shift into Eventide, but her form evaded me. Not even my wolf was there for me. They'd all abandoned me! I screamed into the burning sky, wondering if the Sky Gods had abandoned me too, like They'd once abandoned Ragna. Would Ragna allow me back or would she reject me as well?

I raked my claws into my neck to rip out the flesh where Belenus's mark lived, and blood poured down my chest in between my breasts and over my belly, staining my clothes the color of a broken heart. I shrieked at the physical pain, the rending of muscle and sinew, but it could not compare to the loss of my mate. How could he kill me like this? He knew I'd die from heartbreak, and he chose her anyway.

Hands found me and my face met with snow, buried deep into the foam of winter. I couldn't even feel the cold anymore. My ashen heart spread the numbness like a dead sun radiating poison. The hands, three pairs of them, lifted me and turned me over, holding me in an unbreakable restraint.

A trio of bat-shifters had me pinned, and the faces of more traitors appeared in my line of sight. "You all betrayed me!" I cried through furious tears. "I freed you, I nurtured you, I tried to help, and you supported the man who killed me!"

The silvery fae glanced over at the redhead and my enemy. “Do you feel that?” he asked.

“Why are you ignoring me? You signed my execution!”

The redhead knelt closer. “I’ve never felt that before. What is it?” She started as I snarled at her, warning her to keep her filthy distance.

“Rot,” my enemy said, looking worried. He brushed his yellow hair aside and dared appear concerned about me. What a disgusting actor he was. No wonder I’d been fooled.

“You fucked her!” I screamed at him. “You fucked Eislyn for hours and hours! I had to watch! You made me watch!”

He also dared to look surprised, as if this was news to him. My enemy turned to the others and asked, “What do we do? Is this a curse or some other kind of spell?”

The lies piled offensively, and I screamed at the top of my lungs, nigh tearing my throat, “I’m not making this up! How dare you lie!”

The stern fae reached toward my forehead with a hand dusted in silver. “Hibernate,” he ordered in a low voice, and my torture finally ended. Sweet bliss. Oh, how I welcomed death.

Belenus

“We need to search the area,” King Nechtan said in a cold voice and directed his men to scatter. I started when Emer’s fingers landed on my arm, hastily working to scab gashes that had nearly reached bone. As painful as they were, I was far more worried about the damage Hekla had inflicted on herself. She’d nicked an artery and bled heavily, the rivulets spurting into her dress. I fell to my knees by her head, panicking. My heart clenched as I struggled to recover from the emotions she’d radiated. Our bond had been flooded with her deepest despair and loathing, spreading its agony to me.

"Help me, Emer," I begged and lifted Hekla's head to my lap so I could access her slaughtered shoulder.

"This has to be the most creative assassination attempt I've ever seen," the king fumed as he jotted a message on a small scroll. He summoned a bird handler and released the grey avian with a full tube. "This is too far southwest from the previous rot-witch sightings. They're moving fast."

I vacantly noted that Nofre remained nearby, but Ferrer and Luzia had made themselves scarce, likely too tempted by the sight of fresh blood. All I could say was thank the blazing Sun God they'd just eaten.

I can't find Eventide, Escort alerted, more distraught than I'd ever heard him.

Hekla's unconscious. Wouldn't Eventide be too?

Not usually. One can be awake while the other is asleep.

Fuck, I replied and continued working on my poor mate's neck while Emer held her flesh together. Nofre kept his distance for a while but eventually crouched next to my sister and placed a very hesitant hand on her shoulder.

"Can you sense where any curses might be, Emer?" I asked, then looked up at the winter fae. "King Nechtan? My wolf says that hers has gone unusually quiet."

Emer and the king leaned over my mate's supine form, searching for clues. "It might be nestled in her skull," he said, gesturing to her limp head. "Her affliction is obviously psychological. She appeared to exhibit signs of brainwashing you'd find in torture."

"If her wolf is a separate mind, they might not have been able to curse them both with the same illusion? Maybe they had to block her?" Emer guessed and helped me close up the last of Hekla's lacerations.

If I hadn't been looking at my sister, I wouldn't have noticed Nofre's openmouthed expression. He looked torn, like he wanted to say something but had reservations. I met his eyes and raised my brows in question.

He knew an unspoken order when he saw one. "Is it possible to get her to drink while she's unconscious?" he asked in such a low voice I almost couldn't hear him.

"Why?" I inquired, slowly lifting her head and parting her hair to see if there were any other injuries or curse marks. I hoped to the Sky Gods she served that I wouldn't find anything as complicated as what we'd found on Ragna at Eysteinn's hideout. At least Koray was in this realm, though, so the worst-case scenario was something we could eventually fix.

"I'm… taking a huge risk telling you this…" he whispered, grimacing and turning his gaze to where his people waited.

"Do we need to make a promise, Nofre?"

He pressed his lips together, creating an even paler white line around his lips. "I suppose that would be acceptable…"

My sister reacted first, surprisingly. "I promise I will not share what you are about to reveal," Emer swore and held out her hand. His expression softened, and he shakily took her smaller hand in his to seal their promise.

The rest of us made the same vow, and Nofre rubbed his eyes while taking a deep breath. "We didn't realize until we'd received several cursed fae into the Night Court. One of our fated mates had been cursed with starvation by a fear gorta and had wandered into our territory, near mad with hunger. He lost his control after a nightmare and bit his mate on accident but was cured after having taken in some of her blood.

"We believe," he continued, looking away again, "that not only are we immune to other curses, our blood may act as a cleanser for the cursed. We're so thoroughly cursed that there's simply no room for another spell to latch onto."

I blinked and straightened, astonished. Curse immunity had always been considered an impossibility. So that was why Ferrer remained healthy after his own faery encounter.

"Wow," Emer whispered. "Our healers would be flabbergasted."

Nofre fidgeted uncomfortably, but his eyes flashed with a humble devotion. "I'm willing to donate some of my blood if it helps her," he offered quietly. "She's… potentially my future sister." He mumbled that last part out and Emer bristled.

"You don't know that!" she hissed.

It was my turn to bristle. "Emer, you may technically be able to say whatever you want to say, but sometimes you just fucking shouldn't," I snapped at her. Her face flushed with humiliation, and she fled back to the campsite, leaving a gutted Nofre in her wake.

I shook my head at her immature reaction. Now was not the time for her dramatic outbursts. "Forgive her," I growled and hoisted Hekla up so she'd be leaning against my chest, "but she does owe you an apology. That was cruel."

"I'd just forgotten that rejection was even possible," the bat-shifter replied in a strained voice. Profoundly shaken, his pale skin had lost several shades of pigmentation. He practically resembled a corpse now.

"She's been through a lot. She'll calm down. So what do we need to do here?" I asked, much more concerned about my mate at the moment. I'd have to talk to Emer later about poorly timed tantrums.

"I'll bite my arm and just let it drip into her mouth. You'll need to hold it open for me," he answered and extended his fangs, the sharpest teeth I'd ever seen in my life. I'd say they were even sharper than Hekla's. King Nechtan simply watched in silence, seemingly fascinated by the procedure.

Nofre didn't have to dig deep. He merely punctured one of his bulging veins and held it to her open mouth. "This is so bizarre," he murmured as he fed my mate his warm blood. "I'm supposed to be the one drinking blood here." He laughed weakly and waited a little while before pulling back and pressing on his vein to stop the bleeding.

I closed my mate's bloody mouth and nodded in the direction of the camp. "You've done some good here, Nofre. I hope this works," I said, stroking her hair and washing her face with snow. "Go back to sleep. It's not yet nightfall," I ordered, suddenly feeling exhausted. The weight pressed down, growing heavier the more I thought about Hekla's condition.

King Nechtan quietly interrupted my weary thoughts. "I think we should bind her wrists and feet before you retire in case the blood doesn't work."

I really did not want to bind her, but I couldn't bear watching her hurt herself again. I also wasn't a fan of someone using her to kill me. My poor Hekla was going to feel so guilty.

"Alright." I caved with a heavy sigh and carried her back to camp, hoping she had a spare dress in her bag.

Oh vengeful Sun God, please return my mate to me.

Chapter 27

Belenus

I searched for my adopted sister when I returned to camp and gestured with a jerk of my chin for her to follow me. Once I found a decent space away from male eyes, I created a warm patch of summer to settle Hekla on. "Clean her dress for me, Emer," I requested with a stone-faced expression. She helped me undress Hekla, and I got to work cleaning the blood off my female's skin.

"I'm sorry," she muttered after several minutes.

"It's not me you have to apologize to. You bloody well know that."

She stared miserably down at Hekla's crimsoned dress. "I know."

"I've spent our entire youth bailing you out of trouble, but you really need to open your eyes to your situation," I lectured, scrubbing at a particularly sticky spot on Hekla's collarbone. "When I take the throne, we're going to inherit hefty responsibilities. There is going to be a lot to clean up, Emer, and I'm going to need your help.

"That being said," I warned with a stern look, "before you decide to take on any of those responsibilities, you have a hard decision to make."

"With him?" she asked meekly and I nodded.

"Now, I don't mind if you move to the Realm of the Humans if you want to. I don't mind if he stays at the castle with us. What I do mind, however, is you stringing him along."

"Ah," she whispered, half-heartedly rinsing blood from cloth with warm, melted snow.

"Those people have survived centuries of torture. I don't want you to make any rushed decisions or make up your mind when you're emotional, but Nofre's a good male. He deserves an answer at some point, and I'm asking you not to tease him until then." I frowned and adjusted my unconscious mate's position to wash her stomach and hips. "I know how you are, Emer, but things have become dead serious, and you've got to grow up. Your actions matter more than ever in this situation because you're fated to a male from an endangered species. If you really don't want him, let him go so he can find happiness elsewhere. Perhaps he'll get a second chance mate."

"I don't want to see him with anoth—" she snapped angrily but bit her tongue before she finished her sentence. "I just didn't think I'd ever find or want a mate. Mother an—I mean, the queen and our father didn't exactly make it look like a walk in the park," she explained bitterly. "I didn't know about the mistresses until I was much older."

"I don't foresee Nofre cheating on you," I replied flatly. "Besides, our parents weren't fated. They were poorly matched."

"I don't see him doing that either," Emer confessed, staring at nothing now. Her eyes had glazed over, vapid, and I couldn't read her at all.

"To be honest, he's probably going to worship your unworthy feet. He looked like you stabbed him in the heart when you ran off earlier."

"My feet are quite unworthy." She heaved a sigh, and her gaze finally returned to the wet dress and undergarments on her lap. Steam curled out in long ribbons from between her fingers as her summer reserves drove out the damp. "These will still be slightly stained, but it's the best I can do without soap. At least it'll be comfortable and dry."

I frowned and shook my head in frustration, mentally backing up. "I didn't mean what I said. You're worthy, Emer. You just need to take responsibility now. It's as much about your happiness as it is about his. They both matter, but he's been through enough pain."

She nodded and remained silent until I prompted her to help dress Hekla. I needed to impart one last thought to her. "If you want to know what it's like, Emer, finding Hekla was the best thing that's ever happened to me. I've realized—and take this quite seriously—that she's worth waging war for, and I'd give her anything if she asked for it." I gazed sadly down at my mate's sleeping face as I gathered her into my arms. "She's changed me for the better. She still does, and there's nothing akin to the sense of love, devotion, and completion I get from her. I hope you don't choose to miss out on all that, but you need to do what's right for you."

Then, reluctantly, I bound my mate's hands and feet before walking back to the camp with my silent sister in stride. She turned thoughtful as I settled with Hekla in a dedicated and affectionate embrace. Emer left to find her own space, and I glanced over to find Nofre resting by a fire under the shelter of a tree, watching her from a distance. The poor male looked absolutely heartsick.

King Nechtan woke me, preventing my battered mind from oversleeping. I was bloody tired, sore from so much walking, and beyond sick of winter's bone-deep freeze. It relieved me the bat-shifters ended up being hardy enough to survive the conditions of a long march and a frigid season. They had to hunt more often, though, and I had to accept their frequent coming and going during the night's trek. Thankfully, Ferrer, Luzia, and several other volunteers were on top of the head count and promised to let me know if anyone went missing.

Several hours after returning to our march, I caught Hekla's eyes opening. "Hekla?" I asked softly as my heart rose into my throat, threatening to choke me with anticipation, and her glassy gaze finally drifted to mine.

Eventide? Escort called out.

I'm here. I'm back, Eventide announced. *Hekla is in shock, though. Something nasty surprised us in our sleep and gave her... really, really, really bad nightmares. Belenus, it was bad.*

A mix of relief and anger gripped my chest. *Yes, I think I know enough about it. We... don't need to discuss it. The point is, there's a rot-witch around who's responsible. I just don't know how they got close enough to...*

I claim the right to kill her, Escort proclaimed hatefully. His sizzling rage reminded me to check in with Hekla's emotions. Reaching across our bond, I sensed a flat buzz of numbness, but occasionally, a hint of sadness, jealousy, or shame would trickle across.

"Can you speak to me, my dear?" I asked Hekla, but she replied only with a slow blink, so I turned my inquiry to her wolf. *Can she even understand me, Eventide?*

She's not responding to me either, but I believe so if you're noticing her emotions change. It's not like she's in a coma.

"Right..." I fumbled for the right words as I stared down at my mate's lovely face, her brown cheeks and nose flushed from the cold no matter how I bundled her. "Hekla, you know me. You know I'd rather cut off my cock than even look at that wretch." I fought for some idea to help—any idea. "Whenever those planted images surface, I want you to replace that image of me with something else because that was never me." I chuckled a little and added, "Replace my image in that nightmare with a rot-witch. I guarantee you'll never think of that scene in the same way again."

When Hekla closed her eyes, my cheeks fell alongside my departing smile. I clenched my jaw around a sob and held her tighter as my boots parted the snow. That rot-witch had better hope I never found her. I'd already sentenced her to death.

King Nechtan fell back with his horse to join me. "How close are we to the next hidden door?"

"Should be there around sunrise."

"And what after that?"

I caressed Hekla's shoulders and replied, "If we get to the summer castle in time, I'll need to work on organizing my soldiers and quietly evacuating those closest to me. They'll likely be targeted if they're within reach of the queen's influence."

"And if you don't get there in time?"

I gestured ahead of us. "Then I'll have to send someone in to do it. I can't risk getting close until I find a way out of that contract. I need to know if the team I'd dedicated to that project came up with any solutions. I had higher hopes for someone who'd reached out to some witches in the Realm of the Humans." I held up my other hand to allay any sudden fears. "The Lunar Coven is benign, worry not. They do not worship the rot."

He nodded grimly. "Speaking of witches, we still haven't found the rot-witch, but we'll keep looking."

"Understood," I replied. After that, I updated him on Hekla's slow recovery and gave him some additional details on my plans for the takeover before releasing him to rejoin his warriors.

There were approximately several hours before dawn when we finally neared the door to the Summer Court. I needed to scout the exit point first to see if there was any coverage for the bat-shifters on the other side; I couldn't tell just by looking at the godling's map. Of all the courts they were destined to have to wait in, it was unfortunate it had to be the Summer Court; they would not fare well under our blazing sun, and we'd likely have to make concessions along the way for their well-being.

I called for a halt, transferred Hekla's care to Nofre, and jogged ahead to investigate the door. Luckily, the Winter Court was heavily forested, so the shifters would be able to rest on this side of the door tonight if the other side was too exposed to the sky and thus the lashings of the Sun God.

The uneven blanket of snow continued to be a nuisance, rising to my shins as if thoroughly happy to slow my march. However, as I approached my destination, what had my scowl deepening the most was a subtle change in the air and magic layer.

Lingering around the door was the presence of sourness, and I hissed with instinctive aversion. It was the same rotten, damp, and mildewy aura that we'd detected on Hekla after she'd been cursed. I unsheathed my sword and gathered some summer essence into my hand while peering into the dark. Something lingered at the edge of my vision, but it didn't remain. Slowly, the silhouette hobbled toward me, not appearing particularly dangerous, but I knew better.

Except for the fact that it was a woman, one could have mistaken her for a fear gorta by the emaciation and the rot clouding the air. This was probably the oldest-looking witch I'd ever seen. Hers was not the age that brought wisdom but the age that nurtured madness—especially with the unknown forces provoking these creatures. She stared at me with weepy, bloodshot eyes that hinted at the open door in her mind, a place where hoary, forbidden things were welcomed with hungry arms.

I only had so much magic, so I decided to defend myself against thrown curses. She was in no shape to physically overpower me. Her long, spindly fingers with nails that had warped into talons over the decades—or perhaps centuries—were locked with arthritis and aquiver.

Then, with a mouth open wide, she released a faint hissing scream, one accompanied by more than a singular voice. She giggled madly and continued her waddling towards me, struggling against the shin-deep snow. The eagerness frightened me, but I shoved that fear aside, took a step forward, and timed my lunge, making a judgment call that I believed worth the risk.

She didn't flinch or make any attempt to dodge as I darted to catch her wrists and lock them behind her back. The creature appeared to be falling into something akin to dementia, and she started babbling nonsense as I marched her back to King Nechtan.

"Autumn is fall, spring is fall, summer will fall, seelie will fall. Lust to bawl, families stall. All in all, wrapped in pall," she croaked deliriously, gleeful while performing her macabre poetry. "Shame you fall. So pretty but not delicious. Not enough fat."

I shuddered and scowled, unable to shut her up on our way back to the colony and our allies. I dragged her violently before the winter king and his warriors, but I lost my hold on her right arm when it detached from her shoulder and fell to the ground. I curled my upper lip in disgust and horror, realizing her insides were rotting underneath her pallid, loose skin. Even King Nechtan's stoic warriors released sounds of revulsion as the limb sank through the snow, parting the white with its warm fluids.

"Found," I announced with finality and tried not to breathe too deeply. "Any questions before my—"

I've changed my mind. I don't want to bite that. You kill her, Escort decided hastily.

"Before I execute her?" I amended halfway through my question. "She doesn't appear lucid, so don't get your hopes up."

"That's the oldest rot-witch I've ever seen," the king stated, somehow able to maintain a straight face. I glanced over at Emer, who had a hand placed over her mouth. She blanched, dry heaved, and ran off behind a tree to vomit. Nofre shifted in unease, visibly troubled by her state and torn. He held onto Hekla as I'd asked and—with a jerk of his chin—ultimately gestured for Luzia to go care for her. Many of the shifters looked a touch green at the sight, and I imagined this appeared very much like food that had spoiled.

"What's the rot-witches' goal?" I asked harshly, choosing to no longer handle her with excessive force. I didn't need half the people here losing their stomachs over this interrogation, and her stench had intensified threefold since the detachment.

The rot-witch arched against me and released another quiet scream. I had no idea what it meant. It hadn't sounded like one of pain. "No meals here, no meals," she complained with a wet laugh.

The king scowled and his hand twitched. No doubt he wanted to torture her but knew it was pointless. She'd likely fall apart under a single compelling touch. "Answer him," he boomed, and ice encased her up to her neck and around her skull, stilling her completely. Relieved, I released my grip on her and scooped up some snow to try to wipe the grease from my hands.

Fucking disgusting, Escort mumbled. *Ask if someone has soap. I definitely will...*

The rot-witch sighed, and her cadaverous face relaxed under nostalgia. "So easy get beauty to breed. Autumn is fall, spring is fall, summer will fall, seelie will fall." She hummed and continued, "Winter will fall, unseelie will fall. All in all, the gods will crawl."

"How has spring fallen?" I asked, anger simmering beneath my skin as she continued to test my patience. "Why assassinate me? Is the summer queen involved?" I knew I shouldn't ask multiple questions at once, but I felt like time was running low.

Tiring, she grumbled and slurred out, "No, no, no. Kill the shell. Need you. Spring and fall! Want, want, want. Open and closed. So bad vessel is thin. Not enough fat. Not meal. What waste." Her eyes rolled deliriously to the bat-shifters. "You should be in bed. It's late. So late. Not in time."

Deciphering her rambling now was nigh impossible. "The summer queen," I asserted, "is she involved?"

The rot-witch laughed, which seemed to cause one cheekbone to flatten, and several teeth dribbled from her mouth. "Fuck, fuck, fuck, fuck, fuck, fuck, fuck!" she whispered, but her chant grew progressively into delighted screams just as her body caved in and filled the ice with nothing but rotten flesh and silence.

The silence, like a disease, spread throughout the audience of fae and bats.

Nofre was the first to break it. "They'd sent a dying one on what would have been a lethal mission," he observed and adjusted his hold on Hekla when her head flopped over in her sleep.

The king remarked solemnly, "It's been reported that the dying ones are the strongest… but they expire swiftly after any exertion, physical or magical."

I nodded to them both. I'd have to reflect on everything the rot-witch had said. Then, I turned to face the king and his warriors for one last critical inquiry.

"Does anyone have soap?"

Hekla

The grey-and-black world where I rested, once frigid, thawed. Warmth spread up my limbs and worked its way into my torso. Stiffness melted from my joints, and with a relaxed chest, my body finally felt like it could breathe.

—eems more clearheaded now, a female's voice announced, followed by the sloshing of water.

"Is she responding to you yet?" a soothing, handsome voice asked. That voice reminded me of something. It reminded me of both pain and pleasure, but I couldn't identify it.

Not yet, the first voice answered.

I'll try, my stardust. Hekla, mate, can you hear me? a third voice faded into my head. *Are you coming back to us?*

Did I know that voice? It was masculine, like the one who'd spoken aloud, but was wilder and held notes of feral dominance. This was the newer voice. I hadn't known this one for very long.

"Escort?" I croaked, trying to open my eyes. Jealousy coiled around my heart, a sharp twining, but it wasn't coming from me. How was that possible?

Don't be upset, Belenus, the first voice said—a female. *It was only a matter of time before she responded to one of our voices. Escort is you.*

"I know," I heard the male mumble. "Hekla, wake for me. Please."

Wet fingertips brushed my hair from my face, and the water droplets helped dissolve the leaden weights attached to my eyelids. I blinked in rapid succession until they were able to stay open, and that was when I noticed I could move my arms and legs. The sluggishness told me I was neck-deep in tepid water.

When my eyes focused, I realized it wasn't rocks cradling me but a warm, sculpted male with gold-dusted skin and worried almond-shaped eyes. The man was tired, and his scruff showed that he'd been traveling for a while. His sunflower-yellow hair had been brushed to the side, but strands fell carelessly over a drawn brow. A twig had entangled itself in his short locks; he must have been sleeping on the ground. As worn as he looked, he was as beautiful as he was warrior-like... the most beautiful male I'd ever seen in my life.

His soft lips parted as he searched my face. "My dear, Hekla? My female? Can you talk to me?" he asked gently, adjusting his cradling of my body so I could see him better. My mind slowly returned to me, and memories trickled in to fill the gaps. There'd been nightmares, then nothing. I'd lain in a sleep so deep that I thought I had been dead.

The tingles where we touched made me remember him. It came slowly to me, but when it did, my heart swelled; my mate had been the first to greet me out of sleep. "Belenus?" I croaked out slowly. I placed a hand on the contour of one of his naked pecs, sending rivulets of warm water down his torso. "How long?"

"Oh, thank the Sun God!" he whispered and embraced me, his fingers shaking as they dug into my skin. "I was so worried about you." I welcomed his possessive clutching and listened to how boldly his heart pounded in his ribcage. "Just a little over a day, my female. King Nechtan put you into a quiet sleep so you could heal and wouldn't hurt yourself again."

I gingerly touched my shoulder where Belenus's mark was, relieved to find it intact, and nearly released a sob from my stacking humiliation and guilt. "I hurt you," I bemoaned, then searched for the gashes that I knew he'd already healed. "I hurt you again."

He shook his head in a fierce denial. "It wasn't anything I couldn't handle. I told you that I'd take your hurt, and I meant it. I was just worried about you. I love you. Seeing your tortured face was worse than any cut or broken bone," he confessed, his irises narrowing to amber rings in his examining.

The man's broad chest pressed into me with every slow breath he took. It swelled again, deeply, just before he started speaking again, catching me up on events. I learned, while he comforted me with caresses, what had happened with the rot-witch he'd found. He couldn't share how my curse had been treated, but I was just happy to know it was gone. Belenus had been good to me, despite everything that had tried to tear us apart from day one. He'd tolerated the torture of his court and the strife I'd given him for things he could hardly control.

It weighed on me more now. I really should make my confession.

Belenus's thumb stroked my cheek. "I'm glad you're awake, but I originally brought you here to bathe you," he said softly, showing me a bar of soap he'd pulled from the trickling, lapping riverbank. "A winter fae field healer had several to spare."

The naming of the season had me finally noticing its absence. "We're in summer again," I commented blandly, spying the dry ground and the warm glow of the setting sun. The Sun God was sinking behind a large hill, letting his last rays caress the soft moor ground. On the other side of the river was a smaller forest where the bat-shifters must be.

Belenus gently released me, lathered his hands, and began massaging my shoulders. "We're actually at our destination,

Hekla. The door took us a good distance into the Summer Court. We're about a mile out from the castle, slightly adjacent to the city, and I cast a large glamour with Emer's help to hide us."

That was surprising news, and I took a moment to absorb it. A lot had happened, indeed. I bobbed on the soft pebbles of the river bottom with my toes to stay afloat, but the more he worked, the more his touch relaxed me. I sighed and went mostly limp, grabbing my mate's waist to steady myself against the lazy pull of the river.

"We'll have to figure out how to retrieve the willing fighters and evacuate our loved ones from the castle. We can't allow hostages," I mumbled, thoroughly appreciating his ministrations. The little tingles of pleasure from the mate touch sank deeper into my muscles than any massage could, and I sighed as he lathered my scalp, rubbing thoroughly and sensually.

"I love how you're already such a queen," he rumbled appreciatively, and I smiled, pleased by his compliment. "It's incredibly arousing. You are a perfect match for me in every way, my dear. Don't ever forget that." He ran his soapy hands down each arm individually before hoisting me up and ordering, "Wrap your legs around me, my female."

I gripped his shoulders and secured my legs around his ribs. Belenus moved closer to the bank so that I was just out of the water and continued to cover me in soap. His rough palms molded over my shoulder blades and slid down my ribs to rub my lower back. Deep aches had developed from the days and nights we'd spent walking, and I hadn't realized how sore my muscles had grown until he dug into them.

His eyes never left mine as he cleaned me, not even when his busy hands found my breasts. He just breathed slowly and deeply, maintaining eye contact, though his cheeks and pointed fae ears flushed pink.

"So will we have to disguise the winter fae so their presence here isn't… exposed?" I asked quietly, shivering when he rinsed the suds from my breasts. His eyes dilated on my last word.

"Hmm?" he hummed, distracted. "Oh, yes. We'll do the best we can with glamour magic. My magic here is potent." A hot spark sizzled into my chest. Yes, I knew he was potent in more ways than one. He continued to stare at my face while his soapy palms slid down my belly to the tops of my thighs.

I groaned softly, and he growled lowly in response. The vibration traveled down his chest and right between my spread legs. My core throbbed with need as our bodies communicated without words. I knew I was aroused, and though it was from a great many things, it was mostly from the tenderness of his treatment. A part of me felt so much guilt over attacking him that I didn't feel worthy of his love.

It wasn't your fault, Eventide said, finally speaking to me. I was afraid she'd felt betrayed too. After all, Belenus and Escort belonged to both of us.

I know. My emotions don't... match the facts, I replied uneasily.

You'll feel better after a good mounting, she said casually. As if a hot towel had been tossed onto my head, my face immediately heated, and I looked guiltily up at Belenus. She'd not said that privately.

"Eventide," Belenus murmured with a grin as he pulled back one of my legs to wash the rest of it. "I just got her back. Please don't go making her faint on us." Then, he washed my other leg, sending an attractive smirk my way.

His fingers finally slid from my hips to lather my buttocks, then slowly traced several fingers along until they found my sex. I tensed, and though his washing digits were clinical in their treatment, they did linger longer than necessary. He held my gaze as his fingers lazily traced my folds, and I bit my lip to trap a moan, entranced by the way he studied my eyes; I couldn't bring myself to break the moment.

His motions eventually slowed, and he walked slightly farther out into the river. The currents pulled more forcefully, but Belenus held me firmly to his chest. I very nearly squirmed against him, loving the feeling of my breasts, belly, and core pressed against the hard planes of his body.

Belenus lowered me so my face was level with his, and he nuzzled my nose before tilting his head to lay a soft kiss on my lips. Then, he took in a deep breath to warn me of his next action and ducked to submerge us both under the water. His hands slid all over my skin, wiping away the clouding soap and the remnants of my time spent unconscious.

He resurfaced with me, only moving his lips away so we could take another deep breath. We fell beneath the surface again, and he ran his warm fingers through my hair, letting the river take away all the impurities. Belenus massaged his lips to mine, and I felt a rumble in his chest that I was certain was a satisfied groan. His soft lips, and the pull of the river, made me feel like a darkness was being dragged out of me. What was left from the curse—the mental scarring I worried would linger—was swallowed by the currents.

Then, I truly noticed it, the heat within him.

Belenus spread his essence into my skull and chest, letting his light do the rest of the work. Stunned, I followed the sensations that seemed so much more mature now and blindingly noble. His magic, his summer light, so much stronger than it'd been in the other courts, felt like it could pass judgment and scorch the unworthy. Different. He was different here. Like night and day. Like spring, summer, autumn, and winter...

If I didn't trust Belenus, he would terrify me. Untethered here, he truly was a prince of the summer. I hadn't been able to see his dominion until we were mated and in his territory. The man, though, was a force of nature—the force of an entire season. It had me gaping.

The experience threatened to bring me to tears, forcing Belenus to surface out of concern. I swallowed a sob while he waded us over to the bank, and he looked down at me with half-lidden eyes. Those amber orbs scorched as mercilessly as his essence, and my heart broke into a run.

"Don't cry, my love," he murmured, noticing my overwhelmed state. "Whatever happens in the next couple of days, I'll protect you. I won't let anyone hurt you again." He brushed his lips to mine and murmured, "Touching you will be a death sentence. This I swear."

From this moment on, I had no doubt. I'd just now seen Belenus's true power here, but that made me even more terrified of the queen, who—by his own admission—could overpower him. All the court rules had held back this titan of a man, but as much as he was free to exercise that power now, I knew the queen wouldn't play by the rules either. What in the name of the Moon Goddess would I be able to contribute? What good was an alpha without a pack?

What would Hekla do?

I'd told Ragna to be her own friend. I needed to do something similar, but I wasn't sure what that was yet. I needed to truly take a step back and see everything from a wolf's perspective. At some point, I'd stopped being the wolf in their woods, but I was back now. I was ready to sit at the strategy table. The queen was just another factor. I could handle that.

Both Ragna and the Moon Goddess had referred to me as a guiding light, and that was what I would be. I'd help lead us to victory. I had to do it for these people, for fae like Bidelia, and for the balance of the courts. It seemed colossal, yes, but that's what Hekla would do.

Belenus's eyes searched my distracted ones, flickering left and right, and when I didn't respond to his promise, he said, *You're thinking too much right now.* He slid one arm beneath me so his other hand could run through my hair and press my lips to his in a scalding kiss.

I knew what else Hekla would do. She'd claim her fated mate. After all, she was a spirited little minx. So, I tabled my worries and melted into Belenus's sunlight.

Chapter 28

Hekla

I breathed Belenus in as he ignited my lips with his. He smelled and felt so delicious that had we the choice, I'd never leave his lips. He knew I longed to taste him, so he devoured my ravenous mouth, plunging his tongue inside to find mine. I arched into his unyielding chest, and his grip loosened, allowing me to slide down his torso until I could feel his cock jutting against my bottom.

I whimpered into his mouth, and the sound I knew he loved drew a responding groan from him. "Gods, she-wolf. The things you do to me," he gasped out and crushed his mouth against mine once more. His love and lust radiated through our bond and called out to what was already in the very center of my being. I didn't just need him inside me. I needed him to know he'd claimed my heart.

I grabbed his head with both my hands, tasting him with matching fervor while I mentally prepared myself. I pulled away from his lips, licking mine while catching my breath. "Belenus, my mate, I need to tell y—" I started confessing, but our fiery moment was interrupted by a call from the other side of the river.

Aw, what? Eventide snapped irritably. *We were so close!*

What the shit is it now? Escort growled.

I sighed under the din of our wolves protesting and twisted to see who'd spoken to us. I thought it sounded like Ferrer. My mate turned to hide my nudity behind him, and I held back a second sigh. I guessed he still hadn't shaken old habits. Many of the shifters had already seen me naked, but I could grudgingly respect that Belenus still didn't want to share the view of my body if it could be helped. Zorian was that way with Ragna. Maybe it was more common with mated males than I thought.

"Prince Belenus?" Ferrer's voice repeated hesitantly.

I finally spied him; he was turned away from us, partially hidden by a tree. I dropped my disappointed head onto Belenus's shoulder with a thunk.

Ferrer hastily delivered his message. "King Nechtan is calling for a meeting. All the shifters are rising. He's requesting your presence at your… convenience. Ehm… sorry for interrupting." Without waiting for a reply, he rushed back toward wherever they were camped, pointed ears red with embarrassment.

Belenus, downright disgruntled with his flat brows and his pressed lips, looked down at me to deliver an apologetic look. I was lowered onto a warm, dry boulder where my clothes and shoes waited, and we both dressed like sullen teenagers.

"What were you going to say? Before Ferrer interrupted?" Belenus asked, shrugging on a tunic. The poor fae man was still completely erect.

I shook my head, knowing I needed to wait for another opportunity. "Some other time," I answered lightly, trying not to make it seem like a big deal. The truth was, I wanted to tell him I loved him before we stormed the castle, whenever that would be. As determined as I was, I wasn't a fool. I knew we could both die.

Belenus and I arrived at the camp to find King Nechtan in a discussion with some of his men, Emer, and Nofre. Ferrer looked uncomfortable, no doubt embarrassed about stumbling into our activity at the river. I also noticed he kept glancing stealthily over at Nofre and Emer. The fated mates were tense, but Nofre wouldn't stop his protective hovering. Seemed like nothing had changed between those two while I was unconscious. Ferrer's yearning was new, however, and I tried to feel hope for him instead of sadness.

Soon, I thought. *Soon you'll all have a chance to find your mates.*

"King Nechtan," Belenus greeted as we reached the circle. "Are we ready to discuss?"

"Indeed, we are," he replied. He still wore the bag containing the mac-talla, and I wondered how our little Skye was faring.

Belenus led us to a large section of dirt that had the layout of the castle and the city drawn onto it. I wasn't sure how accurate it was, but the details impressed me. Belenus must have spent a lot of time on this after arriving here. I looked up at his tired face and frowned. Had he even slept?

"We have multiple agenda items," my mate announced sternly, placing his hands on his hips. "One, evacuating those most likely to be targeted or used as hostages. I know Hekla's particularly anxious to recover Bidelia, her mac-talla, and Doctor Egres. I need to retrieve my team, the one that was working on the contract issue, and Koray, if he remained there. I don't know if he went back home."

"He was there when I left," Emer informed.

Nofre released a short, quiet growl but froze when he realized it came from him. He shifted uncomfortably and avoided Emer's irritated look. As they were now, Nofre was going to act like a jealous beast with any attention she gave to the opposite sex. She was going to have to be careful with that, seeing as how it was almost a reflex with them.

I suspected that Emer was going to snap at him, so I jumped into the conversation and said, "We shouldn't pull anyone out who'd be noticed right away. I think it's safe for everyone we mentioned, but I'm not sure who on your team would be missed, Belenus."

"Absolutely," Belenus said. "I also need to meet with Drust. He's a high-ranking guard who I ordered to get an idea of how many soldiers are willing to join our forces. He gave me a sense that the percentage was going to be significant."

"It's not ideal going into this without even knowing if you have an army, Prince Belenus," King Nechtan said gravely, crossing his arms.

"Your concern has been noted," Belenus replied, unfazed. King Nechtan would either help or he wouldn't; we all understood that quite well. "We'll certainly find out soon enough. We won't be removing them from the castle, though. That'll be counterproductive and would grab too much attention. I'll work with Drust on a signal."

"Excuse me, Prince Belenus... what are we to do?" Ferrer asked and Nofre nodded.

I gave them an apologetic look. "We won't be able to get you to the Realm of the Humans until after we take the castle, so you'll have to stay here. I'm sorry about the delay. The door is on the castle grounds, and it wouldn't be safe to h—"

Luzia interrupted, "If you need an army, you have an army." She gestured back to the bat-shifters biding their time. Some were eating, while others were chatting or napping. "You've saved us from extinction. We owe you our lives, vessel of the Sky Gods."

"Don't... don't speak for the others," I ordered sternly, trying to keep the pleading tone from my voice. "This isn't your fight. I'm supposed to get you all home safe."

"I will get a sense of who wishes to help, Luzia," Nofre replied, completely ignoring me. He turned to Emer, pointed a finger at her, and said in earnest, "Whether you like it or not, your fight is my fight. I'm not letting you do this without me."

He stalked off before Emer could say a thing. I expected her temper to flare, but her shoulders merely dropped, and she bit her lip.

Belenus said to me in a low voice, "If they're truly going to volunteer, Hekla, you're going to have to lead them. No one else will be able to control them if they slip and start feeding on people."

I nodded in agreement. That had crossed my mind. They'd be harder to trust than a pack, but at least they'd be controllable.

King Nechtan was simply staring back at the shifters, deep in thought. "Am I to assume the other items on the agenda depend on how the next day goes?" he asked. "We have two days left?"

"Two more sunrises, yes," Belenus said. "If I'm caught after that without a solution to the contract, I'm likely as good as dead."

"I should go and pick up your team instead of you," Emer said. "I don't want you going into the castle so close to the deadline. If I see Koray, I'll bring him back too."

"Best for you to focus on Drust, mate," I said to him. "I'll retrieve my little pack and the doctor."

"Should glamour you," Emer suggested to me and looked over at her suddenly agitated brother.

He ran his fingers through his hair and took a steadying breath. "Hekla, I don't think it's a good idea for you to go," he said through his teeth. "If the queen catches you, she'll either use you as bait or execute you on the spot."

King Nechtan asked, "Who else can go in her stead? It'll be noticed if Emer leaves with such a large group of people."

Did he think me incapable?

I bristled at his question and opened my mouth, but the king cut off my protest before I could even start. "If you're to be queen, you need to understand value and risk. The fact that you're about ready to fight me over this means you don't understand either."

I froze in place and let his words sink into my heated brain. I wasn't thinking like an alpha. I had to think like an alpha. I was a wolf with an army, not a lonely female with something to prove.

"Right," I said tersely, swallowing my pride. So, instead of arguing, I searched for a solution. "What about Oscar? He delivered Arse to Bidelia. He won't know who Doctor Egres is, but maybe he could scent her out if we told him to look for a lycan among the doctors. Bidelia should be able to track her down, though."

"I will get in touch with Oscar," Belenus agreed. "I think he's a good candidate, especially since he's not a new face, and folk fae are more likely to be ignored."

"You should glamour some of my men so they can escort you and see the layout with their own eyes," King Nechtan suggested. "I don't want to just be sitting here. There's much to evaluate, and I'd rather not do it last minute."

"Alright, give me four soldiers. Meanwhile, I'd like you to help Hekla prepare to organize an army. She doesn't know anything about leading an assault," he replied. "If these bat-shifters are adamant about helping, they'll all need to be readied."

I was slowly sinking into a sour mood. They were all right, but it got under my skin.

Don't be upset, mate, Escort consoled. *We're all learning here. Also, these know-it-alls are old as fuck. They've had a lifetime of war already.*

Even alphas need to be trained, Eventide reminded. *We were just kind of dropped into the role.*

That's true, I replied. *I guess I should count myself lucky that we have another person who's going to act as an advisor.*

Putting a lot of trust in him, Escort said flatly. *The king will now know more of our layout than he should.*

Takes trust to build a team, I mused with a sigh. *We'll come out of this knowing exactly where everyone stands...*

If we come out of it, Eventide murmured, but Escort snarled at her.

If Belenus was listening to our chatting, it wasn't obvious. He clapped to get everyone's attention. "Alright, Luzia, you said the shifters are discussing. King Nechtan, you'll give me soldiers and tutor Hekla. I'll glamour your men, make contact with Oscar and Drust. On our way back, we'll gather extra supplies from the city. Emer, you'll fetch my team, then Koray, and you'll return immediately."

"We'll see you by dawn then," King Nechtan stated, scratching at his chin before turning away.

"Stay safe," Luzia murmured and wandered off toward the quiet crowd of debating shifters. Emer hesitated, then followed Luzia. I assumed she was going to find Nofre before leaving. He'd probably go wild if she left without telling him.

They really need to mate, Eventide said and uttered a tsk, *before it turns into a Hekla-and-Belenus situation.*

Belenus jolted me from my thoughts by grabbing my hand and leading me to where our bags were. Out of sight from the others, he pushed me against a tree and claimed my mouth, framing my face with his fingers. Warm lips pressed into mine, and I felt myself slowly relaxing. The thumping of my anxious heart slowed and softened as my attention centered on him.

"I'm so sorry," he whispered into the air between our lips. "I know it's a lot. I know you're upset." He spread urgent kisses down my neck, desperate for forgiveness. Each tingling peck had me shivering more than the last.

"I know you trust me," I replied and hissed in pleasure when his mouth grazed over the mark he'd left on my skin. "You just told me to command an army of shifters. I… ah." I sighed when he tried to move the collar of my dress to access more of my skin.

He voiced his fear in a quiet voice. "I wouldn't be able to focus with you wandering the castle. All I'd be able to think about is the last time the queen threatened to execute you. Please just stay here tonight. Please, Hekla. Let the shifters guard you until we're ready. You're my queen, my precious queen."

"Shh, it's ok. I understand." I pulled his rigid face up to look at me. "I have plenty to do here." I stroked his hair out of his gleaming amber eyes. "I'm anxious to see those three again," I confessed.

"And you will," he growled, kissing me fiercely while sliding his hands up my body. His hungry grip squeezed my breasts over my dress. "I hate how I can't get my hands into this blistering dress. I'm five seconds away from ripping it."

I gave him a grin, showing off my eager canines. "Come back safely, and maybe you'll find it gone."

Belenus pried himself away with a tortured groan and held his hand out for a shake. "Can we make that a promise?"

Belenus

It took everything in me to pry myself away from my mate to pursue the first stage of our mission. I wanted so badly to feel all of her, to know she was alive and well after what had happened. Despite the witch's attack, I desired her more by the day. I wanted to finally be free, genuinely free, to love her the way I should've been able to from the day we met. I loved her in all the ways that truly mattered, but I wanted our love to be seen and accepted because I wanted to show her off to all the realms.

I wanted to not only give her a place in my bed, our bed, but I hungered to place the queen's throne at her feet, to offer the royal dais she deserved to be heard and heeded. She would be good for our people. She would have wonderful, clever ideas. She would be loved and respected, and I knew that from the bottom of my very soul. I just had to get us there. If I had to spill the blood of the unjust to get there, I would.

And we will, Escort agreed savagely. *For our people and our mate.*

As we reached the city with a disguised Slaine and three other winter fae, I felt like I was seeing everything with fresh eyes. This was the first I'd returned since being mated to my future queen, and all I could think about were the possibilities. I could imagine so many projects I could initiate to improve the lives of our people, and it wouldn't just be this city. I wouldn't have to fight the current queen anymore over every little thing.

Even my breaths tasted different. The night air felt fresher now; I could almost taste a better future. I pictured our carriage rolling through the city. I'd be in it with my new queen, holding her hand in mine while she held our heir in the other. I wished I knew what our first child would look like. Would it be fae or wolf? Could it be both? Perhaps they'd have their mother's soft, dark brown skin with a dusting of gold like their father. That would be beautiful.

Our mate would only make beautiful children, Escort asserted.

I definitely agree.

I had to calm myself down after that. Thinking of impregnating my mate, my future queen and wife, was giving me quite the erection to contend with at the moment. I pumped my fists and tried to focus on my goals for today. Fantasizing had to wait. There was far too much to do before we could get to making an heir, and I suppressed a frustrated growl.

The wooden closed sign hung in Oscar's shop's window, but I knocked all the same, persisting until I heard movement. I knew he lived in the apartment upstairs with his daughter, and unless he was visiting someone, he should be home.

My wulver friend, to my great relief, appeared and rushed to the door to usher us inside. I couldn't shake the fear that I'd discover that the queen had taken a loved one into custody just to hurt and manipulate me. This was why we had to move fast.

Oscar led us up to his apartment, but by the raised fur on his neck, I could tell that he was tense. He wasn't fooled by my glamour of the winter fae; he could definitely smell what they were. In hindsight, I was shocked that this wulver held so much trust in me that he'd willingly bring winter fae even remotely close to his daughter, especially after everything Hekla had told him.

"Please return to your chamber, little fawn," the wulver said to his daughter in fae, who retired but not before looking at us with youthful curiosity. I never understood Oscar's obsession with deer, and after years of knowing him, I figured I never would.

Oscar submitted until I quickly told him to rise, and we retired to a table where I swore him to secrecy. I filled him in on everything, which had him more surprised by the word. He fretted over the risks but would occasionally have a bout of excitement at the thought of dethroning the current ruler.

"I told her you weren't capable of doing it," Oscar stated after I removed the glamour that hid my mating mark. He nodded proudly, and I reapplied the glamour to hide it again. "You did scent a little different."

"That could be because of Escort too," I replied thoughtfully.

"So where do I fit in all of this?" he asked. "Do ye need a place to harbor innocents? Soldiers?" His ears had pinned back, and I could easily guess what his reservations were about that.

"I'm honored you think to volunteer before I've said a thing about it. No, nothing that involved. I just need you to fetch three people from the castle. Hekla was about to do it, and I have my hands full with the soldiers. You already know Bidelia and—wait, were you aware your famous mac-talla named himself Arse?" I inquired, resting my elbow on the table with my chin in my palm. My index finger tapped at the corner of a lip where my smile was forming.

Oscar released a sharp, breathy noise that I knew to be his laugh. He shook his head and slapped a hand down on the table in his mirth. "I thought everyone was just swearing! I did not," he wheezed. "We spoke, but it wasn't mentioned. The mood was very serious."

"Anyway"—I gestured the topic away with a hand, chuckling—"if you can fetch Bidelia and Arse from the castle, I also need you to pick up the lycan healer who's originally from Hekla's realm. Her name is Doctor Egres. Bidelia should be able to help you find her, but you could probably also scent her out. She's the only lycan there." I put a serious face on and added, "I know you have your daughter to worry about. I won't force you to do this, Oscar. This is voluntary. If you can't, I'll look for someone else."

The wulver nodded, sobering. "It is because I have family that I should do this, my prince. My daughter deserves a better life, and I know you will treat us better." He jabbed a finger into the table to punctuate his adamance.

Satisfied and more than relieved, I stood from the table and grabbed Oscar's forearm in a strong grip. He did the same, and I locked eyes with him like I would any other soldier. "I will leave first, Oscar. Put some distance between us and find Bidelia or Arse first. They'll help you retrieve Doctor Egres, then I want you to head northeast from the castle where you'll eventually encounter my… army behind a glamour. There will be over four hundred other shifters we've liberated and about fifty winter fae. My sister and Hekla are there. Just make sure no one follows you and return home safe to your daughter. Abort the mission if there is an immediate risk to you or your family, but if you get to my army in time, they will protect and hide you. They already know you're coming. Are my instructions clear, Oscar?"

Oscar straightened and nodded. I took my winter fae escort out of the shop, and we moved on to the castle. I pointed out various locations they'd need to keep in mind for acquiring supplies and orienting themselves if they got lost. The guards at the castle gate were surprised to see me, and as I passed them, I studied their faces, wondering who owned their loyalty.

Exactly why we need to see Drust, Escort said.

He may be in the barracks. If not, we'll inquire subtly, I replied.

Drust wasn't in the first two barracks, and after searching the third building for twenty minutes, I began to worry that he'd been caught and charged with treason. I tried to stay calm, but my heart slammed louder than a hammer to hot metal; it nigh felt like it too.

When we left the building and stepped into the shadows to visit the fourth one, I sensed a man approaching, and an immediate scuffle broke out. I spun to find Slaine and Drust grappling, both unaware that the other was an ally.

"Cease!" I hissed and pried the two men apart before they killed each other. "Drust, it's your prince!"

He stepped back, but his gloved hand still went for the hilt of his claybeg. "Who are these men?" he snapped under his breath. "They're not ours!"

"No, they're not. King Nechtan loaned me some of his warriors."

"They're winter?" Drust's eyes narrowed, and he edged closer to my side. Slaine snorted and crossed his arms while the other winter fae shifted uneasily.

"They're allies," I clarified aggressively. "I uncovered some nasty shit on my tour, Drust. I'm trusting you about our soldiers, so I need you to trust me."

Drust seemed to remember who he was addressing, and his scowl vanished into the night, his visage immediately adopting a cool and professional expression. "My deepest apologies, my prince." He bowed deeply. "I realize we're working under unusual circumstances."

"You're right about that," I replied sternly and patted his shoulder in unspoken forgiveness. "Let's find a private place to discuss our situation."

Drust escorted us into the fourth barrack where I passed enthusiastic soldiers who'd wondered where I'd been this entire time. "Everyone here is safe," Drust informed under his breath, "but let's meet in the cellar."

We seated ourselves at an old wooden table, and I lit the one candle with my summer magic to fill the room with an uneasy glow. Slaine took the third chair, and the other three winter fae settled on some barrels. Drust gestured for them to avail themselves of the fresh food and rations, which the warriors eagerly crowded.

"Fill as many bags as you can, and we'll bring them back to your men," I told one winter fae, who grabbed a burlap sack and started stuffing it with food. At least we wouldn't have to return to the city for supplies. I turned back to Drust and said, "What are the numbers? We won't have a lot of time to organize, and I'm not sure if I'll be able to return after tonight."

"Understood. The surveying was slow, as expected, but I've estimated that we have about forty percent of our soldiers who are willing to revolt." I nodded as I listened to Drust. That was about eight hundred fae. "Fifty-five are unwilling to participate, meaning that they will not help, nor hinder, our forces. They're mostly made of soldiers—many posted in the city—who have young children and fear retaliation."

"For good reason," I murmured over my folded hands. "What about the last one hundred?"

"We suspect they are loyal to the queen for one reason or another. It's likely out of duty or fear of execution."

I sat back in the chair and placed a hand to my mouth. "The problem is not in numbers then. We could obviously clear a straight path forward to the queen."

Who is much more lethal, Escort reminded.

"Correct."

"Then I want our goal to be in stopping these one hundred, not killing them. They are fulfilling their vows, and I cannot fault them for that. They may be just as loyal after I take the throne. I don't want to see anyone die during this if I can. I know it might not be possible, but that is my standing order. You are only to capture hostile soldiers. Injuring or killing in self-defense is permissible, but I want that to be the very last resort."

"Understood," Drust replied.

I sat with my soldier and the winter warriors through most of the night, going through our strategies and signals until we decided upon something that was agreeable to all parties. We'd take this back to King Nechtan for his approval. Hopefully Emer would have returned before me so I could catch up with my team and Koray.

After that... well, I just wanted to dive into my sweet Hekla's arms.

Chapter 29

Arse

Bidelia was crying again, like she had every night since Hekla had run away from the castle. She didn't cry for as long as she used to, but when she did, she heaved gut-wrenching sobs that pulled at my heartstrings. Not only did we miss Hekla's comforting, protective presence, but the queen was also exhausting the servants with unreasonable demands for Belenus's approaching wedding. It was nearly enough to make a mac-talla laugh. How Eislyn was getting married without Belenus was certainly a mystery to me.

His sister had been gone for a while too, and I wasn't sure if she was coming back either. After she overheard her father's name, she fled to find Belenus. I didn't know her well, but she'd healed Hekla, and that was enough for me to worry for her well-being. I heaved a sigh from my spot next to Bidelia. This mac-talla's cranky heart was getting soft.

Dinna cry, I said through our almost week-old bond. *Save yer strength.*

"It hurts," she complained as she wept. "I miss her. I hate the queen. I hate her! It's not fair!"

Nae, it isnae, int it? I agreed darkly. *But ye cannae let the hoor kill yer spirit.*

"I'm so tired of them always getting what they want! They drove her away, Arse! The rules never apply to them! They took her from us!" she yelled, crying harder and slamming a small fist down onto her pillow. "When will it end?"

I didn't have an answer for her. I'd do anything to make her smile, but the future looked dour. No one in the castle had felt safe since Hekla's torture, and preparing the castle for a new queen—one just as bad, if not worse, as the current queen—put morale at an all-time low. None of the servants knew whether they wanted Belenus to break the contract and risk whatever retaliation there would be or marry her and live but suffer hundreds of years under Eislyn's rule. The fact that they even had to think about that made all the servants sick to their stomachs. Belenus was well liked. I hadn't shared much of what I'd overheard with Bidelia. The poor thing was overwhelmed as it was.

Hush, hush. Keep they heid, pup. Whit's fur ye'll no go by ye. Sleep now, Bidelia, I urged, trying not to sound as anxious as I felt. It might be time to find Hekla's human. Maybe we could go back with him to his realm. It might be safer there. I didn't see good things happening here anytime soon, especially for Bidelia. I closed my eyes and decided to find the human tomorrow. Hopefully he was still here.

A quiet knock at the door startled both of us.

"Who could that be at this hour?" Bidelia asked, rubbing her eyes to hide her tears.

Careful, Bidelia, I warned, narrowing my eyes at the door.

The teenage fae gasped when she opened the door and gestured in a familiar face.

Oscar! I shouted. *Whit in the blazes are ye doin' here?*

"Everything alright, Oscar?" Bidelia asked him in fae.

"Bidelia… Arse…" Oscar said, shooting me an amused look that was quickly replaced with a serious expression. "I've been sent to pick you up and take you to Hekla. They're camped outside the city, a bit northeast from here."

"Hekla! They?" Bidelia inquired with wide eyes.

"Belenus and… his army. Emer's there as well," the wulver informed, scratching nervously at his shoulder. "It's not going to be safe here in a couple of days. I have to escort you out tonight."

Bidelia gasped, and I was pretty certain all my pearly whites were on display in a dumbstruck expression.

Nae… I gasped.

"Is Belenus seizing power?"

"Yes, we must go now. I don't want to wait a minute more," Oscar replied. "Prince Belenus is meeting with his soldiers this very minute."

Bidelia reached for the doorknob, and I hollered, *Haud on, Bidelia, yer in yer goonie!*

She looked down at her nightgown and frowned. "My clothes don't have wing holes in them… and I need help to bind myself."

"I could rip holes, I guess," Oscar suggested hesitantly, turning Bidelia around to see how long the slits needed to be.

She worried at her hands and sighed. "Alright, I guess I can maybe sew the seams later." She handed Oscar her dress and twisted her lips into an unhappy pout as he ripped long slits in the back with a knife he kept on his person.

At least it's just yer maid gown, Bidelia, I comforted. She didn't reply; she just took the dress and went into the bathroom to change.

"We need to pick up a lycan named Doctor Egres too. That's our last stop. Do you know how to find her?" Oscar asked Bidelia when she exited the bathroom, her poor crinkled wings poking out the back of her uniform.

"I know where her chamber is," she said with a nod, hauling me into her arms and slipping into the hall. She walked quietly but purposefully, as though she was running a late-night errand.

Oscar probably ruined the picture, but maybe we could say he was sick if anyone inquired.

Bidelia knocked on a chamber door but was met with silence. She knocked several more times, rapping louder with every attempt.

She's nae there, I muttered.

"I do scent a female lycan's trail. It's about an hour old, but it's there," Oscar commented. "Let's try tracking it."

We followed Oscar for about five minutes until we came to a chamber near the castle's hospital. "The trail ends here," he announced, shoving his hands into his pockets and looking down at Bidelia, who was tilting her head in curiosity.

"This is Doctor Elisedd's room!" she blurted, then slapped a hand over her mouth, blushing. "Oh Sun God! I'm afraid of knocking."

"Cannot be helped, Bidelia," Oscar sighed and rapped on the door. "I have a duty to fulfill."

Fortunately, the fae doctor appeared quite sleepy when he answered the door, yawning broadly and scratching at his side. It didn't look like we'd interrupted anything other than a good night's rest.

"Bidelia?" he asked with a concerned frown. "What are you doing out and about at this hour? Is everything ok?" He yawned again and moved his scratching to a pajama-clad arm. "I'm even more surprised to see you, Oscar. It's been a while…"

"I'm so very sorry to disturb you!" Bidelia squeaked, fidgeting uncomfortably. "Erm… we're looking for Doctor Egres. It's extremely important. Oscar seems to think she's around here…" She grimaced, unable to hide her embarrassment.

He kept frowning, but as he woke up a bit more, his eyes popped open in surprise. "Oh! I'll… get her right away."

"Or perhaps she could meet us in a private hospital room? The query must be kept... confidential. Not for hallways," Oscar whispered.

"Well, you might as well just come in then," Doctor Elisedd murmured, looking around and gesturing us into his personal chambers. "Taisa? My female, we have company. Something urgent for you to address."

"I heard what Bidelia said! I don't know what… was it Oscar? I'm afraid I don't know what he said," Doctor Egres replied, tightening her robe and watching us enter the sitting room. "What happened?" We all hesitated, looking at Doctor Elisedd, but the lycan waved a dismissal. "You can say it in front of him. He's a doctor. Confidentiality is half his job," she said, chuckling lightly.

"Erm… this is a really, really, really big secret, though…" the younger fae holding me said, shifting her weight from foot to foot.

It was Doctor Egres's turn to frown now. She opened her mouth to say something, but Doctor Elisedd held up his hand. "It's ok, Taisa. I'll retire with some cotton in my ears." He kissed her on the cheek and strolled back to his bedroom.

"What in the Moon Goddess is happening, pup?" the doctor asked, crossing her arms. Bidelia relayed what Oscar had told her because Doctor Egres didn't speak fae, at least not yet.

"So yer the last one we need to get before we leave," Bidelia said, pleading with her entire being. "We don't want to be caught up between two armies…"

Doctor Egres's response was lightning quick. "No. I'm not leaving."

"But D—"

"First of all, I'm a doctor. If there's going to be fighting here, I want to make sure we're prepared to treat the wounded. Secondly," she said and held up two fingers, "I'm not leaving my mate's side."

"Congratulations on finding your mate," Bidelia said first, then asked Oscar in the human language, "Perhaps Doctor Elisedd could come too?" Oscar looked like he was considering it as an option, but the lycan just shook her head.

"No. Doctor Elisedd would agree with me. We're not going anywhere."

Bidelia opened her mouth to protest one more time but merely received another adamant headshake.

"Och… we tried," Bidelia mumbled, turning to Oscar in defeat.

The doctor gasped upon seeing her back. "Bidelia, what happened to your wings?" she asked. Bidelia tried to turn to face the lycan, but I looked up to see that a hand on her shoulder had stopped her. "They're all battered, and the skin is inflamed…"

"I've had to bind them for… maybe almost four years now, doctor. The queen doesn't like to see them."

"Unbelievable," the lycan growled in fury, and I heard her stomp off to open a cabinet in another room. When she returned, she handed a small jar to Bidelia. "This balm will help with the inflammation. If you keep binding… well, you may already have permanently damaged the surrounding tissue. Come back and see me when it's safe again, and we'll take a better look. Now run along. Give my best to Hekla." She heaved a weary sigh and looked away for a moment. "Tell her not to get hurt. I'd rather not report bad news to Queen Ragna."

"I will," Bidelia said quietly and adjusted her hold on me before leaving with Oscar.

"It was her choice, Bidelia. She's an adult and knows what she's in for," Oscar comforted and tenderly squeezed her shoulder. Bidelia didn't say anything, but her posture drooped into a mope. She probably hadn't wanted to let Hekla down by failing this task.

Failing means yer playin, I said wisely, patting her on the arm.

We left as casually as possible, trying not to arouse suspicion whenever someone could see us. Oscar led us into the chirping wilds, and we eventually crossed a threshold that spooked the fur right off of my head. The surroundings went from a quiet tree line to a crowded forest.

Whit the joukery-pawkery! I exclaimed, fearing my eyes were about to pop right out of my skull. I clutched Bidelia's arm, willing myself not to shake. She needed a brave male to protect her!

I really needed to find one.

Also, whaur is Hekla? I asked Oscar, hoping he could scent her through all these people.

Before Oscar could discern a direction to head in, two individuals approached us, not looking too surprised to have visitors. Oscar didn't submit like usual, probably not finding reason to bow to a fae from another court and… whatever that woman was. The man had a bearing of regal authority, but the women held herself with a casual confidence, striking me as a different kind of leader.

Oscar stepped forward, standing a little in front of Bidelia in a protective manner. "My name is Oscar. Belenus ordered delivery of three. I've brought two as the third declined the invitation," Oscar reported in a formal tone.

"Who may I ask decli—" The tall winter fae in ornate black armor interrupted his own inquiry when his eyes fell on Bidelia. I would have said someone was lying if they told me a winter fae could pale, but this one certainly did! I wasn't even sure if he still drew breath! Maybe if his jaw wasn't clenched so tight, he'd get his blood flowing again…

"King Nechtan?" the woman next to him asked, leaning forward to see what had caught his attention. This was a king? He seemed a bit slow to me.

Oscar assumed the rest of the question, so he simply replied after a moment of awkward staring. "Doctor Egres declined… she said she wanted to remain to treat those who may get injured."

"That's noble… of… her," King Nechtan said absently, his green gaze flickering to look at Oscar for just a second before going back to Bidelia. "I assume this is Bidelia? How old is she?"

Oscar turned to look at her, shrugging.

"Fourteen, Yer Majesty…" she answered, and she clutched me tighter to perform a little curtsey.

"A child," he observed tersely.

"I wish to deliver her to Hekla. They are close. Where is she?" Oscar inquired. The king spun on a heel and gestured for us to follow him.

Dunderheid. Standin around like a stookie... I mumbled to Bidelia. *Whit's they aboot?*

"Guess they don't want me here?" she whispered back to me.

Dinna fash, I said simply, patting her arm again and looking around for any signs of Hekla or Emer. The king led us around another clump of shrubbery, but it seemed like Hekla scented us first because she came jumping out of nowhere to throw her arms around Bidelia and me.

"Bidelia! Arse!" she exclaimed, then dragged the wulver into our awkward hug circle. "Oscar!"

Bidelia just giggled, and by the Sun God, it was nice to hear that sound again!

The wolf-shifter tightened her grip for a second. "I'm so happy you made it! Oh, I missed you so much!" She let everyone go but peppered the top of Bidelia's head with loud, playful kisses. Her giggles turned into squeals of laughter as she fought to escape Hekla's smothering.

There was an unhappy growl from the king who snapped, "What happened to your wings, Bidelia?"

She placed me down on the ground, and I backed up to sit next to Hekla.

Hekla answered for her. "The queen doesn't like to see folk fae wings. She makes the servants bind them." She grinned down at Bidelia and squeezed her arms. "Looks like you gave that up, huh? I'm so glad, pup!"

"The queen forces this on her people? On children?" the king asked, quickly losing his temper. He didn't seem as foggy as he did minutes ago. "Her wings are ruined!"

"I didn't like it either," Hekla replied shortly. "I would have loved to have prevented it. I can promise you that will change if we... when we take the throne."

Bidelia worried at her hands, but then perked up and drew the jar from a pocket. "Hekla, can you help? Doctor Egres gave this balm for the base of my win—"

"I'll do it," the king interrupted with a scowl, taking the jar from Bidelia. Hekla placed a fist under her chin and watched the king kneel behind the young fae. He moved the fabric by her shoulder blades where her wings poked out and delicately applied the cream, muttering angrily under his breath.

Bidelia was frozen with wide eyes, probably wondering why a king was getting his hands dirty applying medicine. That was what I was wondering at the very least. Glancing at the suspicious look on Hekla's face, maybe my mission was a success after all.

I was really quite good at this.

Hekla

I idly petted Arse while I watched the serious winter king dote upon the young castle servant. I didn't have any questions; I knew exactly what had happened, especially after Oscar had quietly described their first encounter not ten minutes ago. I did have some questions about it though. The wulver left promptly, anxious to return to his daughter, and he'd been given strict orders from me to deliver a hug to Oisin. When all this was over, I'd like to see her again. I couldn't wait to tell all my friends about the half-wolves who lived in this realm.

I smiled, thinking that explaining the wulver's ability to speak would probably incite my sub-pack into trying to talk while in their wolf forms again. Except for Ragna's first shift—for obvious reasons—we'd all tried to do it, which had always resulted in horrible but hilarious attempts. It was obviously just for fun. We all knew it was impossible. I closed my eyes for a moment, fixated on a memory from Soley's first shift. Her insistent cacophony had us all in stitches when she'd tried talking with Noon's mouth. That'd been a good night…

I missed them.

"Oh, ye have a mac-talla too!" Bidelia exclaimed when she noticed the bag at the king's side wriggle.

Uh-oh! Guess who's about to replace us as Bidelia's favorite? Eventide said, laughing in delight at the fae teenager. We both dearly loved that pup.

The king's serious façade faded as he crouched by her side. His angry eyes slid from her crinkled wings to her excited face and softened. I could just barely make out a small smile as he pulled Skye from the bag, setting her down on the grass to stretch and yawn.

"This is Skye. Careful, though, she's pregnant. She has some young in her pouch."

I looked down at Arse as the king spoke. "You should go say hi," I encouraged, nudging his little mac-talla bottom.

Arse made his laughing noise, rocking slightly and digging his feet into the dirt. *An' get told ah'm hackit? Ah'll nae do it,* he replied stubbornly.

"Great goddess, it's just a hello," I mumbled at him. "You were wrong about me, you know."

He let out an aggrieved sigh. *Ah ken.*

"Can't be 'afeart' your whole life," I said wryly, twirling a blade of grass around a finger. Bidelia looked over at us and held out her arms, communicating that she wanted Arse to come over to her. Arse released another sigh and withered. He finally caved, unable to resist Bidelia's cute demands. I grinned and leaned back on my arms, glad to see those two had grown closer in my absence.

"Who is this handsome one?" the king asked Bidelia as Arse meandered reluctantly to her side.

"This is my pally! His name is Ar—" Bidelia started saying but was interrupted before she could finish her introduction.

Archibald! Erm... Archibald Mac An Tsamhraidh... Esquire... the third! Arse nearly shouted and Bidelia blinked sharply at his outburst. I placed a hand over my mouth and squeezed my cheeks, partially to keep my jaw from dropping but also to keep from bursting into nervous laughter. Oh what a bold lie that was.

"Erm… sorry. Bit of dust in my throat," Bidelia lied to cover up the interruption that the king hadn't heard. "His name is Archibald Mac An Tsamhraidh, Esquire the third," she babbled it out quickly and immediately clamped her lips between her teeth.

Moon Goddess, bless her for keeping it together. I don't know how she did it, I said in awe to Eventide.

Arse, you're an absolute terror, Eventide barked out, cackling like an idiot since she was the only one who could.

"Archibald, son of summer, you've a most important surname. You must be quite an important mac-talla," the king said to my pet.

"He is very important!" Bidelia announced proudly, putting her fists on her hips as she sat on the forest floor. "He serves the future queen, ye know! He practically saved her during many a banquet!"

Let's give him that one. It's kinda true, Eventide said, and I was unable to hide my smile this time.

He did bravely sneeze away an overeager fae man, I replied with mixed feelings. That'd been a horrid day…

We won't go into details. She snorted.

Y-yes. I am. Well, it's a pleasure to meet ye-oo, 'Archibald' said to Skye, and I gasped.

Arse! I yelled in a private link. *You've been capable of speaking more coherently to me this entire time?*

His head turned slowly, and his little black eyes glittered in fear. *Aye?*

Oh! You are so lucky we're not alone right now! I have half a mind to let Eventide finally eat you! I snarled angrily.

Bidelia looked just as startled.

"Everything ok? They're not fighting, are they? I haven't encouraged Skye to bond with me." The king looked down at the two mac-tallas, then over at Bidelia, his face alight with curiosity.

"I can only hear half of it, but it seems polite…" she answered, tapping her fingers together nervously.

"Oh, I'm glad," the king replied, and I could see his eyes searching for the next thing to say. He obviously wanted to keep the conversation going. "I used to breed mac-tallas, you know."

"Really?" Bidelia squeaked happily, turning to face him, all drama regarding Arse completely forgotten. King Nechtan smiled broadly—looking much younger in that moment—and I marveled at the pair of them. The bond truly was a force to be reckoned with, something Bidelia would realize when she came of age. Though, how had he recognized the young fae before her turning eighteen?

"Yes, there's actually a lot of subspecies of mac-tallas. I have a small section of my library dedicated to them."

"I wanna see!" she exclaimed. "I was trying to be the royal pet assistant. Prince Belenus said we'd talk about it some other time…" She muttered that last part out, sounding so butthurt that I couldn't contain my snort of laughter. Fortunately, I didn't think she noticed.

Pup's too precious for her own good, Eventide remarked fondly.

"Well, perhaps you can visit my castle when you're much older. You'll be my most honored guest." He was looking more taken with Bidelia by the minute. A corner of his lip curled into a smile, and he raised his dark brows, nodding over to Arse. "In the meantime, you should take care of this fierce Archibald. I noticed his sgèile glands are blocked. See how his wings are stunted and a little more transparent than Skye's?"

"Oh! Is that what happened to him?" she exclaimed excitedly, leaning over to see where King Nechtan was pointing.

"It's more common in his subspecies. See the swelling just over the wings? The glands just need to be drained of excess fluid, then the wings will develop. The scales may take longer to come in, so they'll be transparent until the glands fill correctly."

This seems like very personal and confidential infor— Arse protested, glancing over at Skye's calm face. Bidelia just picked him up and squeezed him senseless.

"That's amazing! Did ye hear that, Ar-Archibald? Ye'll get yer wings!" She whooped joyfully next to a grinning King Nechtan.

I don't need wings! he argued grumpily. *I'm fine the way I am!*

"He says he'll think about it!" Bidelia beamed happily through her bold-faced lie.

"I've really never seen such a muscular mac-talla," the king murmured to himself as he watched the fae teenager hug the life out of my pet.

I'd seen enough. He had no signs of arousal, and I was certain that Bidelia, summer's brightest ray of sunshine, was safe in his company. He clearly had no intention of inviting her to the Winter Court until she was of age to recognize him. I stood up and went searching for Luzia.

"Do you think we can assign several shifters to act as Bidelia's bodyguards? Can you recommend anyone?" I asked her while she was snacking on a squirrel. She pinched where she'd been drinking from to look around the various campsites.

"Hmm, let's get two females. I'd trust Olalla and Ines. They have decent appetite mastery," she said and marched through the relaxing bat-shifters to find them.

Oh, you know, just... gotta consider appetite mastery. No big deal, Eventide remarked with a laugh. *What has our life become? Gotta make sure her bodyguards aren't tempted to eat her.*

I'd laugh if it wasn't an actual concern, but our alpha command should ensure her safety. Luzia grabbed Ines, who followed silently until we found Olalla. I instructed the two females to watch over Bidelia, and to defer to King Nechtan if I wasn't around for any emergencies.

An hour later, a familiar scent hit my nose, and I ran toward the barrier to throw my arms around Koray, utterly ecstatic. Emer and a handful of other fae walked into our hidden site, and it wasn't long before King Nechtan joined us with a babbling Bidelia at his heels. I was satisfied to spy Olalla and Ines watching her from a short distance.

"Oh, it's good to see you're alright!" Koray exclaimed, stepping away to make sure I had all my limbs. "I sent word to Soley, and she's been beside herself! They all have!"

I opened my mouth to apologize, but he immediately shushed me. "Nope. You went through a nightmare. We're all just glad you're safe now," he insisted, shaking his head and drawing in a steadying breath. "I'm guessing we beat Belenus here?" he asked anxiously, scratching the back of his head and moving to a tree to drop his bag.

"Yes. I expect he'll be gone til dawn. There's probably too much to discuss with his soldiers already. I hope he finishes what he needs to tonight so he doesn't have to go back until the contract is… sorted… somehow," I said, biting my lower lip and worrying at my hands.

On my last words, excitement lit up his eyes. "Hekla! We're so close! My letter made it to the Lunar Coven, and they sent back some ideas they had! I actually ended up pulling my magic instructor, Dumnorix, into it to discuss my theories!" He pointed over to a folk fae, a thin man with subtle reptilian features. "There's only one or two things I'm hung up on, but I can almost see the solution!"

"No shit!" I gasped, putting my hands to my mouth. "I can't wait until Belenus returns! What did the Lunar Coven have to say about it?"

Koray opened his mouth to reply, but his eyes shifted to the imposing king next to me. "I'm Koray! My mate's friends with this one," he said, holding his hand out and jerking his head in my direction. I laughed, his down-to-earth nature a refreshing change of pace. He was so perfect for Soley.

King Nechtan gripped forearms with him. "A pleasure. I'm King Nechtan of the Winter Court."

Korey then turned to look down at Bidelia. "Glad to see you safe and sound! Where's ol' A—" he began asking but was violently interrupted by two voices.

"Archibald!" Bidelia and I shouted at the same time, startling him. "Archibald, yes! My mac-talla named Archibald, he's around..." I said in a calmer tone but laced every word with meaning.

"Bidelia said he went to forage some grub for Skye, a pregnant mac-talla," the king informed him, returning to his serious demeanor but still raising a brow at our weird outburst. "Apparently, she had a craving."

"I'm really going to need to hear the whole story of your travels," Koray drawled at me, smirking.

"You won't believe half of it!" I grinned.

Chapter 30

Belenus

I returned to our hidden site about an hour before dawn with Slaine and the three fae warriors that King Nechtan had loaned me. I scratched at my itchy stubble as I stepped through the glamour, wishing I'd thought to grab a cream to shave with while I was at the barracks. We dropped off the fresh supplies, and I strolled with Slaine to find the winter king.

"Prince Belenus, how did your meeting fare?" King Nechtan asked, walking away from a conversation with one of his warriors. "Slaine." He nodded to the winter fae, who bowed shortly in greeting.

"Productive," I replied, loosening and removing my sword belt. "Unless something changes, I won't need to return before the day we storm the castle." I caught King Nechtan up on the entirety of the conversation and the agreed-upon plan. "Drust did well sorting the soldiers out. Now it's just a matter of sorting out the contract and getting to the queen. She won't be an easy defeat."

"Speaking of contracts, your team arrived a while ago," King Nechtan replied, placing his hands behind his back. "Your human seems to think he's close to a breakthrough."

My heart all but threatened to jump out of my rib cage at his words. I hadn't wanted to think about their progress, or lack of, in my absence. It hadn't been looking optimistic when I'd left, but then again, they'd barely started analyzing outside of language loopholes.

"Where's Koray?" I asked, trying to stay cool. I didn't want to assume anything at this point, but my body was losing the war against my excitement and disbelief.

King Nechtan nodded in a direction. "Not far from where Hekla's sleeping. He's probably still awake. I'm about to retire myself."

I moved to go find Koray but paused. "How'd our shifters do? How'd Hekla do?" I asked. I'd almost forgotten about everything else in my zeal.

"Shifters did as well as expected. They're pretty rough around the edges, but their speed mostly makes up for it. Given time, they'll be a force to be reckoned with," he answered, looking over at the sleeping shifters hiding in the trees. "Hekla did better. She's a natural leader. The goddess picked well for you, Summer Prince."

I grinned and replied, "That She did, Winter King." I left Slaine and King Nechtan to find Koray, wondering if they'd found progress with the contract language or some other means of freeing me from it.

I found not only Koray, but also one of my original team members and… Dumnorix? I slowed in my approach, spreading my arms and gaping at the master instructor. "What are you doing here? Dumnorix, you joined us? How did you even hear…"

"That was my fault," Koray said, raising his hand in admission while pushing his black hair away from his face. "I needed his input and swore him to secrecy."

I scrutinized Dumnorix, hoping he hadn't been taken unwillingly. The thin fae waved away my dubious expression. "I'm not a prisoner, Belenus. I'm here of my own free will. I think you underestimate how hated your mother is, especially among us folk fae."

"She's no longer that to me," I vented sharply, nearly spitting the words from my mouth. "She's just the queen. Has been since the day she targeted my fated mate."

"And Eislyn doesn't seem like an improvement either. I don't know your mate well, Belenus, but if she's meant for you, I know she'll be a great queen," he said in turn, speaking gently in an attempt to placate me.

That was probably the biggest compliment I'd ever received in my entire life. I sighed and brushed my hair from my forehead, trying to calm myself. "I know that as well. One of the reasons I'm fighting so bloody hard."

"We as well," my team member, Gallcobar, said. I'd brought him in as an expert on fae law, but he had other skills to bring to the table. Speaking of which, it looked like Dumnorix had manufactured a wooden table for their work.

"King Nechtan said we were close to a breakthrough?" I asked them but ended up looking at Koray. He grinned and waved me over to the table, which was covered in notes, bowls, and a plethora of apothecary ingredients.

"So," Koray began excitedly, "I received a response from the Lunar Coven, and they sent back some notes, suggestions, and theories." He handed over a small stack of paperwork for me to peruse while he talked. "It all goes down to the language of the magic. I'm not talking about the contract, but about the magical equivalent of equations and variables found in the involved spells.

"The promise is a series of variables stated as an 'if then' expression. You marry Eislyn, you are safe. You don't marry Eislyn, you are killed. What we want is a solution to the latter, so we focus on how you will be killed. Gallcobar—a genius by the way—explained how executions are carried out in broken contracts." Gallcobar beamed at Koray's praise but also dismissed the words with an embarrassed hand gesture.

"I've witnessed these executions before," I replied gravely, "but I've never inquired about the process. They just... keel over." I withheld a shudder at how brutally sudden the executions were. Tried as I might to forget them, I recalled every single one in vivid detail. "It'd never been a topic I wanted to discuss."

"Can't say I blame you," Koray replied briskly. "Anyway, Gallcobar here said you'll be compelled by the promise to sign the admission in the failure and retaliation section when you're within a certain distance of the contract. After that, the magic in the contract activates, and a spell will force all your organs and muscles to fail until you expire. Needless to say, it's an immediate death."

That certainly made sense with what I'd seen. The bodies just... fell and died. I supposed that it was a twisted sort of kindness for it to be so quick, but the finite power behind such an automatic process unsettled me. I made a mental note to revisit our execution laws down the road. We needed more wiggle room in cases where contractual issues weren't clean cut. Mistakes happened, and I'd hate to see people die over something resolvable.

So much to do...

Thank the gods we have Hekla and Eventide to help, Escort reminded. That relaxed me a little bit. I could definitely rely on our mate to split the responsibilities.

"So we sat down with Dumnorix and went over the notes from the coven. Luan and Senay said that at the very base level, it functions exactly like a cursed object. Mwezi said they have a ton of artifacts locked away that the coven has collected over the centuries to keep people safe. She mentions a ring that compels you to put it on only for it to kill you. She even packaged it in a sealed jar for us to test our solutions on..." Koray then frowned as he looked at the note. "I really, really don't think she was supposed to do that, though..."

He held up a little bottle with a cork stopper for me to study. Inside, clacking against the glass, was a gaudy golden ring covered in diamonds, rubies, emeralds, sapphires, and more I couldn't name. At least it was sealed, but if it did what Koray said it was capable of, it was bloody dangerous, and I didn't want it anywhere near my people. It'd have to be sent back to the coven immediately for safekeeping. Gods above, hadn't the witches anything safer they could have sent us?

"So… cursed objects," I prompted.

"Right," Koray uttered, scratching his jaw with a couple stained fingers. It looked like he'd been handling ingredients already. "The coven only got so far in finding a way to either dispel curses on objects or protect yourself from them."

"How'd they even bottle this up then?" I asked, gesturing to the ring.

"Probably took the entire coven to manage that from a distance," he said, shrugging. "I have no idea, but I'm curious. I'm going to ask them when I get home. It's a good question. Anyway, this is where it gets complicated with the magical equivalent of math and chemistry formulas."

"The fun part," Dumnorix interrupted with a grin.

Koray was too focused on his explanation to miss a beat and said, "I'll spare you the details, but we broke down the execution spell into its base parts and constructed a formula to nullify each stage. Using the notes from the coven, we have everything we need except for one thing, and I can't for the life of me think of what we could use… yet! Yet, Belenus! I haven't given up!" Koray poked the table vehemently to punctuate his determination.

"We're in the process of going through what's available naturally in our realm, but Macdara's asleep now. We'll continue when he wakes tonight. We're adjusting to the new sleep pattern you've all adopted here…" Gallcobar reported, stifling a yawn.

"It's the bat-shifters. They evolved in the Night Court, so we have to adapt to their schedule, especially if they're going to join us in taking the throne," I explained, but from his nodding

I could tell he already knew that. "I know you're all exhausted, and I promise you'll be more than generously compensated when we take the throne. One last question before you retire. What's the nature of this last ingredient you need?"

Koray puffed out his cheeks and exhaled. "Well, we have what we need for the recognizer, catalyst, and applier, but we're lacking the actual core of what's supposed to eradicate the curse."

I sucked in a breath, scrubbed a hand over my mouth, and stared at Koray for a long moment. It couldn't be that easy, could it? I shoved my hands in my pockets and looked up at the clear night sky through the trees. Was this why the Sky Gods gave Hekla her mission when They did? No, the Sky Gods didn't know anything about the nature of Their children. Was this Fate's doing?

Or maybe it was the Moon Goddess? You know how She likes to nudge Fate in favor of Her children, Escort murmured.

It's enough to give a man a headache, I replied, pinching the bridge of my nose. *Changing the fate of the entire Summer Court seems like a lot for the Moon Goddess to ask of Fate, don't you think?*

Maybe not in the grand scheme of things... You fae may live for hundreds of years, but it's still a blink in the eyes of a god.

True... I replied thoughtfully. *But the children of the Sky Gods were hidden from all the gods, weren't they? Ah, I truly need to stop thinking about it. If it's this simple, I'll take it in a heartbeat.*

We're going to have to get permission from the shifters.

I know... we'll do all this when we wake up tonight. The sky was a little lighter. The Sun God would be out in all His blazing glory soon.

"Belenus?" Koray's voice broke me from my reverie.

"Hmm? Oh. Yes, we may have a solution for that, but I need to look into something first," I replied, glancing over at three surprised faces.

"Oh, you can't possibly leave me hanging like this!" Koray protested, splaying his fingers out on the table as he leaned over it.

I would have chuckled at his enthusiasm had I not been so tired. "Get some rest. You've done… phenomenally. We'll meet up at sunset after I make some inquiries."

Dumnorix and Gallcobar bowed, then left to go sleep, but Koray just looked at me in bewilderment. Finally, he threw up his hands and said, "Alright, well, don't let me sleep a minute more. I'm not even sure I'll be able to now." He strolled off with a short, amazed laugh, and I stalked off to find my mate.

She was already asleep, curled under a wool cover. It looked like someone had brought back some blankets, and I imagined it must have been Emer. I lay down behind Hekla, made sure she was wrapped snugly, and pulled her into my arms. I kissed the back of her head before closing my eyes. This was what I'd been thinking about all night. Through all the planning and debating, my mind always went back to her.

For the first time in weeks, optimism flickered in my soul. Maybe tonight I'd allow myself to dream just a little bit about us being in the king and queen's bed instead of on the forest floor.

I woke just as the sun was setting, alerted by the movement of winter warriors and nearby shifters. I stretched an arm out and adjusted my clothes. As always, waking up next to my mate made for uncomfortably tight pants. I peered over Hekla's slow-breathing form at what I could see of our camp and observed several changes.

Emer slept nearby as usual, but my brows raised to find Nofre resting two feet from her. He had slung one of his wings over the side facing her to—I assume—make her feel like there was a respectful barrier between them. Still, this was the closest they've been after settling.

I scratched at an itchy spot at my temple and slowly absorbed the bizarre new scene surrounding Bidelia. Two winter warriors stood stationed on either side of her, and two female bat-shifters sandwiched her in their sleep with their wings crisscrossing her slumbering figure. I didn't see King Nechtan around anywhere; maybe he was uncomfortable having a child in the camp.

Hekla's deep intake of breath told me that she was waking, and I joined her under the blanket for a moment to pull her into my arms. My hands finding bare flesh made my cock strain against the fabric encasing it. Oh, someone had held to their promise.

"You're naked," I mumbled as quietly as possible, immediately palming a deliciously soft breast.

She smiled sleepily at me, blinking slowly against the setting Sun God. The last of the oranges and yellows gleamed in her umbral eyes, adding sunlight to her glittering starlight. The quiet moment had me appreciating them all the more. She did more than steal my breaths, she owned them. "Told you that you'd find it gone," she murmured into my shoulder, caressing it with her soft lips while she spoke. The movement coupled with her batting eyelashes made my stomach twist with yearning. She still made me feel as if we were just touching for the first time.

"Last night went well? With the training?" I asked.

She hummed and nodded. "I think so. Any training is better than none, and they seem a bit more unified, not that they weren't before." She stared thoughtfully at the branches above our heads. "The training seemed to unlock something in them. I think they've all known each other for so long that they have an easier time reading situations, and that just feeds into their teamwork."

"King Nechtan said you're a natural"—I grinned, squeezing her to me—"and that the goddess picked well. I told him I agreed."

She hid her hot face in my shoulder, but I could feel her pleased smile. "And you?" she asked, muffled by my skin.

"We're basically ready unless anything changes." I felt her relax, and I reached around to rub her back. "We're so close, Hekla. You and me and the Summer Court for centuries."

Hekla's relaxation did a full reversal.

Her head shot up, and she regarded me with unease. "Belenus… I won't live that long. Shifters live longer than humans, sure, but…"

I waved away her anxious expression and said, "We've mated, Hekla. My summer magic will keep you alive as long as any fair fae."

"H-how long is that, Belenus?" Her eyes widened, and I was disconcerted to find them full of fear instead of excitement.

"Many fair fae pass on before they reach a millennium…" I said carefully. "Others, like the folk fae, live about five centuries."

"Are you saying I'm going to watch my entire family, and their pups, and their grandpups, and their great-grandpups die?" she whispered, digging her claws into my chest without realizing it.

I scooped her hand away before she could realize and feel guilty. "Yes, and you also get to watch over your family and their descendants. You get to take care of them. Keep them safe."

She swallowed hard and brought her fingers to her full lips. "I suppose that's a more positive way of looking at it…"

"I'm sorry. I keep forgetting what isn't normal for you," I said, shaking my head at myself. She remained still for a while with her face buried in my chest. "I'm sorry," I whispered again and just held her shocked form.

Eventually, she asked, "So how old are you?" I heard her wet sniffle, and it broke my blistering heart to know that I'd made her cry—again.

I sighed and counted in my head to answer her question. I'd lost track after a while. "One hundred and… eighty-eight?" I guessed, crinkling an eye shut.

She grunted. "No wonder you're so immature." She then burst into laughter, snorting into my chest. Her noises tugged a grin out of me, and I chuckled with her. Then, I tilted my head to kiss the top of hers and enjoyed our moment of peace before we'd be forced to rise.

"Belenus?" she asked quietly, and I hummed in response. "How old is King Nechtan?"

"I'm not sure. Looking at him, I'd guess between two hundred and two-fifty," I answered and moved my hand to massage her shoulder and upper arm. "Why?"

"Because Bidelia's his fated," she whispered so lowly that only I could hear. "She's only fourteen..."

My eyebrows shot up, and I glanced back over to where the teenager was resting. "Well, now the guards make sense..." I murmured. Some movement by Bidelia's chin showed that Arse was also sleeping with her.

"How is that possible, though? In our realm, both fated mates must be of age to recognize."

I hadn't known that. No wonder she had questions. "Yes, it is not so here. An adult could recognize a newborn if they were fated, but we have laws for that."

"Really!" She gasped quietly. "I couldn't even imagine."

I smiled. Had I but visited her pack several decades ago, I would have found her a newborn. "The adult can choose to support the family if they wish—from the distance of the biding, that is." I palmed her cheek and caressed it with a thumb, anxious to soothe her worries. "The 'biding' is the name for their time spent waiting for their fated mate to come of age. There can be no contact between them until then. The child is not told. We protect our young, Hekla."

"Why is it so different?" she murmured, partially to herself.

I pondered that for a long moment, idly listening to an evening breeze meandering through the trees. My smile soon faded. The biding Hekla and I would have had meant that I never would have suffered an engagement to Eislyn—unless the queen's plans had indeed gone back that far. Still, it would have spared us both a lot of grief. Instead of sharing that thought, I said, "Maybe it's because we live for so long. Maybe the Moon Goddess wants us to slow down, to keep the adult from marrying another sooner... now that they know for a fact they have someone to wait for. Or maybe it's just to provide an opportunity for us to protect and nurture them from a distance. That's my best guess. It's just our normal, Hekla."

"So how does this work? Does she stay with us until she turns eighteen or…?"

"Already a fierce mama wolf?" I teased her with a cocky grin, and she wrinkled her nose.

"No, a reasonable mama wolf," she huffed. "I just don't know what's appropriate here."

"Like you said. We'll give them an opportunity to meet when she turns eighteen, and she can make her own decision from there."

"At least he doesn't look old," she mumbled and relaxed back into me.

I laughed softly. "This isn't unusual, Hekla." She nodded and leaned up to lay a kiss on my lips. I growled and shifted the blankets so no one could see her naked back.

"I have something to tell you. Can we get time to talk later? Before dawn?" she asked, wrapping her arms around me as she spoke into my lips. I leaned back and looked at her with a surprised grin.

"Pups?" I asked excitedly.

She wrinkled her nose again and shook her head. "No," she said with an amused smile. "Not that."

"Well, shit," I teased. "But, yes. We'll talk later, I promise." I squeezed her to my chest one last time before releasing her to get dressed. More of her love emanated from her as she pulled a dress over her head, and I wondered if she was finally going to confess. Feeling it over the mate bond was cheating, but it certainly wasn't my fault. Half of me wanted to tease her until she confessed, but I kept that mischievous bastard under tight ropes. Until then, though, I'd savor what I could get, and the warmth of her adoration kept my heart pumping strong, fed my fight, and sharpened my claybeg.

"I brought back some fresh rations, so help yourself," I said, kissing her lovely brown cheek as I turned to leave. Emer was rising, and Nofre was already on his feet, stretching and shifting away his wings. Finally able to address the crux of my problem, I crooked a finger at him, and we marched to the edge of the camp for privacy.

"You recall the issue I have to face with the forced marriage, correct? The contract that I have to find a way to break?" I asked him.

He was pulling a shirt he'd brought with him over his head and crossed his arms. "A little. There was more talk of it last night," he said, then scratched behind his pale, pointed ear.

I shifted my weight and stared at the ground darkening from twilight. I didn't exactly know the best way to ask for someone's blood.

Yeah, it's real fuckin' weird, Escort said. *Just do it. I don't think there's a perfect way to ask.*

I blew out a breath, placed my hands on my hips, and looked Nofre straight in the eyes. "Here's the situation. Someone, I don't know who—it could be me, Hekla, or even Emer—will be executed if I don't marry Princess Eislyn. My friend Koray is close to a solution, but he's missing one thing. He needs something that is capable of destroying a curse." I paused before gesturing to him in frustration. "I immediately thought of bat-shifter blood."

His mouth dropped open; I didn't know if it was from shock alone or if he intended to say something as well. I motioned for him to pause. "That being said, Nofre. I will never force anyone to bleed for someone else. This is purely voluntary. If no one is interested in donating... well, we'll have to figure something else out. To be honest, though, it's not looking good for finding an alternative in time. I can't imagine we'll be able to stay undiscovered here forever. Koray may not need that much either."

Vehemently, he thrust his wrist out at me. "No, I am going to help. If Emer's life is at stake, you're welcome to every bloody drop." His dark brows settled into a straight line. All things aside, his devotion to my sister warmed me.

"I don't know whose life is at stake, Nofre," I said gently, reaching out to lower his arm. "It's probably only mine, but I can't be sure. I don't want to take any chances."

The male shook his head with stubborn adamance. "I don't want to take any chances, either. You know I'd do anything for Emer, Belenus. Let me help," he pressed. "We still owe you and Hekla our lives anyway. Blood comes back."

Sometimes. Sometimes it didn't.

I reached and shook forearms with Nofre. "Regardless of what happens between you two, you are like a brother to me now, Nofre. Are you comfortable making a promise with Koray or do you want me to be an in-between?"

He nodded with a clenched jaw. "Let's not waste time. I'll meet with Koray," he said, standing tall and tilting his head to crack his neck. I gestured for him to wait and brought Koray back with me, who was just as excited as he was last night. After Koray earnestly promised to keep the nature of bat-shifter biology a secret, Nofre shared everything he knew about their curse-killing lifeblood.

I wished I could have captured the look on the young man's face as he listened to Nofre. It really was too bad that the kid didn't have any magic of his own. He would be phenomenal. His mind seemed built to figure out the most obscure puzzles, and if he didn't know, he was bloody proactive about finding someone who did. I was so relieved that the situation with Eislyn hadn't destroyed my friendship with him. It'd come close, though.

"It's exactly what we need," Koray sputtered, turning and breaking me from my thoughts. "We can use tonight to run some tests and decide how we'll manifest the counter."

I winced and asked, "Are you using that ring for your testing, Koray?" When he nodded, I lifted a finger in warning. "Do that far from camp. Is that understood? I don't want to risk any of the shifters or the winter warriors."

He shoved his hands in his pockets and nodded vigorously. "Of course, Belenus!"

I looked over at Nofre but continued addressing Koray. "I don't know how much blood you need, but try to spread it out among other volunteers. I don't want to weaken anyone too much." When Nofre opened his mouth to protest, I snapped at him, "No arguments! Everyone stays as healthy as possible. You're still my responsibility."

"I don't know if we'll need to distill any of it or how potent the blood is, but I can't imagine needing more than a liter for the testing and the final product. We'll see." Koray fidgeted as excitedly as the day I took him to meet Dumnorix, and I felt a swell of pride in how much he'd grown. Before leaving to get some supplies, he insisted, "Belenus, I think we have it. I really do! I'll find you later once we run some tests."

I walked away to meet with King Nechtan, shoving my shaking fists in my pockets to hide my nervous excitement. If all went well, we could end up storming the castle tomorrow.

Now I just needed to harden my resolve to attack the queen. I couldn't choke. I squeezed my eyes shut for a moment and scrubbed my hands over my face.

Emer and Hekla are all the family I need, I kept repeating in my head, knowing full well that choking could kill.

Chapter 31

Belenus

King Nechtan, Slaine, and I hovered over my outline of the castle as I walked them through Drust's and my plan. If we intended to strike the following night, we'd have to quickly decide if we wanted to make any adjustments so we could send someone to alert our castle troops.

"Generally speaking, this seems sound, but how many guards came with the spring princess?" King Nechtan inquired, squatting by the dirt drawing and staring at the northern wall.

"Not many. She had a detail of about twenty soldiers," I answered, then sensed that my mate was approaching. My heart leapt, and I turned to greet her with a smile. Though she appeared well rested with her alert umbral eyes, I sensed irritation through our bond. My sister and Ferrer followed her, but Emer appeared to be complaining about something. Hekla's face told me she was moments away from snapping.

What's going on with our sister? Escort inquired. It was weird to hear him refer to her as our sister, but I supposed she was as much his sister as she was mine.

She hadn't warned Nofre that she was leaving when she gathered your team from the castle, and he flew off the handle when he realized she was missing. Now he's hovering so she doesn't sneak off again, Eventide reported.

I gave my mate a sympathetic look as she greeted me with a hug and a kiss, also offering me a ration bar and some fresh fruit. "You're thoughtful," I murmured, nuzzling her forehead. "Thanks for joining us. It was good you brought Ferrer since Nofre will be busy with Koray for a while."

"Promise stuff?" she asked, blinking up at me through her thick eyelashes.

"Yes." I sighed and gestured to the castle layout. I then shared the plan with the new arrivals, wanting to verify that the strategy worked for Hekla and her shifter army. "Did we ever get a number on how many bats are willing to join the takeover?"

"We have about three hundred and twenty-three volunteers," Hekla said, wrapping one arm around me as she addressed the group as a whole.

"There are many who are unwilling to risk further diminishing our population," Ferrer added, pushing his hair from his face. "The older generation is more conservative about it."

"I think that's fair and completely understandable. I'm honestly surprised that we have any volunteers because of that," I replied.

"So with the castle soldiers, my forty-six warriors, and the shifters, we'll have approximately eleven hundred and sixty-nine," King Nechtan surmised, placing a hand to his chin. He stroked the black stubble there that thickened by the day. "That leaves eleven hundred inactive soldiers and one hundred and twenty hostiles."

"There could be unknowns, though," Hekla muttered thoughtfully. "Especially if we're worried about rot-witches. From what Belenus told me, we haven't quite discerned what that rot-witch was saying. Her trying to kill me… well, that would free Belenus to marry. I wouldn't be surprised if we ended up seeing one or two. What do you think?"

"It's possible," King Nechtan replied, and I nodded in agreement. "However, I don't know how we'd prepare for that."

"I'll discuss it with Koray later," I said.

Hekla wrinkled her nose. "From your description, I'm sure I'll smell one coming."

"We'll be able to as well. It was… unforgettable." Ferrer grimaced, looking slightly green at the thought of old, spoiled food.

"So our army's goal is to restrain the hostile units. I do not want anyone killed if it can be helped," I reiterated firmly. Ferrer looked away for a couple seconds and cleared his throat.

"There is a way to… weaken them if we… take enough blood," he shared quietly. His drawn brows told me he felt ashamed for even mentioning it. "A specific percentage of blood loss will result in confusion and dizziness… sometimes fainting."

"I realize that was hard to suggest," Hekla said, laying a comforting hand on his shoulder. He couldn't look at anyone after that. He just shrugged.

"How hard would it be to stop drinking before they're killed?" the winter king asked frankly.

Ferrer's red gaze remained averted. "If we eat before we leave, some of us could handle the temptation."

Both King Nechtan and Hekla turned to me for the judgment call. Emer just shifted restlessly. "Advise those who you trust to do this," I told Ferrer. "We'll use it on those who prove to be particularly problematic only if we have no means of restraining them. Be strict with those you pick. Is that clear?"

"Yes, Prince Belenus. Your order is clear."

I gestured for Ferrer to go about his task and turned to King Nechtan to ask about his contribution. "Forty-six of your warriors?"

His countenance darkened as he frowned, irked that I'd noticed. He merely nodded, choosing not to volunteer an explanation. That alone verified my suspicion.

"Bidelia will be safe here," Hekla reassured, echoing my thoughts precisely. "I have people guarding her, but your warriors are welcome to stay to watch her."

"I was hoping no one had noticed," he said tersely, but when Hekla burst into laughter, his expression turned thunderstruck. She held up a hand in apology and composed herself. The king gritted his teeth and added, "Worry yourself not. You may think us barbaric, but we of winter follow the biding just like you. I have no plans on seeing her again until she comes of age." He crossed his arms and his nostrils flared. "If we're done here..." he asked flatly and looked to me for dismissal.

I nodded, not too surprised about his irritation. Bidelia would be his weakness, and no king wanted their vulnerability known, especially with her being raised outside of his court's influence. Had he been any other winter fae, or perhaps one from an older generation, I might have been more worried about him absconding with her.

"I'll come find you if we're prepared to go tomorrow," he said and strode off rigidly with Slaine.

"What about me?" Emer finally asked, eyeing the departing king with open amusement.

"Do you know how to fight, Emer?" my mate asked. Though she meant it without insult, Emer bristled in offense.

"I can be useful," she snapped at us and fisted her skirts at her hips. "I also have a thing or two to say to the queen before you do... whatever you're going to do!"

"Yes, you know some things. You can put up barriers, but you're not tested, Emer. You've never seen violence," I argued, having a feeling I was going to lose this debate. I wasn't sure it was right to deny my sister some closure. "And what about Nofre? He's going to lose his mind if you put yourself in danger."

You really shouldn't have said that, Eventide said with a fairly audible wince.

Get ready, Escort warned.

In the corner of my eye, I could see Hekla slide a hand over her face.

True to my track record of pissing off those I cared about, Emer blew up and started throwing obscenities at me. She yelled about how controlling men were and that she'd not be left behind no matter what. After telling me that I'd be running into battle with a steel-toed boot up my ass, she stomped off, cursing up a storm.

Hekla's hand slid to her mouth in an attempt to conceal a poorly disguised smile. I withered and sent her my own flat smile, fully accepting the backlash I'd received.

"I'm, uh… going to check on Koray," I mumbled and trudged off to see if any progress was being made.

I found him leaning over the wooden table, drawing something with red ink. Dumnorix was gesturing to the parchment, muttering while Macdara watched from his place next to Gallcobar. Nofre sat against a nearby tree, only partially paying attention to the discussion.

I arrived at the table and Koray beamed up at me like a kid showing off a drawing. "Belenus, I think we did it! We designed the counter, and now we're just adding in some precautionary measures!"

I leaned over to examine the elaborate illustration. It reminded me of what the rot-witch had placed on Ragna's back, which Koray had carefully worked to remove like it'd been a complicated puzzle. The outline was like an arched doorway, curved on the top and flat on the bottom. The inside contained mazelike lines and symbols that I didn't recognize. I had to admire Koray's steady hand; some sections he'd drawn were in fairly cramped spaces and inked with delicate precision.

I stayed to watch the drawing's completion after I made certain I wouldn't be a distraction to Koray's focus. Once he finished, the parchment was passed around to the other mages who reviewed and eventually signed off on the design and its details. Dumnorix placed the paper down on the table, rolled up his sleeves, and rubbed his hands together.

"Alright! Now we designate it as a counter. I'll have to do this part," he explained to Koray before placing his scaled hand on the design and focusing intently on it. After a minute, Dumnorix removed his hand, revealing the faintest traces of diffused sunlight seeping into the red lines, turning the illustration copper. He nodded to Macdara, who carefully set a flat pan of red liquid in front of him. The master instructor lowered the parchment into the mysterious solution, pulled it out slowly, and tilted it like he was panning for gold.

"You want to make sure you get a nice, even coat," he said to Koray. "Are you ready?"

Koray jumped to his feet in excitement, threw off his shirt, and turned away from Dumnorix. The master instructor sandwiched the paper between his palm and the flat plane of the young man's shoulder blade. When the parchment was peeled away, the image of the counter was branded on Koray's skin, just as vibrant and detailed as it was on paper.

"Let's go test it," the young man said with an enthusiastic grin, and we followed him to the edge of the glamour, making sure to stay behind it. Dumnorix grabbed both of Koray's hands and skillfully crafted a skintight barrier to encase them like gloves. It was impressive, I had to admit. I didn't even think I could create a barrier that intricate.

We backed off as Koray unstoppered the jar that contained the cursed ring. The draw was instant and sobering, an unforeseen slap to the face, and we all stepped forward with an irresistible urge to wear the hideous, gaudy thing. The young man stared at us for a moment, released a sharp burst of laughter, and put the cork back in to seal it.

The compulsion dissipated as fast as it'd come, and I nearly lost my balance. "Shit," I muttered, catching myself before I fell over my own blisterin' feet.

"Report?" Dumnorix asked, apparently unsurprised by the ring's potency—or at least he didn't look like how I felt.

"Nothing. Felt nothing." Koray turned around to reveal the counter on his back, and the instructor compared it to the paper copy. He gestured for Macdara to remove his tunic and applied the counter to his back in the same fashion after soaking the parchment again.

"Are you prepared to resuscitate?" he asked Macdara as he removed the barrier from Koray's hands.

"Wait, wait, what are you going to do?" I asked, alarmed. "No, don't test wearing the ring, Koray!"

The young man shrugged, then uncorked the bottle. We were compelled again, lured as aggressively as before. My alarm fell to gut-wrenching fear.

"Koray! Don't! Let me test it!" I yelled, so anxious that I was close to retching. This was my mission, and the risk should have been mine! "Koray! Stop! That's an order!"

He ignored my pleas and commands, and the blood drained from my face when he slipped the ring on his forefinger. An electric-like snap vibrated from the air down to the magic layer, then, there was silence. That was all that occurred. Koray drew his lips back in a relieved grimace when it became clear that the counter held strong against the will of the curse. He shuddered, ripped off the ring, and shoved it back into the jar, freeing us from its lure and thus allowing me to come down hard on him.

"You shouldn't have done that!" I thundered, yanking the jar from his hands. "That was my risk to take, Koray!" Shit, that'd been terrifying. My blood raged through my veins, echoing my fury.

He just shoved his hands in his pockets and said, "Well, it worked!" He chuckled nervously and ran his fingers through his hair before shaking the nerves out of his arms. His nonchalance was particularly rage-inducing right now. Koray, the Key of the Lunar Coven, continued to march to his own blistering rhythm.

I sat down hard and ended up flopping onto my back. "Great blisterin' Sun God's rays of shit," I cursed nonsensically. "Thank the fucking gods it worked." I placed my hands over my eyes, rubbing them and fighting a sudden bout of fatigue. "I want to make it clear that you're staying here tomorrow night, Koray. I'll not have you risking yourself twice."

He didn't reply, to my annoyance, and just turned to let the mages look at his back. I peered up and saw that the counter was gone. All that remained was the arched outline. I exhaled slowly, hoping that it'd work against whatever we'd be hit with tomorrow.

"Can we make enough to protect multiple people?" I asked from the ground and Macdara nodded.

"Just let us know how many, but we should have enough for a couple dozen," he answered.

"That'll have to do, I guess. I can't imagine the contract would target more than a handful of people." I closed my eyes and sent a more fervent prayer to the Sun God.

Please let this work. Please don't let anyone die.

I crossed my arms and studied the post-midnight sky, taking a deep breath and enjoying the spread of stars that reminded me of my Hekla's glittering, dark eyes. Dawn wasn't due for several hours, and I hoped to keep this final meeting short so everyone could be as rested as possible for the takeover. I was personally anxious to retire with Hekla and curious about what she wanted to discuss.

Hekla, King Nechtan, Emer, and Nofre quickly gathered, each displaying a variety of emotions. I could sense Hekla's nervousness through our bond, but she hid it well, straightening her shoulders and holding her chin up proudly. Emer, never one who could—or cared to—hide her own feelings, was openly anxious and flustered. Nofre was serious, but I could tell that Emer's presence and behavior was making him wary. King Nechtan was the only one who seemed calm and collected. I had to wonder if he was almost bored with this takeover. The fae king had seen many wars, all much larger than what we'd planned.

"We're ready to go tonight," I said, making sure to meet every single person's eyes. "We'll rest through the day and gather at sunset. Once the volunteers are ready, we'll begin our march on the castle. I'm going to set up glamour barriers on the way to hide us. It's not foolproof against the queen if she's paying attention, so we must move as quickly and quietly as possible.

"As far as the contract goes, my team has devised a means of protecting against the retaliation. There's no way to know for sure that it'll work, but it's the best solution we have." I gestured to King Nechtan and said, "It's supposed to work on all curses, and we'll have leftovers, so if you and some of your warriors want to be extra protected during battle, you're welcome to it."

After the winter king nodded his acceptance of the offer, I turned my back to the group and lifted my tunic up so they could study the counter that Dumnorix had placed on my left shoulder blade. I straightened my shirt after a minute and turned to face everyone. "I want Hekla, Emer, and Bidelia protected with a counter, so please go find Dumnorix after this. I doubt the contract would target anyone other than Hekla and myself, but it would ease my mind a great deal." I also had a feeling that King Nechtan would insist on Bidelia's protection even though the queen probably didn't care or even know who she was.

I ran everyone through the plan one more time and answered all questions. Emer still insisted on coming along, to Nofre's dismay. He tersely asserted that he'd be her bodyguard during that time and wouldn't take no for an answer. That did make me feel better about her tagging along.

After a half hour, everyone quieted, and I adjourned the meeting to take my mate to Dumnorix where he applied the counter. Hekla then quietly took my hand and strolled with me until we found a private spot.

"Want to go for a run?" she asked in a low voice, squeezing my hand with hers. I didn't need to feel her sweaty palm to know that she was nervous. It was coming across the bond loud and clear.

I smiled down at her and kissed her forehead. "I think that sounds like fun. Should probably give Escort and Eventide some time together before we go into a dangerous situation," I said, thinking clearly before speaking this time.

Hekla, pleasantly surprised, stepped into my arms to deliver an emotional hug. "Thank you," she whispered, "for being open and understanding."

"Escort's not always a little shit," I replied with a chuckle, squeezing her tight against me. "I suppose I owe him."

Yes, you fucking do, big shit, Escort retorted, but his comment lacked malice this time. Maybe we were making progress after all. Now we had nicknames for each other.

In the chirping night of the Summer Court, Hekla moved back to disrobe and placed her clothes on a nearby branch for her to gather later. I didn't bother hiding my groan as I watched her, wanting nothing more than to take her right here, right now. I considered myself lucky that I could transform fully clothed. Had I been nude, she'd have had an eyeful.

She shifted while I transformed, and for the first time, I sat back in Escort's mind and allowed myself to truly enjoy the experience. I'd always been too distracted to focus on what it was like to be a wolf, and now I could better appreciate the wind in his fur as I received his senses.

After a joyous, yipping reunion, Escort and his sweet 'Stardust' ran out into the hills. I sensed some degree of alertness from both of them, knowing that creatures would always lurk in the dark, but for some reason, I wasn't worried about it. The farther we ran, the more secure I felt. It almost seemed like the sensation of being home had now extended into the wilds.

I tucked my mind away to give the two wolves privacy for an hour. I was happy to do it now, understanding the importance and finally accepting it as part of my identity. Ultimately, I realized that I'd actually given Hekla exactly what she'd wanted: a wolf for Eventide. It'd just turned out better than I'd originally planned. I'd done it to please her, then tried to tolerate Escort to prove my love to her, then realized I had to accept Escort as part of myself to truly make her and Eventide happy.

It was worth it.

When our wolves decided to retire and rest, Hekla and I reclaimed our bodies. They'd taken us to an outcropping by a crystal-clear stream that trickled merrily in the balmy night. Whether they'd intended it as a thoughtful gesture or not, it was a perfect site to be alone with my dear Hekla.

I reached for her hands and stood back, letting my gaze sweep over her body. "You are pure ambrosia, my female," I murmured, staring at her firm arms and legs, then raking my eyes over the swell of her hips and breasts. I could already see her excitement in her dilated eyes and in the glistening of the dark curls between her legs.

I was ravenous for a taste of her, but I also knew she wanted to talk. I'd let her talk, but I didn't think I could let go of her. I loosened my grip on her fingers, then slid my palms up her arms and behind her back, pulling her to me a little rougher than intended. She released a gasp when she hit my chest and looked up at me. The angle of her face under the starlight made her eyes glitter all the more.

I slid a hand up her neck to cup her cheek. "How am I so lucky to have you?" I breathed out in wonder, mostly to myself.

Her soft expression grew worried when she glanced around the immediate area. "Are we safe here?" she asked, leaning into my arms. "I still feel like there is so much left to learn about my new realm."

Her question poked at what I'd been feeling, and I thought more deeply about it. "I believe so. I feel… more comfortable now than I ever have. I can't say that I really know why."

"What do you mean?"

"A king or queen pulls power from their entire court and can walk the wilds like they're in the safety of their own chambers. A prince or princess only draws from the surrounding area, but it's starting to feel like more now." I closed my eyes and could almost see the wilds around me through my magic. "The royal summer sunlight sees through all… and I feel nothing but safety."

Hekla leaned her head into my chest, and I stroked her hair. A sighing breeze blew past, calling my attention back to nature. I felt the spongy ground beneath my feet and fixated upon the sound of nomadic water. We were surrounded by the earth, the water, and the sky. I wondered if the godlings of the three domains were showing their support.

"Triskelion must be urging me on," I murmured as I ran my fingers through my mate's locks. "The three godlings," I explained when she looked up at me in confusion. I realized I'd never clarified that. "Supposedly they're the ones who originally tied the royal line's magic to each court. Perhaps they're offering me more before tomorrow… because I feel… more."

"I hope so," she whispered from my arms. "We don't know what tomorrow will bring."

"Tomorrow will bring you to your rightful place, Hekla. The queen's throne waits for you." I wanted to offer comfort and tried to push my fears away for her. "Our people wait for you." I tilted her chin up to lay a soft, slow kiss on her lips. "The king's bed waits for you," I murmured into her skin, holding back a smile when I felt her goose bumps rise under my wandering hands.

A throaty moan escaped her lips, but I was already as hard as steel under my pants. It was a challenge to not be erect around her. She completely sated my mind and soul, but my body incessantly demanded the pleasures of its fated mate, and the prince in me wanted a small army of heirs. The prince in me also quite enjoyed the process of making them. My cock throbbed as I imagined her round with child. I couldn't imagine a sexier sight.

I groaned into her lips, sliding my hands down to hold her hips while I grinded my cock against her. I really should remove these pesky clothes, but I didn't want to release her lips.

Oh shit, that's right, she wanted to talk.

I released her reluctantly, trying to ignore the almost intolerable ache in my groin. "Sorry," I said with a bashful laugh. "You wanted to talk. What is it?"

She smiled and placed her hands on her heated face. "I… almost forgot too." She cleared her throat and rocked on her toes a couple times while she adopted a thoughtful expression. I openly admired the movement of her breasts and hips as she planned her words. I could multitask; I was certain of it.

"I… It's been with me a while, but I couldn't find the courage or right opportunity. I'm no fool, Belenus. I know we could very well die tomorrow." Her expression sobered as she looked far off into the night, like she was staring at tomorrow. "It's been a battle since the day we met, you know. Nothing went according to plan except for when it was just us. Going into town to pick up Arse… late nights in my chambers… rolling around behind closed doors. When laws or people weren't trying to interfere, everything was clear and beautiful.

"It took me time to get the hurt to move off my heart." She looked down at her hands while she worried at them. "I couldn't feel anything under its oppression."

My heart steadily accelerated as she spoke. I knew what she was working toward, and I had to be patient. I had to let her say it even though I wanted to show my gratitude this very minute by making her scream in pleasure. I felt her mild nervousness too, but it was greatly overshadowed by anticipation.

"When its weight was gone… I could fully appreciate our connection again. I'm sorry it took as long as it did. I know this whole ordeal has been hard on you as well." She stepped closer and reached up to cup my face in her palms. We locked eyes and stayed like that for a moment until she bit her lip and pulled my forehead down to rest against hers.

"Don't be sorry," I whispered. "I don't want you to be sorry."

She nuzzled against me to acknowledge what I'd said. My heart was racing at a speed that could challenge even Escort.

"I… I love you," she confessed quietly, arching her back so she could look up at me again. She smiled softly but had a little worry line between her brows.

I released a breath I hadn't realized I'd been holding and crashed my lips against hers, delivering the roughest, most passionate, and penetrating kiss she'd ever had in her life.

Chapter 32

Hekla

As soon as the confession had left my mouth, Belenus's rampaging passion hit me like a charging buck. His mouth crushed mine in a ravenous kiss that left me breathless and reeling. His palms slid over my skin, one moving to cup the back of my head while the other traveled to my bottom and gripped it possessively.

I finally unfroze and released a whimper around his plundering tongue. He groaned deeply in response, so low that I felt it vibrate in his chest. His firm grip on my skull kept me in place while he fiercely massaged our lips around the tongue that kept plunging in to taste me. His jaw moved with mine in a sensual dance, igniting my lust with his seduction.

A shudder like lightning raked through me from head to toe, and I fumbled around with my fingers until I found the bottom of his tunic. I pulled it up his hard body until I couldn't get it past his armpits. I jerked the fabric up a couple times to give him the hint to raise his arms, but he growled into my lips and kissed me harder.

He finally released me, tore his clothes off in the blink of an eye, and laid me down on the soft ground. "No… more… interruptions!" he demanded heatedly, settling between my legs and lowering his head to kiss me again. He licked and nipped my lips gently in his ardor, which swept through the bond like a raging summer storm. I felt his excitement, his satisfaction, and his arousal encase me in a thrilling whirlwind.

He must have needed to hear it so badly. The way he was acting now, it was like he was breathing again, living again, and his hot blood was now pumping with the ferocity of someone who survived a near-death experience. My only regret was that I wished I had said it sooner. I wished I could have given him more time to enjoy it before we'd have to dive into a life-threatening battle.

I knew he'd felt my swirling regret because he pulled his mouth away and said gruffly, "No matter what happens, Hekla, you will be my queen, and we'll have the rest of our long lives to enjoy this love. I won't allow it to be taken from us. Do you trust me now? Do you fully trust that I'm going to win this for us? That we're going to win this together? Do you believe in us?"

I wrapped my arms around his rippling back and looked up at the stars, willing away fresh tears. The Sky Gods themselves had given me a task. They were the ones who'd chosen me. They must have believed in me and found me capable. Had that show of faith given me strength to draw from in my time of need?

It had.

"I have to believe," I cried, caving. "If I do, I'll fight harder. Yes, Belenus! I do! I believe!" I sniffed and tried to let the weight of fear roll off my heart and mind.

Belenus stared down at me with his warm amber eyes. They were so warm and bright tonight; I could have sworn they were glowing. I could almost see his feelings radiate from them like they did across our soul-deep connection. He lowered his gaze, stared at my face through lashes darker than his sunflower-yellow hair, and kissed the tear trails that had formed on my cheeks.

I felt something warm seep through my skin, something I'd felt before with him, and it melted me into a puddle. When he'd returned to kissing my cheeks, I could feel his summer essence through his lips. It hitchhiked onto every caress, mingling with the pleasurable mate touch to add even more intimacy to our embrace. The essence was all the best parts of Belenus, concentrated into something so personal and private that anyone else but me would burn to ashes.

He'd been right when he called it the most intensely erotic act, and even small kisses made me bite my cheek to keep from howling. Each lick of his essence seemed stronger this time too. I didn't know if it was because we were in his court now or if he'd been right about Triskelion's gift.

I gritted my teeth when he followed a tear trail down to my neck and gave slow, languid laps until his lips settled on my mating mark. His velvety soft tongue drew warm, wet lines around his teeth marks, and I bucked up involuntarily at the mind-numbing pleasure. My core wept for him and throbbed mercilessly. I felt a deep urge to claw at something but left my fingernails unshifted, not wanting to hurt Belenus on accident ever again.

"Do you like that?" he whispered into my neck as he licked it.

I whimpered and whined while nodding, too tongue-tied from the sensation to talk. It was like every stroke of his tongue threatened to send me into the eye of his summer storm, where his sunlight shone the brightest.

When he bit down, I arched up into his muscular body and cried out through my clenched teeth. His essence seared through my nerve endings and nearly pulled me over the edge. He was claiming me without a single penetrative act, and I was more aroused than I'd ever been in my life... more than when he'd mounted me for the first time and more than when he came on my stomach. The wolf instincts in me were going crazy, having never felt such an aggressive claiming of territory.

As though he'd latched onto my thoughts, he released my neck and growled, "The water you hear... that's mine. The skies above us? Mine too." He finally pulled himself farther up to settle his heavy cock on my lower abdomen, grinding our hips together to press me into the soft soil. "The ground beneath us. Mine." He pressed his hard body into me and slid down until his engorged member was nestled along my sex. "This body. This female. This queen. Mine." His voice became more savage by the word, making me sob with desire for him.

Mine.

It was something he hadn't said at the very beginning, the moment we recognized each other as fated mates. I had, but he'd been too stunned. Each time he had said it since, though, it felt like he was making up for that lost moment, adding more rapacity for each day those words hadn't spilled from his lips.

With our instincts going wild, him crushing our lips together and rolling his hips to grind his length along my sex, there was nothing else outside of us. All I could see, smell, touch, and hear was him. All I could feel was him, inside and out, though I felt like my heart would stop if I went another minute without him claiming me.

"Please, my mate," I begged through my canines and dug my nails into his back. "I can't wait any more!"

The golden fae male rocking over me leaned to nibble on my earlobe. "Does my queen desire me to feast upon her?" he rumbled suggestively, but I shook my head after he released it.

"No! I can't wait! Mark your territory inside me. Claim it! Claim me! Please!" I whimpered, arching my back to press into him, hoping to tempt him into it. I rubbed my aching breasts into his chest and slid my thumbs up his pointed ears. The last act threw him over the edge, and he buried his face into my shoulder as a shudder shot violently through him.

He reared back, looking almost wild, and sat on his heels. Fingers dug into my thighs before sliding up to my hips, and I was pulled slightly off the ground to meet his erection. He grabbed his cock, harder than I'd ever seen it, and nestled its large head against my humble opening.

He leaned while pulling on my hips to press into me, watching me stretch around his tip. The sight of him so focused on where we were joining sent a massive wave of excitement through me. Arousal slicked out around him and dampened my thighs, allowing him to finally slip through my threshold. I grimaced through the painful pleasure of his wide descent and bit on my arm to muffle an elated cry.

"Do not cover your mouth. I expect to make you howl for me, she-wolf," he said in a low, guttural voice as he pushed in at a torturously slow rate. "I already put up a glamour and sound barrier."

I whined and nodded vigorously, panting as he continued to slide along my channel into my depths. It felt like he was never going to finish entering until he finally bottomed out, pushing hungrily against the soft door to my womb. He released a loud, extended groan of pleasure when his swollen length became fully seated inside me. His sack hung tight outside my entrance, and I could tell he was already trying not to ejaculate. His arms shook, and he drew in a deep, calming breath while we were locked in place.

"You… are perfection," he grunted through a heavy exhale. "You embrace my cock like heat does the sun's rays." He adjusted his hips, closing his eyes tight when I felt him throb particularly hard. He gasped and lay back down over me. "I'll never not be able to say it…" he gritted through his teeth as he rocked his hips experimentally. "Perfect… Hot, smooth, wet, and so very, very tight."

I whimpered louder and slid my fingers everywhere I could reach. The muscles on his arms, shoulders, chest, and back were all as rock hard as his cock. This was a cage that this she-wolf didn't mind being trapped in at all. I ran my fingers through the male fae's hair, fixated on the feeling of his cock dragging back along the shape of my channel. He removed his soaked length until just the head remained nestled inside, then jerked his hips forward to bury himself inside me again.

I cried out finally, telling the night that someone had placed a claim. A fae had caught me and wanted this wolf all for himself. It was a golden fae, as powerful as he was alluring; almost too much for this wolf to handle.

He reached back to pull one of my legs up, encouraging me to wrap them around him. I followed his will, holding on tight while he flexed over me. After several more slow pulls and vigorous thrusts, he settled into a regular rhythm. His forearms framed my head, and he tucked his head down to rest his cheek close to my temple.

His grunting and heavy breathing directly into my ear sent hot and cold electricity down my body to the apex of my sex, where I clenched hard around his pumping member. We released simultaneous sounds of pleasure, and he quickened his pace, his libido overflowing with mine. I was burning up from the stimulation given to me by this fae. He was pleasure itself made male.

Yes, yes, yes, I chanted in my head. *Claim me, mark your territory, fuck me!*

Maybe I had spoken aloud because the fae sped up his pace until he was rutting me with wild abandon. His primal sounds made every dart of pleasure erupt into bolts of ecstasy, and I released a long wail, holding on tight while he ravished my body.

"Yes," he growled in a deep, rough voice. "Show me how much of you is beast, she-wolf." He sped up faster, slapping our wet skin together in a brutal taking. The angle of his hips started pulling something from me other than the delicious pleasure I got from each impact. The heat rose in my belly, spreading outward like the slow lighting of the dawn sky above.

I tightened around his plunging cock, and my stomach coiled in anticipation of the sunrise. His essence had me wrapped just as tight, and I suddenly remembered whose arms were framing my head. Belenus and I locked eyes at the same time, feeling something deeper than bone pull at our attention.

"I love you," I gritted out as his summer storm ravaged me, pulling my senses up to the sky where the sun's warm rays lived.

"Gods, I love you too!" he cried and crashed his lips into mine again, grinding his sweaty pelvis against my clit. It brought us both into the eye of the storm.

I tore my lips from his to release a screaming howl, seizing and clawing at him while a euphoric orgasm splintered through me like lightning. Belenus pumped aggressively a moment longer before following me into spiraling pleasure. We rocked and pulsed into each other. My core clenched his spurting member to rub his seed out in waves, milking him for everything his storm had to offer. He cried his thunder into my shoulder, shaking violently from his own release. A spasming buck would occasionally follow one of his moans as he filled me. His rain poured.

Our writhing dance gradually calmed, and our panting slowed to heavy breathing as we came down from our climaxes. My legs, tired, fell from Belenus's waist, but I pressed my thighs to his, wanting him to stay where he was, if only for a moment longer. His sweat trickled onto my body, mingling with mine as we recovered from our joining.

I nuzzled his cheek with my nose, and when he turned his head to face me, I placed an affectionate kiss on his lips. "Thank you for loving me," I whispered.

"I should be thanking you," he replied in a low murmur, staring into my eyes with an intensity akin to wonder. "I didn't think you could make me feel any happier, but you saying those words…" He shook his head slightly. "I can't even put it into words," he finally said, reaching to brush my lower lip with a thumb, "my beloved female…"

"I do love you, Belenus. I love you so much," I repeated, wanting to give him more of what he seemed to need so desperately. "And I'll tell you every day from here on out, my mate."

"Do you promise?" he asked, moving to trace my upper lip now.

"I promise…" I whispered, closing my eyes to enjoy his reverent touch.

"But what if you forget? What kind of compensation can I expect for breaking such an important promise?"

I couldn't keep the grin from spreading my lips, the ones he continued to trace. Now he was just teasing me. I opened my eyes to find humor, light, and love dancing in his amber gaze. "I'm sure we'll sort something out." I tried to put away my grin, but his own broad smile made it impossible.

"I'll hold you to that then."

The only reason I'd been able to sleep at all during the day was because Belenus's mounting had blissfully exhausted me. It wasn't necessarily an easy sleep, though. I'd woken a number of times worrying that I'd missed the attack on the castle. I also wasn't surprised to find that others were having a rough time of it as well. Even Emer and Nofre were lying next to each other, speaking in low murmurs.

All I could do was curl back into Belenus's arms and try to go back to sleep. Thank the gods for the soothing mate touch as well. I'd be faring much worse if Belenus couldn't sleep by my side.

And no one will threaten to keep us from his bed ever again, Eventide muttered sleepily before we passed out once more.

Chatting and shuffling had me waking to a restless camp at sunset. King Nechtan stood before his nervous warriors, speaking in a terse voice. I imagined that these battle-hardened people weren't necessarily concerned about the fighting, merely the fact that their king would be outnumbered by summer soldiers the entire time, even after victory. It spoke to how much trust King Nechtan was placing in Belenus and me. If I really thought about it… it was staggering. We had his fated mate here too. We had everything here to cripple the Winter Court.

It makes me want to succeed even more, Eventide said thoughtfully. *Joining packs... er, forces, is good for thriving long-term.*

We will win this, I said vehemently, *and the queen will pay for her crimes.*

Yes, she fucking will.

The bat-shifters were busy making sure they were especially well fed before our march, per my orders. We'd be out among a lot of people, more than they'd ever seen, and I wanted to minimize the temptation for them to lose control and feed on soldiers or civilians. I wasn't certain if it was doing them a disservice to think that way, but I wanted to make sure as many variables were thought about in advance as possible.

I tried to get a read on the shifters' moods as I attempted to force food down my nervous throat. They still sweated from the lingering day's heat, but with how they mopped their worried brows, I suspected that fear fed the perspiration. The ones who'd eaten—who were ready to go—fidgeted, finding the waiting intolerable, which I understood more than they'd ever know.

I worried about how they'd react to the unknowns before them. As much as they'd been drilled on sparring, fighting another person was nothing like taking down a monster. Pain stabbed my heart and tension gripped my stomach the more I watched. They were all like pups in a way—a people with an incomparable innocence. I wished they would decide to stay here instead. The gods had tasked me with their safety, and dragging them into Belenus's and my war felt so wrong. I sighed and wiped my own dewy brow. All I could do now was prepare for the worst and fight for the best.

"Miss Hekla?" a voice asked, and I turned to find Dumnorix approaching with Koray and several other fae. "Good evening, miss." The folk fae bowed while holding an armful of leathers.

"Good evening to you." I smiled, wanting to put on a brave, confident front. "What can I help you with?"

"It's the other way around, Hekla," Koray corrected with a proud grin.

"Oh? What did you get up to?"

Dumnorix held up a vest made mostly of boiled leather. "We made you some light armor with a couple pieces Belenus brought back from the barracks. I have an understanding that wolf-shifters prefer to fight in their animal forms, but our archers…" Dumnorix paused and twisted his mouth like he was searching for the right words. "Our archers are some of the very best, and no doubt the queen has many of them who are still loyal to her."

I opened my mouth to tell him that I wasn't offended, but he held up a palm with a pained expression to let me know he still had more to say.

I mean, as fast as I can be, if I'm risking an arrow to the ass maybe don't call me out until we get to the queen, hmm? Eventide suggested.

"That being said, Koray here thought we could put some slits and stretchy fabric in here to make it wearable for… um… Eventide." Dumnorix pointed to the chest, where the breast pieces could fold out to make space for Eventide's wolf-shaped chest. I saw that the sides weren't sewn shut but held with a stretchy material that could accommodate her larger rib cage. "It's not ideal armor for a person going into battle, but it's better to get an arrow in the leg than one straight to the heart."

Koray reached for what was awkwardly tucked under Dumnorix's arm and held up a leather helmet and skirt. Dumnorix said, "These two, you'll have to just take off before shifting. There is no way to make pants work… at least not until this young man invents one." He snorted in good humor, jerking a thumb in Koray's direction.

"You're going to give me a fat ego, Norix," Koray protested, lightly nudging the folk fae in the ribs.

"It's Dumnorix," a fae named Gallcobar corrected.

"It's Norix, unless he'd rather me nickname him Dummy?" Koray replied jovially, looking over at the reptilian fae whose face pinched in conservative amusement.

"I'd rather not..." Dumnorix's nostrils flared from his restrained mirth. "Anyway. Should you choose to use it, the skirt unties easily on one side if you need to shift quickly. Can we make sure the chest piece fits on Eventide?"

I nodded to Dumnorix and quickly stripped to don the loose leather vest and skirt. I fiddled with the ties on the skirt, getting familiar with them before taking it off and shifting into Eventide. The boiled leather creaked a bit as her body filled it, and there were several places where the armor pinched. She squirmed uncomfortably and whined at the fae who crouched with Koray to examine the fit.

They gestured to several spots and Dumnorix made some adjustments. I couldn't see what he was doing, but I felt the pressure in the pinched spots disappear. Eventide wagged her tail to show her approval and did a couple laps around the immediate area to see how it felt.

Not like King Zorian's armor but not bad, she said. *It is so, so, so weird to wear clothing, though. I feel like a people imposter!*

Trust me, no one will mistake you for a human, I replied.

Is that so? Give me a wig, and I'll learn to walk on my hind legs!

I'm sure our fae subjects would love to watch their wolf queen hop around like an idiot.

Can't say it wouldn't be an improvement from their last queen...

I shifted back into my human form, cackling from Eventide's wry comment. No, couldn't say it wouldn't be an improvement indeed.

"Thank you, Koray," I said but looked at all of them, trying to find a loophole to show my gratitude. I tied the leather skirt on again and placed the helmet under an arm. "What you've done, Koray... I don't know how I'll ever be able to repay it, but I will never stop trying."

The master instructor smiled in amusement, but I saw in his eyes that he was touched. "As long as we can call you and

Belenus our new rulers by the end of the night…" Dumnorix stated, bowing once more and heaving a sigh. "The Summer Court is in dire need of change, and you both have given us purpose and hope. Let's keep fighting."

His eyes watered, and he quickly turned to walk away with his fae peers, his shoulders sagging from the weight of fatigue. Koray came up to give me one last hug, seeming as tired as the others. His eyes were a little bloodshot too. He was probably up all night working on this since he knew he wasn't allowed to join the march.

"Wait until Soley hears about all you've done. You'll never get her off you, Koray," I warned, laughed into his shoulder, and released him from our hug.

"That's already a problem," he said, bursting into chuckles. "Not that I'd call it a problem." He grinned before bashfully looking away. He quickly sobered then and placed a hand on my shoulder. "Stay alive, Hekla. I don't want to give bad news to Soley, and you're my friend too." He patted my shoulder and walked away, rubbing his eyes and dropping his shoulders in exhaustion like Dumnorix had.

I went to go say bye to Bidelia and Arse, but the winter king was currently speaking with her. I scented Belenus and turned to face him, smiling in relief. His presence always made me feel lighter, and I very much needed that.

Are you not wearing underwear? Escort asked suddenly. Belenus's face went completely red, and the corner of his lips twitched.

No… I replied, holding back a surprised laugh. *The fae made me some shifter-friendly armor.*

Well, see if you can avoid losing it. Belenus likes it, Escort shared, leaving my mate with an aghast expression. *Easy access.* Belenus looked more betrayed by the second. He was obviously fighting with his wolf because Escort then said, *What? If you don't say it, I will. I told you I make my wants clear. You should too, big shit.*

"This," Belenus snapped out loud, swiping a hand through the air like a sword, "is not the time for that." His angry, flustered face softened, and he reached for my hand. "Are you ready?"

I paused at the question, then ran off to fetch something. When I came back, I wiggled the item in my hand. "I'm ready now," I breathed out, clutching the treasure to my chest. I wasn't sure how I'd carry it as a wolf, though, but I knew I wanted it with me.

"What's this?" he asked, holding out his hand. When I offered the sheathed dagger, he got a better look at it and recoiled. "Ah… yes, please keep that away from me, my dear…" He laughed nervously, stepping away with his hands up in surrender.

I frowned and looked at the dagger. "What? The grand beta and Rakel had it made for me. What's wrong with it?"

"I don't know if they were aware when they designed it, but… pure iron, that is… very… dangerous to us fae. Probably like silver is for you," he informed, stepping closer now that he was no longer surprised.

"Oh…" I replied, looking down at it with mixed feelings. I didn't want to accidentally kill someone I'd just be trying to restrain. I'd have to be extra careful with it. An achy, heavy weight settled in my chest from the burdensome thought.

Belenus reached for my free hand, and we strolled over to give our goodbyes to Bidelia, who was surrounded by her own little army of winter warriors and bat-shifters. Without releasing her tight clutching of Arse, she gave us both a whimpering, tearful hug.

"We'll be back, Bidelia. We'll come and get you, then discuss your career goals as the royal pet assistant, yes?" I teased her, poking her in the belly. She laughed and smacked my hand away from her.

"Promise?" she asked and lifted a hand to rub her tearful eyes. Arse slipped in her distracted grip, and his lower legs splayed to find purchase.

Canny, Bidelia! he complained as he coiled his tail around her arm.

I narrowed my eyes. "Shush, you. The jig is up, 'Archibald.'" The mac-talla sighed and hung limp while Bidelia fought to get a better grip on him.

Make them pay, Hekla, he said quietly. *Dinna... don't die, you two.*

With an anxious stomach and a worried heart, I turned from them and joined the massive gathering at the edge of the glamour with Belenus at my side. He squeezed my hand, went over the plan one more time with the volunteers, and we stepped out into the next glamour that Belenus erected to hide our march. Our army of winter fae and bat-shifters picked up their heads and walked with purpose now. The bat-shifters in particular carried themselves with forced grit. I'd be proud of them if I wasn't so fucking worried.

It's natural to be worried and scared, but I have your back, my love, my mate, my queen, Belenus said to me over our bond's link. I swallowed heavily and smiled tentatively up at him.

I have your back too, my love, my mate, my king, I responded affectionately.

His own whirling emotions blossomed into warm hope, and we walked hand in hand all the way to the castle gates with a force to be reckoned with at our backs. Dread built in my belly as we approached the entryway only to find that the guards were missing. In the large expanse past the gates was a sight of unsettling silence.

"Where is everyone?" I whispered while our teams moved alongside the gate wall to their respective positions. "I don't see anyone. Not even servants."

"Perhaps they cleared the area and are waiting for the signal. I don't like this, though. If that's what has been done, it's too obvious," Belenus said in a low voice and glanced over at King Nechtan.

"This isn't right. They are expecting us, hoping to catch us in a trap," he stated with absolute certainty.

"A pretty obvious trap," Belenus growled, shifting his weight and trying to get a better look at the training yard and barracks. His hand went to his sword hilt as he scrutinized the area.

"So it's not a trap then, is it?" I pointed out. "We both know the other's intent to an extent. We should just proceed with caution."

"Agreed," the prince and the king said simultaneously, and we slowly approached the castle in our armor and with our personal teams of warriors and shifters.

Unsurprisingly, white gold metal flashed under torchlight as summer soldiers poured out of the castle entrance in defense of their queen. A little less than a hundred of them lined up, pointing their spears and unsheathing their swords in preparation. We knew they'd be here. We were prepared for that and ready to start disarming and restraining these fae.

What we weren't prepared for was Drust's appearance. He exited the castle with scores of his own soldiers and stood in opposition to us, pulling out his own weapon.

Cold terror shot through my body, and I froze. This was Drust, right? He didn't have a twin I didn't know about, did he? There's no way anyone could fool Belenus this well… was there? How was this possible? How—

"Drust!" Belenus roared, red-faced with fury. "What's this about?"

The fae soldier didn't reply. His gaze had just locked on Belenus. Neither guilt nor a smirk of victory passed over his features. There wasn't anything on his face.

Suspicious of his emptiness, I took a cautious step forward, sliding my foot in the dirt and keeping my face low. I parted my lips and took the deepest breath I could, hoping the wind would shift in my favor. I side-stepped and hoped that the standstill would remain tense and quiet for a moment longer. I finally caught Drust's scent and there it was.

The faintest hint of rot.

Chapter 33

Hekla

"Belenus! Nechtan!" I hissed through my teeth. "I smell rot!"

The two fae at my side tensed further. "Where?" King Nechtan gritted back, looking furtively about the soldiers. Belenus moved closer to me, sword at the ready for the slightest triggering movement.

"I smell it on Drust. I think they're being manipulated. Look at their faces! There's no emotion! Nothing!"

"Up top," Belenus murmured a warning, and I followed his gaze to find archers positioning themselves on the castle balconies. The bat-shifters we'd designated for archer duty crept quietly up the stone toward the bowmen.

"If they're cursed, it's possible they may have a brand we could disrupt. I've seen Koray do that before. Remember Ragna?" I whispered and Belenus nodded. "We just need to find it."

"This many soldiers… the witches must have caught them unaware to curse so many. They must have been asleep," King Nechtan said in a low voice. "Or put asleep."

"Hold them off, find the mark, remove it, get a soldier back." I made the list out loud and nodded. "I'll inform the shifters. They'll spread the word." I retreated slowly from the scene toward the gate.

As if my retreat had set off an alarm, the queen's soldiers and the possessed fae charged our army. I nearly tripped at the terrifying sight, a wave of armor and sharp edges, but finally got behind the safety of the wall and howled for Luzia. She appeared before me in several heartbeats, wild-eyed with fright.

"Yes?" she asked, breathing fast. She appeared to be on the verge of having a panic attack. I placed both hands on her shoulders, looked her straight in the eyes, and said, "The rot-witches got to our fae soldiers. I need you to tell the shifters to look for any brands they can remove off the possessed fae. I've seen something similar be scratched away, like it's dry ink or something, but I don't know if that'll be the case here. Do not let anyone die. A possessed soldier can quickly become our soldier! We must move fast!" I gestured with a hand over my face. "They'll look blank, like they're daydreaming or something. Go, Luzia! Spread the word! That's an order!"

Her sleek wings unfurled, and she shot out into the night, less crazed and more focused. That was a good sign. I took a deep, stabilizing breath and ran back to the battlefield but tried to stay out of sight.

Belenus! I'm going to see if the rot-witch is still here! I don't know if killing her will release the soldiers, but that's my new mission! I reported to my mate and stalked toward the training yard, needing to get some distance from the fighting to see if I could discover any scent trails. I thought to call Ferrer, but he would be busy managing the drainers and helping Luzia. Nofre would be trying to sneak Emer into the castle. Things did not go according to plan, but that was ok. We just needed to adapt!

Are you sure? You should come back so I can k— Belenus's voice was thick with emotion as he stopped himself and changed his response. *Be careful, my mate.* The pain and worry in his voice almost brought tears to my eyes, and I swallowed a sob.

Louder clanging shocked me into focusing again. I blanched when the first scream hit the air, and my heart painfully skipped a beat. Was that someone dying? Had anyone died yet? I cringed, clutching my chest at the devastating thought, and continued to prowl, searching for my quick solution.

I sped toward any place that would make for a good hiding spot, sniffing, and becoming more agitated with every failure. Was I just wasting time?

Wait! Go back! Eventide shouted, and I took a couple steps back, turning in a circle to inhale everything around me. I opened my mouth to let the air settle on my tongue and found it. It wasn't rot combined with a fae's scent; it was just rot.

We'd found one.

Which way? I hissed, almost unable to think clearly in my excitement.

Left, left, no, right a little, there! she yapped hastily, and I moved into a sprint, running as fast as possible to save as many lives as I could. Every fucking second counted.

I followed the disgusting scent trail to one of the barracks, and once I opened the door, I slapped a hand over my mouth and nose and dry heaved. It was worse in here. It was so much worse.

Oh Sun God, not even your fire could vanquish this fume, Eventide lamented, gagging.

Why couldn't the goddess have blessed us with the ability to turn our noses off instead? I thought vacantly as I scrambled through the room, looking for the source of the smell and the soldiers' possessions.

I removed my hand to see if the scent was stronger going upstairs or downstairs, and I immediately keeled over to vomit. All the food I'd barely managed to get into my stomach earlier came right back out. The smell was too thick, too sweet in all the wrong ways. I heaved again, my vision briefly blurring this time around.

Fuck... Eventide, I can't tell. I'm just going to work from the basement up, I said woozily and stumbled toward the descending stairs. I hung onto the wall, torn between going fast and tripping or going slow and not tumbling down the steps. Though I ultimately decided to go slow, Fate apparently decided I was also going to trip.

I tumbled down the wooden stairs and rolled into a barrel. The sound of wood cracking hit my ears, and brown apples spilled everywhere. After the crash, I heard low, distracted cackling and tapping, which had me scrambling to my feet. With a nauseated grimace, I latched onto a stacked barrel—one that smelled like it also contained spoiled apples—to steady myself. What absolutely had to be a rot-witch was sitting in a chair, stomping her feet on the floor while she tapped her unnaturally long fingers on her knees. She was staring straight ahead at nothing, laughing like she was either having the time of her life or she'd gone insane.

I found one! I screamed to Belenus, balking at the unnerving scene before me. Did she not see me? Was she blind? I had to make a decision.

I unsheathed my dagger, bared my teeth to gather some courage, and lunged to attack her. She finally turned to face me, looking as fresh as a fear gorta with her gaunt form and wild grey hair. Her bloodshot eyes widened as she screamed at me, unleashing a sound that carried more than one voice. It spoke of something else being inside her, something murky, ancient... and not alone.

She caught my dagger arm, but I slashed with my claws and raked her face, gouging her left eye. She hissed and tightened her grip, snapping a bone in my wrist. I screamed as white pain shot up my arm. How was she so strong? I reeled from both the fire searing my nerves and the grey dotting my vision.

Let me out! Let me out! Eventide shrieked, clawing at the back of my mind. *She'll lose her grip!*

In my struggling with the terrifying creature, I lashed out with a foot. She shifted her knee to avoid getting hit, but I still managed to catch her in the hip. She constricted in response, but I had no idea if she was cringing from pain or if she was doing something else. I let Eventide take over—nearly blacking out from forcing a shift on my broken bones—and she slipped from the creature's startled grip. Eventide then tripped on the leather skirt I'd been unable to remove first, and the rot-witch clambered forward in an attempt to grab her.

Shiiit! Eventide screamed in terror, raking her claws into the wooden floor to get upright again.

The rot-witch climbed over her and pressed her clawed thumbs into Eventide's throat, cutting off her airflow.

Her hands are empty! Her hands are empty! I shouted. *Where's the knife?*

I... Despite choking, Eventide tried to turn her head to find it. A glint of iron under candlelight caught her eye, and we spied it just past the witch's knee, momentarily forgotten.

I shifted back into my body, startling the rot-witch again, who screamed in my face and tightened her hold to continue her strangulation. Her nightmarish breath made bile rise into my throat, and I absently prayed for it to stay down while I struggled. My vision blurred as my lungs burned for air. What was left of my eyesight was drowned in tears.

With all of Eventide's attention and energy focused on stabilizing my injured arm, my blind hand with the broken wrist finally found the dagger. I didn't know how to rip throats out with my bare hands, and scratching away at her might take too long. I needed the dagger. I needed speed. Lacking the wind to scream, I faced the white-hot pain as I passed the dagger to my non-dominant hand and plunged the knife into my assailant's neck. I yanked it out and stabbed repeatedly, aiming for her pulsing arteries, until she slumped off of me.

Belenus... I called out weakly, wiping putrid blood from my face and neck. Was he too far away from me to hear? *Belenus, I got her... did it...*

I rolled over onto my stomach, trying to get air back into my body. I winced when I got a good look at my dominant hand; my wrist was already swollen and bruised. This wasn't good at all. The night wasn't over yet, and I needed that arm. Shifting had only made it worse too.

"Fuck..." I hissed as I propped myself up with my good arm. I leaned against a barrel and braced myself against it until I stood upright again. The rotten corpse at my feet was drowned in its own pool of blood and other questionable fluids. Disgusting. The state of myself was almost as bad.

I may never... get this trauma out of my mind, Eventide whispered as I trudged up the stairs, coughing. My windpipe still didn't feel open enough, and I resisted the urge to rub my throat. Maybe it was swollen or bruised...

When I stumbled out of the barracks, I now saw fae soldiers fighting other fae soldiers. My feelings were mixed, but relief dominated them. A growing number of captives were being held next to the wall, tied up or restrained in other ways. Some sat slumped over, unconscious.

Belenus, I called. *Belenus, where...*

Ferrer landed in front of me, and I was too dazed to be startled. "Ferrer," I coughed out, "what's the status?"

He wrinkled his nose, obviously smelling the stench of rot on me, then glanced down and frowned at the wrist I was nursing. "We found brands on the backs of their necks, but before we were able to remove a significant number of them, they all snapped out of their... possession, or whatever it was." He urgently gestured to my wrist. "Is that broken? We need to take care of that."

"No time," I said hoarsely, breaking into a coughing fit. Talking was going to be a bit of a problem. Swallowing was painful as well. "I killed the rot-witch that I assumed was controlling them. Is everyone free? If there's another rot-witch controlling another number of soldiers, I need t—"

"No, no, no," Ferrer said fiercely and lifted me despite the small gagging noise he made. "We've secured the hospital and are already taking our positions throughout the castle. The queen's retreated farther up the tower. I'm bringing you to get checked."

"Ferrer, I can walk," I wheezed, though my voice was starting to go. That couldn't have sounded very convincing. "I need to look strong for my army, Ferrer. That's very important. It's an alpha thin—"

"So you're not aware that you're wobbling, your throat's bleeding, and one of your eyes has gone completely red?" he asked and broke into a run to get past the fighting. That shut me up for a minute, and I accepted the help.

Ferrer would make a good beta, Eventide said with a weak laugh. *He'd stand up to our bullshit like a good beta does.*

Yes, he would, I agreed, blinking slowly and cringing at the throbbing pain in my wrist. Gods, I couldn't wait to get them all to their homeland so they could settle and eventually be safe and sound.

Ferrer sped into the castle's hospital, which was absolute chaos. The injured from both sides had received emergency care here, separated to the best of the hospital's ability to keep the peace. I grimaced at the number of wounded, and tears pricked my eyes. All of this suffering was my doing. I brought them here. I got them hurt. I closed my eyes, overwhelmed by sheer guilt and an unexpected sense of failure. It stung worse than anything I'd just endured.

Ferrer followed a nurse to a room where I was settled on a bed next to two sleeping shifters. I stared guiltily at the floor until Doctor Egres rushed in to take a look at me. I expected her to cast judgment; I was the reason why she was scrambling. She greeted me and began examining my wrist, but I still couldn't meet her eyes.

"What happened?" she asked, leaning over to grab some supplies from a drawer.

"Killed the rot-witch who was controlling the fae soldiers…" I answered quietly. "She was stronger than she looked. Broke my wrist with a squeeze."

"Emer!" Doctor Egres yelled, startling me enough to make me jump. The fae woman ran in with Nofre at her heels, and she released a soft cry upon seeing me.

"There you are!" Emer gasped and covered her mouth in dismay, not seeming to notice Nofre's supportive hand on her shoulder. When I saw Nofre's swollen eyes, which had recently shed tears, my heart sank lower.

Doctor Egres didn't spare a moment longer and said briskly to Emer, "See if you can do something about this broken wrist. I need to find her mate." The lycan turned and hurried toward the door.

"Doctor Egres!" I called out in a panic. She turned and raised her brows. I couldn't bring myself to ask if anyone had died yet, but I felt compelled to say something. "I'm... I'm sorry," I said and nodded to the door. "I'm sorry for cau—"

"I really don't know why you're apologizing," she interrupted and promptly left the room. Emer hurried over, sat next to me, and gently lifted my arm. I couldn't hear anything that anyone was saying. The room simply fell to the fog of numbness.

I didn't know why I was apologizing either.

Belenus

I was talking to Doctor Elisedd about Slaine's unfortunate stab to the buttocks—the winter fae was being an incredibly difficult patient—when Doctor Egres came marching up to the doctor, who was also, apparently, her fated mate.

I shouldn't have been surprised to find out that they were fated. The two doctors had been acting odd and uncomfortable around each other since they'd met. I thought maybe it was because he had some feline in him, but it turned out that the tension in a high-profile professional setting had been incredibly stressful to navigate.

"Everything alright?" he asked the lycan; she was carrying a severe expression on her face.

She tucked a greying strand of hair behind an ear. "Just some minor injuries and a broken bone. Nothing serious," she replied and crooked a finger at me. "Your mate survived an encounter with a rot-witch. Please follow me, Prince Belenus."

My body flooded with adrenaline at her words, and though I wanted to run past her to find Hekla, I nodded tersely and let her lead the way. Also in protest, my heart slammed against my rib cage, finding our brisk pace much too slow.

Just a broken bone, just a broken bone, just a broken bone, Escort chanted. I had no idea if he was doing that for his or my benefit, but the reminder was calming.

We entered another room to find Emer tending to an extremely bedraggled she-wolf. She was covered in blood that my sister worked to wipe clean, blood holding the putridity of decay. If I'd been skeptical, it was all the evidence I would've needed as proof she'd slain one.

"Oh gods, Hekla!" I blurted out and rushed to her side. She gave me a tearful look, and through our bond, her emotions slammed into me. She was drowning in guilt. Shame hung from her shoulders like a leaden shroud, but I had no idea why she was feeling that way.

"I've got this, Emer," I said quietly to dismiss my sister, making it clear I wanted them both to leave. They filed out, and I turned my attention to my female's wrist. The swelling might be ugly, but it would still heal as good as new.

When I moved my gaze to hers, it flitted away in avoidance and settled on the stone hospital floor. The sclera of one of her eyes had gone red, and above her leather vest, her neck hosted a slew of cuts and bruises. She'd been strangled.

"Are you hurt anywhere else?" I asked worriedly and scanned her legs. "Eyes, throat… wrist. Anywhere else?"

She furrowed her brows. "I don't think so. Just coughing and a sore throat. Maybe a little dizzy."

My next question was about what worried me the most. "Why are you feeling so guilty, my love?" I inquired gently and studied her wrist to see where I should start healing it. I could see a little deeper with my magic now, and it seemed to be a fairly clean break. I could fix it.

"Did you see all those wounded?" she choked out and bit on a trembling lip. She paused, glanced over at the injured bats in the room, and rushed out, "That's on me. I brought them here, especially the shifters."

A sob escaped her, and I used that distraction, that spike of grief, to quickly set her bones. She cried out in both pain and surprise, and it all sent more tears rolling down her cheeks.

"Sorry… it's set. I'm just sealing the ends now…" I murmured, trying to think of a response to her answer. "I saw them, Hekla, but there's not a soul out there who didn't volunteer. You're, unfortunately, experiencing the worst part about being a leader before you've even taken the throne." I sighed and pulled her to lean against my chest while I worked on her wrist.

"Remind yourself why we're doing this. It's not just to get out of an execution or a terrible, suspicious marriage. We're also doing this because we know the summer fae need a better leader. Think of Bidelia's wings, Hekla. Neither you nor I can accept living in a society where this torture is a social norm. What we do today will help scores more than those who've been injured."

She nodded quietly and rubbed her nose, sniffling. "I get it… I just… I promised the Sky Gods I'd bring them back, and it's just hard to see them get hurt when I'm responsible for them. I feel like I failed."

"We'll get them to their homeland. It's not like we wouldn't have had problems bringing them through our realm door. You had to leave to find the bat-shifters. I had to follow you. This fight was unavoidable. Had we tried to talk it out, the queen would have just used them against me like she used you."

She nodded again but offered no reply. Her guilt slid into depression, breaking my heart. "What happened with the rot-witch?" I asked, about halfway done healing her. It was a slow process with all the broken blood vessels and inflammation.

When Hekla didn't say anything, Eventide stepped in to answer. *We searched all over the training yard, then finally caught her stench. We followed it to the barracks, and the rot-witch was having a blast down in the basement. You'd... have to have been there... Anyway, Hekla tried to stab her, but that's when she grabbed and broke her wrist.* Escort growled furiously, interrupting Eventide for just a moment. *We shifted, but I got tangled in the skirt because... well... our brain was in survival mode. Come to think of it, I don't even know what happened to our helmet... The rot-witch then tried to strangle us, but Hekla managed to grab the dagger after shifting back and stabbed her in the neck until she fell off of us.*

Something was bothering me, though, and a chill crept down my spine. "Did you behead her? I remember Koray beheading the first rot-witch we ran into. I don't know if he thought he had to or if that's just how he decided to kill her. Lots of creatures in this realm have to be killed in a certain way to make sure they stay dead. I just don't know about these ones from your realm..."

That was when Hekla looked up at me, blanching. "No," she whispered. "I didn't."

I opened the door and called for Nofre. Fortunately, he and Emer were helping nearby. "Send a small team of available shifters to the barracks past the training yard," I ordered. "Search the basements for the rot-witch. If she's there, make sure you remove the head from the body. I don't want to take any chances."

Nofre grimaced, then nodded and strode off to gather a team. I closed the door and shuddered with disgust. It was an ugly task but necessary. Then, I returned to Hekla's side and finished tending to her wrist. Next, I focused on healing her eye before mending the cuts and bruises on her neck. Her sighs of relief grew longer and heavier with the disappearance of each injury, and her little coughing fits stopped altogether.

"Thank you," she whispered, absently touching her neck.

I didn't want the moment here to end because I knew what had to come now. I cleared my throat and rested a hand on her thigh to gently caress it. "I need to get going. We've pretty much cornered the queen at her personal chambers… and it's time to finish what I started," I said grimly, knowing I should try to start shutting down my emotions. This entire situation was almost too painful to bear. And the betrayal done by the one who'd birthed me? Too agonizing to admit.

"Ok," she said, slid off the bed, and grabbed her sheathed dagger from the counter.

"Ah…" I held a palm up to her. "Maybe you should stay here? I don't want you using your wrist so soon after breaking it… Give it some time to rest." I knew she could feel my desperate worry for her safety, but I couldn't help it. A force compelled me to shield her from danger, and I had to at least be heard.

"I'm coming," she declared and stared up at me with resolve. "This alpha has your back."

That's hot.

I ignored Escort's comment and stared back down at her. "A queen through and through," I replied quietly and bent down to kiss her lips before pressing our foreheads together. "I love you, Hekla."

"I love you too," she whispered in return. I sighed and savored one last drop of this sweet moment. Then, I straightened my posture, turned to the door, and opened it for her.

"Let's collect Emer and Nofre. King Nechtan should be around. I saw him with Slaine earlier." I walked out with Hekla at my side and collected both Emer and King Nechtan. When Nofre returned from his errand, I waved him over to join us.

"Is it time?" he asked, immediately moving to Emer's side.

"Yes, everyone ready? Remember what we're expecting," I asked and was met with grim nods. "Alright then, let's head up. Our soldiers will meet us on the last floor we've secured."

We left the hospital for our last march, passing soldiers, warriors, and shifters who were bringing in the wounded or running to gather weapons or supplies. The castle was flooded with activity, and I no longer heard fighting. I looked down at Hekla, desperately wanting to hold her hand, but her only good hand was white-knuckling her dagger.

You see all these people? I asked her, gesturing to the bustling bats and fae instead. *Hundreds of safe soldiers and shifters? That's because you got to the rot-witch so fast. I'm so fucking proud of you, my she-wolf,* I said to her over our link, stealing her profanity. She gave me a weak smile in response.

Eventide and I did our best, she responded, her gaze drifting to all the progress already made in the short amount of time.

I knew Hekla had done her best. She always did. I wrapped an arm around her as we made our way up to the queen's suite. We arrived to find forty of our soldiers and thirty bats waiting for us. They'd already secured the immediate area and stood silently by the grand door, ready to make the final push. To the left, almost in a pile, a handful of her soldiers were knocked out cold, their skin unusually pale under their gold flecks. Half of the spring guards were among the unconscious, and I'd bet the very last of them were beyond this door.

Ferrer stepped forward and jerked his chin toward the unconscious soldiers. "Had to bleed them a bit, but they're alive," he reported. Shame flickered in his red-brown eyes, but I clapped a hand on his shoulder, not wanting him to linger on the negative.

"Well done, Ferrer. You've carried out your orders admirably," I validated and marched past him to stand before the queen's door, my hand on the hilt of my sword. When I grabbed the handle, I nearly laughed to find it locked.

Ridiculous, Escort snarled, echoing my sentiments.

I gathered my magic, the essence of summer sovereignty, into my hands for my next move. It was probably overkill, but I still harbored fury despite every attempt to silence my emotions. Unwillingly remembering the moment Hekla was collared, I focused on the hinges and blew the doors clean off the frame. The wood shattered and scattered inside the garden.

There was the queen in all her finery, sitting for tea with Eislyn at the same small table I'd sat at when she navigated around our own promise. It'd been the last day I'd thought of her as my mother. Though, it felt like months had passed instead of weeks. Nothing about the garden had changed, and yet it all looked different to me now.

You've matured. Don't take her shit, Escort rallied, aiming his hostility at the women before us.

As my soldiers rushed past me to restrain the last of the guards, the queen looked sourly at the splintered remains of the door, as though it was the tea cup I'd shattered the last time I was here. Still bathed with Triskelion's royal glow, her expression tautened with contempt. "Are you quite done with your tantrum, my son?" she asked coldly. "Are you ready for your wedding vo—"

I interrupted her.

"You struck a deal with me. You weaseled out of it!" I yelled. "You harassed, bullied, and tortured my fated mate, the love of my life!" I rose my voice as I strode toward the queen, screaming out all the rage I'd been trying to bottle. That jar had long since shattered, and she would feel it. "You still torment the castle servants, and you mistreat our people! It's over! It's all over for you, here and now! I'm taking over, and by all the gods above and below us, you better step aside because I'm barely keeping it together," I seethed, ending my tirade in a frigid, low voice. I didn't care that my sword arm shook. I didn't care. This was over. I was ending it.

"You have a last chance to reconsider," the queen replied. She was trying to remain collected, but I could see how she leaned away from me—ever so slightly. It was the most fear she'd ever displayed, and it was barely there. Her confidence remained unbelievable.

I nudged my armor to the side and stretched my collar to proudly show off the mating mark my female had given me. In synchrony with my heart, Hekla stepped up next to me to show off hers. She emitted the scariest, deepest growl I'd ever heard her make, but I didn't shush her this time. Whatever she wanted to do now, I'd allow. If she wanted to rip out the queen's throat… she could.

The queen stared at us with barely concealed bitterness and gestured to an officiant at the back of the garden. He approached but did so with averted eyes, a scroll in his possession.

The contract.

Without hesitation, I ripped it out of his hand along with the quill he was holding. The queen pursed her lips when she saw me bring it back to the table, and I slammed it down so I could unroll it. I contained my dark joy at startling Eislyn, who jumped in her seat.

"My betrothed, certainly you must rethink this," Eislyn pled, finally speaking up, but I detected a steely tone beneath her demure pout. "We can still kill her and free you from the bond. You don't want a mutt in your bed, do you? Think of the consequences…"

Hekla interrupted her own sustained growl with a snarl, and the princess's face pinched like she was hiding a wince. Still, Hekla didn't make a move. She was letting me deal with the woman who used to be my mother. This alpha had my back.

"I've had enough of your threats, Eislyn. You're disgusting," I said in a flat voice, rolling down the parchment and feeling the magic compulsion to sign take over my hands. "You've got thirty seconds to leave here and go back to your court, because once I'm king, I will take you into custody and treat you as you are: a hostile invader. Better start running."

She stayed in her seat, ignoring my warning, but I could see her innocent mask become more brittle by the second.

The queen drawled, impassive in both voice and countenance, "If you think you can overpower him yourself, Eislyn, you'd be wrong."

I didn't stop to think about what that meant. Perhaps the queen was giving up without a fight. Good.

As I read the retaliation agreement aloud and declared my failure to uphold my side of the contract, the queen reclaimed her regal bearing and held her chin up high.

Arrogant til the very end, I thought with loathing. I skipped past all the redacted sections, lowered the quill to the paper, and signed my full name: Belenus Ailill Mac An Tsamhraidh.

That was when the queen of the Summer Court, the fair fae who'd ruled for over eight hundred years and the woman I used to call my mother, fell to the ground and died.

Chapter 34

Hekla

No one moved for what felt like an eternity. The queen had expired on the spot after Belenus had signed his acceptance of the retaliation.

"It wasn't any of us," I whispered, too stunned to even know how I felt about it. I looked up at my mate with wide eyes, unable to even sort out what he was feeling over the bond. All I could detect was the muffled buzzing of numbness and shock. Neither of us felt relief, joy, anger, or sadness.

We didn't have enough answers to be feeling anything at all.

I cut my gaze to the spring princess, who'd finally dropped her performance. She sighed in aggravation and leaned back in the chair to cross her arms. It was as if she'd merely lost some game, and in my opinion, she was far too comfortable with that. Eislyn had to learn that this was now wolf territory.

Before she could go anywhere, I marched over, snatched one of her delicate hands, and pinned it to the table with my claws, not breaking skin yet. If she wanted to leave, she'd better use her magic because I knew for a fact my body was stronger than hers.

"What is the Spring Court's interest in the Summer Court?" I asked through my bared canines, bristling.

The princess sighed and made an attempt to ignore me. She leaned forward and said, "It's too bad you won't see your father again, Belenus."

"Look at me!" I snapped. "Do not look at him. Do not talk to him. You are not worthy." Belenus, I believed, was in too much shock, so I continued for him. He needed answers. I demanded them.

Eislyn's nose wrinkled in irritation, and after she failed to get a response out of him, she finally glanced up at me.

I pressed down until my claws finally pierced her skin. "Answer me."

Though uncomfortable, Eislyn reacted poorly to my assertion of dominance and decided to ignore me again, to make it clear she thought me beneath her. When her eyes focused on Belenus again and her lips parted to speak once more, I decided I wasn't having it. I leaned into her hand and dug my claws in until they hit bone. She jolted, tilted her head back, and released a short scream. I still didn't really feel anything. I needed answers to feel something.

The princess caught her breath and glared at me, her cheeks flushing pink in anger. "This is just a small setback," she spat, reaching for my wrist to pull me off of her. Ferrer, appearing out of nowhere, snatched her free hand away and held her wrist behind her back, showing no mercy for her discomfort.

"What is the Spring Court's interest in the Summer Court?" I repeated louder, leaning into her hand. She kept her mouth shut and glared at me in silence. Her pulse beat clearly in her hand. I could get information if I could just get her to fucking answer anything!

"Are spring and autumn in league with the rot-witches?" I asked quickly, switching out the question. Her face subtly flinched, and her body told me I'd hit something sensitive. "I killed one of them, you know," I told her. "Found her controlling the soldiers from the barracks. You brought her, didn't you?"

She gritted her teeth and fought to stay impassive, but I could see it in her face and feel it in her body's response. I had the urge to ask other questions, personal ones, just to get a response out of her mouth, but those were too cruel. Even in my numb state, I couldn't bring myself to be that abusive.

Sky Gods, give me strength.

I also ignored the temptation to use iron against her. The dagger in my recovering hand felt particularly heavy. And yet the eyes on my back were more so.

What would Hekla do? Me? I must be a good example to my soldiers and shifters. They are watching me for my lead. I cannot become like the wretched court fae, I reminded myself.

That was when I started to feel something again. I was angry. After all this, I still had to follow rules that didn't allow me to rip her into pieces. This time, they were self-inflicted. Was this what it meant to be an alpha? Was it this constant struggle to maintain the balance of violence and order?

"Eislyn, creature of spring," I stated calmly, "you are not only a traitor to this court—who invited you here in good faith—but to your kind. You have a small chance at redemption right now. If you answer these two questions, I will negotiate to get your sentence reduced. Where is Belenus's father, and what are the rot-witches after?"

If only she was a shifter, Eventide sighed, lamenting our inability to use our alpha command on her.

If only...

Princess Eislyn looked furtively around the room, searching for help, but her guards were gone, and she had no friends here. She wasn't going to find a thing. She scowled up at me in red-faced fury and released a hissing scream of frustration through her teeth, like a teapot's wail. "I hate you, mutt!"

Without batting an eye, I replied, "That was one. I'll give you two more tries to answer before I go to my courtiers and establish the day of your execution." Another emotion came to me then, but I hadn't created it. No, it was Belenus's emotion. Somewhere in his numbness, I felt a spark of pride. My male was proud of me.

"This isn't your court!" she screamed, spraying the table with spit while she fought to free her hands.

"Yes, it is," Belenus growled quietly from behind me. Ferrer jerked her back to him and tightened his grip.

"That was two," I said, allowing resignation to color my tone.

She licked her lips and rubbed her cheek against her shoulder to get the saliva off her face. "Perhaps if King Aillil hadn't spread my mother's legs, stolen their daughter, and returned for more, he wouldn't have ended up trapped in the Spring Court." Her face broke into a sneer, like she was recalling something particularly revolting. "Pray tell me... is my half-sister here? I'd so love to talk to her now that she's exposed for what she is."

Half-sister?

Belenus's grip found my shoulder, and his anxiety spilled over the bond. That meant Emer was actually related to him. Whether she was adopted or his half-sister, I'd still protect her. Gods, she must now be learning of this too.

I knew Emer was near, but I didn't turn to look for her, not wanting to give away her presence in the room full of soldiers and shifters. Those around her stayed loyal as well, keeping quiet and still. The summer princess's silence, wherever she was in the crowd, made it pretty clear that she wanted nothing to do with the spring princess.

"No?" Eislyn asked the room, looking genuinely disappointed. "That's too bad."

"The rot-witches," I reminded her, pressing into her hand again. I needed her to stop thinking about Emer. She didn't deserve to look at her either.

"Best keep a tight grip on your door to the Realm of the Gods," she drawled, then narrowed her eyes at me.

Hekla, she's— Eventide's interjection reminded me that Eislyn wasn't actually disarmed. Arse had told us…

The seeds!

"Ferrer, step ba—" I shouted and jumped away, but an explosion of vines erupted from around the princess and sent the bat-shifter flying into a marble column. He collapsed into a heap and went still. I snarled and clawed at the vines to cut them away, but each time I severed one, the end split and sprouted two thinner, barbed vines.

The room erupted into chaos with soldiers and shifters converging on the overwhelming brambles, ones that shielded the princess's escape as she struggled to reach the stained-glass window at the end of the garden. I screamed angrily as I clawed through the new vines that ripped at my exposed skin and snagged at my leathers. The smell of my blood joined others as the tangle thickened and thrashed. I released my iron dagger, tossed the sheath, and reached for a swaying vine to see if the metal would make any difference whatsoever.

I sawed through a thick vine, and the end of the plant cauterized, preventing new growth from occurring. Magic plants must hate iron as much as the fae. Emboldened by the favorable edge, I tore recklessly through the bramble in an effort to catch up to the fleeing traitor. Slashing with my left hand, I used my recovering hand to shield my face from the whipping arms she'd left in her wake. Through the din, I could barely hear Belenus calling out to me, but I couldn't slow down.

I wish we knew how many seeds she has! Eventide cried out as I got hit particularly hard on the back of the head. I grunted in pain, stumbled, then paled at the sound of glass shattering. *She's out! She got out!*

I snarled, furious at her progress, and redoubled my efforts to shear past the thrashing plants. I wiped blood away from my eyes when I reached the windowsill and leaned over it, ignoring the small shards of colorful glass that bit into my skin. Belenus's fear hit me now, his eyes on my back from across the room.

Hekla! Don't! We'll try to catch her from outside! he cried out to me, his voice soaked with terror and desperation.

I'll be right back! I'm so close! She's right here! We can't risk her getting to a horse! I answered and climbed over the edge to grab the clinging vines she'd anchored for her escape.

Hekla, no! he screamed.

Below my feet, Eislyn rushed as fast as she could down the vines, descending like she'd done this hundreds of times. I moved my dagger into my weak hand and followed her route as fast as I could, glad that these vines didn't have any thorns. Unfortunately, in a way, I'd brought thorns with me. I gritted my teeth through the prickly stinging of the glass splinters in my palms.

The rustling of my approach alerted the princess to my pursuit, and her head shot up to gape at me. She cursed loudly and braced herself against the wall, forcing roots to dig into the stone. As soon as I realized what she was about to do, the vines under my grip released, and I fell with a shriek. Every vine except for what she was holding onto had detached from the castle.

I stared down while screaming and knew my only hope was to latch onto Eislyn or the roots around her. Though Eislyn tried desperately to get out from under my fall, I landed on her and wrapped my arms around her throat and shoulders. She nearly fell off from the weight of the impact but managed to get her plants to yank her back to the wall. I braced my foot against the stone as she wrestled with me, screaming like the ban-sìths from Bidelia's late-night stories.

When I felt a tendril wrap around my neck, I knew I had to make the call. I just wanted it to be over with so badly. The abuse, the torture, and the betrayal were too much. What she'd put both of us through was unforgiveable. She thought she was going to kill me?

I think not. Eventide prompted glacially.

It was in my weak hand, and it was shaking, but I adjusted my grip on the dagger, shoved it into her neck, and dragged it across, slitting her throat in one brutal gesture. Sounds came out of her neck that would give me nightmares for decades to come, and her grip on the vines loosened. Eislyn slipped out through my spread, braced legs, but losing my grip on her rocked me out of my purchase.

My stomach dropped in terror, and I clawed wildly at the vines, finally grabbing an anchored root to stop my fall. My vision greyed from the jolting stop that nearly dislocated my shoulder, and I gasped when the glass shards in my hand rooted deeper. The adrenaline wasn't enough to block out the pain, which intensified the longer I stayed like this.

Dizzyingly high above sculpted shrubbery and tan flagstone, I dangled from the vine, unable to find a safe way up or down. I waited for what felt like hours—but was probably only minutes—and worried that before I could get help, the plant might lose its grip on the wall and peel away, especially now that Eislyn was dead.

Eventually, a massive commotion came from below, and I looked down to witness a crowd of soldiers, servants, and shifters running out to look for us. Once they saw Eislyn's corpse, they looked up and began shouting in panic.

"I need wings!" I cried out but ended up mumbling toward the end in my fatigue. I hoped for a bat-shifter to find me, but there also had to be winged folk fae nearby, right? Maybe not. I paled from pain and misery, looked up at my sweaty grip on the vine, and noticed that my skin was red instead of its usual brown. My hand was covered in deep lacerations, and I laughed tiredly.

Now let's see if we don't die from blood loss, yeah? Eventide chuckled wearily with me.

There was movement in the air and the sound of wings flapping. I felt a couple of hands lift me away from the wall, and I was returned to the ground by three shifters who'd been the first to spot my peril. I was picked up again, and the crowd followed us back to the hospital where Doctor Elisedd came running toward me. I gave him a big smile to tell him I was feeling great, then promptly lost consciousness.

Belenus

"She's awake, Your Majesty," a servant reported, interrupting my conversation with King Nechtan and King Zorian. My heart jumped straight into my throat, and I gestured to Queen Ragna who scrambled to her feet and dragged two other frantic she-wolves with her. We rushed down to the castle hospital where we were greeted by Doctor Elisedd.

"We'll remove her bandages soon, but she's much improved," he said, walking us to her room.

The she-wolves fidgeted anxiously as I went in first, all three of them waiting for their turn to mob Her Majesty. They understood that I needed to be alone with Hekla first, but I knew from experience the trouble that could come from making a she-wolf wait. The love of my life sat upright in her hospital bed and blinked sleepily at me. Our bond spoke first, and through it came her relief, followed by a swell of love and joy. After that, her face fell a little, and as I sat and leaned over to embrace her, her heart sank into profound sadness.

"It's ok," I said quietly, her sadness making my own throat tighten. My female cried softly into my chest as I held her, mindful of the bandages shielding nearly healed skin. We clung to each other, and I rubbed her back gently, trying not to cry myself. It'd been hard waiting for her, desperately needing comfort after the period of violence and death, but her healing came first. I murmured, "You've only been out for a day. You needed some rest, my love. My heart."

"How are the shifters?" she whispered, her breath warming the tears on my chest.

"They're ok. They're sheltering in the barracks for now. We're taking care of them until we're able to finish the escort. Let's not talk about that now. I'm handling everything." I swallowed heavily as her arms wrapped around me.

"It didn't turn out how I'd thought," she said hoarsely, trying to talk over a whisper now. I grabbed the cup of ice by her bed and urged her to drink. She sipped some of the water that'd melted off the ice and cleared her throat.

"It never does," I replied and placed a kiss on the top of her head, among her lovely dark strands. I closed my eyes tight, almost as tight as my heart felt.

"Why did your… why did the queen put her name on that line, Belenus? Why did she put her life on the line for that wedding? I don't understand. I'm so confused." She buried herself in my shoulder and sniffed. "Why do I feel like shit about all of this? We got what we wanted, didn't we?"

I sighed and moved a hand to stroke the back of her hair, idly brushing out tangles as I found them. "We did... just not in the way we anticipated. I feel like my opportunity to see justice through was taken from me by her. Emer never even got a chance to have her say. Maybe we both feel robbed... I don't know. I've been thrown quite off-kilter." I hadn't quite known how to word it until that moment; it'd kept me up for hours when I'd tried resting. The queen had abandoned the throne to me, and her life, on her own terms.

My sweet mate nuzzled, and I felt her send comfort my way across the bond we shared.

I idly wrapped one of her curls around a finger and continued my update. "Emer went through the queen's chambers to find her journals. Since she's passed, they're no longer locked. She and my father had a lot of problems since their wedding—which I was aware of. Some of what she'd written… I hadn't known. She didn't like him and only shared his room until she bore him an heir… which was me. After that, she swore she wouldn't let him touch her again. It led him to find companionship elsewhere."

I leaned my head on hers and stared blankly at the wall while I spoke. "She discovered that he had an affair with the queen of the Spring Court, Queen Talulla. My… the queen… I'm just going to call her by her first name, Fedelm, now. She's no longer the queen of the Summer Court anyway," I said with a heavier sigh.

"If it's too painful, you don't have t—" Hekla protested, tilting her head to look up at me, but I interrupted her.

"No. I… want to just get it all out. My head's a mess. It'll help me too," I assured her, squeezing her a little before continuing. "The… person who gave birth to me, Fedelm, knew my father wanted another child, and my father admitted that Emer was his after he brought her home. Queen Talulla gave him what Fedelm refused to—another child." I cleared my throat, somewhat uncomfortable explaining my next thought. "The Spring Court is known for fertility, and the queens usually… bear heirs easily. I don't know if that was why her chose her or…" Unless I found my father, I might never know why he went to spring.

"Fedelm was furious," I continued, "and her journal entries became… vicious after that. She was so humiliated that she only allowed Emer to stay on the condition that she'd be introduced to their kingdom as an adopted child that they'd so graciously taken in." I scoffed at the idea.

"After a particularly brutal fight about Emer, my father left, saying that he was going back to Talulla in the Spring Court for a while to get some space. He was gone for a long time; I remember that quite well. Fedelm told me he'd died in an ambush returning from his diplomatic mission. Her journal said that he just never came back or sent word of any plans to return. So, she decided to announce that he'd died, rather than tell the court that their king had left. The court knew their marriage had serious problems, so rather than facing the humiliation of rumors, she made up his demise."

I brought a hand up to scrub over my eyes. I was too tired and too damn weary to cry. I felt like I should, but I just couldn't. "I still can't wrap my mind around all this," I murmured, sliding my hand back down to hold her again. She just stayed silent and waited for me to say more, comforting me in silence.

"She put her name on that line because if she didn't succeed in marrying me to their daughter, they'd let everyone know that the king was alive and had left them and his wife for Queen Talulla. She put her name on that line because she wrote she'd rather die than live with that humiliation. If I had married Eislyn, they'd have returned my father to her, and she was still undecided on what to do about that. She'd written about banishing him or keeping him hidden away, but… honestly, I think it was making her lose her mind."

"But why did they want the marriage between you and Eislyn so bad? What would spring get out of it?" she asked from my chest, her voice muffled.

I shook my head in disappointment. "It wasn't clear. We found some documentation in Eislyn's room that Gallcobar's studying now, but it doesn't look particularly enlightening. I did find out that Talulla married into the Spring Court. She was originally from the Autumn Court. If autumn's where all these rot-witches are coming from, I can see them trying to spread into more territory through these marriages. King Nechtan says that he's beginning to suspect the same thing considering the issues they're facing with that court." I laughed a little at a sudden thought. "No wonder Emer has that Autumn Court red hair. I just made that connection."

"How is she? She must be hurting," my she-wolf asked, then froze as something occurred to her. "Oh gods!" She looked up at me with a grimace, and conflicted emotions crept into her heart. "I killed her sister!"

I stared straight into her worried umbral eyes and said, "Half-sister. And she doesn't care, Hekla. You can rest assured that Emer had no emotional connection to that woman. She hated her. We both did. She was cruel." I felt her relax, and she leaned into me again.

"Emer's hurting from the truth," I consoled, "but she's doing the best she can. I'm on the receiving end of a lot of teasing now that she knows we're actually blood-related—half siblings. I swear she's going to be a pain now. I'm praying hard to the Sun God that Nofre takes her away soon." I laughed and kissed my mate on the forehead, trying to lighten the mood just a little, bring Hekla's smile back. Indeed, it cheered her up, and she released a small, quiet laugh.

"Anyway," I said, wanting to wrap up the stressful news for now. "We're going to keep working with the Winter Court to continue the investigation into the Autumn Court and try to find out more about the rot-witches. A lot of it will be a waiting game, so we'll have to be patient and stay alert."

"We're increasing the number of guards at our door to the Realm of the Gods, right? I'm assuming winter has one too?" she asked, and my heart swelled with pride and bliss. Before I could say anything, she placed a hand to her brow and voiced another thought. "Ah… we need better detection of these rot-witches. We should contact the Lunar Coven for ideas."

I placed a finger on her lips to shush her despite how much I loved what she was saying. She needed to recover—and I wanted her to de-stress after this—but she was still focused. To have a mate who actually cared about important matters took my breath away.

"Gods, I love you so much, Hekla." I tilted her chin up to place a soft kiss on her lips. "Such a queen." I squeezed my eyes shut and rested my forehead against hers. "I'm so glad you're ok. You nearly gave me a heart attack. Don't you ever do something like that again."

She just embraced me in return, her emotions swirling with mild guilt but mostly amusement and affection. "I love you too," she finally whispered.

"Are you ready for your surprise now?" I asked, pulling back to regard her face. She perked up, instantly bright-eyed, and I laughed at her reaction.

You look like a puppy, mate, Escort chuckled.

"What is it?" she asked with an excited smile, and I moved to open the door, wincing as I let in three screaming she-wolves.

Hekla

Aaah! Eventide cried in jubilation.

My sub-pack was here! My mouth dropped open in a happy gape, and I opened my arms to receive the scrambling she-wolves I'd known my whole life. My heart swelled to see the ones it had missed so dearly.

"Careful ladies!" Belenus cautioned, raising his palms. "Watch that table. Bandages! She's still recovering."

"We know, we know, Your Majesty," Ragna said, gently hugging me. Rakel and Soley lightly dogpiled on top, careful not to add too much weight. "We're not barbarians."

My mate smirked at me and then strolled out, closing the door behind him.

Oh, he and Escort are so getting some when we're better, Eventide remarked ferally.

"Can we all just please stop trying to die already?" Soley whined, pulling herself off the pile to claim a stool by the bed while Rakel and Ragna scooted a small couch closer.

"I tried, but your stupid rot-witches have it out for me." I pointed a finger at Ragna, making her gasp in mock outrage and look about for a pillow to throw.

"They are not my witches!" she protested. "I wasn't even the first to encounter one!"

"A likely story," Rakel deadpanned, turning to look at Ragna. I winced at the accidental reference to Rakel's abduction, and Ragna frowned regretfully, but our vessel of the Moon Goddess didn't seem bothered.

Rakel just chuckled and rested her head on her palm, staring at me. "Heard you slayed a princess with the dagger Rude and I gave you. I've never been prouder... or more relieved. Did you name it yet?" Her tone softened at the end. As much as she put on a casual front, I knew she must have been terrified for me. There was a soft center beneath her hard shell—now more visible than ever.

I grimaced. "I tried at first, but Eventide and I were coming up with some atrociously lame ideas."

"What about Fae Killer?" she suggested.

"I mean, that's great and all, but I'm mated to one... so... no."

"Spring Cleaner?" Ragna asked with a laugh.

"Weeder! Hedge Clipper! Hoe Gardener!" Soley yelled. Rakel gave her a bewildered look.

"Ok, you just started naming gardening tools, but I don't know about that last one." She turned to Ragna and asked quietly, "Can you recall if Soley ever hit her head?"

"Maybe the Sun God burns a little too hot..." Ragna replied in a loud whisper, pointing to her temple.

Ignoring them for what was a much more urgent subject, Soley asked, "So what's Belenus's cock like?" She scooted closer and gave me her full—wide-eyed—attention.

"What?" I gasped and Soley sandwiched her palms, looking questioningly at me as she slowly began to separate them.

"Oh my gods," Rakel muttered, palming her face.

The little she-wolf frowned. "Hey, I have to live vicariously, ok?" she explained over her shoulder to Rakel. At this point, Ragna was just howling with laughter. Soley turned back to face me and pressed, "Is it gold like the rest of him?"

I fought viciously to restrain a laugh, to keep my aghast expression intact. It probably looked like the most lunatic grimace in the entire realm. I blew out the huge breath I was holding and threw up my hands. "Ok, it's like I won a race, and I got an enormous gold trophy!" I tilted my head and added thoughtfully, "He did refer to it as his royal scepter this one time... Happy now, Soley?"

My she-wolves fell apart, and the little red-headed terror clapped while she cackled, nearly falling off the stool. "Very!" she cried as she tried to catch her breath.

“Great Moon Goddess.” Rakel chuckled and wiped tears from her eyes. “You better be next, Soley. I can’t handle your antics. Please just jump Koray already.”

“Augh!” she cried out, flopping face-first into the bed next to my legs.

I patted her ember curls in sympathy. “There, there,” I consoled with a grin. “At least Koray’s going back with you!”

“Yeah, but he’s still gonna visit here to study and train,” she moped, muffled by the mattress.

“Just come with him then. I’ll keep you company!”

“I guess…”

I looked up at Ragna and shook my head. “She can’t think of anything else, huh? Her heat is going to suck!” I then addressed the little red wolf who was melting in defeat. “Get Koray working on figuring out how to mark you. You don’t want to go through what I did. Trust me!”

“No, I don’t!” She pounded the mattress in aggravation.

I chuckled and ran my healed hand through her tossed curls. “I missed you all so much...”

Chapter 35

Mekla

I spent one last night in the hospital before Doctor Egres and Doctor Elisedd discharged me. Belenus had stayed with me all night, and I suspected that he had done several more rounds of healing because I felt pretty invigorated the following morning. He brought a fresh change of clothes for me and mentioned a meeting we needed to attend in regards to the bat-shifters.

"King Nechtan needs to leave soon, but he wants to meet one last time with us, the shifters, and the lycan king. I believe the wolf queen will be there as well," Belenus said, smiling down at me as we walked down the halls.

"Oh, wonderful! It was so sweet for you to bring my friends yesterday too. It was very much needed," I confessed, squeezing his hand and leaning against his shoulder.

"I knew the battle was harder on you than it was on me," he murmured. "You've never decisively killed a person before. That will take a while to accept."

"But you lost..." I began to say but then failed to finish my sentence. I didn't know how to acknowledge his loss.

He shook his head, imparting his seriousness through his amber gaze. "She was not my mother anymore, Hekla. I promise you that I won't lose sleep over it. The whole thing with my father was sad and disappointing, but it has nothing to do with us. We're here now, and we're going to take care of our people… and each other."

"And what about your father? We have to assume he's still alive from what Emer overheard..."

"He either abandoned us or is there against his will after he went to visit his queen lover," he sighed. "I'm in no rush to make an inquiry about that, but we'll address it at some point. I'm more worried about the Spring Court's reaction to the execution of their princess. Let's focus on our people first after we get the shifters settled. We have time. There will be a lot of talk before the Spring Court takes any action, and the fae are never in a rush... usually. No doubt we'll be hearing from the seelie soon as well."

He stroked my arm to soothe me, which actually made me realize that I was growing anxious. I checked in with my mate's emotions, and he seemed calm. It was probably for the best that we had a lot to do now. Staying busy would help us move past that bloody day, and there were a lot of positives ahead of us.

We entered a dimly lit meeting room with a long, polished table. Around it sat everyone that Belenus had mentioned—with the addition of Emer who'd sat between Nofre and Luzia. Her involving herself in bat-shifter matters was promising, and I dearly hoped it was a sign that she was planning to accept Nofre as her mate.

"Hi, Queen Hekla," Ragna sang, grinning and showing a little canine.

"Not yet," I replied with a chuckle and took a seat next to Belenus.

"We'll have the coronation when we've completed our escort of the shifters," Belenus explained, rolling up his sleeves to get down to business. "We are acting king and queen since I was the heir, so the ceremony can be delayed without a problem."

Nofre cleared his throat, glanced at Ferrer and Luzia, then asked, "So now that your reign has been established, where exactly will the bat-shifters be going? Will territory in the Realm of the Humans be hard to come by? We'll need enough space for all of us and a source of food."

"King Belenus and I have been discussing that, actually," King Zorian said, which was great because I hadn't had a chance to talk about any of it. He twirled a fountain pen in his large hands and tapped it on his stack of notes. "As there are no records of bat-shifters, I was unable to locate your native region. I do, however, have one offer for you, and if it is not acceptable, we can meet with the other kingdoms to see if there is something more appropriate available."

"What's this offer?" Nofre asked, leaning forward in anticipation, but he didn't look as worried or as vulnerable as Ferrer. The bat with the white streaks in his hair had a palm over his mouth.

"Most of my kingdom is already being used. We have many packs and farmland, but there's a southwestern section that is not yet being legally inhabited."

"Legally?" Ferrer inquired, furrowing his brows deeper in concern.

"There's a lot of rogue activity there. Ah, rogues are wolf and lycan shifters without a pack and are usually criminals. With your help, we could drive them out, and I'd grant you rights to settle the land," King Zorian offered, leaned back, crossed his arms. Red eyes stared at each other across the table.

"We realize it's not ideal to have to w—" Ragna began saying, but then she got a strange look in her eyes. Her posture straightened, and her mate regarded her with a raised brow.

Hekla, I think the Sky Gods are com— Eventide tried to get in before I felt the gods' presence ease into my mind. The skies held more than one presence, and the divine unity of countless gods borrowed my flesh to establish Their will. The possession could not be properly described—the silent chorus of a thousand colors.

A black void. Cold. Hot. Loud. Moving. Bursting. Collapsing. Dancing. Always moving. Always still.

"Hello," Ragna's body said. "It is good to see the Sky Gods' task has been completed."

It took Zorian only a heartbeat to realize what'd just happened. His eyes widened briefly, and he nodded in deference. "Earth Gods… welcome. We were just discussing the bat-shifters."

"Our children have made it. Our vessel did well," my mouth uttered, praising me with myself. The Sky Gods spoke through me like the Earth Gods spoke through Ragna. Though I couldn't see Belenus's face, I imagined he appeared as shocked as what I was feeling from him. The gods then turned my gaze to the three bats, focusing on each in turn. "We are proud of your survival, children. We regret we had not kept you safe."

Nofre, Ferrer, and Luzia stared at me in wonder.

"You are addressing the Sky Gods now," Zorian clarified, gesturing to me. "You know Hekla's Their vessel."

"R-right," Nofre stuttered, then shook his head to gather his wits. "Just never expected to speak to… our gods."

"Earth Gods," the Sky Gods inquired, turning my head to the wolf queen, "do you still have it?"

"Yes," They replied through Ragna. "It is untouched, as you've willed. Many have tried to enter, but we turned them around and made them forget. The land is fertile and ready for your children."

The Sky Gods turned my head to look at my mate. "Do you have a map of the Realm of the Humans?"

Belenus gestured to King Zorian, who pulled one from his bag. "We were looking at it earlier. Spread it out, King Zorian, if you would."

When the map was unfurled, Ragna stood and moved to my side. The Earth Gods placed her finger on the northwest coast, just over the cat-shifter's territory. However, her finger remained hovering over the water, confusing everyone at the table.

"There's no land there…" Zorian murmured, then looked up at his queen from his seat. "Are we missing something here?"

"The land is there. Cartographers were not allowed near it. We were saving the land for the Sky Gods' needs," the Earth Gods replied. "When Their children disappeared, we held onto their territory. We were all responsible for the punishment that led to the witches' actions against the sky-shifters. It was unacceptable that they targeted the Sky Gods' children. The rot-witches fight as dirty now as they did then, and they are becoming better at hiding than ever."

Belenus stood and leaned over to get a closer look at the destination. "I'm sure we have a door that we can use to get them close to their original territory. I'll have to cross reference it with our maps. Is there anything you can tell us about the land? What natural resources can we expect to find?"

Ragna took a seat and folded her hands. "Clean water in lakes, rivers, and springs. It has been stocked with edible vegetation and wild game, but I understand there seems to be a dietary change. I do not have a solution for that. There are forests and caves, but you will have to build your homes. I would have grown more trees had I known you'd evolved an aversion to sunlight."

"I can get a team on that, actually," Belenus said, idly tapping the table by the map. "It'll be slower outside our realm, but we can still speed up forestation."

"I am happy to provide several teams to help build homes," King Nechtan offered unexpectedly, but his green eyes conveyed genuine seriousness. He'd been quiet but seemed intrigued by the project. The bat-shifters at the table murmured their gratitude, looking a little overwhelmed by all the planning.

"We also will have to discuss a means of feeding your people, Nofre," King Zorian said, lacing his fingers together. "You will need to grow your economy, but perhaps we can develop a volunteer blood donation system. We could design incentives around it, like tax deductions, for example. It will have to be heavily regulated. I'm sure you don't need me to explain why." His eyes fell sharply on the bat-shifters, who nodded quickly in understanding. "According to King Keyon, the slave market is finally collapsing in the dragon-shifter kingdom, so many slavers will be eager to find another illegal trade to participate in."

"We are… grateful that you are even considering that," Nofre said quietly, humbly. "We do the best we can with animal blood, but it is just not as nourishing."

"Your biology was not of your choosing," the lycan king said with a resolute swipe of his hand. "We will work with the Summer and Winter Courts for ideas on starting your economy and establishing trade. Your people won't be alone."

"It sounds like our intervention is done, then," the Earth Gods said through Ragna. They outlined the region on the map with Zorian's pen. "You have the land. We have removed the barriers, and it is ready for you." Ragna's hand was placed on Nofre's shoulder. "Earthlight preserve you. It passes by you to settle on the dark of the moon, children of the Sky Gods. We are below you always, carrying your weight."

The bats didn't bother to hide the tears in their eyes.

Ragna was released and wobbled a little, but her mate caught her and dragged her protectively onto his lap. He fussed over her, pushing her hair from her face and caressing her in comfort. The wolf queen smiled at the smallest growl that bubbled from his chest.

"You continue to do well, King Zorian," the Sky Gods said through me. "Your efforts are admirable. The Sky-Blessed is also well suited to her new role." They turned me to my mate. "King Belenus, you have also shown a lot of growth. You put your needs aside for Hekla's task, and we are duly impressed. Thank you for protecting my vessel."

"Of course." Belenus bowed his head in piety. "Though I protect her out of love, not for divine praise."

"As it should be," the Sky Gods replied. "The Moon Goddess must be pleased with your successful mating."

My mate blushed and nodded again, placing his hands behind his back and clearing his throat.

"I will check on you again, children. There is much to be done, and you must all keep your eyes open for the rot-witches. They are learning how to block our eyes." The Sky Gods nodded a farewell, and I planted my feet once control of my body returned. I was a little more used to being taken over than Ragna.

Belenus wrapped an arm around me and asked quietly, "Are you ok?" I nodded and smiled up at him. It was fatiguing at most, nothing I couldn't handle.

"Well, it seems like we all have a lot of brainstorming to do," Ragna declared, sliding off Zorian's lap so he could stand.

"I'd also like to propose additional trades between the Summer and Winter Courts," King Nechtan stated, "but those can be discussed another time."

"I look forward to that discussion," Belenus replied honestly as he escorted the kings from the room. "Are all your warriors r—" He opened the door and was startled to find Bidelia grinning excitedly and holding Arse.

"Tan! Can we make snow treats again?" Bidelia chirped, grabbing at King Nechtan's cape. "Archibald thought dragon fruit might be good!"

I almost expected King Nechtan to be embarrassed, but he just looked sternly down at the young folk fae and said, "I must be leaving now, Bidelia. I am returning to the Winter Court with my warriors now that Slaine is able to ride."

I didn't think I'd ever seen a more disappointed face than the one Bidelia wore. Her jaw dropped like he'd thrown her snow treat onto the ground and stepped on it. Her cheeks then reddened, her eyes watered.

I sense a tantrum coming, Eventide cautioned.

"It's ok, Bidelia. I'm sure you'll be able to vis—" I started saying, trying to get ahead of her explosion.

"No!" Bidelia whined, tossing her head back and stomping her foot. "First Hekla leaves, then Belenus, and now yer leaving me too?" she wailed with tears streaming down her cheeks. She took a big breath and shouted, "I hate y—"

King Nechtan knelt and shushed her before she could finish her fuming.

"Let's give them a moment," I said to everyone else, and we escorted the lycan king and the wolf queen to the gate so they could return to their realm.

"I will come visit again," Ragna promised, giving me a fierce hug before letting me go. "I promise we'll do everything we can to help your bat-shifters."

"Thank you… they feel like my pack, in a way," I admitted. Remembering my status as an alpha now, I eyed Zorian and wondered if I had a snow treat's chance in the Summer Court at getting him to submit. Maybe I could if I took him by surprise.

I pretended to look at something on my skirt, then whirled and shouted, "SUBMIT!" to Zorian. He just grinned broadly and crossed his arms, utterly unperturbed.

"What in the name of the Sun God was that?" Belenus blurted, gawking at me.

I pressed my lips into a flat line, standing with my finger pointed up at Zorian like an idiot. Ragna was bent over, trying to breathe through bouts of laughter.

"It was a good try, Alpha Hekla. I almost felt something," King Zorian said, his red eyes glinting with rare good humor.

"Well shit," I lamented and dropped my hand. "I tried for the sneak attack."

"Keep practicing." He smirked, dragging his laughing mate over to the realm door where a guard waited to transport them. "Take care." He nodded to us and Belenus and stepped through the door.

Before she disappeared, Ragna barely managed to shout around her giggles. "Pack always!"

Belenus

The bat-shifter colony was understandably impatient to leave for their rightful land, to stop the long march and settle into a new life. Nofre had made it clear that the sooner they were settled and able to work on getting their community comfortable, the sooner they'd be able to focus on long-term goals. The idea of getting a blood donation system running made the majority of the bats dissolve into tears. They'd fought for too long against their instincts, and it seemed to them like the world finally cared again. No, Hekla and I would make certain they'd never feel forgotten again.

It was pretty obvious that the other kings were invested in easing their suffering. King Zorian also mentioned that this seemed like a project that the new queen of the dragon-shifters would be interested in joining. He wasn't sure how the cat-shifters would react to their new neighbors, but that'd be a worry for another day. Right now, it was more important to get them settled.

We completed our final escort preparations by nightfall, and all four hundred and twenty-four bat-shifters lined up at the realm door closest to the castle, eyes shining with anxiety, excitement, and yearning.

Hekla's eyes scanned the crowd, and she pointed to some new additions among them. "I'm seeing some fae among the colony. Belenus, are they…?"

I slid a hand across her back to grab her waist and tuck her against my side. I'd been feeling her excitement, but I'd also been feeling a lot of her anxiety. What she'd noticed was a good development, though, and I hoped it'd soothe her worried heart.

"Some found their mates over the last day or so. I imagine some must have snuck into the city out of curiosity or wandered around the castle grounds," I answered, enjoying the deep satisfaction of seeing members of this endangered group find mates of their own. It did surprise me how quickly it'd come for them; some fae waited hundreds of years for a fated mate, if they were even lucky enough to find theirs. Either way, I took it as a good sign. They needed—and deserved—all the boons coming their way.

She fidgeted a bit and worried at her hands. "I want to register them when they leave through the portal and check on them when we send supplies. We've seen firsthand how they can be with feeding, so I need to make sure that they develop laws that protect everyone in the colony."

I knew it wasn't particularly helpful, but I couldn't resist leaning over and whispering, "Every time you say something that makes you sound like the queen you are, my pants suffer greatly for it." I grinned when her mouth broke into a goofy smile, and she glanced covertly around to see if anyone had heard that. It was likely, but I didn't care. I didn't have to hide my love for her anymore. I had plans to parade her around for centuries to come.

"You did say you needed pants that fit better," she muttered out of the corner of her mouth, looking up at me with impish amusement. I laughed, leaned her back dramatically, and kissed her on the lips, smiling when I heard some whoops and clapping from onlookers. I released my breathless, aroused mate and gestured to the guards and volunteers who'd arrived with packhorses.

"Did we get everything?" Hekla inquired, rosy-cheeked.

The fae held up their checklist. "Tents, medicine, sleeping pads and bags, clothes for different climates, tarps, rope, torches, lanterns… and everything else we discussed. Many of these are divided into the bags left by the realm door for each shifter. Everything else will be carried by the horses. We saved a lot of space by not needing cooking gear."

A voice piped in from the right. "Their mates will though."

I turned to see my half-sister approaching with a small smile, a bag slung over her back. Did that mean what I thought it did?

"Ah! I hadn't thought about that," Hekla said, palming her face. "That's a good point, Emer. Perhaps we can send another group tomorrow with those things. I thought it'd be just Emer, b— Er… I…" Hekla stumbled when she realized she didn't know if Emer was actually going with Nofre or not. It looked to be the case, but until she spoke the words aloud, neither of us could bring ourselves to assume.

"No, it won't be just me," she replied sheepishly, looking down at her toes while rocking on her heels. I took in a deep breath and released it, feeling another weight slip from my shoulders. "I've decided I'm going to accept Nofre as my mate. Seeing the old queen—the odd, empty state she was in before she died—I realized that anyone could have done better than her in raising a family. It made me want to embrace what I have with Nofre." She shook her head thoughtfully. "I know I can be better. We're not doomed to be like our parents. It just took me a while to realize that. Nofre's…" she said, trailing off as she watched him converse with Ferrer, "he's the best male I've ever met."

Hekla strode forward without a word and embraced her soon-to-be sister-in-law. In a thick voice, Hekla choked out, "I will make sure you get the best frying pan we have!" Emer burst into laughter, which seemed to diffuse some of her tension and timidity over the subject. Hekla held her out at arm's length. "In that case, can we rely on you to represent the mates who've joined and will someday join the colony? I want to make sure the couples are equally represented in having their needs met."

Emer's eyes gleamed at the question, and she sobered. Perhaps now she realized that she could contribute—that she was in an ideal position to make a huge difference in the lives of others.

"I will," she accepted with a set jaw and a squaring of her shoulders. "I'll gladly represent and see to their needs." Her eyes flickered to me, and I nodded. We were on the same page. She knew this was how she could grow up and fill an essential role. She was ready to be responsible for something now, even a task as colossal as this.

"I'm proud of you, Emer," I told her, unable to bring myself to say anything more at the moment. So much had changed over the last couple of days, and I was still reeling. I'd be sad to see my only blood relative leave, but I was glad for the reason. Visiting also shouldn't be too difficult. However it had been arranged, the Moon Goddess obviously had plans for her. With a calm heart, I watched my half-sister stroll over to Nofre, Ferrer, and Luzia, only to take her mate's hand and lead him away for a private conversation. The bat-shifter was about to get some exceptionally good news.

"I think we're ready," Hekla muttered nervously, wiping her palms on her hips.

"Yes, this will take a while. Let's get started," I agreed, and we marched up with our first team to follow them through the realm door.

We landed on starlit, springy pine needles amongst giant, ancient redwoods. It was immediately obvious that no one had touched these lands for the entirety of the shifters' absence. Where we'd arrived appeared pristine, with no signs of littering or habitation.

"Oh, it smells delectable!" Hekla gushed, taking in a huge lungful of air. "Eventide is fighting to get out." She laughed in glee and took my hand. Yes, even Escort yearned to feel the pine under his own paws. Perhaps I'd bring my mate here for a run instead of the gardens—a surprise outing for Eventide and Escort. They'd like that.

Our first team, a large group of soldiers, spread out to set up a perimeter and check for nearby predators. We also brought scouts and hunters to get an initial lay of the land and look for a source of water. Volunteers then crowded around the pack animals, removing lanterns and torches to light up the campsite.

Hekla and I made sure they didn't set up too close to the realm door because we'd be bringing a lot of supplies over in the coming weeks and more once they discovered a place to start building their homes. We both agreed we'd continue to support them in sending resources and able-bodied volunteers until they were self-sufficient. Though she'd seen her task through to completion, Hekla didn't feel like she could ever walk away from them, and I respected—if not adored—that about her.

Since I had help this time, it wasn't long before we got all the bat-shifters teleported over into their original realm. I would never forget their expressions. I could only describe it as them coming to life for the very first time. On the march, they'd improved, but there had been a listlessness that lingered. Here? Something here stirred their souls.

Luzia and Ferrer walked over to us wearing identical looks of wonder. The she-bat breathed, "There's something so bone-deep familiar about this place."

"Maybe your ancestor was a messenger pigeon-shifter," I said wryly, and Hekla chuckled at my side.

"I don't know what that is, but… I'll take it as a compliment?" she replied uncertainly. "Everyone seems to be settling in fine. The rucksacks you've provided each of us contain good supplies that will last for a while. We are… grateful, to put it mildly."

"Luzia will be more grateful when she can experience what other people in this realm taste like," Ferrer intoned dryly. Her nostrils flared, and she punched him in the shoulder.

"You weren't supposed to share that, you clot!" she hissed angrily. He just gave her a bleak side-eye and crossed his arms. Luzia jerked a thumb at Ferrer and said, "Well, this one is pining for a mate. He's acting like a naive, romantic pup. You should see how he mopes whenever he sees Nofre and Emer."

"Incorrect. I don't need anything or anyone, and I do not mope!" Ferrer seethed through his fangs and stalked off with clenched fists. Luzia snorted and walked off in a different direction.

"Just like siblings." I chuckled, shaking my head. "Why do I suddenly feel like a parent?"

"Probably because you're going to be one," Hekla said quietly from my side.

What? Escort asked.

"What?" I echoed, snapping my gaze down to look at her. Her smooth hand found mine and squeezed it. "What was that, Hekla?" I asked again, not sure if I'd heard her correctly.

She moved in front of me and slid her arms around my back, laying her head against my chest. I felt her take a long, calming breath. "Doctor Egres brought a report earlier this evening right before we left. My bloodwork tested positive for offspring." She tilted her head up to look at me, resting her chin on my chest.

"I'm still processing it myself," she added with a chuckle, then placed a finger across her lips and looked up at me expectantly.

My throat went dry, and I could barely hear Escort over the deafening hammering of my heart. "Pups?" I whispered hoarsely, feeling warmth glow in my abdomen like the sky before a sunrise.

"Or faebies, as my grandmother likes to call them," she with a laugh, and I could feel some of her tension fade away to be replaced by excitement.

And grandpa, Eventide added.

Oh my shit, Escort blubbered. *When?*

Hekla shrugged and smiled up at me in growing bliss. "Can't really say."

Probably the first time, which was Eventide and me, Escort said immediately, only because he knew it'd trigger the shit out of me.

Belenus, we don't know. It could have been any of the first few times. Be a good boy, Escort, Eventide commanded with a bit of alpha coming through her tone.

Big shit knows I'm just messing with him. Escort laughed.

I shook my head to take a step back and get perspective. "Why in the name of the Sun God do I care? I'm going to have an heir! I'm going to be a father! I... I can't... Hekla, forgive me."

She opened her mouth in surprise when I hoisted her up like a trophy and paraded her around the campgrounds. "My mate, my queen is pregnant!" I announced.

The entire colony of shifters, their mates, and our volunteers filled the night air with screams, hoots, yells, and clapping. The woods was in an absolute uproar, and I feasted on Hekla's amusement and mild embarrassment. Oh yes, the parading had begun.

I continued marching my cackling mate around, yelling, "I love this female! We fought for our love and our kingdom. You helped us claim a place where we no longer have to hide that love, and you all helped create a place where my heir will grow up in safety. For that, we give you our thanks and our continued, devoted support!"

"Then name 'em after me!" one older shifter hollered through the celebrating, waving a hand in the air to get my attention.

"What's your name?" I asked loudly, chuckling as I turned to fully face him.

"Fulgencio!"

I immediately shook my head and shouted, "Nope!" The crowd laughed, and some slapped a grinning Fulgencio playfully on the back. I spied Nofre chuckling with an arm around Emer, who was cackling as hard as my Hekla, fanning her red face. My heart warmed to see them closer, and I wondered how long it would be until I became an uncle. After living with such a fractured sense of family, I nigh glowed to see a healthier one on the horizon. I owed far too much to the Moon Goddess and made a note to build a larger shrine to Her.

When Hekla started squirming, I settled her feet on the ground but didn't let go. I couldn't. I crashed my lips into hers, delivering my deepest affection with a kiss equally deep. My palms found her smooth cheeks, cupped them, and caressed lovingly. After getting the taste I needed, I tore myself away, but just for a moment to whisper, "Gods, I love you. I love you so much, my precious female. Look at you, giving us an heir as soon as we claimed our home."

"H-home…" she panted breathlessly into my lips, ignoring the rowdy cheering and whistling, or maybe not hearing them altogether. I nodded and kissed her again as soon as she finished getting the word out of her mouth. Joy swept through us both, and I couldn't tell who was feeling more of it. The bond told us we simply shared the same euphoria, and my chest tightened. Emotional now, her confession had me thinking of her fatigue. I wanted to take her home. She'd been awake all day, and I wanted her to rest. There was more work to do tomorrow, but now I had to make sure she didn't take on too much. I smiled again, mentally preparing myself to fight my female on that.

I scooped her up into my arms again, despite her protests about being a strong alpha, and bowed my head to the colony around us. "We're going to take our leave now, but we'll continue to send supplies and check on you. I need to take my pregnant mate home to put her to bed."

"I bet you will!" someone called out, which triggered more raucous laughter. I grinned into Hekla's hair, kissed the top of her head, and turned, striding toward the realm door to go home.

The halls of the castle no longer witnessed dirty looks, and the folk fae—though some were still a touch nervous with the change—walked about with proudly displayed wings, tails, and horns. The overall mood of the servants and other inhabitants was one of good cheer and gratitude, something I'd never seen before in my life.

Though Hekla and I had years of work to do, the castle was finally a safe place to call home—for everyone.

Chapter 36

Queen Hekla: One week later

I was drowning in she-wolves. Ragna, Soley, and Rakel hovered over the poor maids preparing me for my combined marriage and coronation. Bidelia was babbling excitedly as she wrapped a little black bow tie around Arse's neck, despite his curmudgeonly protesting. I knew he loved her attention, though, because he let her get away with a lot—way more than he allowed me. It wasn't the first time I thought about giving Bidelia his ownership papers. They were inseparable.

Maybe when she's older. We'll ask 'Arsybald' what he wants, Eventide proposed giddily. She'd been just as excited about the wedding. It hadn't meant anything to us at first, but having Belenus and me claim each other per his culture's tradition was a thrill of its own. It was just another opportunity to show thousands that Belenus was mine, and doing that publicly meant more than ever.

All ours!

Once the maids finished, my she-wolves fell into a rare moment of silence. I smoothed the skirts on the gown and turned to look at myself in the mirror. The cream corset was being adjusted by Ragna, loosened a little because she knew from experience that I might feel faint under the hot, summer sun.

"Now that you're with pup like me," she said, looking over my shoulder with a warm, happy smile, "you're going to have to be more careful with dizzy spells. Your body will warn you. Just make sure you listen to it."

"I don't have symptoms yet, but I'm sure it's only a matter of time." I laughed, beaming back at her joyful expression. Soley fluffed the layered gossamer skirts of gold and blue, the colors of the last thread of sunlight on the horizon before it was swallowed by the deep blue of the evening. Rakel lifted the gauzy, midnight-blue cape so it wouldn't drag on the floor and studied the tiny diamonds sewn into it. I didn't know who designed the dress, but I was wrapped in everything the sun and skies offered, and my she-wolves murmured in approval and admiration. My reflection smiled back at me—a joyous alpha in a wedding dress.

"Are you ready?" Rakel asked, tilting her head to make sure nothing was missed. "I'm glad you left your hair down. You look like a sky goddess, Hekla."

"Yeah," I breathed out nervously. "I am ready!"

"Then let's go, go, go, Queen Hekla!" Soley chirped and ran forward to get the door. Ragna linked arms with me, and Rakel held onto my cape that doubled as a train.

Bidelia skipped along in a cute gold-and-green dress that brought out the colors of her gold, emerald, and sky-blue butterfly wings. They remained crinkled, but I would do everything in my power to see if they could be fixed. Doctor Elisedd said that we might have to wait until she stopped growing to try. Arse still stubbornly declined his own treatment for his wings, but I imagined he'd cave someday.

My she-wolves handed me over to my crying father once we reached the carpet, and we marched toward the altar so he could give me away to Belenus. Bidelia had prematurely thrown her last handful of petals and ran off to find her friend, 'Tan,' a nickname far too inaccurate for the pale fae ruler. She sat gleefully next to the calm King Nechtan of the Winter Court, trying to be polite but—like a little ray of sunshine—couldn't seem to stop radiating excitement. Her little feet kicked the air rhythmically as she fought to contain her enthusiasm. I didn't have the heart to seat them separately, knowing this would be the last time they'd see each other for four years, and he'd behaved himself quite well with her.

Nofre and Emer were currently traveling for reasons I tried not to think about, but all of the bat-shifters who'd wished to attend were seated under a large, thick tarp to protect them from the sunlight. Needless to say, with the bats, the fae, my subpack, their mates, and my family, the crowd attending the wedding and coronation was colossal. Though the sea of faces intimidated me, friendly faces offered relief. I smiled when I spied Oscar and his daughter, giving them a little wave as I passed.

When my blubbering father passed me over to Belenus, my entire world centered on him. I stared at his clean-shaven, flirty grin and fell into his warm, loving amber eyes. His hair had been trimmed and styled to perfection, like how it'd been when I first arrived. And in his wedding attire, he looked downright dashing, a smart white and gold-trimmed paludamentum thrown over a shoulder. His grin turned knowing when I suddenly felt a touch weak in the knees. How could I not be affected by this fae? Belenus was everything I could have asked for and more.

I fought to pay attention to the officiant because Belenus's amber eyes were too hypnotizing. We didn't mind-link at all, but I knew what he was saying with his body. What he'd confessed weeks ago still held true—he would make it very clear tonight how much he wanted me. The fire in his eyes whispered that he hadn't nearly gotten enough. With his smoldering gaze and the way he subtly rubbed his thumb and forefinger together, he shared what he'd be doing with his magic later. By the time the officiant wrapped up his speech and prompted us to make our vows, the heat from my cheeks rivaled the sun. I was done with fae games, but there was no ignoring his call to play.

After we slipped our rings on each other, Belenus's mouth crashed on mine, and he leaned me back again into a dramatic pose, eliciting a roar from the crowd. We almost had to be pried apart for the crowning, of which I have no memory of because all I wanted to do was escape and rip Belenus's clothes off of his hard, hungry body. My wolf paced inside, wanting to get to my mate now that we'd been introduced as the ruling mated pair.

We addressed dinner as a challenge, both of us needing to escape as soon as possible. And since it was my turn to tease him, I made sure to target only the sausages on my plate. To encourage him into a hasty retreat, I licked and sucked completely inappropriately on the ends when I thought no one else was paying attention. As much as I missed my mother and enjoyed discussing the news of my pregnancy, I had other things on my mind.

Though, the more heated glances I sent him, the more I started to notice a change in Belenus. He seemed a little stronger since the coronation, and his hair seemed a little… brighter. The gold flecks on his skin also reflected a touch… more brilliantly? I poked his shoulder to get his full attention again and ran a finger over the back of his hand.

"You seem different, mate," I noted, examining him with curiosity.

"Triskelion's blessing is fully settling in," he murmured, bringing his hand up to stare at it. Wonder brightened his radiant amber eyes. "I've been feeling my court's magic slowly become more available to me. Now that I'm king, it's all at my disposal. With so much magic under my skin, it changes my appearance a little…" He stared at his hand in fascination. "It's bizarre to see it happening to me."

I stared pensively at him, and after the surprise calmed, I narrowed my eyes. This could be used to my advantage. "I think this warrants an investigation, wouldn't you agree?"

His face cracked into a roguish grin, and he leaned in to ask quietly, "What are you wanting to investigate, wife?"

"I think we need to check the rest of you," I whispered into his ear, brushing my lips against the tip on 'accident.' "Make sure you're ok. Everywhere."

"Yes," he breathed, raising his brows and setting his lips into a grim line. "I'm especially concerned about my cock. You should thoroughly examine it."

We made our excuses without delay, citing a medical concern and fooling absolutely no one. Belenus swept me up into his thrilling, muscular arms and raced to the royal chamber that was finally ready for us as of today. My mate had wanted all of his parents' things removed, so it'd taken time to redecorate and remodel.

Once we were in the royal bedchamber, Belenus untied my dress, then ripped it up and over my head. He groaned at the sight of me in my damp undergarment and worked quickly to remove the rest. "Gods, Hekla, I could spill my seed just by looking at you." He moaned and shucked his own clothes, discarding them onto the floor. I helped him with his shoes, and when our skin felt only warm summer air, he cradled and lowered me onto the bed.

"I need you," I called to him in a low voice. "I couldn't stop thinking about you the whole time..."

"You have me, my wife, my queen, my mate," he said, sliding between my legs and spreading them. "Only you get to have me. Only I get to have you." He reached between us to notch his cock into the entrance of my sex. We were much too ready, too eager for teasing or foreplay. The wedding had been teasing. Dinner had been foreplay.

We moaned in chorus as he nudged between my folds to plunge past my threshold. My arousal spilled out, dripping down my thighs and buttocks as he pushed his pulsing member deeper. The sparks of the mate touch stole my breath, but there was something more spellbinding about Belenus now. I could detect the smallest hint of his essence just under his skin, and for several heartbeats, I weakened, melted beneath him. My sex throbbed, threatening to spin me into a climax.

"Oh Moon Goddess, Belenus, I can feel your magic." I tilted my head, tested by his sublimity, and slid my hands up his chiseled arms to grip his back. He grunted to acknowledge what I'd said as he continued to ease into me, staggeringly hard. I heard him take slow, controlled breaths and realized he was trying not to climax either. That alone made my stomach flip from lust, and my core clenched around him possessively.

His fingers held the sheets in a death grip as he took a moment to breathe. "You… you feel…" He was at a loss for words and simply lowered his head to lay soft, tingling kisses on my neck. He finally relaxed as he pushed in the rest of the way.

I gaped as his exquisite form and essence filled me to the brim. Belenus was completely mine, and I could still scarcely believe it. I wasn't sure why the Sky Gods had chosen me, why the Moon Goddess had given me Belenus, and why the Summer Court needed me as its queen, but I'd take every single joy that came my way.

"Oh, she-wolf," Belenus breathed into my ear as he lifted his hips, sliding his erection out of my sex just a bit before pushing back in, "I could do this until the day I died…" He rolled his hips slowly and sensually, taking a different approach to our mating this time.

"Me too," I gasped out, arching into his muscular chest as he undulated over me. His gentle, provocative movements had me so aroused, so stimulated, that chills and goose bumps pricked at my skin. He'd invited me into a lazy, carnal dance that heated up my body from the very marrow of my bones. I growled in acceptance and stretched under him, moving in time with his rolling hips.

"Tell me, she-wolf," he groaned, shuddering after I'd released my wolfish noise, "do you still want for anything? You know I'd give you anything you asked for…" He flexed his abdomen, sending his swollen, rock-hard length deep into my depths again. I spasmed under him, curled my toes, and released an excited pant.

Through my foggy, aroused mind, I considered his question. I had a home, a mate, a purpose, friends, and family. What more did I need? I couldn't say I wanted for anything. Still though, a dusty place remained in my soul where my pack used to be. There wasn't anything I could do about that. I knew I'd be packless forever...

I swallowed heavily as I held onto Belenus. It couldn't be possible... could it?

"Belenus?" I whispered, running a leg along his flexing thigh in an affectionate, sensual gesture.

"Yes, sweet wife?" he murmured and shifted his weight to lean down and kiss me.

"If I could make a pack... would you join it?" I asked nervously, biting my lower lip.

"If that's what you want, I'd do it in a heartbeat," he answered, moving to plant gentle, wet kisses on my brow. "Though I'm not sure if it's possible."

My curiosity possessed me in that moment, and I was unable to wait. Straddling a place of pain and pleasure, I ran a claw down my palm, leaving behind a small red line of blood. He slowed his motions and drew his brows in, not recognizing the significance.

"Hold your palm up," I requested falteringly, searching his eyes as I put myself in a deeply vulnerable place. I felt no judgment from him through the bond—merely curiosity. He held his palm up, and I cut a long line down it, identical to mine. He didn't wince in pain, just stared down at me and waited patiently. "I don't know if this will work," I said nervously. He wasn't a shifter, but he had a wolf spirit...

"Just try," he encouraged and brushed a strand away from my face.

I swallowed and grabbed his hand, placing our bloody palms against each other. I projected an alpha command into the sacred lines of my own people. "I, Hekla Nighean An Tsamhraidh, alpha of the summer queen's pack, accept you, Belenus Ailill Mac An Tsamhraidh, into my pack."

Something did happen, taking me utterly by surprise. I hadn't really believed it was possible. The sudden sensation of a pack link forming between the two of us had Belenus and me jerking in shock. The intensity of the tether's appearance flared like the first ray of sunlight and swirled with energy like the ever-restless sky. The empty place inside of me was now filled and connected directly to my mate.

Belenus hissed and adjusted his weight over me.

"Are you ok?" I asked worriedly, astonished by the link's appearance, but he only chuckled weakly, and I felt his cock swell and throb within me.

"Yeah…" He laughed into my shoulder and rolled his hips, forcing a moan out of me while I waited for him to say more. "Just when I thought I couldn't feel closer to you…"

That cut through all my defenses, and my eyes watered. He didn't reject it or tell me to undo it. Was he ok letting me have this?

As if he'd read my mind, he said into my ear, "I told you, I'd give you anything." He nuzzled my jaw sweetly with his nose. "If this makes you happy… I'll gladly fill the role." He pulled his heavy cock out and thrust it back in to punctuate his eagerness. I gasped from the sudden movement, and broiling fire coursed through my spine.

I scrabbled at his back and arched into him again, losing myself in how much I loved my mate. He'd done what he said he was going to do. He became more mindful of his words, became less judgmental of my culture, and ended up embracing everything about me, including what he'd eventually found within himself.

"I love you!" I cried through my sobs, tears rolling down my cheeks. "Thank you, thank you, thank you!" I tightened my legs around his hips and pulled him into me with each of his thrusts. "Thank you, Belenus!" I whimpered and clutched at his back muscles, panting with blooming passion. I was too stimulated, too overwhelmed, too happy, too excited, and I knew Belenus felt it as well because his movements became rougher.

"I love you too," he replied in a thick, emotional voice. He leaned onto his elbows and started slapping his hips into mine, plunging his stiff length all the way in to kiss my cervix. I whimpered and rubbed my breasts against his chest, reveling in the mate touch and the essence that poured out of him and into me. I no longer felt like something was missing. Belenus had made me whole again, to perfect completion, something I'd never thought possible.

"You are sweet perfection. I'm going to worship you until my dying day," he vowed between pants, sending his cock sliding back and forth along my weeping channel. Each plunge was a reminder of how he completed me in every way and how we both had a long lifetime to celebrate that. "Oh Sun God, I don't know how much longer I can last. You're so beautiful, so tight, so warm, so wonderful." He rained kisses over me as he accelerated, his moans caressing my skin in sensual puffs.

"Give me your seed," I begged and caught his mouth with mine. I kissed him fervently, holding tight as he reached his fastest pace, rocking me into the king and queen's bed. I whined and whimpered into his lips as I tilted my hips to meet his impacts. Though the sounds forced their way out of me, I knew they spurred him. Fully embracing all my tricks, I slid my hands up his neck through his shorter hair and rubbed the points of his ears.

He growled voraciously into my mouth, and his breathing deepened, grew desperate. He reached between my legs and massaged my aching, swollen flesh, groaning with carnal lust. "Come for me, and I'll give you what you want, she-wolf," he said in a deep voice that made my abdomen twist into scorching, pleasurable knots.

As he dripped the sweat of his exertion onto me, I took a deep breath of his scent, basking in the lemon trees and summer storms. He was everywhere now—in my lungs, my pores, my mind, my sex, and my soul. I could stay like this forever.

He did what he promised he'd do during our wedding, and a climax burst out of me. Through me, I swear the sun escaped the horizon in the most brilliant, blinding sunrise. My body was caught on the rays of light that passed through me, bringing waves of ecstasy with each flare. The loud cry that escaped me made my mate fall into a rutting frenzy.

"Yes! Howl!" he yelled and thrust in one final time to release his seed. He roared through his teeth and braced himself over me, shaking violently from his climax as I pulsed against him with mine. His eyes squeezed shut, and his hips jerked with every release that my massaging channel urged out of him. "Shit!" he cried out, gasping and wrapping his arms around me, then rolled us over so I was lying on his chest. His hips continued to buck up with each spurt, and I swayed helplessly over him, allowing my core to milk out his offering, his essence, and his love for me. My mind and body were abuzz with euphoria, and even though my climax was ending, the euphoria was not.

"Gods, I love you so much," he groaned again, dragging me down to wrap me in his loving, golden embrace.

"I love you too… so very, very much," I replied, nearly choking up with emotion. I was so happy, and I could feel that he was experiencing the same overwhelming joy. I couldn't imagine anything better than sensing my mate's equal bliss.

I sent a prayer of gratitude to all the gods. I thanked them for giving me a fated mate, for watching over us during our quest for the throne, and for deigning to let me have the last, tiny sliver of myself that was missing. I now had a pack, and his name was Belenus.

Author's Notes

Dear readers,

As you know by now, all of my novels are written as an exposure therapy exercise for childhood trauma. It's too emotionally difficult for me to explain again here, especially the sexual assault I survived, so if you wish to understand the context of these notes, please read the Author's Notes in *The Mistake and the Lycan King* and the Author's Notes in *The Dragon Knight and the Coveted.*

There were two elements I focused on in this sequel: powerlessness and escaping the bubble of a warped reality.

Powerlessness:

Ultimately, try as I might, escaping or sustaining damage while trying to tolerate the abuse was always the answer because some things could not be helped, at least not in a way I felt possible. I rarely felt safe growing up and dealt with a continuation of fear.

My days in elementary school after I'd been touched consisted of being alone at school while I hid from harassment, then avoiding the second predator that entered my life. Then I'd face another part of my day—cry and avoid another person.

Yelling, screaming, partial undressing, and hitting led to hiding and plans of running away—which I packed for many times but always came to my senses. That led to chronic nightmares that I still have to this day. I felt powerless against the nightmares from the beginning.

At that point, I unknowingly accepted my powerlessness, both at school and elsewhere, and escaped inward. I cried, I dissociated, and slept most of the time when I could, choosing to face my chronic nightmares over reality. I tried to draw on inspiring women from novels I'd read and keep my head up high in public, but somehow, that just made it worse.

I couldn't make Hekla's experience with the fae court exactly like mine, but all the elements were there. I'd craved love and affection. I craved being noticed by the right people and ignored by the wrong people. I felt powerless to control any relationships, and all I could do was run away.

Except for one friend who lived just down the street. She taught me everything I was supposed to learn since we met in elementary school. She gave me self-confidence and love and is probably the reason why I'm alive today. No one tolerated my emotional outbursts like her. To this day, I honestly don't know why she stuck around. I was a mess—a clingy, jealous, depressed, angry, and confused mess.

I ultimately developed PTSD, then a personality disorder, and eventually blocked out so many bad memories that I can barely remember my childhood, but I'm slowly starting to recall more through therapy. The more I can recall, the more I can address and figure out why some things hurt more than others.

This book is my way of acknowledging the suffering in silence that I've done—the feeling of wanting to be seen and protected by the right people but being let down by those I could have sworn were supposed to keep me safe. This book is my way of acknowledging the times where I wished I could have lashed out at the abusers but was obsessed with following the rules out of self-preservation and was ultimately controlled by my fears.

Most of all, though, this book is to remind myself that I got through it and that I'm safe now. I survived it, and I dragged my ass into therapy. I'm where I'm supposed to be now.

Once, I thought I didn't have a reason to feel bad because I was certain someone else had it much worse, but all that did was invalidate my very real experience. It's ok to feel bummed out about the bad things. It's also ok to feel grateful for the good things. That's the beauty of compartmentalizing, a skill I'm still working on.

Escaping the bubble of a warped reality:

Adding from what I've written above, Belenus was my experience with life after I went to college. For the first time, I was surrounded by absolute weirdness: healthy relationships, genuinely content individuals, and alternatives to rules that were terribly unhealthy and destructive. I know that some things look happier on the outside and that comparing lives is not the best practice, but I was nearly brought to my damn knees when I saw a plethora of healthy relationships—all sorts of them.

I grew up thinking that unhealthy things were normal. This is reflected in Belenus's view of how the fae court works and his insistence that you couldn't play by any other set of rules. The Moon Goddess's story about the pup who bites was another example of this.

I was not a biting pup, but I was told that I had a 'monster' in me at a very, very young age, and that it would manifest later. I was told that I had to accept growing up a certain way, but I fought it. Maybe that's why shifter stories move me so much—how the internal 'monster' is really a benevolent being. I've finally dismissed the 'monster' as a myth thanks to DBT therapy, but I can't ignore the similarities there.

Relatively fun facts:

My readers asked for vampires after I wrote *The Mistake and the Lycan King*, but I had to think long and hard on how to work them into my world lore. The corpse version of vampires doesn't work for what I need; I cannot reconcile the lack of a heartbeat and the circulatory system that would be required to create things like… an erection. Just, too many issues for me to resolve. So, I decided to make them vampire bat-shifters, though, in my world lore, vampire bats are referred to as blood bats since vampires just don't exist. Anyway, my bat-shifters needed more adjusting to be like classical vampires. They needed the sunlight sensitivity, so I decided to use the fae realm to evolve them, trapping them in a court of endless night to force that vulnerability. They needed the bloodlust, so I made them cursed by needing to drink what their inner blood bats require. Vampire bats also have extraordinary mobility, being great jumpers and fast runners, so that checked off the supernatural traits as well. I've made my bat-shifters capable of echolocating in their human forms, similar to human echolocation, via clicking. Nofre, Ferrer, and Luzia represent the three species of vampire bats. Nofre's bat, Steal, is a common vampire bat. Ferrer's bat, Iron, is a white-winged vampire bat, hence the white streaks in his hair. Luzia's bat is the hairy-legged vampire bat, which is, hands down, one of the cutest animals on the planet. I'm glad my readers urged me into working a new species into my novels, as I hadn't expected the opportunities they'd provide—challenging avenues to explore for my exposure therapy.

As far as the fae creatures go, I drew from what I loved when I was younger, as creature lore was both a comfort and obsession for some reason. Disney's Fantasia first grabbed my attention with the Waltz of the Flowers and the Pastoral Symphony. Triskelion, first, is an ancient motif I found fascinating my whole life, and it inspired my fae godlings Tri, Ske, and Lion. On the other fae creatures, almost every named faery creature in this book, like the fear gorta—and yes, the boobrie—came from across Scottish and Irish folklore except for the mac-talla, which was born from my own heart. The name means 'echo' in Scottish Gaelic and is a reference to how translation is like an echo in disguise. I have a soft spot in my heart for creatures that are viewed as pests, thus the creation of an opossum with moth wings. Growing up, I became a little confused about how I saw the fair folk from my childhood looking more like Tolkien elves in modern popular fantasy. I'm sure there's a rabbit hole I could fall down some day and explore. And seasonal courts? Researching outside of what I grew up reading has been overwhelming. Faery lore in general spread and became so diverse across countries and culture. The etymology is endlessly fascinating too.

Belenus was a Celtic god of healing and has been associated with Apollo as a sun deity, though I'm reading that there is still some debate on this. The name has various translations but basically means 'bright or shining one.' He is also associated with pastoralism, a form of animal husbandry that is often combined with nomadism. I didn't realize how well this would all fit into *The Packless and the Fae Prince* when I named him in *The Mistake and the Lycan King*. I suppose it was meant to be, just like Gero from *TDKatC*.

Why Hekla is an 'alpha' and not a 'luna': In regards to the modern day wolf-shifter and werewolf novels, I heard the term, but I don't know where the 'luna' role in a fictional pack came from or who coined it. Scientists and animal behaviorists have historically referred to the leading wolves in a pack as the alpha pair, though, there is discussion that the term 'alpha' is no longer accurate at all, and that wolf packs are generally families led by a breeding pair.

I remain rather speechless by all the support I have been receiving and the validation from other survivors. My shifter family seems to grow by the day, and that alone puts an emotional lump in my throat. Thank you for walking by my side when it often feels so unbearably lonely. You all saved, and continue to save, my life.

Moonlight preserve you,
Asha Nyr

www.ingramcontent.com/pod-product-compliance
Lightning Source LLC
Chambersburg PA
CBHW020602310726
48979CB00008B/1306/J

9798988535072